Reggie & Me

ALSO BY JAMES HENDRY

Back to the Bush: Another Year in the Wild (2013)

'Witty and hilarious, *Back to the Bush* captures life in a game lodge brilliantly.
I could not put it down!' – NICKY RATTRAY

'*Back to the Bush* is just as readable and entertaining, if not more so, than
A Year in the Wild. It is filled with pathos and bathos and much to make you
chuckle, laugh out loud, and even shed a tear or two. There is an unexpected
twist in this riotous read.' – BRIAN JOSS, *Constantiaberg Bulletin*

A Year in the Wild: A Riotous Novel (2011)

'There's family conflict, romance, funny anecdotes, poaching and all kinds of
intrigue – in other words, something for everyone.'
– KAY-ANN VAN ROOYEN, *GO*

'It's both delicious and deliciously funny. It draws easy-to-imagine pictures of
madness and mayhem; hilarity and horror. And it gives the most fascinating
insights into what goes on behind the posh scenes of larney lodges.'
– TIFFANY MARKMAN, Women24

'*A Year in the Wild* is more than an amusing and entertaining account of game
lodge goings on; it is also a coming-of-age tale of two brothers who explore
life, love, lust and loss.' – CHRIS ROCHE, Wilderness Safaris

Reggie & Me

A NOVEL

James Hendry

MACMILLAN

First published in 2020
by Pan Macmillan South Africa
Private Bag x19
Northlands
Johannesburg
2116

www.panmacmillan.co.za

ISBN: 978-1-77010-642-0
e-ISBN 978-1-77010-643-7

*This is a work of fiction. Any resemblance to actual places, events or persons,
living or dead, is purely coincidental.*

Editing by Craig MacKenzie and Nicola Rijsdijk
Proofreading by Katlego Tapala
Design and typesetting by Triple M Design, Johannesburg
Cover design by Hybrid Creative

For my beloved Mum and Dad,
who taught me English.

PART I

1976–1989

I

Hamish Charles Sutherland Fraser arrived on this planet via emergency Caesarean section on the twenty-fourth of October 1976. As a clichéd harbinger of things to come, Hamish's entry into this existence was not easy for him or those concerned with his well-being. His mother, Caroline, experienced a protracted labour of twenty-four hours before her doctor finally decided that the irksome foetus had no intention of becoming a member of society of its own volition – and certainly not before the 09h08 tee-off time at the Country Club Johannesburg.

Caroline and Stuart (father to be) had been focused on little else but procreation for some seven years. Adoption was whispered, but then Caroline fell pregnant and considerations of raising someone else's offspring had been no longer necessary.

Hamish did not come from an exotic and heroic dynasty – not that anyone could trace at any rate. His blood contained traces of ancient Scottish nobility, soldiers, brigands, businesspeople and, very far back, an Irish monk who'd failed to overcome his Darwinian drives. On his father's side, Fraser's Fishmonger of Perth, Scotland, had earned sufficient tom for Stuart's mother to make a decent if not overly comfortable living. Stuart's father's absence necessitated his son's presence at the shop after school and on weekends, and the smell of fish innards never quite left Stuart's nostrils. His presence during business hours became necessary when Captain Charles Fraser was killed on Sword

3

Beach, Normandy, in June 1944. What remained of him was buried in an unmarked grave just above the high-tide mark.

Despite the challenges of a frugal Scottish existence that relied on the vagaries of the fish market, Stuart had finished school with an admirable academic record, whereupon his mother had decided she'd had enough of sleet, snow and fish guts, and emigrated to South Africa. Stuart had gone along, and secured a bursary for a university education. By the time Hamish was born, Stuart was a well-to-do financial director with a Perthshire lilt.

Hamish's maternal grandparents had slightly more African origins, Caroline's mother being of 1820-settler stock. Born in South Africa to Scottish parents, Caroline's father had grown up in Johannesburg and amassed a large fortune by concocting fantastical mining deals in remote parts of southern Africa on land he neither owned nor had any prospecting data on. His swindling ways eventually caught up with him and some of his booty was seized on the commencement of a lengthy prison term. The old man was incarcerated when Caroline was the tender age of thirteen, and he contracted fatal emphysema not long after. This familial turmoil was to contribute to a not-insubstantial list of neuroses possessed by his daughter.

Caroline's father's ill-gotten gains (those the law hadn't unearthed) had ensured that she and her mother, Elizabeth, never wanted for anything material. Caroline grew up in a salubrious Johannesburg suburb, went to an expensive but severe boarding school that made her father's prison look like a holiday resort, and then read for Law at Stellenbosch University. She practised for a time but packed it in when Hamish arrived.

Hamish's parents had been introduced by a mutual friend. At the time, Caroline was engaged to another lawyer, who wrote poetry, played the lute and didn't wash his hair. She dropped the fellow like a hot coal on meeting Stuart, who looked a bit like Robert Redford, played the guitar and couldn't speak on account of a broken jaw sustained on the rugby field. Six months later, in the summer of 1969, Stuart and Caroline had recited their nuptials and begun the serious business that all organisms evolved to achieve – though the procedure had proved more difficult than expected.

So it was with great fanfare that Hamish arrived at the family nest ten days after his birth. Cousins, aunts and uncles were there to greet him, a Scottish standard flew over the threshold, and Stuart's brother, Walter, played 'The 79th's Farewell to Gibraltar' on his bagpipes – much to the disgust of the Fraser Burmese, which had to be extracted from a tree later that evening. Hamish's only remaining grandparent, Caroline's mother, Elizabeth, by then aged fifty-eight, shared the cat's distaste and had to be coaxed from a bench at the far corner of the garden.

'Whenever there is a family celebration, that obstreperous man has to befoul the atmosphere with his savage's instrument – I shouldn't wonder if the poor baby isn't already stone deaf,' she complained from behind a rose bed. '*We* won the battle of Culloden – not the barbarous Scots!' She still thought of herself as an Englishwoman living in the colonies despite having spent less than one per cent of her life in England.

Caroline settled the peaceful infant into a lovingly decorated nursery some seven years in the imagination. There was a mobile above his pillow, a red clockwork owl from which a lullaby emanated when its string was pulled, and a wooden crib draped with soft white linen, which Hamish was to share with a stuffed orange dog named Peach.

A few months before Hamish's birth, Caroline and Stuart had decided that their new addition would necessitate full-time domestic help. The interview process consisted of a ten-minute conversation with the neighbour's housekeeper, who had a friend in need of employment.

Christina Lebogang Baloyi began working for the Fraser family on the Monday after Hamish arrived home. When Stuart brought Christina into the nursery to meet her young charge, Caroline was in a state of high agitation, tears streaming down her face, her blue-eyed boy yowling his tiny head off, little fists balled in what the inexperienced mother read as distressed rage. The more she dithered, the more he resembled a landed salmon, squishing the contents of his flannel nappy onto the table and himself.

Standing just five feet and two inches off the ground, Tina, as she became known to the family, took control. She gently moved Caroline out of the way, grabbed the infant's ankles, hoisted them up and began to wipe. Hamish calmed immediately – as did his mother.

'You feed him now,' Tina instructed, handing over the clean and newly swaddled infant.

Assuming that Tina would allow the process of breast-feeding to unfold in privacy, Caroline sat down on the nursing chair. But the new housekeeper-cum-nanny put her hands on her vast hips and watched as Caroline draped a towel over her shoulder, removed her right breast from a loose-fitting shirt and attempted to latch her son. Stuart departed post-haste.

The new mother had had plenty of time to learn the theory of caring for infants. She'd read the contents of a bookshelf filled with the latest tomes on the subject for modern (Western) families, making notes in the margins and leaving countless bits of coloured paper protruding from the pages. As such, she felt herself a theoretical expert in the art of administering milk.

'No, Manna,' Tina instructed, addressing Caroline by her own contraction of 'madam'. 'Not like that.'

'But Marvin Eiger says that this is how to do it!' said Caroline.

Tina had no idea who Marvin Eiger was or what he had to say about breastfeeding, and neither did she show the slightest interest. She walked to the chair, pulled away the vanity towel and lifted the infant, holding him as though she was going to feed him.

'Manna must carry him like this,' she demonstrated. 'His head like this so is easy for him drinking – you see?'

'Oh ... um ... yes ... I think so.' Caroline forgot her embarrassment in her concentration.

Tina handed the child back. 'Now you try.'

Hamish took to the breast immediately. Sun streamed in through the east-facing window as the boy began to gurgle contentedly. Caroline felt a surge of motherly bliss.

Satisfied that the feeding was progressing with the correct method, Tina began to move the cloth nappies from a drawer to the shelf above the changing table. In the ensuing silence, Caroline began to feel awkward.

'Do you have children?'

'Yes, Manna. I got four children.'

'Oh? Where are they?'

'They at home in Witsieshoek – with my mother.'

'I see.' Caroline tried *not* to see the implications of this. 'How old are they?'

'The firstborn is boy, 1960, the second is girl, 1962. Then third-born, boy, 1969, and last-born, boy, 1970.'

'That's why you know so much about babies!'

'Yes, Manna – but I look babies since before I am small. All girls in the village are looking babies. From very young.'

Caroline thought of her friends and the dazed exhaustion on their faces during the first years of child-rearing and wondered if a bevy of older children, aunts and cousins would have eased the load. Her notions of the poor rural areas were fused with an unsophisticated bucolic nostalgia – cattle and goats walking the grass-covered hills herded by old men with pipes, woman tending vegetable gardens, their children playing simple games in the healthy dust nearby ...

'Your children are at school then?'

Tina continued repacking Hamish's clothes in more convenient places.

'Sometimes at school, but sometimes school is closed or teachers don't come.' Tina shrugged and closed the last drawer. 'It's finished that side. Move him other side now,' she instructed before departing for the kitchen.

Caroline looked into the summer garden, peace enveloping her, and ten minutes later, Tina reappeared.

'That's good – now you make the air come out.' She wrested Hamish from the breast, flopped him over her shoulder and patted his back. 'Or else he is crying too much.'

Caroline gasped at the firmness with which the stocky woman handled her precious boy.

The infant belched. Tina handed him back to Caroline, who laid him back in his crib, where he instantly fell asleep.

In the kitchen Stuart was finishing a piece of toast and marmalade, the *Rand Daily Mail* spread out in front of him.

'All okay?' he asked, not wishing to engage too closely with the minutiae of mammalian nursing.

'Very much so!' Caroline settled herself opposite him at the antique yellowwood table. 'Tina showed me exactly what to do and everything worked perfectly.'

'Excellent.' Stuart carefully folded his newspaper and stood. 'Now, Tina, let's show you your room and get you settled.'

While Caroline relievedly poured herself some tea, Stuart led Tina out of the back door and down a flight of paved steps into the back yard. There they met Parkin, the Fraser Labrador, a good-natured creature of astonishing laziness and corpulence. She lay outside her kennel, wagged her tail enthusiastically but didn't bother to stand. Tina balked, and made sure to keep Stuart between herself and the hound.

'She danna bite,' Stuart reassured.

Next to the wrought-iron gate leading into the driveway stood two enormous bags made of plastic sacking – Tina's worldly belongings. Stuart picked one up and manhandled it towards the end of the yard. Tina took the other with a practised sweep of her powerful arms.

'This is the laundry.' Stuart indicated a small room with an ironing table in it. 'Caroline will teach you how to use the machine.' Next to the laundry, Stuart opened a stable door and dragged the sack inside. 'And this is your room,' he said, wiping his brow.

Tina peered through the entrance from the dappled sunlight of a wild cherry tree.

The door opened into a narrow sitting room. Shafts of light shone through a wide cottage-pane window onto an old sofa set against the back wall.

Tina walked in and looked around slowly. There was a smell of glue from the new carpet tiles. Stuart followed her in and opened a window.

'I'm sure that smell will go awa' in a day or two if we leave the windows open.' He stepped across the room through an opening and into a square room furnished with a single bed, an old, slightly lopsided wardrobe and a rickety bedside table. A window looked onto an unkempt jasmine bush creeping up the southern wall of the property. 'This is the bedroom.'

The small bathroom was tiled with black-and-white linoleum and instead of a folding seat, the loo had two curved pieces of wood screwed into the bowl rim.

'Will this be alright?' said Stuart, nonplussed by the lack of expression on his new employee's face. He had, after all, spent a whole Sunday carpeting the place.

'Yes, Massa.'

'Good.' He checked his watch. 'I'll leave you to get settled then. Oh, one last thing, when is your burthday?'

Tina looked up, slightly confused.

'What date were you born?'

'I don't know, Massa ... I think is 1943.'

'And the day?'

Tina shook her head and shrugged.

'Well, then let's give you a date. How about the Queen's burthday – that seems appropriate. The twenty-furst of April.'

Tina shrugged and smiled for the first time. 'Is good, Massa.'

'Excellent. I'll see you this evening.'

A few minutes later, satisfied with the arrangement of his domestic affairs, Stuart reversed his Mercedes 230.4 down the driveway. Tina looked about at what was by far the biggest space she'd ever had to herself. Then she took a few minutes to unpack her clothes into the wardrobe. On a plastic camping table in the sitting room she placed two aluminium pots. Her sewing kit, a small bolt of shweshwe cloth and a half-knitted jersey went temporarily on the sofa. She placed a battered radio, a long length of copper wire extending from where the aerial used to be, on the window sill of the sitting room, extending the wire out of the window and wrapping it around the top burglar bar.

She sat down on the sofa. Dust motes floated in the sunlight that pooled at her feet. A house sparrow hopped to the entrance and looked at her before departing on whirring wings.

2

One year and two weeks after Hamish's first birthday, Roger Richard Horace Fraser was born. He came into the world without fuss or fanfare. He cried when appropriate and never when not, and slept through almost from birth. It should be noted that Hamish had yet to develop the ability to self-soothe and took an inordinate amount of his parents' and Tina's time (not to mention patience). Still, Hamish's initial years passed without much in the way of major upheaval. Caroline and Stuart became accustomed to parenting, although the former experienced as many sleepless nights worrying about her babies as she did tending them. Tina settled into life and her indispensable role with the new family. While Caroline's need for neatness bordered on irritatingly obsessive, Tina was allowed a free hand with the boys.

Hamish began his formal education at the age of three, at a Montessori preschool called Jumping Jacks, which was set on an enormous property at the end of the Frasers' street in Inanda. Caroline and Stuart had high expectations – their son had spoken his first word at just nine months and so, quite naturally, they assumed that their son was a prodigy. His efforts at bipedalism were equally exceptional and many were the acknowledgements of the Frasers' peers, whose children, much older on account of the Frasers' conception troubles, provided the paltry benchmark that young Hamish consistently surpassed.

While the parents considered their son an athletic genius, they were slightly worried about his social skills; Hamish showed himself to be so shy that he was barely able to use his speedily absorbed words with anyone other than Tina and his immediate family. It was apparently a supreme effort for him to look at people's faces.

Caroline and Stuart hoped that school would encourage him to become comfortable with other children. It was a matter of time, they were almost sure, before his gift of intelligence would be moulded by Jumping Jacks' modern approach to academics, and a plethora of birth-day-party invitations would set him on the path to popularity.

As it happened, Jumping Jacks offered almost complete freedom to the young Fraser, and the extensive grounds provided ample space for solitary amusement – which was something of a blessing, as Hamish's shyness could morph into an ugly and vicious temper. One July morn-ing, the boy found himself indoors on account of an icy winter wind. Sitting at a table with a bowl full of wax crayons, he was attempting to draw Parkin when a boisterous four year old collided with the table, sending the green crayon in Hamish's hand scraping across his paper.

'Nooo!' Hamish slammed his balled fists onto the teetering table, grabbed the ruined picture and tore it to shreds. 'You messed my pic-ture! You *stupid* boy!'

The commotion attracted Mrs van Dijk, the head teacher, who arrived in the doorway just as Hamish flung his tiny chair after the per-petrator, collecting her in the midriff.

She grunted, straightened and walked slowly into the art room.

'Come over here, Hamish.'

This wasn't the first time Hamish's temper had landed him in the dwang – he'd spent a good deal of time in his father's study being berated for tossing toys at his brother. But it was his first public outburst, and the authoritative voice of Mrs van Dijk made him afraid.

'I'm sorry … but that stupid fat boy knocked my table and messed my drawing!'

Mrs van Dijk held out her hand, and the next thing Hamish knew he was sitting opposite her on a small chair in the head's office.

'Hamish, I want you to listen to me and not say anything until I am finished. Do you understand?'

The boy nodded, hoping that the Almighty he'd heard about in Sunday school might swoop in and remove him from the awkward situation.

God, however, left him to his fate.

For her part, Mrs van Dijk knew that making the boy sit silently in her presence would prove far more effective than shouting or beating. And squirm Hamish did as the teacher pretended to think about what she was going to say.

'Hamish, firstly, it is very unkind to say that people are fat. It is mean. Do you understand that?'

Hamish nodded.

'Secondly, you may not throw furniture. Ever.'

Hamish sat bolt upright as his anger flared.

'Hamish,' the woman said very firmly. 'Sometimes we get cross when people make mistakes. Andrew made a mistake – that is no reason to get angry and throw something.' Her masterful tone softened. 'When you get angry, the only person you hurt is you – Hamish is hurt when Hamish gets angry.' She let the words hang for a little while. 'Can you see how unhappy you are now? There is always sadness when you get angry, Hamish. Will you try and remember that for me?'

'Yes,' said the scowling boy.

She made him sit for another few minutes, trying not to laugh at the child's pinched frown.

Afterwards, and despite the cold, Hamish made his way to the bottom of the garden, where a gnarled old walnut tree stood in seclusion. The tree was easy to climb, with soft bark and horizontal limbs on which a little boy could dream away the time. In summer, he'd discovered, the leaves were too thick for anyone sitting in the foliage to be observed from the ground.

He climbed to his favourite spot and sat looking out through the leaf-less branches.

When the walnuts had ripened that autumn, he'd spent many hours collecting them from the ground and carefully removing the blackening husks – somehow always managing to cover his pants in streaks of unwashable dye. He'd then cracked the shells using a hammer and anvil fashioned from two stones that he kept in a hole near the tree's roots. It had intrigued him to find out if the nut was whole or occupied by an insect or its larvae, the latter being a satisfying triumph.

It wasn't that Hamish loved walnuts – eating them made him bilious. He'd often just taste the flesh of a nut and then toss it away. No, it was more primal than that – something about picking food directly from nature appealed to him.

One January morning in his second year (aged four), Hamish found himself staring out of the window during a lesson on lace-tying. He wandered out into the summer morning, kicked off his shoes and headed for the walnut tree, revelling in the feeling of the cool dew on his little feet.

The old walnut tree grew in the corner of the school grounds – its boughs stretching out over the stout, split-pole fence separating the school from a suburban livery yard. Hamish walked past the jungle gym, through a little grove of pine trees strung with ropes for balancing. Making a perfunctory check for nuts on the ground, he noticed that the dew film had been broken around the base of the trunk and a scowl darkened his face.

'Do you like ponies?' asked a voice from above.

Hamish was ill-prepared for this – his tree wasn't somewhere he came looking for company. With a flash of irritation, he noticed that the voice emanated from his favourite perch. The speaker was difficult to make out – a head silhouetted and haloed in green-gold.

As his eyes adjusted, Hamish registered that the head was covered in an explosion of dark hair and that its owner was female – a distinct and exciting realisation.

Hamish's terror of one-on-one interaction left him in a dilemma. He could turn and go back to lace-tying, or climb the tree as planned and engage the intriguing creature above.

'This is my tree,' he snapped, finding his limbs climbing upwards of their own accord.

'I like ponies,' the girl replied. 'My mum says I can have a pony if I'm good. Have you ever rided a pony?'

Hamish reached the fork where his branch grew out from the main trunk. Normally, he would ease himself up and then slide to his perch on his backside, a thin limb across his chest for safety. But to his horror, he noticed that the girl was standing – not sitting – on his branch, her knees carelessly leaning on the safety limb.

'There's a very big pony in the grass.' She pointed, turning away. The breath caught in Hamish's throat as she released the safety limb to point.

Another dilemma: remain where he was on the trunk or climb to where he could see what the girl was talking about. An awkward moment passed as he struggled to overcome his sudden fear of falling.

'Are you scared?' she asked.

'No!' he lied.

Hamish took a few deep breaths, steeled himself and shuffled up until his feet were level with the branch. He remained attached to the trunk like a limpet, wondering how on earth he'd ever managed to climb the tree before.

'You can't see him from there.' Her tone was gentle. 'Come and stand here with me.'

Paralysed by a combination of fear and shyness, Hamish reached for the safety limb, leant on it and began an awkward shimmy towards the girl. He stopped a foot from her and lifted his head.

In the paddock, a huge chestnut thoroughbred was grazing in the long summer grass, its coat sparkling in the morning sun. Hamish's heart slowed its pounding. The two children stood in silence for a while.

'I want a pony like that one,' said the girl.

'That one's too big for you.'

'I don't care. He's a shiny brown pony,' she replied wistfully, returning her gaze to the horse. The girl sat down on the branch and, with relief, Hamish did the same.

'What's your name?'

'Hamish Charles Sutherland Fraser.'

'I'm Reggie.'

'Reggie.' Hamish committed that important fact to memory. 'I'm four years old,' he offered.

'I'm also four years old.'

'I live down the road and I have a brother called Roger,' Hamish said, warming to the unusual pleasure of conversation. 'Have you got a brother?'

'No.'

'Do you like walnuts?'

'Yes.'

Hamish remembered a nut in his pocket. On impulse he took it out and offered it to her. 'You can have this one.'

She took it from his outstretched hand and their eyes met for the first time. Hamish looked away quickly, blushing. In the nanosecond that he managed to hold her gaze, he noted the colour of her navy-blue eyes.

'Thank you, Hamish Cha … What's your name again?'

'Hamish Charles Sutherland Fraser!' he said, astonished that she'd forgotten.

'Do you like ponies?' she asked again.

As Hamish considered the question, the chestnut lifted his head and snorted. Pollen puffed from a grass inflorescence and caught the sunlight.

'Yes, I think I like ponies.'

Hamish would always remember the smell of that summer's morning – fresh-cut grass from the school garden, walnut fruits and Reggie. The last of it was undefinable for his young senses. It was a human scent, not one of detergents and shampoo.

Hamish had made his first friend.

It is worth mentioning that by this point, invitations to play (given and received) had dwindled to nothing. For the first few months of his Jumping Jacks career, Hamish had been expected to socialise with children his age at afternoon teas, the majority of which he'd spent asking his mother when they were going home. Caroline, enjoying tea and confectionery with new friends, had often been forced to pack up, red-faced, after her son's over-honest assessment of his playmates and their homes:

'Mum, I don't like Katie. She doesn't smell nice and she's got snot on her face.'

'Mum, there's lots of dog poo on the grass here.'

'Mum, this juice is horrible and also the biscuits.'

'Mum, Gregory's house is ugly and he made a wee in his pants.'

Latterly, Caroline had avoided taking her firstborn anywhere. When Roger went to play with his friends, Hamish stayed at home with Tina.

'Hamish! Come here!'

It was pick-up time, and Caroline was attempting to extricate Hamish from the gravel under her car, where he'd slithered as she was strapping Roger into his seat.

'There's a jelly bean.' Scuffling.

'That's disgusting, Hamish. Leave it alone!'

'It's a green one!' Protruding navy-blue sandals the only evidence of the child.

'Hamish! Come. Here. *Now!*'

'Also a red one!'

'Hamish Charles Sutherland Fraser, get out here THIS INSTANT!' Caroline quickly surveyed the area before dropping to her hands and knees to grab at the sandals.

'Excuse me?' a soft voice greeted.

Being spotted on all fours in the gravel trying to fish her son from under her car was just the kind of social embarrassment Caroline's nightmares were made of. With a reddening face she stood, took a deep breath and turned around as small pieces of driveway fell from her knees.

'Hello,' said a dark-haired woman about Caroline's age, dressed in a threadbare pale-green suit. The woman offered a hand. 'I'm Sarah Fine, Regina's ... eh ... Reggie's mother.'

The little girl stood obediently next to her parent, a brown stuffed rabbit in her arms.

Caroline's confusion must have been apparent.

'Reggie says she's a friend of Hamish's ... That is Hamish, isn't it?' The woman pointed underneath the car.

On hearing his friend's name, the boy emerged, a red jelly bean protruding from his left nostril.

'Yes. Unfortunately, it is.' Caroline dusted off her hand and took Sarah's. 'I'm Caroline Fraser. Sorry – Hamish hasn't mentioned Reggie, but he doesn't mention a great deal unless it's to lodge a complaint or argue with me.'

'You want the green one, Reggie?' said Hamish, pulling the crushed and sandy bean from his pocket.

'Hamish, that'll make her ill!' Caroline grabbed the proffered gift.

'I wondered if you might like to bring Hamish around for tea – perhaps on Friday afternoon?'

Caroline wanted to refuse politely, but Sarah was warm and not as gaudily dressed as the other mothers, and Caroline observed the easy manner between Reggie and Hamish – something she'd not witnessed before.

'That's very kind,' she replied. 'I suppose he couldn't embarrass me further.'

Two afternoons later, Caroline and Hamish pulled up outside a small property in the suburb of Orange Grove. The surrounding bottle-green wall was three-feet high and topped with a mesh fence covered in jasmine and honeysuckle. The Frasers entered through the garden gate under an arched pergola strung with a tangle of small yellow roses, and emerged into a little garden, the centrepiece of which was a bursting vegetable patch. Colourful flowerbeds stretched on both sides of the gate, and roses – white, pink and yellow – hid the western wall. At the back of the property a humble red-brick house, the eves of its verandah strung with baskets of fuchsias, rested in the shade of an oak tree. Caroline was surprised and a little jealous – she considered herself green-fingered, but the detail and care in this exuberant patch rendered her temporarily speechless.

The mothers shared tea while Reggie and Hamish collected acorns, dug in the soil and took turns on a low swing. Sarah made a quick charcoal sketch of the kids sharing their milky tea and home-made chocolate cake at a little wooden table under the oak – their smiling mouths covered in icing. She gave it to Caroline, who later placed it carefully in an album of her son's memories.

Caroline found Sarah a welcome relief from the more pretentious mothers at Jumping Jacks. Completely sure and comfortable with herself, Sarah had put her new friend at ease to the extent that Caroline had been able to share her worries about Hamish. The boy was becoming an increasingly difficult prospect: he was often melancholy, and his outbursts had caused his grandmother to remark on more than one occasion, 'My dear, there is something not right with that boy.'

It was the first tea date that Caroline had been able to relax at and enjoy, and not once did Hamish ask to go home. In fact, he was mortified when, as the sun turned carmine in the western Johannesburg smog, his mother informed him that they would be leaving.

3

Hamish continued to flounder academically and socially into his last year at Jumping Jacks. He spent as much time as possible with Reggie, but she had other friends, and his chronic shyness precluded his joining their activities. If the two of them began a game together, her friends would sometimes try to join them but, threatened by their proximity, Hamish's temper would flare and he'd tell them to go away. When they failed to acquiesce to his demands, he'd withdraw to the walnut tree.

While this behaviour resulted in him being left alone for long periods, one of Hamish's teachers discovered that the small, introverted boy had a penchant for performance. It happened during a music session one day.

The children were learning 'Twinkle, Twinkle, Little Star', which Hamish found about as entertaining as learning to tie his laces. The music teacher, a particularly perceptive and dedicated woman, gently singled out Hamish as his gaze wandered through the window to the late-October green of the garden.

'Hamish, would you like to sing a song for the class?'

Hamish stared at her, and then at the faces of his classmates, in abject horror.

'Do you know any songs?' she asked gently.

It just so happened that Hamish did know a song. It was a Xhosa song that Tina had taught him. She'd also shown him a little dance to go with it.

'Yes,' he said, rooted to the floor.

'Well, I think you should teach us. Who wants to learn a new song?' she asked the class.

'MEEEEEEEE,' came the deafening chorus.

'Reggie can help you if you like,' coaxed Miss Cummings.

Reggie walked over to Hamish and reached out her hand. He took it, and the next thing he knew he was on the tiny stage at the front of the music room looking down on his classmates. Quietly at first, he began:

'Saguquka sathi bheka, nants' iPata Pata,

Saguquka sathi bheka, nants' iPata Pata,

Saguquka sathi bheka, nants' iPata Pata,

Saguquka sathi bheka, nants' iPata Pata ...'

When he'd completed the song, perfectly pitched with the Xhosa clicks all in place, Miss Cummings began applauding, genuinely impressed, which set the rest of the class clapping. Hamish was astonished and delighted. So he sang it again – loudly – and this time he added the dance. In no time at all, the whole class was butchering the lyrics to Miriam Makeba's 1967 classic, attempting the dance moves and clapping while Hamish belted out the song at the top of his lungs.

The singing brought a flurry of interest from the class next door. Another group, hitherto playing outside, also came rushing in. Quite suddenly, ten children were thirty.

The gentle and perceptive Miss Cummings was no disciplinarian.

'Um, children ...' she urged as the lesson escalated into a mosh pit for minors.

One child found himself a drum, which made everyone else lunge for instruments, setting upon maracas, shakers, triangles and xylophones. Those too slow to grab an instrument used the furniture or fought over items already claimed.

The racket attracted Mrs van Dijk, who assumed there was a riot or a medical emergency – both of which would require her stern leadership. By the time the head teacher arrived from her biscuit-baking lesson in the kitchen, a beast hitherto unrealised in Hamish had emerged. The powerful but utterly unrefined star of the show had climbed onto the piano stool while kids thrashed instruments, furniture, the walls and each other, any semblance of music long gone.

Mrs van Dijk quickly singled out Hamish as the root of the problem. She waded through children onto the stage, pulled him off the stool by his waist and held him out to Miss Cummings.

'Get this child out of here!'

Hamish, who considered the impromptu concert a roaring success, was confused. He began to squirm as Miss Cummings bore him out into the garden, released him in the sandpit and told him to sit still.

'Don't worry, Hamish. You sang and danced very nicely,' she placated, seeing the distress on his face. 'Now, tell me where you learnt that song.'

'Gogo Tina teached me.'

'Who is Gogo Tina? Is she your granny?'

'No. Gogo Tina is our housekeeper,' Hamish announced with disdain, as if everyone in the world knew this.

Tina often looked after the boys in the afternoons when Caroline was busy, though entertaining Hamish was no easy task. He couldn't concentrate for more than ten seconds unless an activity took his fancy, and these activities could be counted on two fingers: tree climbing and digging up his mother's beautifully planted seedlings. Knowing a thing or two about raising children, Tina had realised the child needed physical activity, so she'd taught him the simple dance routine one afternoon as Miriam Makeba's voice crackled over the little battery-powered radio Tina carried everywhere.

Hamish had a good sense of rhythm and tone for a little boy, and he'd caught on quickly. When the song had ended, he'd begged for a repeat, so Tina had turned off the radio and sung while they'd done the dance. Once Hamish had learnt the steps, he'd started imitating the sounds coming from Tina's rich contralto. He loved the click sound, especially when combined with a stamp, and after an afternoon of fairly obsessive practice, he'd had the song and the routine down pat. From then on, every time he'd gone into the kitchen or found Tina doing housework, he'd refined his performance. What was henceforth referred to in Jumping Jacks circles as 'The Pata Pata Incident' was the culmination of three months' practice.

The afternoon of the Pata Pata Incident, after Mrs van Dijk had thoroughly castigated Miss Cummings for her disciplinary shortcomings, the two women agreed that the otherwise seemingly talentless boy may have one redeeming feature.

So it was that Hamish and Reggie were cast in the school play as Father and Mother Christmas.

The great Christmas performance began at three o'clock one Friday afternoon in early December 1982. Hamish loved his bright-red costume, shiny black Wellington boots, long white cotton-wool beard and the cushion sewn into his jacket. The boy's excitement was matched only by his mother's feverish dread that her son would conjure a fiasco and taint the family name forever.

Tina dressed the fidgeting boy in the costume she'd sewn from scratch.

'Hamish,' she said, adding the final touches, 'you must be good today; okay?'

'Yes, Gogo.'

'You mustn't be naughty. You must only do what you practise. You understand, Hamish?'

'Yes, Gogo, I understand.'

Elizabeth, Tina, Caroline, Stuart, Hamish and Roger walked to the end of the street, where the school nestled in a small forest, and territorially rolled out their picnic rug. The plan was for the Frasers to sit with the Fines, who were late as a matter of course because there was always some pressing revolutionary engagement to which Professor Fine, very active in the anti-apartheid movement, had to attend.

Elizabeth took charge of Roger, a task she enjoyed because her youngest grandson's manners and demeanour were a source of enormous pride. The grandmother's musings on Roger's virtues were disturbed by Tina grabbing Hamish and upending him, whereupon a melted and half-eaten Caramello Bear fell out of his left boot, leaving a chocolatey streak down the leg of the hitherto pristine costume.

'You say you'll be good today!' Tina scolded.

Five minutes before the start of the performance, Sarah and Reggie arrived looking flustered, Professor Fine conspicuous by his absence. Hamish detached himself from Tina and ran to meet them, the enormous cotton-wool beard flapping over his eyes so that he tripped over the nearest outstretched leg. His fall was broken by a creamy sponge cake fringed with delicate strawberries that was sitting in the middle of another family's picnic blanket.

The destruction of the confectionery provoked the first swear word of the afternoon: 'Bloody hell!' yelled George Sandcross, who was poised to serve his family their tea.

The outburst silenced voices and turned heads. Undaunted, Hamish stood, placed a Wellington boot on a cheese sandwich, knocked over a juice bottle and continued his charge.

He reached Reggie halfway across the lawn, having stomped in a bowl of grapes, kicked over a teapot and squashed the toes of a now-howling toddler. He took Reggie by the hand and dragged her towards his family.

'Reggie's here!' he bellowed at the top of his little lungs, strawberries dripping intermittently from his ruined costume.

Caroline reached for the Valium in her handbag and sidled over to where Roger was eating a peanut-butter sandwich with his grandmother – as far away from the melee as their picnic rug would allow.

'That ridiculous troglodyte needs to be taken in hand,' said Elizabeth in disgust. She turned to Caroline. 'He is a menace to civilised society.'

'Hamish!' snapped Stuart, who was on his hands and knees cleaning up the ruined strawberry sponge and trying to placate its owner. 'Settle down!'

Hamish retrieved the unattended, seeping Caramello Bear wrapper and thrust it at Reggie. 'This is for you,' he said proudly.

Before Father and Mother Christmas took to the stage, the children and their parents sang carols, the volume of Stuart's enthusiastic renditions of the bass parts giving an inkling as to the genetic origin of Hamish's flair for performance.

The rest of the afternoon went off relatively smoothly. Hamish performed his little speech word-perfectly and rather theatrically for a boy his age, the words having been written by Mrs van Dijk (evidently a rampant liberal).

'Christmas is a time for giving,' Hamish started. 'It is a time for us to remember that we are lucky to have homes to live in, food to eat and clothes to wear. We also need to be grateful for our families and the time that we have to spend with them.' He paused for effect. 'We remember that not everyone in South Africa is able to be with their families at Christmas and we hope that they will find peace and happiness soon.'

The political allusion was lost on some, offensive to others and a poignant reminder to a few. Stuart looked down at his teacup and saucer, and then at Tina, on whose lap Roger had fallen asleep.

After this, Hamish and Reggie sat on two chairs with sacks full of gifts made by the children for their families. Mrs van Dijk read out the name of each child, who then approached the stage, gave her a hug and received a present. The gift-giving progressed smoothly until Andrew Carmichael, a corpulent fellow who'd been known to scribble on Hamish's artwork, arrived. Hamish held out the gift and then snatched it back.

'My granny says only good boys get presents, and you're not a good boy. Say sorry.'

Andrew was stunned, and there were stifled giggles from the audience. Miss Cummings, who was assisting the Christmas couple, hissed: 'Give it to him, Hamish!'

Hamish stared at his nemesis for some time before handing it over.

After the last carol, the Frasers, Tina and Elizabeth walked cheerfully home, whereupon Caroline poured herself a huge glass of wine before she'd even put down her handbag.

That year, the Frasers hosted a vast family Christmas, which included Stuart's two siblings and Caroline's brother, their spouses, six teenage offspring and Elizabeth.

While Stuart carved the ham, Elizabeth (fuelled by three champagne cocktails) stood Hamish and Roger back to back and took great delight in pronouncing the younger taller than his older brother. It irked Hamish slightly that he was smaller – it was the first time anyone had noticed.

It wouldn't be the last.

4

At the end of 1982, Hamish graduated from Jumping Jacks with an academic record best described as non-existent but for his unusually impressive grasp of walnut biology. In contrast, when Roger completed his nursery schooling a year later, he could read, write, add, subtract, multiply and divide. He could also tie his shoelaces. (Hamish couldn't keep his shoes on for long enough to learn how to tie them.)

Trinity Pre-Preparatory School the following year was to be something of a rude awakening.

Hamish's first shock was the discovery that Reggie and he were no longer to be schooled together. His second was the notable absence of all femininity but for that clinging tenuously to his teacher, Mrs Arnot. With his parents, Hamish went to meet her the day before school began. Aged somewhere in her late forties, with cropped dark hair and a round face, she seemed sweet and gentle. The next day, out of eye and earshot of protective mummies and daddies, gentle Mrs Arnot morphed into a vicious harpy and it wouldn't be long before she was lashing Hamish with her handbag on the way to and from chapel on Thursday mornings.

On his first day, Caroline and Tina clothed Hamish in his new uniform – a white shirt, navy tie, grey shorts, a grey blazer, long grey socks and shiny black shoes that gave him nasty blisters on his heels. The uniform was completed by a grey cap, the first of at least a dozen that Hamish would lose during his three pre-preparatory years. On his back he had a brand-new blue satchel made for a boy four times his size.

Mrs Fraser was notoriously tardy, and so they arrived in the classroom five minutes after the rest of the boys were seated. At the door, Caroline hugged Hamish. Tears dripped from her eyes, apparently drawn by an intuitive understanding of the trials he was going to face.

The tiny new arrival walked gingerly into the morgue-silent room. Mrs Arnot smiled thinly and looked at her watch.

'You are late, Hamish.'

She allowed a few moments for the boy to bathe in the stares of his new peers. Hamish stood, adrenalin flowing, sharpened senses taking in the details of the room. A clean blackboard dominated the front wall; to the right a reading alcove with low shelves of books. Posters with letters and pictures covered the other walls.

'Sit over there,' Mrs Arnot said eventually, indicating a chair and desk in the middle of the room.

Hamish took a few steps forward, tripped over a satchel and sprawled onto the floor. The pale linoleum tiles were cold on his hands and smelt of detergent, shoe polish and small boys whose parents weren't up to the task of cleaning them. Laughter fluttered through the room then ended abruptly.

'Boys!' Mrs Arnot barked.

From his prone position, Hamish was surprised that no one came to check he was okay. At Jumping Jacks there was a rigorously enforced code: if a child was hurt, then anyone close by *had* to help. Now, there was just an awkward silence as Hamish struggled to stand under the weight of his satchel and then arranged himself at his desk.

He sat for ten minutes as Mrs Arnot handed out exercise books, endlessly reinforcing the need for these to be taken home and covered in brown paper. His boredom ramped at a tremendous speed such that after twenty minutes on the hard wooden chair, he rose and made to walk out. Halfway to the door, a searing pain shot through his right ear.

'And where do you think you're going?' Mrs Arnot bellowed, the ear lobe between her thumb and forefinger, a nail digging into the soft flesh.

'Answer me, boy!'

He recoiled at the smell of her cigarette-laden breath, her face an inch from his, which just increased the pain in his ear. The answer seemed so obvious, he felt he surely didn't have to explain.

'Answer me! Where are you going?'

'I want to climb a walnut tree.' His lip began to quiver.

'A walnut tree? A *walnut* tree? Sit down and don't you dare move unless you have put your hand up and asked. Do you understand me?'

'Yes.'

'Yes, Mrs Arnot – you say, "*Yes. Missus. Arnot*"!' She yanked on his ear with each syllable. 'Go and sit down!'

Hamish walked meekly back to his chair, acutely aware of forty eyes gawking at him.

A little while later, a dull ache in his skinny backside made Hamish raise his hand as Mrs Arnot was telling the class to draw their favourite animal. She stared, surprised that her initial assault hadn't cowed the strange child into submission, and considered ignoring him. There was, however, the chance that he might be about to soil himself.

'Yes, Hamish?'

'Please may I go and climb a walnut tree?'

Mrs Arnot's mouth flopped open, eyes bulging.

'NO ... YOU ... MAY ... NOT!' she snarled in crescendo. 'There are no walnut trees here, and you may only go outside during break time and at no other time. DO. YOU. UNDERSTAND. ME?'

'Yes.'

'Yes, *who*? YES ... MRS ... ARNOT!'

'Oh ... um ... yes ... um ... Mrs Arnot,' Hamish said to his desk.

'LOUDER and LOOK at me when you're talking to me!'

'Yes, Mrs Arnot!'

Hamish's next question remained where it had formed in his head. No walnut tree? There must be some mistake. How on earth could he be in a place with no walnut tree? He didn't understand what break time was, or why he'd been refused permission to escape when he'd asked as instructed.

Confused is how Hamish spent much of his first school year. The educational approach taken by Jumping Jacks and Trinity could not have been more different, and Hamish, being unused to any sort of structure, found it deeply troubling. He quickly worked out that Mrs Arnot was not a person whose wrath he wished to incur, but how to avoid this eventuality was to prove more difficult.

While some boys could read and write a little when they arrived in Grade One, most could not, and so the class began with learning the alphabet – sounding the letters and then stringing a few together.

A few weeks later Mrs Arnot announced, 'Boys, today we are going to learn to write the letter "a", like you say in the word "apple".' She stared in mild disgust at the sea of small, snot-encrusted faces. 'Everyone say "a is for apple".'

Examining his sharpened HB pencil – sharp because it had yet to be used – Hamish failed to say 'apple' because it was a word he had already mastered some years previously.

'Hamish!' snapped the teacher. His eyes shot up as a shiver made its way down his spine. 'Say "a is for apple"!'

'Um … "a is for apple",' he whispered.

'I can't hear you, boy!' Mrs Arnot liked to vent her frustrations on the indolent.

'Eh … "a is for apple"!' Hamish repeated.

'Now put your pencil down, pay attention and do everything I tell you. Understand?'

'Yes' – he paused and then remembered as the bellow formed on his teacher's lips – 'um … Mrs Arnot.'

The teacher turned back to the board with an irritated sigh and wrote an enormous lower-case 'a' on the board in yellow chalk.

'See how I do it?' she asked, and then drew another one.

Hamish stared at the empty page in front of him. It seemed so full of promise despite the poor-quality paper – the off-white sort unsuited to a small boy of Hamish's poor hand musculature. He took up his pencil once more.

'Watch again.' Mrs Arnot drew a third example very slowly. 'Don't open your books yet, boys – you must watch first. I will tell you when to write your first letter.'

As she repeated the drawing for the fourth time, she failed to notice the Fraser boy making his first attempt at literacy. George Abbot, Hamish's neighbour, cast his eye towards the page next to him. Never shy to raise the alarm to a crime, he put up his hand. He knew he wasn't allowed to speak unless given permission and this golden rule he would never break, despite his desperate desire to tell Mrs Arnot about the carnage unfolding next to him.

Hamish's full-page, grand entry into literature continued as his peers watched Mrs Arnot's fifth example of an 'a'. George Abbot's hand began to pump violently up and down.

The writer's unrefined pencil skills drove the instrument through the thin paper and by the time he had completed the front half of an 'a', there was a cut in the page that extended to the two beneath.

George Abbot's face turned puce and his extended forefinger began to quiver.

Hamish felt a rising sense of panic. How on earth was he going to hide this? He scrabbled quickly in his little pine pencil box and pulled out the unused eraser. As the sixth 'a' appeared on the board, he set to the page with the rubber. It took three strokes for the page to detach completely from the spine of the book.

Hamish went cold.

George Abbot was uttering small groans with each frantic extension of his arm. The movement finally caught Mrs Arnot's eye. She swung around in irritation, but her face softened as she beheld one of her favoured pupils.

She smiled. 'What is the matter, George?'

'Mrs Arnot,' he gasped, 'look! Hamish has teared his page and writ on the table!' He pointed to his neighbour, who was too terrified to take his gaze off the catastrophe in front of him.

Mrs Arnot all but hurdled the front row of desks to get to Hamish. When she took in the scene – the abuse of the pristine exercise book, the ugly stripe across the wooden desk and the detestable Fraser boy trying to hide his crime by sitting on the page he'd ripped, she exploded.

'Hamish, *what* did I just say? What did I JUST SAY?!' she screeched.

Hamish stared up at her, his face green. His failure to answer this question had nothing to do with dumb insolence or terror – he genuinely had no recollection whatsoever of her instructions.

Mrs Arnot took his blank expression for impudence.

His left ear took the first contact. She grabbed it, hauled him out of his chair and pulled him to the front of the class.

'Put your hands on my desk!' she yelled.

Tears pricked Hamish's eyes as he committed to memory the small vase of red carnations on the desk. He despised carnations from then on.

'I'm sorry, Mrs Arnot,' he snivelled. 'I didn't mean to!'

The next sound was a solid 'thwack' from the leather strap of the teacher's handbag whipping the back of the boy's legs.

It wasn't the pain that forced the tears out of Hamish's eyes and down his cheeks. It was the shock of violence.

'Go and sit down and don't you dare touch your book unless I tell you to.' Mrs Arnot's voice was an icy hiss.

On returning to his desk, it was his neighbour's smug look that dried Hamish's tears and flared his temper. He pushed George Abbot's neatly arranged pencil box onto the floor.

'You are a stupid moron,' he snapped, and regretted it immediately as the air behind him displaced with the speed of Mrs Arnot's advance.

'I'm sorry!' he said, tears welling again. 'I didn't mean to!'

Hamish spent the next hour and the whole of break sitting on the floor, staring at the corner of the room.

Six weeks later, each boy was invited to the teacher's desk to read a simple sentence consisting of three-letter words. When Hamish's turn came, he walked up to Mrs Arnot, blanching under her angry glower.

Hamish was something of an enigma to the cantankerous teacher. On meeting her pupils, she liked to pigeonhole them: bright or dim. This child fell into the former at first impression and then moved to hanging uncomfortably in-between.

'Read this line,' she instructed.

Although prone to selecting favourites and partial to the odd bout of violence, the teacher was not beyond feeling sympathy for dim-witted fellows who tried hard. She fed Wayne Johnston (a vast but thick-skulled fellow) spade-loads of soft, cajoling encouragement as he tried and tried again to come to terms with the first three letters of the intro-ductory reader.

'Don't worry, Wayne,' she'd coo. 'We can try again later.'

She could tolerate plain naughtiness – it was predictable and easy. Richard Fountainberry merely needed a beating once a week and a ses-sion with the headmistress every fortnight.

She felt little sympathy for Hamish, however. He was obviously not thick. His language skills were good – he spoke more eloquently than ninety per cent of his peers – but his snotty, supercilious accent and imbecilic inability to concentrate for more than two seconds made him the object of botheration rather than sympathy.

Mrs Arnot pointed at the first word on the page.

Hamish had one chance. He peered at the letters 't', 'h' and 'e'.

'And!' he exclaimed.

'No!' the teacher snapped, almost triumphant. 'Hamish, you can't read – now go and sit down!'

Hamish and the other dunces were to receive extra tuition through the medium of a remedial reading pamphlet with letters of a size inversely proportional to the slowness of the recipients. Along with the pamphlet came a letter in Mrs Arnot's hand explaining tersely that Hamish was academically slow and that the contents of the remedial reader should be drilled into his obviously not thick but clearly impervious skull so that he could resume his place as a functioning member of the class.

When Stuart arrived home that late-summer's evening, looking forward to bathing his little boys, setting them to bed and then enjoying supper with his wife, he was assailed before he could reach the front door.

'Oh, Stuart!' His wife burst out of the house. 'The most terrible thing has happened!'

Stuart halted.

'It's Hamish,' wailed Caroline waving Mrs Arnot's missive.

'What's he done now?' asked Stuart, putting down his briefcase so he could take hold of his near-hysterical spouse.

She handed him the letter. Stuart cast an eye over it and frowned. 'It's probably nor a big deal. He's just a wee bit different; we know that. We'll just have to help him a bit, that's all.'

'But he's behind!' she said. 'Already! We spent all that money on Jumping Jacks and for what?'

'He's superb at climbing trees.'

'Stuart!'

'And nor bad falling out of them.'

'Oh, please!'

'I'm sure he'll be fine. Let's go and have a glass of wine.'

This they duly did. Bath-time was delayed on account of the perfect March twilight. While the parents chatted on the verandah overlooking the lawn and a flowerbed bursting with white St Joseph lilies, Hamish and Roger laughed as they threw a ball and then raced Parkin to fetch it. Stuart re-read Mrs Arnot's letter and then tossed it aside with only a twinge of worry.

5

In the kitchen, Tina placed the perfectly roasted chicken onto a platter and surrounded it with roast potatoes. When the beans and carrots had been drained, she walked through to the verandah to tell the family that their dinner was ready.

'Thank ye, Tina.' Stuart stood up. 'It smells delicious.'

Tina smiled as the boys came running onto the tiles, panting.

'What's for supper, Gogo?'

She put a hand on Hamish's head and smiled. 'Roast chicken!'

'Not *again*!' the boy replied.

'Hamish!' snapped Stuart. 'Get into the study now!'

Two minutes later, Hamish found himself in his father's sanctum, the door shut. An antique wind-up clock chimed quarter-past seven. Hamish looked around at the bookshelves, the brass lamp on the teak desk, the cabinet full of tin soldiers. The clock grew louder in his ears with each second.

Stuart forced himself not to break the silence. Eventually, he spoke.

'Hamish.'

'Yes, Dad.'

'You're old enough now to understand that you must be grateful for the food you eat. A lot of people in the wurld go to bed without any supper.' He stopped – bite-sized pieces of information were more effective with Hamish than long tirades. 'Do you understand?'

'Yes, Dad.'

'Repeat what I just said.'

'That there's lots of people in the world that hasn't got supper.'

'There *are* lots of people in the wurld that *haven't* got supper,' Stuart corrected.

'Yes, Dad.'

Later that night Stuart was propped up on the bed, staring out of the window. The newspaper lay unread on his legs and his glasses dangled from his mouth.

Caroline looked up from her nightly cleansing ritual. 'What's worrying you?' she asked.

Stuart sighed. 'Our sons and the wurld in which we're raising them,' he replied. 'Perhaps we could do more about the country – you know, join the progs or something. Like wee Reggie's father ... or perhaps we should be raising our kids in the UK.'

Caroline wafted over to the bed and sat at her husband's side. 'I'm an African – I have no ties to Britain, despite my fascination with Princess Di. I don't want to leave. Soon things will be fine and everyone will be equal.'

'Maybe we should try and help with Tina's kids' schooling, or find out about it at least?' he mused.

'I think that's a very good idea.' Caroline kissed her husband's forehead. 'You are a tremendously kind man, Stuart Fraser, and I love you very much.'

A few days later, Stuart asked Caroline to invite the Fines around for supper.

'All of them?' she asked, thinking how nice it would be for Hamish to see Reggie, given his failure to make any new friends at school.

'As opposed to half o them?'

'No, man, I mean him as well – Albert?'

Caroline and Stuart had met the activist professor once or twice, but always very briefly as he hurtled to a meeting or steamed in through his front door with a brief greeting before vanishing into his study.

'Yes, if he's around. I think it'd be good to talk to him – you know, about the country and where he thinks things are going. I don't suppose he'll come, but you never know.'

That Friday, at five-thirty, all three Fines arrived in a battered Volkswagen beetle that covered the Inanda estate in a great deal more smoke than Stuart's braai fire.

Caroline was nervous for two reasons. First, she felt Professor Fine might take a dim view of their luxurious situation. Second, and more terrifying, Elizabeth had invited herself to join them. She had phoned on Thursday evening.

'Caroline, I'm coming round for supper tomorrow,' she'd announced.

'But, Mother, we have guests tomorrow. Could you not come on Saturday for tea?' Caroline well knew this would precipitate the dealing of sympathy cards – a pack of them.

'I do not understand why it is that you have to be so difficult, dear,' Elizabeth had sniffed. 'It seems as if you are purposely trying to exclude me from my grandchildren's lives.'

Caroline had no stomach for a thirty-minute negotiation and agreed to her mother's attendance at the braai, forgetting that Elizabeth's political views could not have been more juxtaposed with Albert Fine's. He was an activist in the fight against apartheid and almost certainly a clandestine member of the South African Communist Party. Elizabeth could regularly be heard yelling 'Commie Jew!' at motorists who took exception to her homicidal tendencies behind the wheel.

A week previously, Caroline had accompanied her mother to a boutique in Hyde Park where the older woman had hoped to purchase an outfit for the annual general meeting of the South African Rose Growers Association.

'I am the chairlady of the South African Rose Growers Association,' Elizabeth had launched at the young shop assistant. 'I'm sure I need not tell you how important it is that I look elegant, but I do not wish to garb myself in the manner of a garish clown like you young people insist on doing.'

As the girl began to respond, Elizabeth had finished: 'Something like Her Majesty might wear would be excellent.'

Whether or not the nineteen year old had any idea as to which majesty the older woman was referring was unclear, but she managed to find a pale-pink suit that was judged acceptable.

Eventually, the bill was tallied and the figure presented. When Elizabeth saw the number, her jaw clenched and her eyes snapped up at the quivering assistant.

'Good God, girl! I say, is this boutique owned by Shylock and Sons? That's bloody iniquitous!' Elizabeth was in no way short of funds but it was simply her wont to complain about every bill and, in so doing, suggest some sort of Semitic conspiracy.

With this experience fresh in her mind, Caroline made sure that her mother arrived before the Fines. On the verandah, she supplied Elizabeth with a purposefully weak Campari and soda.

'Mum, I want you to listen to me, please,' Caroline began.

'My dear, I always listen to you. What is the matter?'

'Nothing at the moment but, please, I want to remind you to not make any anti-Semitic or anti-communist or racist remarks tonight. The people coming over are Jewish by name – they don't practise – and Professor Fine is an anti-apartheid academic.'

Elizabeth took a long sip of her drink and gazed out over the pool. Then she looked at her daughter and scowled.

'My dear, who you keep company with is not my affair, and how on earth you could affront me by suggesting I might insult your guests … well, I never did … I'm speechless.'

Thirty minutes later, the Fines emerged onto the verandah with Stuart. Reggie, as usual, was polite to a fault.

'Hello, Mrs Fraser. Hello, Mr Fraser. Hello, Mrs Sutherland. Hello, Roger. Hello, Ham—'

Hamish grabbed her by the hand and began pulling her towards the garden. 'Come and look at the fort that Roger and me built!'

'Hamish,' growled his father, 'it's the fort that Roger and *I* built, not Roger and *me*. Now say hello to Professor and Mrs Fine.'

Hamish did as he was bade and the children disappeared into the shrubbery.

The professor, standing about five feet and eight inches, was dressed in a moth-eaten tweed jacket and ill-fitting brown corduroys. It was his genes that gave his daughter her curly dark locks, but while hers were neatly tied back for the occasion, his were in open rebellion. The volume of salt-and-pepper hair was almost as impressive as the beard he wore. A whiff of body odour completed his appearance.

Elizabeth's nose twitched.

As Stuart was about to offer drinks, Tina emerged carrying a tray of home-made cheese straws and a bowl of olives.

'Sawubona, dadewethu,' said Albert to Tina.

Zulu wasn't Tina's mother tongue but she spoke it well.

'Yebo sawubona, baas.'

'Angiyena ubaas dadewethu, ngi ngumfowenu. Unjani na?'

Tina was gobsmacked. This was the first white man who'd ever suggested she was an equal – a sister no less.

'Ngiyaxolisa, mfowethu. Ngiyaphila, unjani wena?' she replied, embarrassed.

Albert continued the conversation for a few minutes while the Frasers watched in astonishment and Elizabeth with a vague look of distaste. Sarah's eyes went to the children playing in the garden. As Tina withdrew, beaming, Stuart took a drinks order and disappeared inside.

Elizabeth was the first to speak. 'I say, where on earth did you learn to speak black?'

'Black? Black isn't a language.' The professor's face pinched.

'Mum,' said Caroline through gritted teeth, knowing that no amount of kicking under the table would stop her.

'Isn't it? Well, that sounded like black to me. It certainly wasn't the tongue of Chaucer.'

'Mum, please!'

Sarah rose wordlessly from the table and walked into the garden.

'It was isiZulu, just one of at least nine indigenous languages that white people in this country have studiously avoided learning, despite the fact that we make up such a minute proportion of South Africa's population.'

Elizabeth drained her glass of crimson Campari and looked dismissively into the twilight. 'Well, I'm sixty-four years old and I've never had cause to speak black.'

'That's because you, like most whites, are prepared to sit by and observe as a totally amoral dispensation perpetrates crimes against humanity on a daily basis.'

Elizabeth simply couldn't resist. 'My dear man, why are you Jews so dramatic always? By all means, speak black or Sooloo if you like, but I'll thank you not to poison my grandsons' minds with your bilious red propaganda and notions of racial equality.'

'Mum! That's *enough*!'

'Here we g—' As Stuart emerged with a tray, the professor leapt out of his seat, leant across the table and pointed a grubby finger at Elizabeth's nose.

'You fucking racist cow!' Albert yelled, spittle flying from his mouth. 'It's people like you who are aiding and abetting endless misery for millions of black people with your attitudes that belong in the Dark Ages!'

Elizabeth sat back in her chair, one eyebrow slightly cocked, her face a picture of serenity. 'You have the fingernails of a labourer,' she said, considering the digit pointing at her. 'I suppose that goes with being a Bolshevik.'

Sarah came running back onto the verandah. 'Albert,' she groaned, 'please don't do this here, it's not the time.' She took hold of the wrist that was thrust towards Elizabeth.

But Albert tore away from her touch, his fist colliding with the drinks tray. Glasses flew in all directions and shattered as wine, whisky and beer dowsed all present and the tray flipped up into Stuart's face, the steel edge cutting into the bridge of his nose. The host reeled back, his head slamming into the edge of the cottage-pane door.

'Why don't you fuck off back to Britain!' Albert's voice broke as he stormed into the house. Less than twenty seconds later, the Volkswagen backfired like a piece of antiquated field artillery and reversed up the driveway.

A cape robin, oblivious to the human conflict, called from the garden tap.

On the verandah, the commotion brought the children running from the garden and Tina from the kitchen. She quickly saw that this was not a place for the young and took them away for a snack.

Stuart, bleeding from both sides of his head, took control. He turned to his remaining guest.

'Please, come and sit down.' He indicated a cane sofa away from the mess.

Wearing an expression of resignation, Sarah flopped down on the cushions.

Then Stuart turned to his wife, who had tears streaming down her face. 'Come on, darling, everything's o right.' He guided her gently to the sofa.

His mother-in-law stood up and made to join them.

'Nor you,' Stuart snapped. 'You've gone too far this time. Get off my property immediately!'

Elizabeth glared at him. 'What are you talking about? My daughter needs me – look how upset that violent communist has made her.'

'No one needs you right now. Take your bag and go.' There was venom in his voice.

For the first time that evening Elizabeth lost her serene visage. 'I will not be spoken to like that!' she spat.

'You'll be spoken to any way I see fit under this roof. You have disgraced me and my family for no reason other than your own petty prejudices.' A drop of blood fell from his nose onto the floor.

'Please go, Mum, just go,' sobbed Caroline.

41

Elizabeth ground her teeth and picked up her handbag.

'One more thing,' Stuart said as she was about to step off the verandah. Elizabeth spun round.

'If I ever hear you trying to impress your vile attitudes onto my sons, you will never be left alone with them. I hope I make myself crystal clear.'

The grandmother departed in high dudgeon.

For a while the only sounds were the robin's song and the tinkling of glass as Stuart cleared the shards. Once complete, he poured two large glasses of red wine and handed them to the women. He stoked the braai and, as the smell of the coal mingled with the fragrance coming from the garden, peace returned.

The remaining Fines, now without transport, remained at the Frasers for the night. Stuart offered to take them home, but Sarah said she didn't feel like facing her husband. Hamish was hugely excited about the sleepover: while the adults were eating, Reggie, Hamish and Roger cleared the linen cupboard of towels and made a blanket fort, in which they eventually drifted off to sleep.

During the course of the dinner (fillet steaks, exquisitely marinated lamb chops and a not-insubstantial volume of excellent red wine), Sarah explained that Albert's outbursts were frequent and angry. He wasn't a violent man – he'd never harmed Reggie or Sarah – but he was obsessed with issues of social justice, and his temper was vicious and unpredictable. Sarah knew that the family's meagre savings were being dished out to funds supporting the families of incarcerated or murdered struggle activists.

'Every time I write a cheque, I'm afraid it will bounce.' She sniffed. 'Our electricity's been cut off more than once ...'

Albert was bombastic, Sarah said. As far as he was concerned, if a person wasn't lying underneath the bulldozers stopping the forced removals, they were as good as conspiring with the apartheid government. She admired his dedication and commitment – it was why she'd fallen in love with him – but she was never sure if Albert realised how

his work affected his wife and child. He would hear no word on the subject and simply began railing if she suggested that he might spend more
time with his daughter: 'What about Mandela's kids and the countless
others who have no fathers?' he'd yell before slamming his study door.
Reggie was used to it – she'd never known anything different.

'I've started seeing strange cars on the street outside the house – I'm
sure it's the security police. It's bloody terrifying.'

The evening ended late, and while Caroline readied herself for bed,
Stuart sat on the edge of the verandah with a nightcap. Parkin lay next
to him, wagging her tail. The dim stars shone through the trees and
the generous measure of Talisker caught the light spilling through the
teak cottage-pane windows. Stuart sipped the amber elixir as the distant
sound of a police siren tainted the serenity of his garden. He couldn't
help but compare himself with Albert – a man who was sacrificing his
happiness and quite possibly his physical safety for the well-being of
others. Here Stuart was, sipping an expensive whisky from a crystal
glass on an extensive acre of Africa, his only real worry being where the
family would holiday next.

Retreating into the house, Stuart looked in on his children once more.
There wasn't a peep from Roger's room. Hamish was snoring as normal, splayed dramatically. Reggie lay in the foetal position, cradling a
fraying orange teddy.

In their bedroom, Caroline was taking out her contact lenses.

'You know,' Stuart began, 'maybe we should feel ashamed.'

'Maybe,' she answered, 'but I'm not sure what to do about it. Stuart,
is it really that bad in the rural areas? Is it not isolated – albeit brutal –
patches of oppression?'

Stuart shook his head. 'We meet Tina every sunny morning and she
greets us with a smile and we think, "Gosh, it's nor really that bad is it?"
That's the brilliance of the state machinery.'

Caroline sighed. 'I suppose the problem is that it's so easy to live like
we do.'

'Shielded from the actual horror of what's going on,' Stuart finished.

The next day, Tina received a cheque and a promise that should her children need uniforms, books or anything education-related, she merely had to ask.

6

At four-thirty in the morning on a Saturday in mid-December, Stuart took Tina to the bus station in the middle of Johannesburg. He'd given strict instructions for the rest of his family to be ready and waiting the instant he returned, for a departure no later than six o'clock. As Stuart pulled into the driveway, Hamish, butt naked, ran out of the house, a plastic cup of chocolate milk sloshing down his front.

Stuart grabbed his son, dragged him into the house and factored in a delay of at least sixty minutes.

Inside, even Roger's serene disposition had been ruffled by the excitement of the impending holiday. At the kitchen table he was trying, and failing, to stuff his not insubstantial collection of Matchbox cars into a little brown suitcase. The hinges eventually snapped off and miniature automobiles exploded in all directions.

From the far end of the house, Caroline bellowed, 'Stuuuuaaart!'

Mr Fraser could gauge the state of the world from the tone of his wife's voice. He factored in a further sixty-minute delay, left his children driving toy cars through puddles of chocolate milk and walked through to Hamish's room, where he found his wife in amongst a pile of children's clothing and close to tears. The suitcases she'd carefully packed the night before had been emptied at first light by Hamish, who didn't agree with his mother's choice of holiday togs. Indeed, seven pairs of underpants, five socks (none matching), a model aeroplane and his

45

bedside lamp were what Hamish intended to fulfil his summer dreams.

The Frasers finally turned out of their driveway at five to nine. The boys were snivelling slightly, having received a lashing (tongue in Roger's case, hand in Hamish's). Stuart and Caroline were on no speaks, but both were relieved to be on their way.

The Frasers' route took them down South Africa's main artery, and Stuart and Caroline re-established friendly relations as the summer countryside passed them by.

In the flat farmlands of the Orange Free State, good summer rains had turned the maize, wheat and sunflower fields to abundant green. There was a brief stop on the side of the road just beyond the lamentable town of Kroonstad for some coffee, sandwiches, boiled eggs and sausages. They bypassed Bloemfontein, and Hamish stared out of the window as farmlands gave way to the arid scrub of Karoo sheep farms, the flat-topped hills a subtle backdrop of green, grey and purple. Overhead stretched the impossibly blue vault, with flocks of cumulus drifting lazily by. Roger, not quite as enamoured by the scenery, alternated between sleeping and paging through a picture book.

Caroline had packed some snacks for the boys and these she doled out at intervals. The cooler box was cunningly placed between them so that they'd be unable to attack each other – or, more accurately, so that Hamish wouldn't be able to irritate his little brother to the point of violence.

Caroline passed the time knitting and while she concentrated on a particularly difficult section of the cardigan she was creating, Hamish's little hand reached repeatedly into the cooler box, where he'd discovered the irresistible combination of boiled sweets and dried guava roll. Roger noticed, but chose not to say anything.

Just outside the farming outpost of Springfontein, Roger looked over to his brother and considered that his face had turned a livid shade of troll. Two minutes after that, three guava rolls, ten sweets, and a masticated mixture of hard-boiled egg, pork banger and cheese sandwich emerged from Hamish's mouth in a multicoloured projectile torrent. The driver's seat took the brunt of the stream, but so strong was the objection of Hamish's bowels that a fair amount splashed up over the top of the cream-leather seats and onto Stuart's shoulders.

As Stuart realised the source of the warm spattering on his head and upper body, he slammed on the brakes and swerved off the road. The violent lurch unbalanced Hamish, whose head turned towards his brother. Roger saw the next few seconds in slow motion. His eyes doubled in size and the slightly smug look on his face turned to terror as Hamish's mouth opened for a second deluge. The car screeched to a halt on the verge and Roger lunged for the door, but not before he'd received a goodly covering of sick down the front of his new stripy T-shirt.

Before the third emanation, Hamish had been pulled from the car by his seething father. Stuart was squeamish and it wasn't long before he too was retching into an unfortunate farmer's wheat field.

That night, the Frasers slept in Colesberg on a stud farm belonging to an old family friend of Elisabeth's. After a supper of roast Karoo lamb, Hamish, having recovered from the excesses of his confectionery theft, lay listening to the semi-desert night. The open window next to his bed framed a paddock where, bathed in the blue light of the full moon, a dark bay gelding pulled grass from a hay net. Hamish thought how much Reggie would have liked the horse as he fell asleep to the delicious smells of the Karoo.

The family arrived without further incident in the little seaside hamlet of Great Brak.

As the car pulled up to the double-storey white house, two people of a sort that Hamish and Roger had yet to encounter rushed out. They were, in the South African sense, 'coloured'. Cena and Tyrone Tobias were employed to service the house and cater to the whims of its tenants. They spoke only Afrikaans, although they understood smatterings of English. Stuart's Afrikaans vocabulary was diabolical and his accent worse.

'Hello, I'm Stuart,' he said, holding out his hand.

Tyrone took it. 'Angenaam, baas,' he said, looking down.

His wife repeated the greeting, her hands clasped in front of her apron.

'Oh, um,' replied Stuart, 'would you, eh, rather call me Mr Fraser or better still, Stuart?'

'Ja, Mr Stchooyit,' Cena replied.

Presently, Caroline manhandled her two sons up to the front door. Hamish stared in mouth-gaping amazement at the two new faces. Although they carried a cocktail of South African genetics, a goodly proportion of the Tobiases' blood was that of South Africa's first people. Both in their seventies, their faces were leathery and wrinkled in a way that Hamish had never seen before. Neither had front teeth (or indeed any teeth in Cena's case) and this amplified their furrowed visages.

'Mum!' Hamish tugged at Caroline's shirt sleeves.

'Shh!'

'Mum, this lady has got no teeth and her face looks like a huge raisin!'

Caroline went pale but Cena wheeled around cackling with laughter.

'Nee, my seun!' the tiny woman squawked with a toothless grin. She took Hamish's little hand and put it on her face. 'Kyk hoe voel my ou vel!'

'Are you a Sotho like Tina?'

'Nee, ek's nie 'n Sotho nie.' She frowned. 'Ek's 'n kleurling!'

For Christmas, Hamish and Roger received fishing rods. Stuart was no fisherman, but Tyrone was the keenest fisher in the Cape Province, and in order to escape the drudgery of cleaning the house and tending the garden, he offered to teach the boys the rudiments of angling.

So it was that on Boxing Day, just as the sun was peeping up over the horizon, Hamish, Roger and Tyrone headed off on foot for a jetty that extended into the Great Brak River. From the rickety wharf, Hamish inhaled the scent of the sea and the comforting smell of pipe tobacco that hung around Tyrone. The boys had carried their little rods and small plastic buckets. Tyrone carried four rods and an old tin box with his fishing knives, hooks and tackle. For bait, Stuart had been instructed to supply frozen sardines.

There was no common language between the boys but the old man shared his passion without words. At the river, the boys watched as Tyrone attached sinkers, swivels and hooks to their lines. Roger took full note of how the various knots were achieved; Hamish was distracted by a flock of terns wheeling in the sky, the early sun rimming their wings with gold.

'Kyk hier, seuntjie,' Tyrone admonished gently before demonstrating how to cast a line into the water. Both boys managed this task after a few tries, then Tyrone baited the hooks and indicated the water. 'Nou gaan ons 'n bietjie vis vang!'

Three lines sailed out into the glassy river …

Almost immediately, Hamish began frantically reeling in his line, convinced that the slight drag caused by the incoming tide was a monstrous fish. The piece of bait emerged from the water at a terrific speed, and before Tyrone could stop him, Hamish's sinker had caught in the top eye of his rod. The sudden cessation of movement caused the rod to jerk in the young fisherman's hand. Hamish watched the sardine slip off the hook and plop into water just as Roger dropped his own rod and yelped in agony as Hamish's hook embedded in his leg. Unaware of what had caused his brother's distress, Hamish involuntarily jerked his rod. The hook came free of Roger's leg along with a piece of his left calf.

Hamish was horrified. Tyrone went pale and dropped his rod.

Roger sat down and wailed as blood flowed.

'Oh, fokkit,' said Tyrone, kneeling at Roger's side.

'Rog, I'm sorry, I'm sorry!' cried Hamish. 'Rog!'

'Wag net, seun,' Tyrone said to Hamish, holding out his hand.

The old man sat next to the wounded child and assessed the damage. The number of booze-fuelled, pay-day bust-ups he'd witnessed as a youth had given Tyrone a fair idea of what constituted a lethal injury, and this wasn't one. The wound was bleeding but not deep, so he took a handkerchief out of his pocket, tied it around the calf and scooped up the little boy. With a stern look, he beckoned Hamish to follow.

It was a five-minute walk back to the house. By the time they approached the front door, Roger's wail had become a snivel. Tyrone carried the boy into the kitchen, where Stuart was making coffee – looking forward to a child-free dawn with his wife and his holiday read. Roger began crying again when he saw Stuart and the father's dreams evaporated.

'What happened?' He looked at Tyrone and then at Hamish. From Hamish's baleful look it was clear he was responsible.

The old man placed the boy on the kitchen table and took two quick steps back towards the door. He explained the incident using hand signals and Afrikaans, his eyes flickering from Stuart's face to his right hand.

Despite his rudimentary Afrikaans, Stuart caught the gist.

'I send you off with my boy and he comes back missing his leg!' he said to Tyrone with mock severity.

'Jammer, baas,' Tyrone stammered.

Hamish was astonished – he'd never seen a grown man cowed before.

'Please,' Stuart said, shaking his head. 'Ek is nie ... um ... cross ... kwaad met jou.' His final attempt at humour was to tell Tyrone that not even God was able to predict the erratic nature of his eldest son's actions. The sentiment and the shocking way it was delivered broke any tension.

Caroline appeared presently and after the predictable hysteria at the thought of her injured babies, she set to mending her youngest son's flesh. Stuart poured three cups of coffee and handed one to Tyrone, offering him a seat at the kitchen table. He then turned his attention to Hamish, who was obviously mortified by what he'd done.

'Sorry, Dad,' Hamish said sniffing. 'I didn't mean to.'

The morning after the hook-in-the-leg incident, Hamish woke at dawn again. He let himself out of the house and took his rod down to the wharf. He had no sardines so he took half a loaf of bread to bait his hook. With the sun rising at his back, Hamish tossed a line into the still, silver water. He was careful to reel in very slowly and after about half an hour, his patience paid off: a small steenbras took the hook and swam off. Hamish's little coffee grinder sung as the line disappeared into the distance.

The boy immediately clicked the lock on the reel and began frantically winding the handle. The tiny rod bent to breaking as Hamish fought the fish. After what to him felt like an hour, but was more like two minutes, the unluckiest fish in the estuary emerged onto the wharf.

Hamish was thus confronted – completely unprepared – with a flapping steenbras. But he knew his father would know what to do, so he grabbed the rod in one hand and the line just above the fish's mouth with the other, and set off at a brisk trot.

A breathless three minutes later, Hamish arrived at the kitchen door. This morning it was his mother on coffee duty.

'Mummy, Mummy, look!'

Caroline turned around to see the hapless fish flailing in her son's hand. She was not a person who killed her own food; indeed, if it didn't come from a shop, Caroline tended to regard nature's bounty with deep suspicion.

'Oh God, Hamish, what have you done now?' she said, turning green.

'I catched a fish – all on my own!' Hamish grinned.

'But it's still alive!' His mother retched.

'I don't know how to kill it,' replied the boy.

Caroline was about to yell for Stuart when Tyrone walked into the kitchen.

'Yoh, klein baas! Jy'd vis gevang by jouself!'

'Oh, Tyrone,' began Caroline. 'Asseblief kan jy die vis doodmaak – dis verskriklik om hom so te sien ly!'

Tyrone grabbed the fish in one hand and with the other he directed

51

Hamish to a backyard sink. There he demonstrated how to extract the hook and then he pushed his fingers into the gills and snapped the neck. The crack of the breaking bone made Hamish take a step back.

Tyrone laughed. 'Volgende keer as jy die vis vang, dan maak *jy* hom dood!'

The steenbras (all eight inches of it) was then handed to Cena for preparation. Hamish was deeply distressed when he found out at breakfast that his fish was insufficient to feed the whole household. He made sure, however, that Roger (who was still limping slightly) had a good portion. Roger ate his distasteful mouthful graciously.

7

On the first day of Grade Two, Hamish woke with a sore throat. He lay for a little while, looking at the uniform hanging over the back of his chair. Roger came bustling in, immaculately dressed for his first day of Pre-Prep but for his tie.

'Hamish, can you show me how to put this on?' he asked, holding up the navy strip.

Soon there was a large granny knot in the tie, and Roger was having difficulty breathing. The younger boy left to find his father while Hamish fell back on his bed and closed his eyes.

A few minutes later, Caroline came softly into his room with a cup of chocolate milk.

'Hamish, it's time to get up now – nearly time for school. Aren't you excited?' she affected, knowing the answer. She placed the cup of tepid liquid on his lap as he sat up. 'Are you feeling alright?' She put her hand to his forehead. 'You don't have a temperature.'

She pulled the covers off the bed.

'Drink up and get dressed. You know Dad doesn't like it when you're late.'

After his chocolate milk, Hamish lay back down and in three seconds was fast asleep. The next thing he knew, his father was yelling.

'Come on, Hamish! Get up, boy!'

Hamish slumped out of his bed and wandered into the bathroom, where he gave his teeth a perfunctory once-over before dragging on his uniform.

The five weeks since he'd last worn a tie resulted in an abomination, the fat end two inches long and the thin end hanging three inches below his belt. He was utterly unmotivated to fix the problem. His shoes were also too much effort, and he slouched through to the kitchen for breakfast in his socks. Tina managed to elicit the first and only smile of the morning, having arrived back from her Christmas break in Witsieshoek late the previous evening.

Hamish smiled as she picked him up and enveloped him in a cheerful hug.

'Was wrong?' she asked.

'Nothing, Gogo. I'm a little bit tired today.'

'Where are your shoes?' asked Stuart.

'In my room, Dad.'

Hamish ate half a bowl of over-sugared cornflakes and left a piece of marmalade toast uneaten.

While Roger waited at the back door, it took the combined efforts of Tina, Caroline and Stuart to ready Hamish for his departure. His satchel looked like it had suffered a road accident (inside, Tina found a sandwich on which five weeks' worth of gleeful mould was thriving). His pencil box contained three broken stubs and two marbles. The blazer was in an almost acceptable state only because Caroline had reattached the buttons the night before. His brand-new tie (the old one soiled beyond use) had acquired a fresh milk stain during his meagre breakfast.

The traditional photograph of the boys' first day of school would show a grinning Roger and, looking somewhere into the middle distance, his dishevelled brother, now a full inch shorter.

As the car pulled out of the driveway, Caroline turned to Tina, knowing that even if the answer to her query was inaccurate, it would be honest.

'What do you think is wrong with Hamish?'

'He is afraid, Manna. He hasn't got friends.'

Staring up the brick driveway, Caroline's eyes teared up. There'd

54

been a few invitations to play during the previous year, but Hamish had hated every single one. Regular visits to and from Reggie had continued to form the bulk of his social life.

'Why doesn't he have friends?' Caroline sniffed.

'He's not like Roger, Manna. He doesn't like people – he's not nice to them.'

A few minutes later, the Mercedes pulled into the car park at Trinity Pre-Prep fifteen minutes after the intended arrival time. Stuart led the two boys across the field, one attached to each hand, Roger slightly ahead and Hamish slightly behind.

Hamish tried to accompany Roger and his father to Mrs Arnot's class, but Stuart shook his head.

'No, boy, you need ta go ta Grade Two. You're a big boy now. You must go on your own. I'll see you tonight.' He kissed his son's head and turned him towards his classroom, where, as per the previous year, Hamish was the last to arrive.

There was one seat left in the middle of the class. Mrs Wallingford indicated it to Hamish.

'Good morning, master Fraser,' she said sternly.

'Good morning, Mrs Wallingford.'

'You are late this morning, aren't you?'

'Yes, Mrs Wallingford.'

'You must say sorry when you are late.'

'Sorry, Mrs Wallingford.'

'Hamish, you must say sorry to the whole class, because you have kept all your friends waiting.'

Had Hamish felt more alive, he'd have replied, 'These people are not my friends.' But he was dazed by the abrupt cessation of his freedom. 'Sorry, everybody.'

'Good fellow,' said Mrs Wallingford cheerfully. 'Now go and sit down.'

At break time Hamish imagined that Roger and he might eat their sandwiches together. He found his brother playing soccer with ten Grade One boys and thought better of disturbing the game. Instead, he made an attempt to join a game that his own class was enjoying.

'Wayne,' he asked the closest boy, 'can I play?'

'It's Johnny's ball,' said Wayne, tearing off after a pass.

Hamish waited patiently until Johnny was closer.

'Hey, Johnny? Johnny! Can I play?'

Johnny looked at his diminutive classmate. 'Ja, but only if you're good.'

'Ja, I'm good.'

'Okay,' said Johnny, 'you can play left back.'

Hamish tried. He chased the ball wherever it was, playing every possible position (he had no idea what a left back was) but whenever he received the ball, he was immediately dispossessed. After ten minutes he gave up. He wandered towards the northern side of the field through a grove of ugly eucalyptus trees to a secluded pine (a poor substitute for his beloved walnut) he had discovered late the year before.

On Monday mornings Tina always added a little treat to Hamish's lunch box – normally a flat red lollipop. Not being a great sharer, Hamish always took his Monday snack on a low-hanging branch of the pine.

One freezing winter's morning in June, Hamish was eating his peanut-butter sandwich in the tree, looking forward to the lollipop and wondering when the summer would return.

Suddenly, the loud voices of Nicholas Cullinan, Robert Bosch, Christopher Cooper and Toffee Botha broke the silence of the tree's ambit. Cullinan was the largest boy and ringleader of a group that called itself the A-Team, after the television classic. They announced their arrival with a very poor attempt at singing the first three notes of the theme tune.

'Dan dan *daaan!*' growled Cullinan (aka Hannibal) as the gang descended from the field.

Hamish swung round to see the four boys circling.

'Hey, you!' shouted Cullinan. 'Give me your lollipop.'

'Ja, give him your lollipop,' added Robert Bosch (aka BA).

While there was menace in Cullinan's unusually high-pitched voice, Hamish felt irritation more than fear. Who the hell did this foul boy think he was instructing Hamish to do anything, let alone demand his precious Monday treat?

Toffee Botha (aka Murdoch) approached and pushed Hamish's lunch box to the ground. A half-eaten peanut-butter sandwich and a juice bottle fell into the dry needles below.

'BA,' commanded Cullinan, 'bring me that juice.'

Bosch did as he was told, whereupon Cullinan dropped the bottle and jumped on it with both feet. The plastic buckled, and liquid exploded into the dirt.

Hamish's irritation turned to rage, but before he could say anything, Christopher Cooper (aka Faceman) shoved him hard from behind. Hamish tumbled out of the tree and into the small muddy patch created by the ruined juice. The three stooges held him down – two on his legs and one on his arms – and Cullinan straddled him, sitting down heavily on his stomach and knocking the wind out of the smaller boy.

'This is my lollipop now.' The gang leader tore it from Hamish's grasp, pulled off the wrapper and popped the delicious redness into his mouth.

Hamish fell into fury. 'You dumb, stupid moron! That's *my* sucker!' he yelled. 'It's *mine*!' Tears welled up as he thrashed ineffectually.

'No, it's mine,' replied Cullinan. He pushed a knuckle from his balled right fist into his victim's sternum.

Hamish thought he might burst with pain. He screamed as his breath returned in ragged sobs.

'Want some of my lolly?' Cullinan asked.

'It's *my* sucker,' Hamish sniffled.

'Here, you can have it back,' said Cullinan. He took the sweet,

57

dripping with saliva, and pushed it into Hamish's gasping mouth.

The victim gagged, turned his head and spat it out.

Cullinan stood up to deliver his final line: 'I love it when a plan comes together.'

With that, the A-Team departed.

For a minute or so, Hamish lay panting, crying and spitting, the thought of Cullinan's saliva in his mouth more horrific than anything else. His back was freezing and he realised he was lying in a muddy puddle of juice and the remains of his peanut-butter sandwich. As he stood, the tears flowed again – he didn't even like the juice nor did he enjoy peanut-butter sandwiches, but he had watched Tina make those sandwiches for him and pack them lovingly into his lunch box. The sandwich was a connection to comfort and love – to his mum and dad, Tina, his brother and Parkin the dog. The flattened and muddy food was an obscene violation of home. Racked by uncontrollable sobs, Hamish gathered his lunch box and scrambled up to the field.

The break bell was ringing and children were charging across the grass to sit in class lines before the orderly march back to lessons. Hamish wanted to see just one person.

Roger was at the front of his class, sitting patiently on the ground, waiting for instruction. Hamish sat down next to his brother.

'What happened?' asked Roger, alarmed at the snivelling and grubbier-than-normal appearance of his sibling.

'They took my sucker!' was all Hamish managed before the tears came again.

Mrs Arnot was on break duty. She spotted the befouled child sullying her class's line.

'Hamish Fraser! Get into your own line! Do you want to be back in Grade One?'

'But the A-Team took my sucker!' Hamish wailed.

Mrs Arnot neither knew nor cared who the A-Team was and was utterly unconcerned with their crime. 'Don't you dare talk back to me – get to the back of your own class line right now!'

Hamish's tears dried instantly. He stood and, just for a second too long, stared the teacher in her eyes.

The reaction at home to this incident was predictable. Caroline was convinced they needed to convene a meeting with the headmistress, who in turn would have to call in the A-Team's parents and demand they discipline their bullying sons. Stuart said that Hamish was going to have to learn to deal with bullies – sooner or later his son would have to negotiate the world's social complexities.

Tina's reaction was prosaic. Young children fought with each other, the smaller ones normally lost, therefore Hamish should be taught to fight.

8

'Let's send him to this.' Caroline walked onto the veran-dah brandishing a pamphlet from the letter box. It was a Saturday morning and Stuart was examining the weekend edition of *The Star*, a steaming mug of black coffee next to him. Parkin stirred under his feet.

Stuart looked up. 'Send whom teh what?'

Caroline proffered the pink paper and her husband frowned.

'Pony camp?'

Caroline sat down on the cane sofa. 'Yes, pony camp – it's perfect for him. He can meet kids of other ages in a fun environment. You said yourself that he needs some sort of physical outlet given how utterly hopeless he is at ball sports. Also, he can meet people – girls especially – outside of the stuffy atmosphere of that school. Reggie can't be his only friend forever.'

Stuart leant back, looked into the garden and shrugged. 'Isn't riding ponies for gurls?'

'No! Lots of boys ride – well, some at least. You know how he loves riding in the mountains.'

'I don't suppose it can do any harm,' said the father, returning to his paper.

The Inanda Club, part of which was an illustrious livery yard, nestled in the suburban forest about five blocks from the Frasers. Two days after the end of his second year of scholastic underachievement, Caroline drove Hamish to the club. He was apprehensive. In fact, he was terrified. Not at the thought of riding – he'd done that many times in the Drakensberg. Rather, it was the thought that he'd be away from his family for a week with a bunch of complete strangers. His parents had convinced him to go only by explaining that he could phone if he wasn't happy and they would fetch him.

The little boy, now eight years old but two years smaller, looked out of the car window as the tyres rattled over the driveway. On the left, beyond a neat row of syringa and pine, were paddocks in which horses grazed or dozed in the shade.

Caroline led her son to an office building. Behind it stretched four rows of stables – space for some sixty horses. To the right of the path was a circular arena for beginner riders and two rectangular sand arenas with an assortment of jumps. Hamish's attention was drawn to a huge liver-chestnut thoroughbred sailing over a four-foot spread.

Outside the office, under a pergola strung with jasmine, a line had formed in front of an austere woman with permed, dark hair who was consulting a clipboard. Around her, four teenage girls were helping to separate young campers from their parents, and hefting their belongings into the clubhouse. The Frasers were the last to arrive, and joined the back of the queue, Hamish patiently holding his mother's hand.

Eventually it was their turn.

'Hello,' Caroline said to the woman. 'Um … I'm Caroline Fraser and this is my son Hamish.'

The woman looked up at Caroline and then down at the little boy. A faint smile flickered in her eyes.

'I'm Annabelle. Welcome to Inanda.' She ticked off Hamish's name and then placed the clipboard next to her on a wire table and folded her arms. 'Have you ridden before, Hamish?'

Instead of shrinking back behind his mother, the boy looked up at the riding teacher's face. There was something about her matter-of-fact tone that appealed to him.

'Yes, I've ridden in the mountains on my holidays,' he replied.

Annabelle arched her right eye-brow upwards. 'Ah, a mountain rider.' She looked at Caroline, who shrank away slightly under the confident woman's stare. 'How many times has he ridden?'

'Oh, um, about ten, I suppose.' She looked down at her son and back up at Annabelle. 'I don't know how good he is, but he seems to like horses.'

'Well, that's a good first step!' Annabelle looked back at Hamish. 'And you're about six, are you?'

The boy's hitherto placid face pinched in a vicious scowl. 'I'm eight and two months!'

'Oh!' said Annabelle smiling. 'Well, you're not a very big boy, but as long as you're brave, that's okay.'

Not considering himself particularly brave, Hamish looked at the floor. At that moment, a thirteen-year-old girl with a vast plumage of curly red hair and a smile of perfect white teeth emerged from the clubhouse.

'Imogen,' said Annabelle, 'please take young Hamish into the clubhouse and find him a space to sleep.'

This was the moment he'd be separated from his mother – for six whole days.

Imogen held out her hand. 'Hello, Hamish. Come, let's go and say hello to the others.'

Hamish looked up as his mother, whose eyes filled with tears as she forced a smile. 'I'll see you next Sunday, darling.'

Before the goodbye could become any more painful, Imogen took Hamish's hand, picked up his bag and dragged him into the clubhouse.

The boy's bedding for the week was to be a camping mattress and sleeping bag that Stuart had last used for a canoe trip to Loch Ness in the Fifties. While thirty years older than everyone else's, the equipment smelt of home.

62

The next morning, Imogen woke the eighteen little campers at dawn. Hamish said very little as he stood in line to receive a cup of the sweetest tea he'd ever tasted. He then found a rock to sit on outside the clubhouse as the sun came up. Angela, a precocious eight-year-old with ash-blonde hair and a supercilious twist to her wide mouth, strode over and looked down at him.

'I'm Angela and I'm eight years old. I'm riding Uncle Dick. He's the best horse in the world. Who are you and who are you riding?'

Hamish scowled. 'I'm Hamish Fraser. I don't know who I'm riding.'

Angela sat down next to Hamish on a tiny piece of protruding rock and the boy flinched as her backside made contact with his.

'Well, don't worry about that,' she said. 'There's lots of ponies here – Annabelle will give you one. I started riding in Grade One and I've just finished Grade Two. There's Annabelle – let's go and ask her who your pony is.' The little girl dropped her cup on the ground, grabbed Hamish's hand and dragged him towards the riding instructor.

'Annabelle, Annabelle!' Angela squealed. 'This-is-Hamish-and-he-doesn't-have-a-pony-who-is-his-pony-can-you-tell-him-who-his-pony-is-he-*must*-have-a-pony-for-the-camp!'

The woman looked from the bright face of the girl to the shocked boy.

'Good morning, Angela. Good morning, Hamish,' Annabelle said evenly.

'Good morning,' replied Hamish.

'Yes, but *who* is this boy's pony, Annabelle?'

'Angela, calm down – I'll tell Hamish and the other children who they're riding in a few minutes.'

A little while later, each child had been allocated a pony for the week. Many of the children had been riding for a year or two already and some would be riding their own steeds. The novices were dispatched to a row of stables in which lived a collection of ancients – docile ponies tolerant of the kicking, shouting and rein-tugging inflicted on them by the progeny of the white middle class.

Hamish was allocated Rex – an arthritic gelding well north of thirty years. His coat, once lustrous dark bay, was flecked with grey. His back bowed and his muzzle was almost completely white. On sighting the horse for the first time, Stuart would remark that Rex would be of more use in a glue stick than a stable yard. Elizabeth thought the pony had an unfashionable Roman nose, giving him the appearance of an equine Barbara Streisand. But to these and myriad other shortcomings, Hamish was blind. His favourite movie was *The Black Stallion* – and to him, Rex looked exactly like the film's great Arabian.

The children were separated into groups according to their experience. It quickly became apparent that the young Fraser had some natural aptitude for riding, so he was installed in the front of the novice class. When, just three days later, he was trotting and cantering unaided, he was promoted to the intermediate riders.

This, his first actual success in life, brought some confidence.

The mornings at pony camp began with the rising sun. After their tea, the children would collect empty hay nets and wander, bleary-eyed, to the hay barn. Dust rising off the bales would elicit a storm of sneezing, and, on one occasion, Harry St Claire (aged eight) let out a screech as a Johannesburg rat with a yen for more bucolic times scuttled across his path. Stuffing the nets with spiky grass was an unpleasant task for the soft hands of Johannesburg's elite. The grooms looking after the horses not occupied with pony camp filled their nets at the opposite side of the barn, chatting and laughing – their calloused skin impervious and their sinuses accustomed to the dust.

Once Rex was chomping away on his hay and the sparrows were chirpily collecting crumbs of horse feed in the sun outside, it was time for Hamish to muck out the stable. Wielding the dung shovel taxed his small muscles, but he was inspired to greatness by the fear of being out-done by Angela. Her pony, Uncle Dick, a tractable light bay older than the Sphinx, was stabled next door to Rex, and the two children made regular forays to inspect each other's progress, lavishing useless advice. (The workout proved far more beneficial than standing in the middle of a cricket field waiting for a ball he had no hope of catching or trying desperately to figure out where on the soccer field the left back was supposed to operate.)

After the morning ride, it was grooming time. Hamish had to stand on a bucket to reach most of his pony, but Rex was compliant and enjoyed the sensation of having his body tickled. Then it was tack-cleaning and some theory lessons, which Hamish found surprisingly interesting. After lunch, there was free time, during which the kids swam in the club pool.

On the second afternoon, Hamish found himself paddling around in the shallow end feeling self-consciously alone. Leanne and Imogen (both thirteen) were lounging nearby, keeping an eye on the water in case one of the younger ones failed to surface.

'Hamish,' called Leanne, 'come over here.'

She was smiling, so he swam across to them and peered over the pool edge. The two girls were lying on their fronts, the hot flagstones warming their bellies.

'Hamish ... why do you speak with such a posh accent?' asked Leanne.

'What does that mean?' asked Hamish.

'It's when you speak like you're from London or something,' explained Imogen.

'I'm not from London. I'm from the Sandton Clinic.' Realising he'd just made a little joke, Hamish grinned.

'Well, you speak like you're from London or like someone in a book,' said Leanne, 'but it makes you sound older.'

Hamish took this as a compliment, realising that he rather enjoyed pony camp.

As twilight fell, the pony campers refilled hay nets, topped up water buckets and brushed down their horses. The sparrows returned for their final scraps, and the thrushes and robins sang from the syringas.

Happy children devoured their dinners, satiating appetites built up by a long physical day. After teeth-cleaning (Hamish was fastidious about this task, while some others were gathering a layer of fur over the course of the camp), the campers settled on their beds, Hamish between Angela and Imogen.

He lay on his back, revelling in the feeling of a satisfying day, and watched Imogen painstakingly brush her immense volume of red hair, the fragrance drifting down to him.

'Sleep tight, posh Hamish,' she said.

As Angela prattled on about Uncle Dick's merits and his new almost-friends bantered quietly about the day's events, Hamish drifted into a deep sleep.

The camp ended with a gymkhana that Sunday. Hamish woke in a nervous frenzy, determined to win his classes. He was entered in the Best Turned Out Horse and Rider, the Sack Race and the Walk Trot Canter.

The groom for the ponies who were just a few strides short of the dog-food cannery was Colin Sibanda, an illegal Zimbabwean immigrant in his early forties. He had joined the staff at Inanda only a few weeks before Hamish began riding and accordingly was assigned to the least fancied of the yard's residents. Colin was in Uncle Dick's stable helping Angela to saddle up when Hamish went into a panic.

Rex confounded the theory that equids sleep standing up – he lay like the dead on his sawdust bed and thus woke every morning covered in muck. The first event was the Best Turned Out, and Hamish knew that a horse in such a state of disrepair wasn't going to pass muster. His anxiety was increased by the fact that he'd just seen the competition: Fairy Star, a little Welsh pony, was standing near the arena, gossamer coat glimmering. She belonged to Harry St Claire, who happened to be in the other Grade Two class at Trinity.

Hamish ducked under the pole separating Rex from freedom and darted into the next-door stable, where Colin was giving a few final brushes to Uncle Dick and helping Angela to saddle up. The little girl, whispering to the aged steed about how much she loved him, was immaculate in a pair of cream jodhpurs and a white shirt with brass tie pin, her blonde hair in a neat net.

Panicked rage exploded from Hamish.

'Colin, my horse is dirty! It's not fair – now Angela and her *stupid* horse will win! Why haven't you cleaned Rex?'

Colin was used to white children treating him like the manure he shovelled for them. He looked down at the impudent, red-faced boy. 'I help you now,' he replied calmly.

Angela stared at Hamish in misplaced astonishment. 'Uncle Dick is *not* stupid!' she squealed, tears filling her righteous blue eyes.

'Uncle Dick *is* stupid and Colin is not doing his job!' the boy raged.

It was at that second that Stuart and Caroline appeared.

'Hamish!' Stuart bellowed.

Uncle Dick started at the noise, his muzzle knocking Angela to the ground, which set forth a loud wailing.

Stuart reached into the stable, grabbed his son by the arm and lifted him out. He dragged the child a few metres away. Stuart did not beat his child as a matter of course, but he was to make an exception that morning – he put the boy down and hit his backside three times with a flat hand.

'If I *ever* hear you speak to anyone like that again, I'll make sure you never ride a horse again. *Do you understand me?*'

'Yes.'

'I can't hear you!'

'Yes, Dad.' Tears streamed.

'Now you'll get back into that stable and say sorry to that man. You will *never* talk to him like that again. And then you will say sorry to that girl. Go!'

Hamish made his way sheepishly back to Uncle Dick's stable, where Caroline was apologising to Angela's mother, who wanted to know why her daughter was in tears and why the front of her brand-new shirt was covered in Uncle Dick's saliva, with his dung on the back. She looked at Hamish in disgust.

'I'm sorry, Angela,' Hamish sniffed.

'Tell her what for,' hissed Stuart from behind.

'I'm sorry for shouting and being rude to you and Colin.'

'Accept his apology,' eased Angela's mother in an accent that could have graced the halls of Kensington Palace.

'It's okay,' sniffed the girl, wiping her snotty nose with a remaining portion of clean sleeve.

'Now go and say sorry to the groom.'

Hamish walked into Rex's stable, where Colin was brushing the dirty pony, wanting to be anywhere else. In his experience, where there were squabbling whites, black people normally copped the blame.

'Sorry, Colin,' Hamish mumbled. He looked down at his black school-shoes, now covered in dust.

'Say it properly,' growled his father.

'I'm sorry, Colin, for being rude to you.' The boy began to cry again.

'Hello ... um ... I'm Mr Fraser, this boy's father. I am sorry that he spoke to you like that. Please will you forgive him?'

Colin looked up briefly and continued to brush the horse. 'Is no problem.'

By this stage, ponies and riders were emerging from all over the stables on their way to the arena, but there was one more injustice to right.

'What on earth are we going to do about your shirt? It's ruined!' Angela's mother bellowed.

'If I may,' interjected Stuart, 'your lass is the same size as my son. It's his fault that, um ... I'm sorry, what is your daughter's name?'

'Angela.'

'Well, Angela should wear Hamish's clean shirt and he'll make do with the dirty one.'

'We insist,' said Caroline, desperate to make amends.

Hamish did not win the Best Turned Out Horse and Rider. He came eighteenth – out of eighteen. The pony's coat was fair to middling but the fact that the rider's shirt looked as if it had passed through Rex's digestive tract precluded any participation in the awards ceremony.

The Walk Trot Canter race proved more successful. The rules were simple – walk one lap, trot the next and canter the third.

'Ready, steady, go!' Annabelle shouted.

There was a great flurry of activity but very little movement as children kicked in an effort to encourage eight of the world's oldest ponies into a brisk walk. Rex was out front (because of a false start), but then spotted a tuft of grass growing next to the arena and swerved with surprising agility across the phalanx of trailing competitors. Butternut – more mule than horse and topped by an overfed ten-year-old girl with a bright-red face – ambled around Rex to take the lead. Uncle Dick and Angela ended up wedged between Rex and the split-pole arena fence as Uncle Dick also set to the grass, but then Rex bit his neighbour on the muzzle. The latter bucked, and the last thing Hamish saw of Angela as his pony rejoined the race was her plummeting into the dirt. Like a riderless steed in the Grand National (in slow motion), Uncle Dick set off after the rest. The first two laps took the best part of a torturous five minutes – the jostling for position taken very seriously by the children and ignored almost completely by the ponies.

As they came round the bend for the final lap, the crowd (well, the parents and one or two grooms who found this gymkhana malarkey to be excellent for a laugh) began to cheer for their favourites. The riders forgot about technique, and twenty-eight limbs flailed, giving the impression of seven miniature windmills atop a sea of slow-moving horseflesh. As they passed the start line, Harry – mounted on Fairy Star, who was the youngest pony by decades – achieved a canter.

Something clicks over in the mind of a horse, no matter the age, when surrounded by galloping companions. Uncle Dick gathered what remained of his strength and began to canter. As the riderless pony surged past, Rex was inspired to acquiesce to Hamish's cajoling and he too began a spritely canter. Delighted to be catching up, Hamish simply went with the movement. As the two old ponies took off, the remaining five exploded to life and in a few seconds seven ponies (one sans rider) were charging down the straight in hot pursuit of Fairy Star.

Just before the first bend, Harry turned to judge the margin by which he was going to win. His eyes nearly popped out as he beheld the cavalry charge behind him. So fixated was he that he failed to steer his pony around the corner. Fairy Star jumped neatly over the arena fence and Harry, unprepared, bounced backwards over his pony's imperious bottom and into the sand. Uncle Dick followed the grey mare, and clattered through the fence.

Hamish hauled on his right rein and just before he jumped either over or through the prostrate Harry, Rex swerved. The other riders weren't as well balanced, and their ponies followed Uncle Dick and Fairy Star to freedom.

Rex and Hamish won the race – they were the only ones to finish. The prize-giving was delayed as parents, grooms and teachers tended to the injuries (physical and psychological) of the competitors and their mounts. Finally, Hamish was awarded a red rosette with '1st Place' embossed on it in gold.

Stuart smiled. It was the first time he'd felt pride for his son in this way, and it wasn't because Hamish had won, but because he'd kept his cool. Hamish's first outright victory went straight to his head, however, and he waved frantically at the politely clapping assemblage of parents and siblings.

Elizabeth, sipping champagne from a camping flute and ever more convinced that her grandson was possessed of an inferior brain, remarked, 'That beastly child thinks he's just won at Aintree.'

When the great rider joined his family at the side of the arena, Roger looked up from his collection of Matchbox cars with which he'd been patiently playing for some hours, and smiled at his brother. 'Well done, Hamish.'

Hamish looked at his sibling as though he was an irksome insect and flopped down in the middle of the picnic blanket, knocking over

Caroline's glass of orange juice. 'I think Rex is a bit slow for me because I'm such a good rider now. I will be needing another horse. And I want a roll with cheese.'

Stuart gritted his teeth. 'You —' he pointed his finger at Hamish '— over here. Right now.'

His father's tone indicated that he'd done something wrong, but Hamish had no idea what that might be.

Once again, Stuart grabbed Hamish by the arm and dragged him to a secluded paddock. 'Hamish, come on, boy! D'ya understand what it means to be humble? D'ya know what the word "humble" means?'

'No.'

'It means that when you win, you don't go around shouting about how good you are. When you win, you don't treat people like they are wurth less than you. Do you understand what I'm saying?'

Hamish stared at his father, who could see that his son was failing to compute.

'When Roger won the Maths prize, d'ya remember how he thanked you when you congratulated him? He didn't walk around like he was the king of the wurld. You are not the king of the wurld. You have done well today, but you must say thank you to people who say well done. D'ya understand now?'

'Yes, Dad.' Hamish scuffed his shoes in the sand and ground his teeth. He couldn't fathom how Roger's Maths prize could possibly compare with victory in the Walk, Trot and Canter.

Stuart sighed, looking up at the summer sky. 'I'm proud of you, Hamish, but please, you have to try and understand how you affect other people. Okay?'

'Okay, Dad.'

'Okay, boy, let's go and have a nice picnic. Say thank you to Roger for being nice and say sorry to Mum for knocking over her drink.'

Just before the Frasers left for home that day, Stuart and Caroline sought out Annabelle for an honest assessment of their son's riding ability.

Annabelle was frank, and declared that Hamish showed genuine promise as a rider, with an understanding well beyond his years. He was arrogant at times, she said, but he'd made an enormous effort at the pony camp. Compared with his unfavourable school report, which lamented his lack of effort in just about all facets of school life, this was a positive ray.

9

On reaching Standard One the following year, Hamish was required to audition for the choir. Mrs Sharp, the kind and gentle music mistress, called each boy up to the piano and played them a few notes. They had to pitch the notes and then sing 'Twinkle, Twinkle, Little Star'. It took Mrs Sharp half a minute to install Hamish in the choir – he sang his four notes perfectly and halfway through a rather theatrical performance of the nursery rhyme, she told him to sit down. It was with great pleasure that Hamish watched Andrew Marsdorf wail 'Twinkle, Twinkle, Little Star' like a startled goat – Marsdorf always laughed when Hamish dropped a cricket cherry or attempted to kick a soccer ball.

Having sung in choirs for much of his life, Stuart encouraged the musical outlet. He hoped that being part of the choir would give his boy an understanding of being in a team that sport had failed to. Hamish, however, merely enjoyed being on stage, giving very little thought to being in a team, and was as judgemental as ever of his peers' efforts.

'That was excellent!' gushed Caroline after an alfresco performance at the Summer Concert in February. The Pre-Prep's twenty best singers had given a rendition of 'Ching-a-ring-a ring ching' – a childish ditty with a pretty tune about the Exodus. (The fact that it came from the blackface tradition was lost on or ignored by the choir mistress.)

'Thanks, Mum,' replied Hamish, remembering with effort the correct response to praise. 'But Ryan has a horrible voice and his breath smells,' he added (not untruthfully – Ryan Newnam had terrific halitosis, an affliction of which he seemed entirely unaware.)

Unfortunately, Ryan and his mother, from whom a vague whiff of body odour emanated, were standing close by. The offended parent swung round.

'I'm so sorry,' said Caroline, her face crimson, as she dragged Hamish away to where the rest of the family was seated.

As the recorder orchestra began to sully the warm evening air, the Frasers settled into their picnic. To one side sat the St Claires – family of Harry, owner of Fairy Star. His father, Toby, an eccentric cockney immigrant and brilliant tax evader, laundered his wealth through a bevy of expensive horses that he let to others and sometimes rode (badly) himself. He sat on a camping chair, exuding *joie de vivre*, dressed in white flannel trousers, a blue-and-yellow striped blazer and a straw boater. A glass of Bollinger rested in one hand and a plate of expensive snacks balanced on his knee. His third wife, Harry's mother, apparently of Eastern European descent, was adorned in a flowing dress of bright emerald.

'Your boy sang real nice tonigh – lots o talen,' Toby raised his glass to Stuart. 'Fink I eard young Amish all the way from ere.'

'Thank you, I think,' said Stuart, abashed.

Toby ruffled Harry's thick blond hair. 'And you, Arry, lovely clear voices you boys ave.'

On the other side of the Frasers, the court of Philip and Jill Cooper was hosting the entourage of Felicity and Ronald Henderson. As relieved applause faded on completion of the recorder orchestra's destruction of 'Mary Had a Little Lamb', conversation turned, inevitably, to politics.

Ronald Henderson, banking mogul with unmoving and perfect coiffure, sighed, dragging his eyes from his evening copy of *The Citizen*. 'Have you heard about that school in Alexandra being burnt to the ground? I don't understand why they burn the one thing that offers hope!'

This was a magic bean to the fertile ground of Elizabeth's Chardonnay-fuelled prejudices, and she leant in. 'It's disgusting what those people do – how do they expect the police to react? They are vandalising state property built to help them!'

Philip Cooper, executive at Anglo American, concurred. 'Yes, it's difficult to see what violence will achieve in this context – of course the education is inferior, but at least it's *something*.'

Ronald forked a piece of quiche Lorraine into his mouth. 'We've moved a number of assets offshore. Frankly, I'm not sure business is sustainable in this climate, or under any dispensation in South Africa. The kids are down for British high schools, just in case things get out of hand here.'

'I've told Caroline and Stuart they should do the same,' agreed Elizabeth. 'I can't bear to think of my grandchildren growing up in yet another failed tinpot African country.'

Such crass sentiments were seldom voiced, although possibly shared, by the two astute business leaders – both of whom were masters at giving strong opinions that said absolutely nothing. Two picnics west, Toby was different. For one, he had twice the mind of the two Oxbridge-educated executives, and for another, he saw no point in owing allegiance to any flag. As far as he was concerned, human history (and he knew a lot about it) was a demonstration of how harmful flags and religions were, and he'd concluded that he owed allegiance only to his family and to himself (not necessarily in that order). Informed by this world view in a country run by religious and racial zealots, it wasn't surprising that he'd chosen fraud as the source of his gargantuan wealth.

As the junior string orchestra made their way onto the stage in the twilight, Toby began. 'Tell me, Philip, if you don mind, if no by violence, ow would *you* suggest the black people of vis country emancipate vemselves from the … eh … the "yoke of slavery", as i were?'

Toby irritated Philip Cooper, who cut an imposing figure and was used to be being addressed with reverence. Philip was not British by birth, but his Queen's English had been perfected during three years at Magdalene College, Cambridge. The small, balding, immigrant East Ender had no formal education, and worse, he was slouching in his chair with a cigar hanging from his mouth. Anglo was one of the country's largest employers of black labour and the upstart Cockney's inference that the mining conglomerate's workers were nothing more than glorified slaves, rankled.

'Well, Toby, I am not a believer in violence – I believe in peaceful protest and engagement. We all know apartheid is dreadful —' (nods of agreement all around) '— but I'm also not one to believe everything being spouted by the ANC propaganda machine.'

'Well ven, Philip, ol pal, I've a question to ask: should Britain no ave declared war on Nazi Germany?'

'Don't be ridiculous – of course they should have. But you cannot *possibly* compare Nazi Germany with apartheid.' The last bit was delivered quietly, as Philip realised he may have stumbled into a trap.

Toby pushed home. 'Well, I pu i to you, my son, vat for the average black man being fired upon in Soweo of a weekend, i seems very much like Nazi Germany. Now, you're a man of the church, righ?'

Cornered like a rat while the string orchestra set to sawing at their instruments, Philip replied: 'Yes, I'm a lay preacher at St Martin's.'

'Well, innit so vat *your* bishop – Tu'u – has compared apartheid with Nazism?'

'Bishop Tutu is also against all violence!' snapped Philip.

This was the sort of situation Toby revelled in.

'Yeah, but he *did* say vat aparheid is like Nazism. No only vat but e's ad some arsh fings to say abou wha we migh call the white middle class and veir general apafy to the plight of veir black brovvers.' Toby drained his glass. 'So I pu i to you, who are complainin about the parlous state o vis nation, vat you face something of a conundrum and i goes like vis.'

He removed his boater to examine the ribbon.

'If you are to live as you do – in a state o luxury and relative riches, in a counry where the black masses are traumatised by a governmen vat *your own bishop* has declared akin to Nazism – a governmen vat companies like Anglo supply wiff millions o rands worff o taxes, then perhaps, my son, you are part o the problem, ravver van part o the solution.'

'How dare you!' Ronald Henderson was stung out of his chair; a

76

chipolata sausage sailed into the air and landed in the grass. His family gathered blankets for the poor every winter, and regularly gave old clothes to their maids' and gardeners' families. 'We have supported the Progressive Party and the Liberal Party since their inceptions. We do not support apartheid and never have. I take exception to being called "part of the problem"!'

His wife had been pushed over the edge. 'As for that bloody bishop,' said Felicity, 'that man doesn't understand that politics and religion must be separate – the church is not the place for soapboxes and political insurrection. I mean, he's now calling for sanctions! Do you have any idea how that will affect us as a country – that beastly man is going to halve our wealth and drive the rand into the dirt.'

Toby had one more button to push. 'Feliciy, I can' claim to be a church man, so correc me if I'm wrong, but I don' recall the good Lord Jesus and his disciples – many of whom me ends as gruesome as veir master's – ever makin concessions in order vat the moneyed middle classes migh maintain veir portfolios.'

Felicity's greatest offence was that he'd lumped her in with what he called the middle classes – her family kept a palatial Westcliff residence and her husband's earnings were substantial. 'Please pass me a serviette,' she barked at Ronald, who dutifully handed her a table napkin. Felicity dabbed at her mouth while considering a repost.

Jill Cooper, whose IQ was inversely proportional to the mass of gold jewellery that festooned her, came to her friend's aid. 'Toby, you can't talk like that to people like us. We're good people who do a lot for the poor, and that upstart little black bishop is going to make things worse for everyone. People listen to him, you know – he needs to think about what he says. He's even won that peace prize!'

'Indeed, some Swedish peace prize.' His point made, Toby replaced his hat. 'I apologise ... I mean no offence.' He turned his attention to the stage as the string orchestra finally concluded their next tune. 'Now vat's some rending of "Baa Baa Black Sheep", hey. Bu i may ave been "Insy Winsy Spider" – difficul to tell?!'

At the end of the Easter term of 1985, the entire school assembled in the cathedralesque Trinity chapel to receive the College's ceremonial leader, the Bishop of Johannesburg. One Desmond Tutu arrived to conduct the Eucharist for the heirs of the white middle (upper in some minds) class, on a sunny morning in April. For the occasion, Mrs Sharp had drilled the melody of John Rutter's 'The Lord Bless You and Keep You' into her young charges, and the choristers from Standard One to Matric were to combine for this piece of Trinity history.

Hamish was deeply excited. He knew who Bishop Tutu was because Caroline, suddenly possessed of a need to find spiritual meaning, had recently been confirmed in the Anglican Church. She harboured a huge respect for the bishop and had told Hamish stories of his brave activism in the lead-up to the service.

On the morning of the visit, the choristers squashed uncomfortably into the stalls in front of the rood screen, which afforded them an excellent view down the nave. A sea of boys stretched to the back under the gallery where organ pipes topped with polished brass trumpets reached the vaulted stone ceiling. Just before the rear doors opened, the great instrument thundered out the introduction to 'Be Thou My Vision', and Hamish's eyes nearly popped out. He'd never heard the organ before – all their practice had been with a piano. As five-hundred voices, led by the choir all around him, burst into voice, goosebumps rose on his arms and legs. With gusto, he joined his thin treble to the throng.

The diminutive bishop – almost two feet taller with his mitre extending to heaven – walked solemnly up the aisle carrying the ceremonial silver shepherd's crook, his purple robes flowing. As the entourage made its stately way towards the altar, smoke from the censer floated up, intercepting the shafts of autumn sunlight that cascaded through the eastern windows.

As the procession passed Hamish, the bishop, perhaps drawn by the bellow emanating from so tiny a boy, looked to his left. He caught Hamish's eye and winked. The boy's chest swelled as he belted out the last verse. For the rest of the service, Hamish was captivated by the energy of the delivery and the unique timbre of the bishop's voice.

After the communion, the choir performed an anthem. They stood in their stalls either side of the nave as Bishop Tutu made his way back to the altar. He stopped as the boys began to sing. He smiled and then turned to make eye contact with each chorister until the last peaceful amen.

Hamish was unusually chatty in the car on the way home that day.

'... and there was this *smoke* blowing up from a silver thing on a chain and the organ was so *loud* and I sang louder than *anyone*!'

'And what did the Bishop say?' Caroline asked.

'He said thanks and then we sang to him again – he even looked at *me*, Mum, and he smiled! I think I'm going to be a bishop when I'm big. How do I be a bishop, Mum? Roger, you can also be a bishop.'

His mother smiled. 'Maybe Roger doesn't want to be a bishop.'

'Yes, he does, don't you, Rog? Even you saw him with his silver sheep-catcher!'

Roger knew better than to have an opinion while his brother was holding forth on a subject with this level of enthusiasm.

'Hamish,' Caroline eventually stopped him. 'That's enough – be quiet for a second.'

'But I want to be a bishop!' whined Hamish.

'You can be. Now just be quiet for a little while and stop badgering your brother.'

'Mum, why were you late to fetch us today?' Hamish asked a few moments later, when he'd eventually become bored.

'Um ... I had to see the doctor about something.'

Roger, ever concerned for his family, sat forward. 'Are you sick?'

'No, no, Rog. Um ... he wasn't really a doctor you see if you're sick ... well, he is, but I'm not sick. Um ... never mind.'

Hamish sat forward and the boys exchanged a glance.

'Then why did you see the doctor?' asked Hamish.

'I'll tell you when we get home …'

'Tell us now!' insisted Hamish.

'Well, um, it's that … well, eh boys, you're going to have a new little brother or sister,' she stammered.

'Where are you getting us a brother or sister?' asked Hamish.

'I don't think I want a new brother or sister,' said Roger, frowning at Hamish.

Caroline had anticipated the question from her eldest, and still had no idea how she was going to answer it. She chose to assuage Roger's concerns first.

'Rog, it will be like having two Hamishes —' Roger looked alarmed '— or maybe it'll be a sister.'

'But where are you getting him *from*?' Hamish persisted.

'It might be a she!' deflected the mother.

'Why don't you *know*?' Hamish countered.

'We'll only know when he or she arrives …' Caroline drove faster, willing the trip to end.

'Arrives from *where*?' Hamish snapped.

'From my tummy!' blurted Caroline. There was silence but for the roar of the engine working too hard. 'You know, like you boys came from my tummy.'

Hamish and Roger remembered something about this.

'But how did he *get* in there?' Hamish persisted.

'Back home at last!' said Caroline pulling into the driveway. 'We'll talk about it later; I have to run to the loo.' She leapt out of the car.

Six months later, Julia Jane Garlake Fraser was born. She arrived at the Inanda house, again with Uncle Walter belting out a welcome on his bagpipes and Elizabeth complaining acerbically about the 'Barbarians north of Hadrian's Wall'.

10

The beginning-of-school photo that was stuck with a magnet to the fridge throughout 1986 showed a scowling Hamish now an inch and a half shorter than the serenely content Roger.

On that day, Stuart dropped Roger at the Pre-Preparatory first, and then drove Hamish up Cambridge Road past the western façade of the College. It was a humid January morning and thunder clouds darkened the sky over the humble wooden cross that topped the massive stone chapel's buttressed edifice. Many found this view inspiring; Hamish was intimidated. He had no love for his Pre-Prep experience, but was daunted by the new environment. And although Stuart could feel his son's fear, there was nothing for it but to pretend all would be well.

Stuart eased his Mercedes to a halt just outside the Prep school's archway, where the huge wrought-iron gates were drawn open. Boys were filing through – some in happy groups reuniting after the long holidays, others alone and pensive.

'Out you go, boy. It's going to be an exciting day!'

Hamish looked at his father with a raised brow and sardonic twist to his mouth. His rising cynicism was broken by the hoot from a goal-orientated executive in an even larger Mercedes.

'Come on, Hamish, out you get – you'll be fine.'

The boy was a feeble physical specimen and a social imbecile, but he wasn't a coward. Hamish bade his father a terse farewell and, with difficulty, slung his large satchel onto his back as he walked towards the

81

archway. Through the gates, the sound of boys' feet and voices echoed off the vaulted ceiling.

For once, Hamish was not the last to arrive in his new classroom, that of Mrs Potter. He selected a desk in the middle of the room – the one that offered the largest radius of unoccupied social space. He noted Neil Long and Wayne Johnson tossing a tennis ball at each other; Bradford York, Philip Cobbler and Johnny Goodenough swapping marbles; and Paul Simpson and Andrew Marsdorf comparing their new cricket bats. Hamish pretended to be very busy unpacking the contents of his satchel into his desk.

As class began, he was flanked by Angus Campion (a corpulent and less-than-athletic boy) and Harry St Claire (fellow rider and chorister). Harry had a good sense of humour, and if there was a single boy in the class who liked Hamish, it was Harry. The feeling was almost mutual, although Hamish thought Harry did a dreadful job of brushing his hair in the mornings.

As the year wore on, Hamish would discover that Mrs Potter was a kind and fair woman, who showed no favouritism. While Hamish's dire ability to spell showed no signs of improving and his writing remained neolithic, his sense of humour was the greatest indicator to the teacher of his intelligence. A developing sarcasm that was inappropriate most of the time and unrefined all the time often left her giggling quietly when her back was to the class.

The athletics season was in the third term, and, as is the wont of little boys, many thought themselves exceptional athletes capable of Olympian speeds, distances and heights. Each Monday morning, Mrs Potter asked the boys to share one goal for the week ahead. She encouraged them to have realistic aspirations and to share these honestly with the class. Most of the goals for the third week that September involved House Sports Day, for which they'd all been training furiously. Many of the boys shared their dreams of winning an event, although most knew that Wayne Johnson would win all but the hundred-metre sprint, in which Paul Simpson was destined to smash the existing record.

The only person dissuaded of the latter inevitability was Angus Campion. His father, he confided to Hamish just prior to the goal-setting session, had given him the secret of great speed.

'What is this secret to speed?' asked Hamish flatly as he regarded the blancmange-like apparition next to him.

Angus looked conspiratorially from side to side. 'You promise not to tell?'

'Okay.'

'You have to run on your toes,' Angus whispered.

Hamish had been running on his toes since he could stand and was sufficiently self-aware to know that although he wasn't going to challenge Paul Simpson for glory, he was leagues faster than Angus 'Fatty' Campion. Before he could persuade the fellow of his delusion, Mrs Potter began to pick boys at random to share their goals. Fourth was Angus Campion.

He stood. Hamish held his breath.

'My goal for the week is to win the hundred metres at Sports Day on Friday.'

There were a few muffled sniggers, despite Mrs Potter's strict admonition that there was to be no laughing during these sessions – all boys had a right to their dreams. The absurdity of the delusion, however, was too much for one Hamish Charles Sutherland Fraser.

'Campion, you run like a strawberry jelly … Even a strawberry jelly running on his toes won't beat Simpson in the hundred metres.'

Cackles of laughter rippled from Paul Simpson and his group, who were clustered towards the back of the class.

'That's my *secret*!' exploded the maligned fat fellow.

Hamish was appreciating the laughter he had elicited when Angus grabbed him by the collar, hauled him out of his desk and threw him to the ancient wooden floor. The violence ceased with Mrs Potter's sharp rebuke.

'Stop it! I will not have that sort of behaviour in my class. Both of you will put on your blazers and report to the headmaster!'

'I'm so sorry, Mrs Potter!' pleaded Hamish, all humour instantly forgotten.

'You can be a very nasty little boy, Hamish,' she said icily. Campion was too terrified to speak. 'And you, Angus, must learn that we do not attack people, even when they are nasty to us. Go!' She pointed at the door.

Mr Oliver Dicks, headmaster of Trinity Preparatory, was not a man to be trifled with. He came from the old school and would certainly have thrashed the boys six each were it not for a progressive ban on corporal punishment at Trinity. He was stooped, always draped in his academic gown and walked with a stick, reminding Hamish of a large bat with bushy eyebrows. But it was his smell that Hamish found most appalling: Mr Dicks used liberal quantities of Lifebuoy soap and smoked forty a day, giving him an odour somewhere between a hospital and an ashtray. He was, by Hamish's reckoning, the oldest and most terrifying human being in the world.

The boys walked down the corridors to their doom, Angus (crying), just slightly in front while Hamish looked into the classrooms, at the boys at their work, the teachers instructing ... It all looked so pleasant in comparison with what he and Angus were facing.

An interminable wait outside the office ensued, with the administrative staff walking into and out of the inner sanctum casting disgusted looks at the criminal boys. By the time they were shown into the headmaster's office, Hamish was nauseous with fear, and tears were still leaking down Fatty Campion's extra-puffy face.

For a few minutes, Mr Dicks did not look up as he read through something on his blotter. Hamish looked alternately at his feet, at the grey comb-over Mr Dicks had affected and at the office's wood panelling. Next to the blotter, steam rose from a china coffee cup and mingled with smoke from a cigarette resting in an ashtray. Hamish was thinking of how prettily the morning light caught the steam and smoke when Mr Dicks cleared his throat and looked up. Beelzebub himself.

'What have you two boys done that warrants your disturbing my busy day?'

Silence.

'You, Campion, speak!'

Fresh tears erupted from the boy's eyes. He'd haltingly made it through half the story before Mr Dicks stopped him with a growl. The headmaster had been disciplining boys for forty years; it took only two sentences for him to work out that the uncoordinated, overweight child was the brunt of some joke, and he had no desire to hear the whole sordid tale. Campion was there because of a retaliatory attack, and Mr Dicks thoroughly approved of boys sorting out their differences with their fists.

'Stop that foul snivelling, blow your nose and go back to your classroom.'

Feeling a massive weight lift, Hamish too turned to go.

'Not you, Fraser!'

Fatty jumped, spun around and sped away like Paul Simpson at the start gun. The weight thumped back down onto Hamish.

'Fraser, look at me.'

Hamish lifted his eyes, lip beginning to quiver. The headmaster rose and leant over the antique mahogany desk until his face was three feet from the boy's.

'I will not tolerate bullying of any sort. I have no doubt that a small boy like you is picked on by bigger boys. I am sure you do not like being picked on. Do you, Fraser?'

'No, sir.'

'Well, teasing a boy about being fat is bullying, and today you, Fraser, are a bully and I will not tolerate that in my school. Do you understand me?'

'Yes, sir.'

'Bullying is a most cowardly act! A few years ago I'd have thrashed you six.' Mr Dicks indicated his recently retired cane resting in a mounted glass cabinet behind the desk.

Hamish shivered, his face flushed with genuine shame.

'Yes, sir. I'm sorry, sir.'

'Now get out of my office, and by this time tomorrow you will have written two hundred lines saying, "I shall never be a nasty bully to anyone ever again."' He leant closer, spittle flying from his ancient, thin lips. 'If they are not here by the first bell, I shall reconsider my sparing of the cane. Out!'

Hamish scuttled away like a startled skink.

Hamish could easily have hidden a thrashing from his parents. Writing two hundred lines, however, and concealing the time it would take from his family, would be something more difficult.

At break, Hamish began his penance. He took a pad and his mangled ballpoint to a secluded part of the field and began writing. Five minutes before the bell rang, he'd completed thirty lines and was feeling a little better, though his eyes still stung with embarrassment when he thought about being accused of bullying. He stood, scrambled up the grassy bank and made his way back across the field.

Between boys tossing balls, pushing each other, yelling and horsing about, he did not see the A-Team coming – the gang always struck after the first bell, catching lonely stragglers.

'Dan dan *daaaaan*,' sang Nicholas Cullinan.

Hamish winced – half at the tone-deafness and half in fear. As he spun round to assess the threat, Robert Bosch pulled away his pad. Hamish lunged for his precious thirty lines, dropping his pen, lunch box and blazer, which, with the efficiency of a hyaena clan, the A-Team instantly possessed: Cullinan jumping up and down on the blazer; Cooper snapping the pen in half; and Bosch tearing off pieces of pad paper and scattering them to the wind. Taken by the breeze, the thirty lines flew over the bank and into a storm drain below, while Hamish was pinned to the ground by Toffee Botha.

Cullinan put the victim's juice box on the ground next to his head and stomped on it with practised precision, delivering the predictable departing line: 'I love it when a plan comes together.'

Hamish was late for class, the right side of his face covered in soil and grass cuttings stuck with orange juice. Unfortunately for Hamish, Mrs Potter was not feeling any particular affection for him on that day and he narrowly escaped a second batch of punishment.

Hamish was often dishevelled and uncommunicative after school so Caroline didn't worry too much when he climbed into her car that afternoon, his face still covered in muck. She chatted to Roger, who was thoroughly enjoying his time in Standard One – although his choir audition had been unsuccessful.

Hamish spent the rest of the afternoon cosseted alone in his room. Caroline left him be – her afternoon occupied with entertaining the baby Julia in the garden and then hosting tea for a friend with a similarly aged daughter. By the time Stuart arrived home at six o'clock, Hamish had completed his lines and placed the papers in his satchel. He felt a huge sense of relief to have completed the punishment without either of his parents noticing.

The next morning, Hamish was rushing out of the house, stuffing his pencil bag into his satchel, when he tripped on the edge of a raised brick in the driveway. The satchel and its contents sprawled onto the paving. Fuming, Stuart leapt out of the Mercedes, where he'd been sitting revving, Roger already in the back.

'Hamish, why can you never, *ever* be on time? It's so bloody irritating,' Stuart yelled, gathering the fallen jetsam.

Hamish saw his punishment pages too late. Stuart almost didn't read the spidery scrawl, but the unusually regular pattern of the two hundred lines arrested his attention.

Hamish froze.

A crested barbet that had been eating pawpaw on the bird table in the chestnut tree flew off. How Hamish wished he were a barbet.

'What. Is. This?' Stuart's calmness chilled Hamish to his core.

Hamish looked down at his untied shoelaces.

'Get into the car immediately.'

They drove in horrendous silence all the way to school, Roger knowing better than to break the charged atmosphere. On arrival, the younger bade his father a swift goodbye, leaving Hamish and Stuart alone for the drive up to the Prep school.

'Hamish, I'm going to ask you once more, and if you do not answer me immediately, I'm going to come into school and ask your teacher. It's your choice.'

Hamish began to cry, and explained in halting snivels what had happened. Stuart kept his counsel until Hamish was about to alight from the car.

'You will go to Angus Campion today, and you will say you are sorry for being nasty. You will do this because that is what a gentleman does when he has done wrong. That shows strength.' Stuart turned to face Hamish in the back seat. 'Strength is not in your muscles or in your brain. It is in your heart. It is in your ability to feel compassion for others, your willingness to make sacrifices for them and your ability to admit when you are wrong.'

The boy stared at his father.

'I can see you know you have wronged this boy – now go and apologise.'

Hamish removed himself silently, and went to hand his punishment to the headmaster just as the first bell rang. The old man didn't look up from his blotter as the red-faced boy was ushered into the office.

'Put them on the desk,' he growled.

Hamish did as he was told and turned to leave.

'Good God, boy.' Mr Dicks looked up at the pages. 'You write like a spastic dung beetle. That had better improve.'

'Yes, sir.' Hamish, who was halfway between the door and the desk, was unsure as to whether he'd been dismissed.

At the sound of the second bell, the headmaster looked up.

'WHAT ARE YOU STILL DOING HERE?' he yelled, and Hamish ran.

He found Angus Campion gathering for assembly with the rest of the boys in the quadrangle. The round boy was standing alone, hands is his pockets. Hamish gritted his teeth, his father's words fresh in his ears.

'Angus? Angus, I'm sorry about yesterday. I didn't mean to be nasty. I'm sorry,' he blurted awkwardly.

The two boys regarded first each other and then the stone of the quadrangle before Hamish wandered away. He'd done his duty but felt emotionally drained – like after a hard Physical Education session.

II

Each Wednesday morning, assembly took place in the amphi-theatre. Mr Dicks gave general school announcements and instructions and then read the sports results. Applause would accompany boys receiving Man of the Match awards as they walked up to shake the scowling headmaster's hand. The adulation was always loudest for Darren Cockerel, nearly thirteen – house monitor, captain of soccer and cricket, holder of three athletic records – who was routinely announced for taking a fifer, smashing a fifty or scoring a brace. There was a Darren Cockerel, more or less, in every class. Paul Simpson was the Darren Cockerel in Hamish's.

While Hamish accepted that he was the shortest boy in his class, he had a vastly over-inflated sense of his physical prowess and lived in the delusion that his body was almost as well-muscled as Paul Simpson's – whose belly had been bricked with an eight-pack from infancy. Why Hamish lived in this state of denial probably had to do with his desire not to be categorised with the non-sportsmen of the class – the 'co-ords' for want of a better term. The fact was that from the very beginning of his school career, Hamish had shown neither aptitude nor interest in school sports – cricket and swimming in summer, soccer and tennis in winter. Most viewed riding ponies as a pursuit for young girls and effeminate boys – certainly this was the distaste with which Mr Lawrence, head of Physical Education, considered Hamish's efforts on horseback.

Roger wasn't a great deal better at sport, but he was more of a size with his peers and his ability to concentrate ensured that he learnt the skills that nature hadn't blessed him with. He also wanted to fit in, and for this he had an instinctual skill that Hamish lacked.

Some unsporty boys took up musical instruments and achieved greatly in their exams and in concerts. Their names too made the roll of honour at Wednesday amphitheatre, but the applause from the school was muted and polite rather than enthusiastic. Almost no one aspired to be like Gregory de Ridder, an astonishing pianist, nigh-on genius, and contemporary of Darren Cockerel's. The latter was idolised by every boy younger than him and most in his own class; the former was admired by a few of the piano students. It was the swashbuckling warriors-to-be who were spoken of in the staff room at break time and pointed out by younger boys, not those who would go on to study at the Royal College of Music or the Julliard School.

When it came to school sports, Mr Lawrence had given a consistently poor assessment of Hamish's abilities, beginning all the way back in Grade One:

> *Hamish does not enjoy sport. He is physically weak and his lower back is unusually curved, which should be looked at by a physiotherapist. During cricket, I often have to reprimand him for wandering off or lying on the grass. His batting is poor and he is unable to bowl. Soccer is also difficult for him because he cannot control the ball and makes little effort. He is able to swim freestyle well enough but is slow in the water.*

This first unfavourable assessment of Hamish's physical ability had arrived two weeks before the house athletics day in 1983. Stuart wasn't overly worried about the apparent lack of aptitude, except he realised that failing at sport would push Hamish towards the bottom of the social pile – a pile he was comfortably propping up already. Business deals were done on the golf course; the local squash league was a proxy for the social pecking order. Stuart didn't suppose this was a uniquely

South African situation – indeed, he assumed that hunter-gatherer societies of old had been the same. Men bonded while hunting. The bravest mammoth hunters claimed social standing and the trappings that came with it.

Hamish, as far as he could tell, was no mammoth hunter.

And so, for the next fortnight, Stuart had taken his son onto their tennis court each evening and tutored him on the art of running in a straight line. Hamish had one event in Grade One – the sixty-metre dash – and his parents were determined that their son, even if he came stone last, would run in a straight line, on his toes and not fall over or lose focus for the twenty or so seconds it would take to complete his event.

'On your marks ... get set ... GO!' Mr Lawrence had bellowed on that warm summer morning.

The shout had given Hamish a fright, so he'd set off fractionally later than the other nine boys. Angus Campion (already a few stones more substantial than his peers) had collapsed after ten paces and Philip Cobbler had fallen over his laces before he'd run a step. Neil Long and Bradford York had made the early running but Hamish, jaw set in determination, had lifted himself onto the balls of his feet, pumped his spindly arms, and passed five of the other competitors halfway down the track, catching the others with relative ease.

Sitting in a knot of parents on the grass bank next to the track, Caroline had been unable to watch. Stuart's heart was in his mouth when, with ten metres to go, Hamish had taken the lead.

'Come on, Hamish!' Stuart yelled, an outburst that was considered very poor form.

Hamish was not used to being cheered on. Indeed, when he did hear his name called with such enthusiasm it was almost universally because he'd done something wrong. With two metres to the finish line, he'd stopped dead and looked to his father.

Long, York and another five boys had passed him before he stepped over the line.

On the second school day of his Standard Two year, Hamish was fin-ishing a drawing of an ox wagon during a history lesson when the bell rang. He looked up, oblivious as to what his next lesson was to be. Most of the other boys were standing, which confused him because Mrs Potter didn't normally allow much wandering about the class between subjects.

Mrs Potter solved the mystery: 'Come on, those of you still sitting – it's PE now. Up to the change rooms and then down to the field, quick as you can.'

Hamish felt his throat close and a coldness develop in his legs. For the umpteenth time, he'd forgotten his sports kit – that morning he'd man-aged to get it as far as the car, but in the boot of the Mercedes the togs remained. He pictured it nestled in the parking garage of his father's office building, wondering absurdly if he'd be able to run to the tuck shop payphone, call Stuart and get him to deliver the bag in the ninety seconds he had before PE.

In the house change room, Hamish managed to borrow a white vest from Philip Cobbler (who was a good foot taller), but no one had any extra shorts. Down on the field, Mr Lawrence waited with his clipboard and a long, bendy rubber pencil – his punishing device. It wasn't that Hamish feared the pencil; it was the shame of being singled out in front of the class while trying to think up a gormless excuse. 'I forgot them, sir' never sufficed for Mr Lawrence.

Hamish slouched down to the field in his grey school shorts, bare feet and over-sized vest as the rest of the boys joked around him.

'Wayne, I'll swap you a galaxy goon for four milkies.'

'Four milkies? No ways – twenty milkies. No, not for sale. I don't even like milkies.'

'Throw here!' Neil Long called to Johnny Goodenough, who was never without a ball in his hand. The red Slaz he tossed to his best mate whizzed over Hamish's head.

Hamish looked up into the boughs of the oak trees. He could see a flock of small, unidentifiable birds flitting about in the leaves and wished he was up there with them.

'Fraser!'

Hamish's attention was arrested by his teacher's strangely high-pitched, nasal tone. Mr Lawrence couldn't say the vowel 'i' (it came out as 'u') and neither was he able to utter the consonant 'h' (he replaced it with a 'y').

'Thus us the furst day of PE and you yaven't got your kut! Come stand over yere!'

Hamish sighed and moved from the rest of the boys, who were gathering on the grass in front of the teacher.

'Where us your kut?'

The boys watched, looking forward to the application of Mr Lawrence's rubber pencil.

'I forgot it in my dad's car, sir,' said Hamish.

'Why dud you do that?' (The stupidity of this question made Hamish scowl reflexively.) 'Don't look at me like that, boy!'

'Sorry, sir. I don't know why I forgot it, sir.' Hamish looked down at the neatly mown grass. An ant crawled onto his foot.

'Ut's because you stchoopud after the holidays!' Mr Lawrence came to an epiphany.

The boy's face clearly displayed his disdain for the revelation. The teacher, blessed with a level of intelligence barely beyond that of the ant foraging on Hamish's big toe, became irritated.

'Come over yere to meet Excalubah!'

Delight rippled through the class. Hamish duly took three steps forward and gritted his teeth as two blows struck the back of his legs. Mr Lawrence was an idiot but he wasn't a sadist, so the pain was insignificant compared with the embarrassment.

'Go sut down,' the teacher instructed.

In the Prep school, Mr Lawrence picked captains from the best sportsmen in the class and instructed them to select teams for the day's game. Whether he ever realised the cruelty of this practice wasn't certain.

Paul Simpson and Wayne Johnson were appointed as captain selectors for that day's cricket match. What followed was as predictable as it was unpleasant for those not blessed with good hand-eye coordination. The two sporty boys came to the front of the class and stood on either side of Mr Lawrence.

'Okay, puck your players, captains.'

Paul Simpson went first, and pointed at his best friend in the world. 'Andrew.'

Then it was the turn of Wayne Johnson, who had almost mastered the power of speech, aged ten. 'Dylan.' Dylan Crane went to stand behind his captain.

One by one the boys of Standard Two were picked: first the friends of the captains and then the sportsmen. Being neither, Hamish tried to catch the eye of both captains, nodding his head vigorously in an effort to avoid the ignominy of being left in the pool of co-ords. Eventually he caught Paul Simpson's eye. The bigger boy's mouth turned up slightly and he moved his gaze on to Neil Long.

'Neil.' Paul nodded his head and Neil Long stood with relief.

The group whittled down slowly to four: Hamish and a group of three friends. Angus Campion, Alan Moses and Richard de Villiers had found things other than sport in common. They passed their breaks swapping comic books and role-playing their favourite characters – Spiderman, Superman and Batman. (Hamish, observing such a game one day, had remarked that Campion was more Fatman than Batman.)

'Fraser.' Hamish heard Wayne Johnson sigh his name in resignation.

When Fatty Campion (who would be picked last until his final PE lesson in Matric) had made his way to the back of Paul Simpson's team, Mr Lawrence unfolded his arms.

'You boys need to learn yow to choose your batting lineups – for practice for real matches. U'll guve you two minutes.'

'Fraser!' Wayne Johnson pointed at him moments later. 'You bat number nine.'

Paul Simpson won the toss (unsurprisingly, since he won everything) and decided that his team would bat. Johnson's team took to the field.

At this level of the game, the best batsmen were normally also the best bowlers, so Johnson opted to open the bowling himself.

Hamish longed to be the wicket keeper – he reckoned even he could catch a ball with those big padded gloves.

'Hey, Wayne,' he ventured. 'Can I be wickie?'

His captain glared at him. Johnson mostly used sentences of two or three words long, and these were spaced well apart as his brain searched among the twenty-five in his vocabulary.

'You … mad,' he scoffed at the smaller boy. 'Johnny's wickie. You can't catch.' His finger lifted towards the midwicket boundary. 'You go there.'

At least there was shade on the boundary, Hamish thought. And acorns. Not quite walnuts, but he could examine them for insect life and test their taste. Hamish checked a few shells for evidence of insect drilling as Wayne Johnson trotted to the end of his run-up. Johnson was built like a twelve year old and he bowled with the speed of a possessed freight train.

Hamish smiled wanly as the first delivery nearly felled Andrew Marsdorf – a boy he'd come to dislike with the same enthusiasm that Wayne Johnson brought to bowling. Marsdorf was the sort of fellow who found the distance he could spit a source of pride.

Johnson took two wickets in his four-ball over and conceded no runs. Next up was Dylan Crane, who had the unfortunate task of bowling to Paul Simpson. The first ball was slammed in Hamish's direction but went so far over his head that it cracked into the top of the oak tree and dropped gently to the ground over the boundary. Hamish retrieved it, deeply relieved that he hadn't been called upon to put his hands in the way of the shiny red missile.

The next two balls were dispatched for four to the cover boundary and Hamish lost interest. As Crane trundled in to bowl his last ball, Hamish took a bite of the acorn he'd just peeled. His eyes slammed shut as a sensation of extreme bitterness assailed his tongue.

Yet again Simpson found the middle of the bat, this time rocking onto his back foot and hooking the ball towards the midwicket boundary – where Hamish was now doubled over, retching. The fielder vaguely heard yelling but so intense was the assault on his tongue that he failed to heed any warning. The ball bounced once and hit Hamish in the ribs. He collapsed.

Everyone on the field, including Mr Lawrence, laughed hysterically. Hamish lay on the ground for a minute before standing up and rubbing the right side of his rib cage. He had the presence of mind to bow deeply at his laughing peers.

In these PE games, everybody had a chance to bowl four balls unless they feigned injury – Stuart Moses, for example, couldn't possibly bowl as he had an ingrown toenail, an 'ailment' that would 'hamper' him for the rest of his school career. When Wayne Johnson called Hamish as the tenth and last bowler, Hamish dropped his acorns and jogged over to the end of the pitch. It should be noted that no one had ever actually taught Hamish to bowl, so the logical thing to do was emulate Wayne Johnson as best he could. Hamish walked back to where he'd watched the captain start his run-up – about twenty metres from the crease.

At the batting crease stood Paul Simpson, who had yet to be troubled by anything he'd faced that day. Hamish was suddenly determined that he would unseat the class's best batsman, especially when he heard Neil Long mutter, 'It's Fraser, okes. He's a co-ord.'

The new bowler gritted his teeth, turned and charged. He completely misjudged his delivery jump and took off metres past the crease. He slung his right arm round past his ear and let go. Vaguely Hamish heard Mr Lawrence shouting 'No-ball!' as he propelled the red cherry, every muscle in his scrawny body contorting to make him look like a flailing demon.

He didn't see where the ball went because the explosive bowling convulsion made him lose his footing and fall to the sisal cricket matting.

Paul Simpson's superb hand-eye coordination would have been sufficient to deal with such an extreme no-ball had it bounced. Hamish's only delivery, however, was a beamer. Everyone on the field watched in horrified fascination as the projectile fizzed straight from Hamish's hand towards the batsman's head.

From his prone position, Hamish interpreted the oohs and aahs as admiration for his swift delivery. A moment later, he became aware of people running towards Simpson. Then he heard Mr Lawrence's voice.

'Fraser, you udiut! What yave you done! You can't bowl beamers like that from yalfway down the putch!'

Simpson staggered, hands clutching his face, and stifled a sob as the adoring class rushed to his aid.

'Paul, Paul, are you okay?' whined Mr Lawrence, who was as in awe of Simpson as his peers were.

The stricken boy moved his hand from his face to reveal a spilt and bleeding bottom lip. He only cried when he saw the blood on his hands. Mr Lawrence had no stomach for open wounds: he covered his mouth with his hands, turned the colour of milk and fainted, while the more squeamish of Simpson's admirers fell away gagging.

Hamish wasn't squeamish in the slightest, but he did feel deeply ashamed.

'Sorry, Paul,' he said, approaching the injured boy. 'You must go to the san and see the matron. I'm really sorry, Paul.' To the wailing and exclamations of the class, Hamish took off his grubby borrowed vest and held it up towards his victim's mouth. 'Put this over your mouth,' he instructed calmly.

'Sir's lying on the floor,' yelled Stuart Moses as Simpson walked off towards the sanatorium with at least three helpers.

As the remaining boys turned to look, Mr Lawrence slowly sat up and put his head between his legs.

'Fraser,' he gasped, 'you can't bowl again after what you dud to Paul!'

And so it was that Hamish Fraser did not turn his arm over again for the remainder of 1986.

12

Friday visits to and from the Fines continued. Time with his best friend and his riding lessons were the only things Hamish looked forward to during the school week. Reggie had many other friends at school, but none with whom she had a bond like that she shared with Hamish.

So it was one Friday in 1987, as the first tongues of autumn reached into the Johannesburg evening, that Reggie shared a concern with Hamish. The parents were on the verandah quaffing wine while the two friends sat in the chestnut tree on the driveway, sharing the odd word, but by and large enjoying the twilight in comfortable silence – the only sound provided by a robin singing the end of the week from the flowerbed below.

Then the atmosphere changed – Hamish sensed it as did the bird, which ceased its song as the last light faded.

'Hamish,' said Reggie. She was picking at a rough piece of bark between them.

'Yes, Reg.'

'My mum is sick.'

'She'll get better … What's wrong with her?' replied the boy, unable to think of anything wiser to say.

'She says it's going to take a very long time to get better.' Reggie looked out through the turning leaves.

The robin retreated into an ivy hedge.

'She has to have an operation next week and then something called chemo-something. It's going to make her hair fall out.'

The autumn dusk rustled the foliage in the tree above and a single yellow leaf drifted slowly down past the children and onto the soil below.

A chill ran down Hamish's spine. He knew what this meant. His very first experience of the cinema had been to watch *Champions* – the story of British jockey Bob Champion, who'd overcome cancer to win the 1981 Grand National. Hamish listened to the soundtrack often, always skipping over the melancholy parts that indicated the hero's proximity to death – they gave him a powerful sense of dread.

'Well, Bob Champion got cancer and then he won the Grand National in England. Your mum will be okay.'

Reggie said nothing and Hamish could tell she wasn't comforted. He too picked at the bark, the branch suddenly feeling prickly and uncomfortable.

'She won't die,' he said hopefully.

When Sarah had explained to Reggie that she was seriously ill, the ultimate eventuality had been specifically excluded. Now the little girl's heart split in two. Just a few tears came at first, and then convulsive sobs so strong Hamish thought she might fall out of the tree. A crushing vice gripped the two children as the girl sobbed and the boy sat helpless. He couldn't hug her – they were sitting in a tree – so he reached out and placed his hand on hers and she gripped it so hard his fingers went numb.

After what felt like a hundred-million years, Reggie's sobs retreated to the extent that she could speak. She turned to Hamish, navy-blue eyes puffy, cheeks red and nose streaming. Her jaw clenched as she dug her nails into the skin of his hand.

'My. Mother. Is. NOT. Going. To die!' she screamed, spit catching him in the eye. 'She's *not* going to die!'

Before Hamish could recover himself, Reggie had dropped out of the tree and was running down the driveway.

The boy was bereft, and climbed slowly down, jaw clenched in frustration and anguish.

On the verandah he found a deeply subdued scene. Reggie was curled up on Sarah's lap. The mother's face was streaked with tears, her cheek buried in her daughter's chocolate curls. Hamish thought he was in serious trouble and made to escape before he was noticed, but his mother – who could sense his presence at a hundred paces – looked up. She too had been crying; his father looked pained.

'Come here, Hamish,' Caroline said softly, reaching out her hand.

Hamish steeled himself and walked to his mother, who lifted him onto her lap. The five of them sat in silence for an interminable period. Hamish looked from Caroline's necklace to the binding on the cane chairs and then the three twinkling bulbs in the verandah chandelier – again and again his eyes travelled to these things as he willed the moment to end.

When it did, the Fines departed, Stuart carrying the sleeping form of Reggie to the car. Before they left, Sarah hugged Hamish.

'Everything's going to be okay, see?' She kissed him on the head.

In that moment – as would happen to him from time to time – Hamish had a premonition. He knew, without doubt, that nothing was going to be okay. That this woman was lying and that his best friend's worst fears were going to be realised.

The following morning – a Saturday – Stuart woke Hamish with a cup of hot chocolate at seven o'clock. He drew the curtains to reveal a sky turned gunmetal, flotillas of angry cloud scudding by.

'How are you feeling today?' asked the father.

'I've got a sore throat,' Hamish croaked, staring out of the window.

Stuart wasn't surprised: it seemed to Stuart that Hamish's body was an excellent gauge of his emotional state, so the inflamed throat was almost inevitable.

'I'm sorry, little fellow. Stay in bed and we'll see how you feel a bit later.'

Hamish sat up and drank half of his hot chocolate (his father never made it as sweet as his mother did, or as rich). He snuggled back under the covers and watched the sky: cold and blustery with flurries of autumn leaves, but the grey racing clouds carried no rain and the brief patches of blue sky flashed with a sun that brought no warmth.

After half an hour of tossing around, Hamish climbed heavily out of his bed and made his way to the kitchen. The back door was closed, which made the normally cheerful room dark, and he felt the chill of the floor on his bare feet. He pulled the door open and was struck in the face by a gust. Persevering, he turned down the brick steps leading into the back yard and then to Tina's room. The top half of her door was open and from the warm interior – Tina's room never seemed to be cold – he could smell comfort.

He stood on his toes and peeped over the bottom door. Maizemeal bubbled on the two-plate stove in the corner. Tina was sitting on her sofa knitting a woolly cap for the coming winter. She felt the beam of the small blue eyes over the door.

'Sawubona, mfana,' she greeted without looking up. 'Come inside, it's cold. You want porridge?'

'Yes please, Gogo.'

'Sit here.' She indicated a spot next to her and then stood to fill two plates.

There was very little talk as Hamish ate the sweet soft porridge and milk. When he'd finished, he curled up on the sofa and fell fast asleep.

Hamish was ill for the whole weekend and into Monday, which dawned still, cool and clear.

'Mum,' he said as she propped him up on his pillows with the correct mix of cocoa, sugar and milk, 'I can't go to school today.'

'Why is that, Hamish?' She looked at him suspiciously.

'I'm still not well.'

'You look fine and you don't have a temperature.' Hamish knew he'd have no chance with his father, but his mother was much easier to bend. He went with logic rather than whining.

'I'm infectious and will make the other boys sick,' he said, looking maudlin.

He spent much of the morning in his pyjamas in Tina's room, lying in a ray of sun on her sofa, unable to shake his melancholy.

That Friday, Sarah underwent a double mastectomy and Reggie came to spend the weekend with the Frasers. Albert was simply unavailable, as he spent every Friday bailing out activists rounded up by the security police, sparing them a weekend's interrogation and torture.

Before the visit, Caroline had joined the boys at the kitchen table as they ate a lunch of fish fingers.

'Hamish, I need you to listen to me very carefully. Can you please do that?'

'Ja,' he'd said absently, considering the merits of a puddle of tomato sauce.

'Hamish, you know that Sarah had an operation today. Do you remember that?'

'Yes, Mum,' he replied, rolling his eyes.

'Don't look at me like that! And you know Reggie is coming to stay with us tonight?'

'Of course, Mum.' The boy grinned.

'And you also know that we're going to take her to see Sarah in the hospital?'

Hamish had forgotten this bit, but he nodded.

'You need to be tactful – that means you only say things to make Reggie feel better. Understand?'

'Yes, Mum.' The grin vanished.

Roger stuffed his last three fish fingers into his mouth and departed post-haste.

'Don't mention anything about dying when we're with Reggie today. It's your duty to make Reggie happy.'

Hamish looked up at his mother and pushed a fish finger around the plate.

'But her mum is going to die,' he whispered, voice cracking. 'I know it.'

Caroline looked away, over the pots of African violets on the window sill. Sarah had waited too long before having the lump checked.

'We don't know that – she might just as easily get better.'

When Caroline took the little girl to see her mother that evening, Hamish went along but was made to sit in the waiting area, where he watched the nurses behind the reception desk, the hurried movement of white coats, the worried faces and tears of visitors. A rising dread filled him. Hamish's eyes began to leak, but he remembered the stern words of his father the night before: 'Hamish, remember, this is a very difficult time for Reggie. You must be strong for her.'

Hamish realised that in all the misery surrounding him, he had the least excuse for wet eyes. He sniffed once, wiped his face and gritted his teeth.

A little while later Caroline and Reggie emerged, his friend's face a picture of stunned, confused sadness. Her chocolate curls were a mess and her navy eyes were glassy with tears. As Caroline spoke to the duty sister, Hamish stood and hugged Reggie, awkwardly pinning her arms to her side so that the jersey she was carrying fell to the floor. He released her and retrieved the garment, banging his forehead on her knee on the way down.

Reggie spent increasing periods with the Frasers during Sarah's illness, most weekends, while Albert palmed her off on school-friends or the school boarding house during the week.

In the August school holidays, the Frasers took Reggie away with them to the northern Drakensberg. Sarah, who was by then far too weak to leave the house for more than a few hours at a time, had pleaded with Caroline to take the little girl away from the atmosphere of impending doom that permeated their Orange Grove cottage. With winter and Sarah's weakening, the garden had become a lifeless shadow of its former self – the flowerbeds bare and the hanging pots on the verandah sagging with strands of brown and grey.

The holiday was perfect because there was hardly a moment for

Reggie to contemplate her disintegrating world. For Hamish, the activities that filled their days meant he didn't have to sit awkwardly while Reggie gazed into the middle distance, tears rolling down her cheeks. This had been happening with increasingly regularity – the two of them would be engaged in a game, swimming in the Inanda pool or climbing in the chestnut tree when Reggie would stop suddenly and just sob.

The friends rode horses every afternoon (Roger played tennis with Stuart) as the sun sank behind the Little Berg. In the mornings the family hiked up into the mountains through the yellow winter grasses, the proteas and their buds waiting for the spring. They drank from freezing mountain streams. It was an idyllic seven days – and, as it turned out, something of a last hurrah.

On their return to Johannesburg, Sarah's decline accelerated and by the time the new school term began, she was in a hospice. Her abiding worry was naturally for her daughter's well-being. She and Albert had decided it would be a poor idea for him to raise their child. The idea of asking the Frasers to adopt Reggie was mooted, but Albert wouldn't hear of it.

'I will not have my daughter raised by bourgeois bigots! My parents will take her,' Albert had said.

'Your parents?' Sarah had coughed, licking her pallid lips. 'You hate your parents, your parents hate me, and I doubt they'd recognise their granddaughter if she tripped over their threshold.'

Albert had stared out of the window as a coughing fit overtook Sarah.

'There will be no love in your mother's house. Your pride should be hurt by the fact that you're incapable of looking after your own child – not by the thought of her being raised in a loving home by people you consider strangers.' Sarah rolled onto her back, staring at the ceiling.

Albert wheeled round.

'I have important work to do – I have to make sacrifices. You think I enjoy living the way I do? With no money, with the cops on my back all day and without a relationship with my daughter? That's how it has to be – sacrifices must be made for the struggle.'

(It must be said at this point that while Reggie had been neglected to the point of criminality by her father, innumerable victims of the apartheid state had been saved from jail, smuggled out of the country or fed by the actions – direct or otherwise – of Albert Fine.)

'Albert,' Sarah sniffed, 'you are a fanatic.' There was a soft plop as a tear dropped onto her starched pillow.

So it was that a few weeks before Sarah succumbed, Reggie moved permanently into the home of her grandparents. The senior Fines did not want for material wealth, but they abhorred their son's politics and though they could hardly have been described as religious, they could never forgive Sarah for not being Jewish. They hardly knew Reggie when she moved in, but saw in her a chance to right the wrongs they perceived in their own son.

Along with Reggie's removal to their palatial spread in Observatory came the removal of almost all contact with the Frasers. No matter how Caroline tried to organise meetings for the two friends, Shirley Fine made an excuse: Reggie was playing with new friends. Reggie was at ballet. Reggie was ill. Reggie was doing her homework and could not come to the phone. Their last phone call ended thus:

'Look, Caroline – is that your name?' Mrs Fine didn't wait for an answer. 'Reggie needs to move on. You and your son remind her of her old life, which we didn't approve of. We are having a difficult time disciplining her out of her bad habits without distractions from her past. Now I don't mean to be rude, but I'm going to ask you not to phone us again.'

The line went dead.

Sarah Fine died five days before Hamish's eleventh birthday. He always remembered this, because the excitement of his day was ruined by the funeral.

It was a small service at St George's in Parktown. Sarah wasn't religious, but she loved the old stone building and had asked to have her funeral there, much to the disgust of her parents-in-law. The Frasers found a pew in the middle of the church. Hamish, dressed in his school uniform, stood closest to the aisle looking out for Reggie. Just before the service began, she walked past him on her way to the front, where her mother's coffin lay. Their eyes met and Hamish reached his hand towards her. As she extended her hand to his, a wan, teary smile forming on her face, Shirley stepped between them and chivvied the little girl along.

Reggie looked helplessly over her shoulder.

Hamish sought her after the service, but his friend was nowhere to be seen.

After supper every Thursday for the next six weeks, Hamish asked his mother if Reggie was coming over the following day. Just before the Christmas holidays, Stuart and Caroline went to his room one night as he readied himself for bed. Stuart sat on the plastic desk chair and Caroline on the bed next her son.

'Hamish,' began Caroline, 'we need to talk to you about Reggie.'

The boy sat up and looked from one to the other, perplexed.

'You're going to have to get used to not seeing her any more, my boy,' Stuart said bluntly. 'It's become very difficult since Sarah died. Her grandmother wants her to live without memories of her past.' The blue eyes narrowed in anger.

'Why doesn't she like us? I don't want other friends.' A quivering lip.

'There are lots of reasons, boy,' said Stuart. 'They didn't like Sarah and —'

'Is it because we're not Jewish?'

'Well, that might have something to do with it, but it's probably more complicated than that. The thing is, you need to try and make some other friends.'

'But nobody else likes me.'

This was not entirely inaccurate, but while Hamish's mother's heart nearly burst at this utterance, Stuart was more prosaic.

'Hamish, I know it's not easy for you to fit in, but as I've said again and again, you're going to have to learn how to make friends or your life is going to be very lonely.'

During the course of the next few months, Reggie and Hamish exchanged a few letters but Hamish found this more frustrating than anything else. Much of their communication had been non-verbal and trying to express himself on paper was impossible.

58 3rd Avenue
Inanda
Johannesburg
2196
8ndof Siptember 1987

Dear Reggie,

It is me Hamish Charles Sutherland Fraser. How are you?
    I am fine.
    Happy Birthday for today. I hope that you got good presints and that you are having a nice party. ~~Maybe I can come to your party.~~ *My dad says you carnt come to my birthdya this year becos your granny doesint want to bring you.* ~~This makes me sad.~~ *It would be nice if you cood come but I know your granny doesint like us. Only Harry is coming and we are going to the Pilansberg to camp for two nights. It would be fun if you came camping with us dont you think?*
    I do not have a lot of time so I must go and do my homework. I hate homework and I also have to feed Parkin. She remembers you.
    Love from
    Hamish

48 Grace Road
Observatory
Johannesburg
2194
Fifth of December 1986

Dear Hamish,

Thank you for your last letter. I had a fun birthday party and I hope that you also enjoyed yours. I asked my grandmother if I could go camping with you but she said that you did not send me an invitation. I told her you did but then she said it was disgusting to go camping with two boys. She is not a nice person.

I have had a good year at my new school and I won prizes for English and for drama. Do you like drama?

We are going on holiday to a place called Southbroom this year. There are quite a few girls from school going there so I think we will have a good time.

Happy Christmas and New Year.
Love
Reggie

By the end of the year, Hamish and Reggie's communications had dried up – their connection eroded.

13

For Hamish, the next school year passed without incident or achievement. His dislike of what he perceived as a deeply tedious existence was tempered by choir concerts, his enjoyment of leaving school each day and his exploits in the riding arena. By this stage he was riding three times a week on a sparky black pony called Bultarka. He was also old enough to ride his bicycle to and from the stables – only five blocks away – and he relished the independence.

One March afternoon, Hamish lingered after a late lesson. He had an Afrikaans essay to write, so going home held no appeal. Instead, he helped with feeding the horses their buckets of bran, oats and horse nuts. By the time he'd finished filling Bultarka's water bucket, twilight peace had descended over the yard.

Outside his pony's stable there was an ancient oak tree, and over the years the grooms had nailed hooks into the trunk to hang halters, hay nets and string. Below it were two weathered pine stumps. Colin often sat on a stump in the evening, rolling himself cigarettes from newspaper and Boxer tobacco and fixing hay nets with orange bailing twine.

That evening, Hamish joined Colin as the sun disappeared. A bulbul called among the leaves above and from the stables came the contented and rhythmic sound of horses tugging grass from their nets and chewing. In the distance, as if in another world, the sound of traffic was just perceptible.

Colin had just returned from a trip to Zimbabwe, so Hamish thought this a good conversation starter.

'Where do you come from, Colin?' he asked.

'From Plumtree,' replied Colin.

Hamish thought this sounded like a storybook place. 'Where's Plumtree?'

'It's east in Zimbabwe.' The cigarette glowed in the side of Colin's mouth every time he inhaled. Hamish hated the smell of commercial cigarettes, but the rolled tobacco of Colin's was strangely comforting.

'Oh. Did you go home for holiday?'

Colin shook his head and sighed. 'No, I went for funeral.'

'Oh. I'm sorry about that.' Hamish's experience of death was limited entirely to Sarah Fine. 'Was it one of your parents?'

There was a short silence before Colin answered. 'No, my brother.'

In the distance, a police siren wailed.

Hamish persisted. 'Was he sick?'

Colin stared hard into the net on his lap and shook his head.

'No – we don't know what happened to him. It was politics – it's not only here in South Africa that people are dying. Police come and take his two friends and him at night and then we don't hear nothing. A farmer near my village find his shoe and his jacket but nothing else.'

'But maybe he's just lost.' Hamish clutched at a straw.

Colin shook his head. 'They find bones near his shoe and then some clothes.' His voice broke slightly and then silence ensued.

'I'm so sorry, Colin,' said Hamish after a few minutes. He felt so lame.

The bulbul went to sleep and Colin continued the meditation of the nets. As the day faded from pink to purple, the boy stood, tapped Colin lightly on the shoulder and departed.

From a competitive point of view, riding hadn't all been plain sailing, and to say that Hamish's first foray into the world of show jumping was unsuccessful would be akin to ascribing that adjective to the Titanic's maiden voyage. Bultarka had taken the bit between his teeth at the first jump, exited the arena via the southern fence without breaking stride and dumped Hamish in a nasty thicket of paper thorns. Hamish had shown a lot of courage in climbing back into the saddle and had becalmed the pony by the end of the day.

So it was that in the autumn of 1988, Hamish and Bultarka were formally registered with the Transvaal Horse Society. For their first graded show, Annabelle entered the pair in the children's C grades. From this point on, Hamish could no longer turn up in a grubby T-shirt – there was a compulsory formality to the shows and Caroline spent liberally in order to ensure that the boy would arrive (although almost certainly not leave) looking the part.

Early one Saturday morning, Hamish and Caroline arrived at the stables to help with the task of boxing the horses to the show-grounds in the countryside north of Johannesburg. There were two children going to the show that day: Hamish and Amy. The latter was about to turn fourteen and this was to be her last show. She and her pony, Timothy, were a highly rated A-grade pair, and to Hamish she represented the pinnacle of kids' riding.

Hamish was turned out in a new white shirt, cream jodhpurs, polished boots and, in a small suit bag that remained in Caroline's car, a tweed jacket. His mother, knowing her son only too well, had placed an old T-shirt over him until the last possible moment – desperate for his debut to make a good impression on all fronts.

The ponies boxed with relative ease and presently they were on their way, Annabelle driving the pick-up and Colin sitting in the load bed in case anything should fly out. Hamish felt honoured to be travelling with Amy. The two of them sat on a narrow and buttock-numbingly uncomfortable bench at the front of the horse trailer while the ponies pulled grass from their hay nets.

'Are you nervous?' Amy asked as the trailer rattled along.

He looked up at her. 'A little bit.'

She smiled and he felt his face flush as she looked away. Amy was four inches taller than Hamish. She had auburn hair tied neatly into a hairnet for the show. Her large brown eyes were shaded by a powder-blue peak, which she wore in the absence of her riding helmet. She had a strong jaw with a faint dimple on her chin. Below that, she was, to Hamish's mind, beautifully proportioned. Her arms and legs were lean and muscled – almost stocky. Amy gave off an air of detached authority and, if he'd been able to verbalise the jumble of unrefined emotions that suddenly assailed him, he'd have realised he had a crush.

Hamish had the guile of a wildebeest, so Amy immediately realised the effect she was having. She smiled and looked out of the window, unoffended, and in fact rather pleased. Hamish made her laugh – not always on purpose – but she enjoyed his sense of humour and refreshing bluntness. He was also quite cute. Not like Garry Benson (the boy she'd kissed at the school social a week previously) – he was a warrior-type and all the girls wanted to be with him. Hamish was tiny but he had a large, raw personality. She also enjoyed the fact that she was in complete control of this situation.

She turned back to him. 'Well, I think you are going to do very well today.' She reached over and touched his knee.

Hamish felt a surge of unmitigated joy.

'Thanks,' he said, turning his face to look out of the other window. 'You, um, will ... eh ... do well also I'm sure ... You'll win as usual.'

She giggled. 'Maybe, maybe not.'

As suburbia gave way to smallholdings, Hamish thought how bright and green the day was.

'Are *you* nervous?' He pretended to adjust something on Bultarka's halter rather than look at her.

'Not now. I will be just before the bell though. You look very smart today, Hamish.'

She was teasing him now, and he flushed again.

'Thanks. You, eh ... look ... um ... pret ... ah ... good too.'

He longed suddenly to be out of that horsebox but at the same time hoped that the two of them would never leave its rattling intimacy. Eventually the spell was broken by Annabelle wrenching open the trailer door to let them out.

The entire family had been dragged out to watch Hamish compete. Stuart was not a horse person and neither was Roger. Julia, aged three, wasn't much fussed but loved the adventure. Elizabeth had insisted on attending. When the Transvaal Horse Society had been mentioned, she'd conjured up images of the Badminton Horse Trials – a bevy of Sloanes dressed in Harris tweed, deer stalkers, exotic picnics, champagne and a glimpse of one of the famous Phillips family. She'd dressed for the occasion, the obligatory hat even more exuberant than usual.

'There seems to be rather a lot of dust here,' she'd complained as they drove into the show grounds. The urgent activity of horses, riders and cars had excited a goodly amount of highveld dirt into the atmosphere.

'What were you expecting?' muttered Stuart.

'What was that?!'

'It's Africa and we haven't had rain for two weeks – it's going to be dusty.'

The family then spent twenty minutes wandering among the milling horseflesh and children. Elizabeth was nearly run over by a chestnut pony whose rider had lost any semblance of control. By the time they'd found Caroline, who'd arrived in her own car earlier, the grandmother had been thoroughly disabused of the notion that there was anything glamorous about children's show jumping.

In the shade of a syringa, the Frasers and Pratchetts (Amy's mother and father) set up camp on the side of the arena. When Stuart arrived, Hamish and Annabelle were walking the course. The boy actually looked quite smart in his little tweed jacket, black hat and new boots.

Stuart's heart sank on hearing that there were ten fences arranged in a convoluted track. For the life of him, he could not see how Hamish – who couldn't remember how to spell 'necessary' two minutes after reading it – was going to recall the position and order of the jumps.

From the arena, Hamish and Annabelle walked down to where Colin was sitting on a bucket, back against a thorn tree, Bultarka's reins looped easily around his arm, the pony dozing where he stood.

'Good luck, Hamish!' he said cheerfully, as Annabelle boosted her pupil into the saddle and then led him to the arena gate, where an officious round woman was standing with a clipboard.

'Are you Hamish Fraser?' she snapped at him.

Hamish looked down at her, feeling rather proud. 'Yes, Madam, I am.'

'In you go then.'

'Right, Hamish,' Annabelle said, 'remember what I told you – you've done all you need to prepare. Just trust yourself to ride well and do not worry about the outcome. Go and have fun.'

Hamish nodded and kicked the black pony into the arena, where he suddenly felt very alone. He realised the only thing he could hear was the sound of his own breathing. Then the bell rang and it was his turn to ride. He gathered in the reins, sat deeply into the saddle and applied some pressure with his legs. The pony, sensing the excitement, arched his neck and broke into a sprightly canter. They circled once, passed through the start flags and approached the first fence.

The round passed in a blur but gave neither rider nor pony the slightest trouble. Hamish felt utterly elated as he made his way back to where his family were sitting with the Pratchetts.

'Oh, Hamish, well done,' said Caroline, her eyes brimming with tears.

'Well done, boy!' Stuart said, clapping his son on the shoulders, before heading off in search of the catering kiosk for what, for him, would become the only redeeming feature of his endless Saturdays among the dust, dung and snobbery of the shows: fresh bacon-and-egg rolls.

He bought an armload and returned to the group to hand them out. Hamish munched contentedly as they watched the rest of the competitors in the class.

Amy and Timothy came a close second in the first A-grade class. Inspired, Hamish pushed much harder in his second class. He was exultant and breathless as he finished the jump-off round, and despite being first to ride, he held the lead until the very last competitor – a completely fearless ten year old – pipped him by two seconds. Hamish's second place earned him a huge hug from Annabelle, a chuffed pat on the back from his father and his mother cried (but there was nothing unusual about that). He felt his father's eyes boring into him as he thanked the Pratchetts for their congratulations.

'This isn't exactly the Derby, is it?' growled Elizabeth. 'I mean, it's a little early to be comparing the boy with David Broome.'

But Hamish had no interest in who David Broome was as he sat down on the grass next to Amy, who was leaning back on her elbows chewing a stalk.

'Well done, Hamish,' she said without looking at him.

By this stage Elizabeth had had quite enough.

'This is beyond tolerance,' she complained to Caroline. 'For godsakes get me out of here!'

'You might at least congratulate Hamish,' her daughter replied.

'For trotting over a couple of poles while I suffer here in the dust of a thousand nags, the stink of their dung and swarms of blood-sucking flies? Not likely.' She folded her arms – still convinced that her least favourite grandchild was mentally and physically deficient. But Elizabeth's lack of magnanimity meant nothing to Hamish. He was on top of the world.

Later that afternoon, Amy cleaned the field in her second class – her final appearance on Timothy. The occasion brought with it a lot of emotion, as she and the pony had forged a strong bond over a period of four years. While she completed her lap of honour, Hamish walked down to where Colin and Bultarka were waiting. The groom was sitting on his bucket, back against the tree trunk, eating a butterless half-loaf with some luminous pink polony of indeterminate origin – the standard 'groom's lunch' as sold by the Transvaal Horse Society.

'You guys ride well today!' Colin said cheerfully.

'Yes … thank you, Colin,' Hamish replied as Amy and Timothy walked up.

Her feet were out of the stirrups, legs loose below the saddle, reins held at the buckle. Timothy stretched forward to a water bucket and drank with loud slurps as Amy flung her right leg over the pommel and dropped silently to the ground, eyes shining.

'Well done,' said Hamish, slightly in awe – both at her achievement and the immaculate condition of her clothes, but for the inside of her jodhpurs, where they'd rubbed against the saddle. He self-consciously shifted his tie to cover the egg stain on his shirt.

'Thanks,' she replied, unbuckling the girth.

Hamish watched as she pulled off her helmet and the hairnet underneath, and then shook out and smoothed her hair. He realised he was staring just as she looked up, and quickly cast his eyes to the horizon, trying to look aloof but instead appearing squinty-eyed and myopic.

By the time they departed for home, the world's least comfortable bench was the only place in the universe Hamish wanted to be. Rattling along, his leg touching that of the pretty girl next to him, he felt flushed with achievement. When he turned to look at Amy, she was gently stroking Timothy's muzzle, a tear rolling down her cheek. She reached up with her left hand and wiped it away with her thumb.

'Why are you sad?' he asked after realising he'd been staring at her face and neck for ages.

'Because I have to sell Timmy now – this is the end of riding for me. My folks don't want to spend the money any more.' Amy shrugged. 'I've just made the national gymnastics squad – I love gymnastics and riding, but it takes up too much time to do both.'

'Oh,' said Hamish, his mind grasping for something useful to say. Then he remembered that after Reggie's mother had died, Caroline had explained that it was best not to offer advice or platitudes. 'I'm sorry you feel sad.'

'Thank you, Hamish.' Then she tilted her head and rested it on his shoulder. It wasn't comfortable, given that the shoulder was bony and lower than her own – but Hamish thought he might burst. She sat up a few moments later when the trailer hit a bump and drove Hamish's collarbone painfully into her temple.

The Johannesburg shadows were lengthening as the horsebox crunched down the brick driveway of the Inanda Club. Faint tongues of autumn reached through the afternoon as Hamish and Amy led their horses out of the trailer and down to the stables.

Amy was leaning on the gnarled trunk of the old oak as Hamish emerged from Bultarka's stable to hang the halter on its peg. The late afternoon sun warmed the western side of the trunk and the friends moved instinctively round to catch the last rays.

'I think you should buy Timothy,' Amy said after a while.

'Maybe I'll talk to my Mum and Dad,' he replied. 'But I think he'll miss you.' The deflection was not lost on her.

'You can take him up through the grades again and you'll be kind to him.'

The sun had just set when they heard the rattle of metal buckets as the grooms approached with the evening feed.

'Hamish?'

He looked up. Amy planted a lingering kiss on the boy's mouth, her lips slightly parted.

Hamish's whole being fizzed – he responded instinctively, putting his arms round her waist and puckering his lips. Just as he was about to ruin the moment by attempting to involve his tongue, Amy moved her face away and they held each other firmly for a minute. He felt the plop of a tear on his shoulder. As Amy ended the embrace, she smiled.

'Take care, Hamish – of you and my pony.'

Hamish never saw Amy again.

In later life, Hamish might have stored the experience in the private part of his memory, knowing that to share what had happened would break its spell and cheapen it. He had no such compunction aged eleven – he was simply bursting to tell someone that he had kissed a girl (not that she'd kissed him). He wanted to tell Roger but didn't really know how to broach the subject – they seldom talked about such things.

On Monday mornings there was a choir practice, and Hamish was fit to exploding by the time Harry took his place with the rest of the trebles.

'Harry,' Hamish began without a greeting. 'Harry, this awesome thing happened this weekend!'

'Fraser, shut up and turn to page five,' scolded Mr Danhauser, the choirmaster.

'Yes, sir, sorry, sir,' said Hamish.

He had to wait until the tenors botched their entrance to the Kyrie of Fauré's Requiem before he could speak again.

'Harry, I kissed a —'

'Fraser, I told you to shut up!' Mr Danhauser boomed from the front. 'Now get out! You can write me a five-page essay on why I should allow you stay in the choir!'

'But, sir —'

'Now!'

Hamish gathered his blazer and skulked out of the room. The essay he wrote detailed his experience at the show and culminated in Amy's kiss. He took it to Mr Danhauser – who, as with all punishment of this nature, tore it up and threw it out without reading it.

14

In his penultimate year of Preparatory school, aged twelve, Hamish had joined the senior choir in which the upper registers of the Prep choristers were added to those of the broken College voices. Hamish was deeply moved by the sound of the eighty-strong choir in full voice.

His favourite performance of that year was the carol service. The choir rehearsed from September and, to Hamish, the sound was familiar and wonderful. Since he could remember, Stuart had played the Nine Lessons and Carols from King's College Cambridge on the turntable at Christmas time. Hamish thought the Trinity choir sounded exactly like the boys of King's.

At the service, the first verse of 'Once in Royal David's City' was sung by a diminutive fellow in the year above Hamish. Benedict Arthur had a treble of piercing clarity and a confident knack for performance. His soaring rendition of the solo first verse held the congregation of boys and parents mesmerised.

Hamish resolved there and then that he would be performing that verse in his final year of preparatory school. (As a result, he would develop an abiding terror that his voice would break and shatter his dreams. Unbeknownst to him there was no danger of this, for while the voices of many of his peers started to jump about in that unattractive adolescent way, Hamish's would not break for the next four years.)

Excellent as young Master Arthur's performance was, it did not come close to the baritone solo in 'The Three Kings'. Simphiwe Buthelezi was one of the few black boys at Trinity – the sons of African ambassadors, clergymen, academics and a few black businessmen who had managed to make it big despite the best efforts of the apartheid state. Buthelezi was the son of an Anglican deacon, and he had a voice that made people think they were listening to the Lord God Almighty Himself. It was rich, round and natural, and had a power that Hamish instinctively knew he would never possess.

There was also nothing cowed or shy about Buthelezi – his parents, using the inspiration of the Archbishop, had instilled in him a sense of his own worth and pride in his blackness. The carol service was his chance to demonstrate this, and he cracked the vaulted chapel ceiling with his booming baritone.

In the dining hall after the service, the main topic of discussion over tepid Earl Grey, instant coffee and stale biscuits was not the tone of Buthelezi's voice, not the quality of his diction, not his perfect performance of 'The Three Kings' and the small improvisations that had made the delivery unique. It was the colour of his skin.

Hamish, tiny and without outwardly remarkable characteristics, walked almost invisible in the sea of chattering parents and bigger boys, and thus found it easy to empty a biscuit plate into his blazer pockets without being noticed. This achieved, he found a corner of the room in which to consume them. There was a knot of parents close by and Hamish listened to the conversation with interest.

'That black kid can sing, hey,' said a perfectly turned out banker in a pin-striped suit.

'Ja,' replied a fat balding one about Stuart's age, 'but all blacks can sing – my garden boy sounds like that all the time.' He raised his teacup to his lips and slurped. 'And dance!' he added. 'You've seen them in the streets – they've all got rhythm.'

An insipid-looking woman with an overexcited perm and sequinned jacket swallowed her bite of biscuit. 'It's their genes – like running, they're designed to run.'

'And throw stones – they love to throw stones.' This from a tall blonde woman with a hurricane-resistant coiffure.

'No,' corrected the banker, 'they're much better at throwing half-bricks.'

The banker's eyes darted to his friends, who laughed before the perm spoke again.

'How does he afford to come to this school?'

'His father must be doing something dodgy – supplying dagga or cigarettes in the townships probably.'

Hamish felt his anger rising.

'Or half-bricks!' They all roared and then, quite suddenly, the banker noticed a small boy sitting on an unused table in the corner.

The malevolence in the boy's face made the moment awkward.

The fat man coughed and addressed Hamish. 'How long have you been sitting there?'

Hamish drew himself up to his full four feet and six inches, his chest puffed out in righteous indignation.

'Long enough to hear that you're a racist!' he snarled.

Years around the boardroom table with the captains of South African industry meant that the banker was seldom thrown off his stride. He slowly set his teacup on its saucer and met Hamish's eye.

'What's your name?'

'I am Hamish Charles Sutherland Fraser.' He stared straight back at the banker.

The perm stifled a giggle.

'There are many things you don't understand about this country of ours, boy. Many things that only adults can understand.' His tone dripped with condescension and arrogance.

'But there are many things I *do* understand,' said Hamish, buoyed by the sight of Stuart chatting to Buthelezi's father in a group not far away. 'And I know racism when I hear it.'

Hamish stalked off before any of them could reply.

He arrived at his father's side to hear him say in exuberant tones,

'Your son really has the most tremendous voice – has he always sung?'

'He has grown up in parishes all around the country – many in rural areas. There is always singing in the church,' replied Father Buthelezi in a voice that sounded tired. The priest took a sip from his tea.

Stuart swallowed the remainder of his biscuit. 'Do you think he'll sing professionally?' he asked eventually.

'No, I don't think so.' Father Buthelezi placed his cup back on the saucer and looked directly at Stuart. 'He has very limited options in South Africa, so we are trying to get him a scholarship to a US university. If we don't manage that, then it will be Kenya most likely.'

'Ah … well … yes, I suppose that would be best.'

Hamish watched the interaction with growing discomfort – he'd never seen his dad squirm before. Father Buthelezi was in the truth business, not the feel-good business, and with the truth subtly laid bare, he said, 'Thank you for your compliments on my son's singing. Good evening.' He nodded at Hamish and walked over to the tea table to replenish his cup.

For their part, the ladies of the entertainment committee were slightly nonplussed by serving a black man, and allowed him to pour his own tea as they pretended to be busy filling milk jugs. They also wondered if the missing biscuits were somewhere under the priest's cassock. (They were in Hamish's blazer.)

In December that year, the family travelled down to the sleepy sea-side town of Kenton-on-Sea, where Stuart and Caroline had bought a house, sight unseen, as a holiday property. Tina was persuaded to join the family for Christmas in order to help with setting up the house and nannying Julia – now four years old and showing early signs of an iras-cible nature. Stuart, Hamish and Tina were to drive down to the coast towing a brand-new trailer loaded to the gunwales and topped with children's bicycles. Caroline, Roger and Julia would fly down a day later.

After a night on a stud farm in Colesberg, the driving party stopped for breakfast in the farming town of Cradock – a settlement not known for its liberal values. At about eight o'clock, Stuart wedged the car and trailer into a parking bay outside a charmless roadside restaurant, and he and Hamish climbed out.

Tina was reticent. On the way into the town, fading election posters from the Conservative Party had festooned the telegraph poles and streetlights.

'Come on, Tina, it will be fine,' Stuart said opening the passenger door to encourage her.

'Aiee, masser.' She slowly emerged, shaking her head.

The three of them walked into the eatery and sat at a table. There were no other customers and the comforting smells of coffee and bacon did little to lift the oppressive atmosphere. From behind a counter in the dingy recesses, a vast white woman emerged and waddled over. The first thing Hamish noticed about her was her moustache.

She looked at the breakfasting party for an awkward and wordless few seconds.

'Good morning,' said Stuart.

'Môre,' she replied curtly.

'Ah, yes, may we see a menu, please?' asked Stuart. He would have tried speaking Afrikaans but figured that she'd be less insulted by his English than by his butchering of her language.

The moustache bristled. 'Ek praat nie Engels nie.' Her eyes flicked to Tina and back to Stuart. 'Ons dien nie swartes nie. Jy en die seun kan eet maar die swarte eet nie hier nie.'

The great irony of this situation was that Stuart had to ask Tina to translate for him. This she did while staring at the coffee-stained tablecloth, and Stuart's hitherto friendly visage faded instantly. Hamish ceased unscrewing the lid from the salt cellar.

'You will serve all of us or you will serve none of us. We are all hungry and we come here as a family.'

The woman, who apparently understood English perfectly well, replied, 'Ons maak nie kos vir vuil swartes.'

Tina made to leave. 'Come, masser, we go now please,' she pleaded.

'We are not going anywhere!' shouted Stuart, looking at the moustachioed waitress, then at his son and the woman who had all but raised him. His face reddened with indignation, his temper suddenly at boiling as the woman turned towards the kitchen.

'Wat die fok gaan hier aan?' A giant emerged from the kitchen at what would have been a run but for the size of his wobbling belly, which was covered in enough khaki material to make a two-man tent. He was probably about Stuart's age but a good four inches taller and forty kilograms heavier.

Hamish well knew what 'fok' meant but he'd never heard it uttered by an adult in anger.

'Wat die fok maak 'n swarte en 'n rooinek kaffer-boetie in my fokken plek?'

The astounding volume and ferocity in the man's voice took the boy's breath away. He dropped the salt cellar and it smashed onto the ground.

Stuart stood, his chair clattering over behind him and faced the oncoming threat. It was at this point that realisation dawned on the Fraser patriarch: the biggest person Hamish had ever seen was not about to engage in an intellectual discussion on the merits or otherwise of apartheid policies. He was going to bludgeon his point home through the medium of his fists. Stuart also realised that this was a man who understood and longed for violence, especially when it came to two of the things he hated most in his world.

Stuart took a deep breath and put his hands up in a gesture of peace. He forced his anger down, the necessity of protecting Hamish and Tina overcoming his pride.

'We are leaving,' he said gritting his teeth.

'Ja, fokkof, jou rooinek kaffer-boetie.' The boom of the voice shook the bones in Hamish's skull.

Tina grabbed Hamish by the hand and pulled him towards the door. Stuart, seething, followed.

The trio drove on in silence for the next hour until Hamish finally spoke.

'Dad, why was that guy so cross?'

'Sit back in your seat, Hamish,' Stuart said, feeling angry, embarrassed, emasculated and sad all at once.

The boy did as he was told.

'But why was he so angry, Dad?'

'Let's talk about it later. I have to think about the driving now.'

Wordlessly, Tina resumed her knitting. She wasn't surprised or even angry – she was simply relieved.

In the small town of Bedford, Stuart found a roadhouse and went in to buy takeaway breakfasts for three. After that the holiday atmosphere returned somewhat and by lunchtime they were in Kenton, unloading the trailer.

While Stuart drove off to Port Elizabeth to fetch the rest of his family, Tina and Hamish picked their way to the bottom of the unkempt garden, the grass shin length. Bees worked in the flowering weeds, zitting grasshoppers hopped out of their way. At the bottom of the garden, they found a path that led through the tangled dune bush where the cicadas played a deafening tune in the heat. The path wound down to a tow path on the tidal Kariega River. Looking downstream about a kilometre, Tina saw where the river mouth met the Indian Ocean.

She stopped and stared. 'So much water! I never seen the sea!'

Impatient to leap into the waves, Hamish grabbed Tina's hand. 'Come, Gogo, we're going swimming!'

Tina allowed herself to be led towards the beach where, as the boy swam in the waves, she sat on a towel gazing at the rolling ocean. By the end of the holiday, she had become something of a boogie-board enthusiast, leaping onto a blow-up lilo in her bright-green costume and an ornate blue bathing cap.

The house needed a lot done to it – the carpets (covered in fleas) had to be removed, walls painted, furniture bought and cheerful art hung from the walls. Tina's main function during this time was to play nanny to Julia and to a lesser extent the two boys, while Caroline and Stuart fixed the house with the help of a Xhosa woman named Daisy Ntunjwa.

Daisy and Tina struck up a friendship almost immediately – Tina's Zulu and Daisy's Xhosa were similar enough to be mutually intelligible, and the house was soon filled with the sound of happy chatting.

Once she had figured the Frasers would not object, Daisy decided to try and bring her son Ayanda, aged eleven, to spend some time with Hamish and Roger. Just after New Year, as Kenton disgorged the chaos of holidaymakers fighting over bread rolls in the supermarket, Daisy approached Caroline.

'Mummy,' she began, 'I can bring Ayanda for playing – his English at school is not good. Maybe your boys help this?'

Thinking this a tremendously liberal thing, Caroline agreed readily.

Ayanda arrived the next day and the three boys were introduced over some glasses of iced Coke. Awkward silence ensued as they looked at each other and the cane verandah furniture. Hamish regarded the fiddlewood tree as a flock of white eyes flitted about. The uncomfortable silence grew. Just as it became unbearable, Roger struck on an idea.

'Ayanda, do you like to swim?'

The Xhosa boy's face lit up.

'Let's go swim in the river! I'll go and get some towels.' Roger jumped up.

'Have you got a cozzie?' Hamish asked the well-muscled boy, who frowned. 'Um ... swimming shorts ... have you got shorts for swimming?'

Ayanda was dressed in his only pair of jeans and shook his head.

Hamish ducked inside and ran through to the laundry, where his mother and Daisy were unpacking some shopping. 'We're going swimming in the river but I need a cozzie for Ayanda.'

Caroline's eyes widened. 'Hamish ... um ... well, I am ... um ... not sure that Ayanda can swim,' she half-whispered, but loud enough so that Daisy could confirm or deny her son's aquatic abilities.

Daisy cricked her back and smiled down (she stood at six feet) at Caroline and her son. She winked and nodded. 'Ayanda always is in the river at home.'

Caroline reached into a pile of freshly ironed laundry. 'Well, we'd better give him one of Roger's cozzies – yours won't fit one of his legs.'

A few moments later, the three boys stood on the southern bank of the river. The sandy path was lined with succulent tidal plants and across the channel a huge flock of terns rested on a sandbank. Two hundred metres away, on the opposite bank, a small herd of cattle wandered out of the dune thicket and onto the sand, followed by a young Xhosa herd boy. It was a week into January and a few peaceful holiday stragglers drifted in paddle skis or walked along the river towards the beach.

The boys left their towels on the bank. Prawn holes belched water as they stepped onto the grey tidal sludge. Roger hated the feeling and moved like a disgusted cat. Then they were paddling tentatively into the shallows.

While Roger and Hamish hesitated about taking the plunge into the chilly water, Ayanda waded up to his thighs and swam for the sandbank fifty metres opposite. He swam freestyle with his head out of the water like a water-polo player. The two Frasers followed quickly, Roger imitating Ayanda's style. They emerged onto the bank and walked over to an area only submerged at high tide – a thin, warm crust covered soft sand and air pockets.

Ayanda dropped his knees through the crust and lay down with a satisfied sigh. Hamish and Roger, who'd been taught to be fastidious about keeping sand off their bodies, stared at the Xhosa boy, who rolled onto his back, grinning.

'It's good and hot!' he invited. 'First knees, then stomach and over on back!'

Hamish gave it a try. A thrill shot through his body as his chest broke through the crust and the exquisite warmth of the sand enveloped him. He took a deep sniff of the sand – it smelt like the sea and its creatures.

Of summer and holidays and happiness.

The three boys lay there until the two paler ones felt their skin starting to burn.

'We must go back,' said Roger. 'I'm burning.'

'What is burning?' Ayanda asked, rolling onto his side.

'My skin,' said Roger. 'Can't you feel you are burning?'

'I don't think I'm burning,' he replied with a shrug and lay back down.

Roger rose, brushed the sand from his chest and headed for the water. Hamish remained with Ayanda, his skinny chest turning beetroot.

A few minutes later, Ayanda said, 'I come to your house, so it is good you come to my house.'

'Yes,' said Hamish lazily.

'Tomorrow – I tell Mama. You are staying in my room with my brother!'

As Ayanda stood and made for the river, Hamish's brain, slowly at first and then with increasingly rapid alarm, registered that he'd just accepted an invitation to spend a night with a strange family. He suddenly felt cold.

To say that Hamish was not socially adventurous would be a gross understatement. Indeed, the few nights he'd spent at Harry St Claire's mansion, despite the luxury and kindness lavished, had made him homesick. He found making any sort of small-talk intensely painful and generally only managed a conversation with strangers if he was soapboxing or asked directly about his riding exploits. If the stranger happened to be a female younger than twenty-five, he became a dribbling statue.

Following Ayanda and Roger slowly back up to the house, he wondered how on earth he was going to make an excuse that wouldn't offend Daisy or his new friend. But it was pointless: Ayanda raced on ahead and by the time Hamish had stepped onto the verandah, Caroline had been told and Daisy and her son were walking off into the house chatting animatedly.

'I believe you've been invited to stay with Daisy and her family tomorrow night!' Caroline turned to Hamish, eyes agog – she knew her son only too well and saw immediately that he'd somehow fallen into this situation.

'Um …' replied Hamish.

'Well, let's talk to your dad, and see what … um … he thinks.'

Hamish felt a faint glimmer of hope that he'd be reprieved.

'Talk to Dad about what?' said Stuart arriving from the garage bearing a heavy paving stone for use on the dune path. He set the stone down and stretched his back while Caroline explained.

'Oh,' he said after a while, taking a hankie out of his pocket and mopping his brow. 'Well, that's a wee bit unusual … um, what did you say to Daisy?'

'Well, what could I say?' whispered Caroline becoming a little panicked. 'I told her … I, uh … I told her that would be lovely!'

'Mu-um!' whined Hamish.

Stuart shrugged. 'I can't see any harm in it – they live on a farm in the middle of nowhere. It might na be what he's used to, but Hamish will be safe, I'm sure.'

'Da-a-ad!' Hamish saw his reprieve disappear.

'I actually think it'll do you some good, boy – it's just a night.' Stuart smiled mischievously. 'Besides, your dear, polite mother here has accepted on your behalf and we can na change that now – can we? It'd be rude.'

Just after three o'clock the following afternoon, Stuart dropped Daisy and Hamish on a dusty road fifteen kilometres inland from Kenton.

'See you tomorrow, boy,' said Stuart as he handed Hamish a little backpack.

'Bye, Dad,' said Hamish, a slight quaver in his voice.

Stuart sped off before his son could change his mind. As the dust receded, Daisy turned to her guest and smiled.

'Come, Hamish – we go over here.' She indicated a rail-less stile leading over a barbed-wire fence. A well-worn path stretched through the veld beyond.

Daisy stepped onto the weathered wood, balancing with catlike grace, and in three quick movements was up and over. Hamish tossed his bag to the other side and then climbed over on all fours.

He followed Daisy along the path, winding east through a field where a herd of fat Jersey cows grazed. In front of them, the gorge of the Kariega River and the verdant farmlands stretched under the summer sky. To the north, the rolling countryside of the Eastern Cape: patches of tangled euphorbia, wild plum and stinkwood grew in-between the cattle pastures and chicory fields.

Hamish smelt it first – the wood smoke mixed with a hint of cow dung. Then he saw the Ntunjwas' home perched halfway down the hill. Below it, to the north-east, the river meandered through its picturesque gorge; raptors wheeled in the sky above, looking for prey in the cliffs. Closer to the homestead, Hamish heard the sound of chickens and the tinkling of bells tied to the necks of a raggedy herd of ten goats. Smoke rose in a thin pall from behind the house.

As they arrived, Ayanda and three little girls dressed in a collection of ill-fitting dresses came to greet them. Ndileka (four), Lindi (six) and Thandi (nine) spoke in animated Xhosa and cast glances towards the small white boy staring in wonder at the mud- and dung-covered house.

'Ayanda take you to where you sleep,' Daisy said to Hamish, who followed the younger boy around to the front of the house.

There they met Sipho, the eldest, a strapping lad of thirteen, who was repairing a hole in the chicken coop. Next to that an exuberant veggie patch grew, a moth-eaten scarecrow in its midst. Two cows, one uniform brown and the other piebald, grazed beyond the chicken run, their soon-to-be-weaned calves lying in the shade close by. Home-made gutters transferred water from the rusted corrugated-iron roof into

corroded oil drums from which the Ntunjwas drew most of their washing water.

Sipho nodded a greeting at Hamish, but seemed otherwise unfazed
by the new arrival.

'Come inside,' invited Ayanda.

The floors of the immaculate four-roomed house were made of dung
and soil – Hamish marvelled at how level they were. The front room
served as a kitchen and living room, the walls adorned with a collection
of endlessly repaired furniture. The central table was surrounded with
six chairs of wildly different origins. A thin coat of yellow paint covered
the cow-dung plaster, giving the walls a cheerful mustard colour. House
Ntunjwa was spotlessly clean and nothing was out of place.

Ayanda led Hamish through a low door to the boys' bedroom, where
a thin shaft of light from a small window illuminated a collection of
rolled-up reed mats stacked neatly against a wall and a hardwood wardrobe that, if its heavy port-side list could have been repaired, might have
fetched a fortune in an antique shop.

Ayanda indicated the floor and smiled. 'Boys sleep here!' Before his
guest could verbalise his surprise, the host said, 'Come, we go fetch
water,' and departed.

'Sleep where?' Hamish thought, slightly dazed as he returned into
the light.

'There is toilet.' Ayanda pointed towards a structure made of corrugated-iron scraps about twenty metres away, much of it covered in
a tangle of granadilla vines. 'But only for pff pff.' The host made loud
farting noises and pointed at his bottom. 'Bushes everywhere for psss.'
This he indicated by holding his finger in front of his fly.

Hamish laughed and willed his bowels to hold until his return home
the following morning. Psss in the bush was one thing; pff pff in a rusty
pit latrine with newspaper for reading and wiping was quite another.

Ayanda retrieved two twenty-litre plastic containers from where they
were stacked.

'You help Ayanda fetch water?' Daisy said to Hamish as she emerged from the chicken coup.

'Yes,' said Hamish, happy for any activity that would negate the need for him to try to hold a conversation.

The boys walked down into the valley on a rock-strewn and precipitous path, each carrying a plastic drum. As Hamish slipped and stumbled, he marvelled at how Ayanda's flat, bare feet didn't register any sign of pain on the sharp stones. A few hundred metres from the river, the path turned north toward a copse of tangled *Schotia* and *Rhus* with a giant milkwood at its centre, and the boys disappeared into the deep shade.

Ayanda led them to a corrugated-iron cover with a thorn branch resting on top of it. Water trickled from under the cover, carving a shallow channel that disappeared under a num-num bush and emerged the other side into a large pool. Ayanda removed the metal to reveal a spring that pumped clear water into an overflowing shallow well. Then he reached up into a low *Schotia* branch and pulled out a plastic two-litre Coke bottle that had been roughly cut in half. With this, he began to painstakingly decant water from the well into the containers. Hamish watched in fascination at the patience brought to bear on the slow task.

'Why don't you just use that deep water over there?' Hamish asked, pointing to the pool.

Ayanda looked up and smiled. 'Cows drink there. They make mud and pff pff and psss in the water,' he said by way of explanation. 'I must careful of mud in this water.'

The hoof tracks, dung patties and strong smell of cattle were suddenly obvious to Hamish and the two boys laughed.

Twenty minutes later, the containers were full and the ancient milkwood invited with low-hanging branches. Hamish's love of tree-climbing had never waned, and the two boys wound their way up and peeped through the top of the foliage. The floodplain was bathed in soft yellow light, the grazing fields uniform emerald, fringed with thickets of every possible green, and punctuated every so often by flashes of blue plumbago and red *Schotia* flowers. The boys sat in silence for a few blissful minutes until Hamish noticed a white bakkie speeding along a farm track, two large brown dogs visible in the back.

'Who's that?' he asked.

'The farmer – this his place.' Ayanda waved a hand at the floodplain. 'My father works for him. Come.'

He quickly descended, picked up one of the containers and waited for Hamish, who picked up the other one as nonchalantly as possible, knowing it was going to be a mighty struggle for him to convey his water up the steep slope. Although the boys were almost of an age, the white one was blessed with the physique of a dowelling rod and a life unfettered by the strains of manual labour.

'Can we stop for a rest?' Hamish asked halfway up the hill. His face was red and he was gasping for air.

Ayanda turned around surprised. 'You are sick?'

'No, I'm just a bit tired.'

Ayanda nodded, but didn't give voice to his confusion as to how this short walk could be physically taxing.

They sat on their containers looking at the view for a while before continuing, more slowly this time, towards the comforting smell of a wood fire at the house.

'You are tired!' said Daisy sympathetically when she saw the exhausted smaller boy. 'Come, we have tea now.'

Daisy, Ayanda, Hamish and the others gathered around the cooking fire, where an ancient tin kettle was boiling. Inside it, tea was stewing – milk and mountains of sugar already added. They all sat in the dirt and received a tin mug, which seared Hamish's lips as he took his first sip. When it had cooled sufficiently, he felt a surge of pleasure as the sweet, steaming drink worked its way into his belly. Around him, the family chatted in Xhosa, the children under the misapprehension that Hamish knew what they were talking about.

When tea was over, it was time for more chores. The three youngest set to cleaning – sweeping the area around the building until it was free of leaves, wiping all the surfaces in the humble home and washing the tea things. Daisy removed to the vegetable garden and instructed the two boys to milk the cows.

Ayanda retrieved two plastic jugs from inside and led Hamish around to the cow pen on the western side of the house. At this point, both boys made a dreadfully inaccurate assumption: the host that his guest knew how to milk a cow, the guest that his host would realise that he hadn't the foggiest idea. The little herd of four, used to the unchanging rhythm of each day, were waiting at the entrance to their pen.

Ayanda pointed at the Jersey. 'You milk that one.'

Hamish stared at the animal, who'd hitherto looked like a gentle member of a bucolic children's book, but was now casting what Hamish interpreted as menacing looks in his direction. Ayanda slid back the log from the pen entrance and the cows went in. Then he took a piece of orange twine from a rusty nail, tied it around the piebald's horns and attached the other end to a fence post. Hamish took another length of string, assuming it was for the same purpose, and approached the Jersey.

She eyed him and snorted. Hamish stopped. He could already hear the milk squirting into Ayanda's jug. He took another step forward and the cow turned away with disdain. She nuzzled her calf, which Hamish took for a sign of her returning to good humour – he stepped up to her head and slipped the loop of the string over her horns. So far so good. He tugged on the string to make the bovid move forward a step. The cow stood firm and then mooed loudly. Her calf repeated the call. Hamish gave another tug. 'Come on,' he encouraged.

She relented, took a step forward and then drove her forehead into Hamish's hip. The boy yelped as he left the ground, landing with a groan a few feet away. Hysterical laughter erupted from the smaller children leaning against the fence. Hamish rolled onto his back and a swarm of flies alighted angrily from a fresh patty disturbed by his left elbow.

The yelp had brought Daisy at a run, and a torrent of angry Xhosa flowed. The children scuttled round to the other side of the pen, where her powerful spank couldn't reach them. Relieved that the skinny child appeared unharmed, Daisy ducked under the fence, grabbed the string on the Jersey's horns and wound it around another fence post. She smiled as Hamish retrieved his plastic jug and pointed at Ayanda.

'You teach me please – how to milk this evil cow!'

The bigger boy, his milking complete, handed Daisy his full jug and then knelt in the dirt next to the becalmed Jersey's udders. He took hold of a teat, massaged it briefly and then pulled it from the top down. A jet of milk shot into the empty jug. Hamish winced at the harshness of the tug.

'You now,' said Ayanda. 'That one.' He pointed at one of the other teats.

Hamish replicated the action more gently and a few drops came out.

'More strong!' said Ayanda.

Hamish tried again and this time a jet of frothy cream came forth. The satisfaction he felt was immense, and after ten minutes Ayanda had to draw him away.

'It's finished – now babies must drink.'

As the sun disappeared behind the hills, the boys made their way back to the front of the house, where they met David, the Ntunjwa patriarch. He was sitting on a hand-made stool next to the fire in weather-beaten blue overalls, the arms tied at the waist, and a holey once-white T-shirt.

He looked up and smiled wearily as the boys approached. 'Molweni.'

'Molo, Baba,' they replied in unison.

Ayanda and David exchanged a few words as the father filled a pipe with Boxer tobacco and lit it expertly. Daisy indicated a stump, polished by countless bottoms, and Hamish sat down.

As the pipe smoke mingled with the smell of the wood fire and the meal of samp and beans boiled on the coals, the family gathered in the growing darkness. The chickens clucked quietly, settling into their hutch, and a fruit bat began to tink. An expectant air hung as David began to speak. He had no English, but he paused every so often for Ayanda to whisper a translation.

The story was a memory of David's life – of a time when he was around the same age as Ayanda and Hamish. He told of building a new family home much the same as the current Ntunjwa residence, but with a thatch roof and far less furniture. He described going to cut and carry the huge corner poles and digging the holes for them in the hard earth. His voice became gruff as he imitated how his father, by then a crooked old man, had yelled at him and his nine siblings when they tired.

Slowly the house took shape in Hamish's imagination. He pictured being part of the crew – gathering the saplings to wind between the poles, taking metal buckets to fetch the termite-mound cement for the daubing and, finally, seeking out where the family's four cows had left their dung so it could be plastered onto the walls.

It was a story richly told and no doubt one that the family had heard many times, but as the night grew around them, they listened with all the attention of a first rendition. Their patriarch's rich, comforting voice and the iron discipline he insisted on made for a mesmerising atmosphere.

After the story, the family ate. Hamish received the first share, a mound of samp and beans so large he began to look for somewhere to hide it. When the meal was complete, the young girls gathered the plates and went off to wash them by candlelight.

Hamish stared into the dancing flames, saying nothing but also not feeling the passage of time as the low flames turned to coals. Another short story from David – this one about setting traps for francolins as a herd boy – signalled the end of the evening, and the family rose to go inside.

The three girls spread their mats on the kitchen floor while the boys readied their room for slumber. Hamish had no idea how he was going to sleep on a reed mat. He lay on his back between Ayanda and Sipho and pulled a threadbare blanket up to his chin.

The air in the room was close and smelt strongly of human beings who'd worked all day then sat next to a smoky fire, and who did not have the luxury of running water. The small window didn't allow for any air movement and Hamish felt slightly claustrophobic as he lay there, the other two already breathing with the depth of sleep. He didn't think a great deal about the afternoon or his sense of contentment – that would only come much later.

Pale dawn lit the small window. Ayanda and Sipho were folding their blankets. Hamish felt a strong urge to pull the blanket over his head and pretend to be asleep, but Ayanda didn't give him the chance.

'Molo,' he said loudly, ripping the blanket off his diminutive guest. 'Wake now for tea and washing!'

Hamish groaned as he stood to help fold the blankets and stow the reed mats. All of them had slept in the clothes they'd worn the day before, so there was no need for dressing.

They stumbled outside into the dewy, clear morning, the valley a cacophony of birdsong. Daisy and the girls were already preparing for the day. The mother expertly stoked the fire before placing the blackened kettle on the edge of the flames. The three girls, completely naked, were washing. The two smaller ones stood in the metal bath rubbing soap on themselves and giggling as Thandi poured jugs of cold water over them. Hamish stared as he considered what the experience would feel like on a dark and windy July morning.

'Molo, Hamish,' Daisy greeted.

'Molo, Mama.'

'You sleep good?'

'Yes, good, thank you. And you, Daisy?'

She nodded.

When the girls had finished, Sipho and Ayanda carried the bath to the veggie patch and emptied it carefully along a row of spinach before taking it to the back of the house.

Hamish watched in some embarrassment as the two boys stripped off completely, but soon he was standing naked as well, not knowing what to do with his hands.

'You have been to the bush also!' said Sipho, observing the skinny white boy's nethers. Then he laughed, slapped Hamish on the back and began to wash.

Hamish was too shy to ask what Sipho meant or why Ayanda retained his foreskin.

When they were done, they shared a tiny hand towel before dressing themselves, still damp under their clothes. They returned to the fire for sweet tea and runny maizemeal as the valley brightened.

The meal complete, Hamish helped milk the cows again – this time he took the piebald.

'Where is your father?' he asked his milking partner as white liquid squirted satisfyingly into his jug.

'He must be to work before morning,' came the reply from behind the recalcitrant Jersey.

Hamish and Daisy met Stuart at the road around eight o' clock that morning. All the children accompanied them along the path and then shook their guest's hand solemnly before he climbed the stile and fell into the grass on the other side. The fall broke the formality of the greeting as all the children – including the object of amusement – laughed hysterically.

'You come again!' said Ayanda.

'Yes,' smiled Hamish, with meaning.

They drove home mostly in happy silence. Hamish looked at the gorge, the banks and fields and felt connected to them.

'What was your favourite part?' asked his mother over honeyed scones and tea later that morning.

'Did you know that there are springs with salty drinking water on the river?' said Hamish, staring into the garden with a frown. 'Ayanda and the others have to fetch water to cook with every day – they have to walk all the way down this rocky hill and then back up again.' He bit into his scone. 'Every single day.'

15

After a lengthy and highly enjoyable holiday in Kenton, Hamish passed into his last year of preparatory schooling. He was gratified to be at the top of the pile and, at the first assembly, was confident that his name would be included in those read out as Prep-school prefects. As far as he was concerned, he couldn't imagine a more perfectly designed human being for the role of leadership.

Of the seventy-eight boys in the Standard Five class, twenty had been chosen: five from each of the four houses. His house, Johnston, was third in the list. Mr Dicks read out the names with ponderous solemnity.

'The prefects in Johnston House for 1989 are George Abbot, Philip Cobbler, Alan Jameson, Sipho Khoza and John van Schalkwyk. Well done to all of you.'

There was applause from all the boys except Hamish, who assumed that there was a catastrophic error. Until the end of assembly, he continued to hold out hope that Mr Dicks would realise his mistake.

Back at his classroom where a Maths lesson was about to begin, there was an excited buzz as the prefects congratulated each other, fixing new badges of authority to their lapels. Ambitious George Abbot intended to take his new responsibility very seriously, and the irritated Fraser boy provided the perfect opportunity: as Hamish walked into the class, he tripped on the raised threshold. His temper snapped and he kicked the tin waste-paper bin in the corner of the class. It flew into the dais, upended and sent papers, apple cores and pencil shavings scattering.

'Pick that up, Fraser,' said Abbot, pointing a finger, 'or I'll report you!'

Hamish wheeled round. 'Fuck you, Abbot.'

In the absence of a teacher, this was not unusual language for the boys walking the hallowed cloisters and echoing corridors of the august Anglican church school. The boys liked to swear at each other in the manner of the latest age-restricted movies. It made them feel older.

This was too much for the pious George Abbot.

'I'm a prefect!' he shrilled, tapping his newly affixed badge. 'You can't talk to me like that!'

Hamish feared authority – from adults. For the authority of his peers, however, he felt nothing but resentment, especially when it came from the likes of the brown-nosing new prefect. Abbot was fastidiously neat and a snitch of the first order. He also smelt of talcum powder.

'Abbot, you are a schloop, and that's why you're a prefect. It's not because you're better than me.'

The class was watching now. This encouraged Hamish, who began to imitate the new prefect. 'Sir, sir, sir, sir,' he opined, 'Fraser hasn't polished his shoes, sir.'

Giggles began from a few of the onlookers because Hamish's impersonation of Abbot's whiny voice was excellent.

Hamish sat in one of the front desks and pumped his hand, index finger extended into the air. 'Sir, sir, sir, York hasn't done his Maths homework.'

The giggles became laughs.

'Sir, sir, sir, Fraser left his PT togs at home. Sir, sir, sir, Simpson is being nasty to Goodenough – I'm going to be a prefect, sir, so that I can tell on people *all day long*!'

Abbot's face flushed. As mean as Hamish was being, he wasn't wrong, but he failed to see how the scorned new figure of authority would cope with the problem.

'Fine!' Abbot yelled. 'Then I'm taking you!' This meant he was going to deliver a report to a teacher. No one dared approach old-man

Dicks directly – he hated snitches – but the deputy headmaster was new, young and easily influenced. Indeed, one of the major reasons Abbot had been named prefect was due to the effect Mrs Abbot's olive skin and fluttering eyelashes had on Mr du Toit. When, at the last parents' and teachers' meeting, she'd indicated with a husky whisper that she thought her son would make an excellent prefect, Mr du Toit had vigorously agreed.

As the deputy head was settling into his post-assembly coffee before planning the term's cricket fixtures, a red-faced and tearful George Abbot burst into his office without knocking.

'Sir, sir, sir,' he wailed, 'Fraser kicked a dustbin and when I told him to pick it up, sir, he swore at me, sir, with the f-word, sir, even though I'm a prefect, sir!'

Mr du Toit, the arousing scent of the raven-haired Mrs Abbot still in his nose, agreed that this was unacceptable. 'Tell Fraser to come and see me immediately!'

Five minutes later, Hamish presented himself, stomach churning, at the second master's office. Ten minutes after that, he had a ten-page essay to write about why swearing is unacceptable at a church school. As his rage ebbed, he became aware that his behaviour would have displeased his father.

Once he'd recovered from the shock of not being raised to the leadership group, Hamish refocused on his one goal for the year: to sing the 'Once in Royal David's City' solo at the carol service. He'd never really set himself a goal before, but he was single-minded in the pursuit of this one. From the very first choir practice, he concentrated as much as he was able and when his mind wandered, he ensured that he didn't talk to anyone about it.

His task was made easier by the fact that Harry's voice had started to drop, which meant his friend was singing with the altos (as was the case with many solo-quality voices). Sipho Khoza was already with the tenors. Hamish was one of only three Standard Five boys still singing with the trebles. His main competition came from the powerful voice of William Hamilton in Standard Four – a red-faced little cherub that everyone liked (except Hamish). Alex Dickson, also in Standard Five, was a supremely confident singer for whom a surge of adolescent testosterone was the only thing standing between him and choral glory.

Mr Danhauser appreciated Hamish's efforts – it was clear that he took his singing seriously. But Hamish's performances were erratic. If the stars aligned – he was concentrating, not thinking about Jane (the new girl at the stables), hadn't consumed a sugary drink just before practice and wasn't showing off – then he sang beautifully, never missing an entrance and producing a very pleasant tone. At other times he missed his entrances and tended to bellow, which made him sound like a distressed warthog. It was not the sort of timbre anyone wants to hear in celebration of the Lord's birthday.

The choir's major work that year was Mozart's *Requiem*, with a full orchestra and professional soloists – an immensely ambitious undertaking for an amateur school choir. The performances took place in the chapel over the course of three nights in July. Despite the fact that a number of Johannesburg's elite were heard to mutter something along the lines of 'Why don't they do stuff from *Cats* or The Beatles?' the choir's performance was roundly admired. The exceptional Mr Danhauser was congratulated by staff and parents alike.

Hamish held himself together for all three occasions and by the end of the performance run he'd done his cause no end of good. But he was always in the third place – William Hamilton and Alex Dickson were simply more reliable.

Thoughts of singing went on hiatus for the month of August 1989 as the winter term came to an end and the Frasers drove to The Cavern Berg Resort in the Drakensberg along with another family, the MacDonalds, for a week of hiking, riding, tennis, wine and port (the latter two for the adults, of course). The month was to prove a seminal time in South Africa.

Dennis MacDonald was a member of parliament for the opposition Democratic Party. On the first evening of the holiday, while the rest of the adults sipped their predinner tipples, Dennis to-ed and fro-ed between the reception telephone and the lounge. Rumours were rife that President PW 'Die Groot Krokodil' Botha's number was up and that his cabinet had turned against him.

Dennis was in an ebullient mood when he emerged from the office for the final time. He strode across the bar and into the lounge, his bald head shining.

'What news, Dennis? Should I be booking passage to the Highlands?' asked Stuart, who'd been sitting next to a roaring fire chatting with two other couples.

'It's good, it's good.' Dennis sipped at his Pinotage and waited for all attention to be on him. 'I predict he'll be out by the end of the week.'

'Who?' asked Clarice Johannson, mother of the twelve-year-old blonde Hamish was failing to impress on the lawn outside.

'Botha.'

'Botha? Where's he going?' Confusion was not an unnatural state for many of the white middle class, though 'wilfully ignorant' is probably a more accurate term. Clarice's husband, Bjorn, a senior executive for one of the country's largest mining houses, had an inkling of the political storm about to engulf the country in which they were raising their daughters, but had chosen not to worry his wife about it.

'What's happened in Cape Town, Dennis?' Stuart steered the conversation back.

'My sources tell me the cabinet – led by De Klerk – is about to push him out.'

'Who'll take over?' Caroline was vexed.

'De Klerk, certainly,' replied Dennis. 'And we could well see the end of apartheid by Christmas.'

The room went momentarily silent, apart from the crackling fire and the sound of the near-adolescent children laughing outside. At their offsprings' distinctive timbres, each adult felt a pang of parental apprehension.

'My man will ring as soon as there are any developments,' Dennis said, ending the silence.

Sophia Killian squeezed her husband Sean's hand and thought of her domestic worker looking after their palatial schloss in Westville near Durban. She resolved to give Dorcas a salary increase and to fix that leaking toilet in her bathroom just to ensure no ill-will should she suddenly be enfranchised.

Hamish and the other youngsters were outside in the early darkness. Their games had ended and they were sitting in the chilly air sipping Lemon Twist. Lisa, the girl Hamish (and the other four boys) had taken a fancy to, was much more interested in the easy-going James MacDonald. Hamish watched as the older boy teased her, making her giggle, and wondered how on earth anyone could address a female of such magnificence without feeling dizzy.

Hamish stood and wandered over to the verandah edge, where an unruly jasmine was just coming into flower. It was a fresh, starry night and the boy's breath misted in the winter air. Below, the blue moonlit valley stretched to the east, farmhouse lights flickering in the distance. He drew in the scent of the jasmine – the first suggestion of the coming spring. A breeze blew up the valley and with it came the smell of dry thatching grass, dust and something else. It was a human smell – wood smoke on cloth. He looked across the lawn and noticed the night watchman sitting in the shadows, invisible but for the glint of the moon off his short stabbing spear.

Hamish thought about greeting him and felt suddenly ashamed. His Zulu, after two years of study and more than a little cajoling from Tina, was only just good enough for him to say hello.

The boys returned to school with the oak, plane and jacaranda trees that lined the walkways and gardens of Trinity College in full flush – nature mirroring South Africa's long-awaited spring. It was an immense contrast to the blustery, leafless winterscape he'd left a month previously.

Front of mind, however, was choir and his goal. The 1989 pro-gramme came from a variety of sources, the most interesting pieces being extracts from the *Navidad Nuestra* by Ariel Ramirez – a Christmas cantata in Spanish. It was a challenging work with syncopated rhythms and unfamiliar harmonies, so the choir was to spend a good deal of the term practising this rather than the familiar carols the congregation would sing. 'Once in Royal David's City' was one of these, and every practice Hamish would take his place with the trebles, hoping that Mr Danhauser would announce the old favourite and then prevail upon him to sing the first verse.

Stuart and Caroline knew of their son's all-consuming desire to per-form the solo – not so much because he'd told them but because it was a constant refrain around the house and in the spring garden. Every time Hamish walked past the piano outside the dining room he'd play the middle C, and then launch into the first verse while going about what-ever it was he was doing.

'Hamish,' asked Stuart one warm October evening as the family were eating supper on the verandah, 'are you hoping to sing the solo to "Once in Royal David's City" this year?'

'I hope so,' replied his son. 'I know it really well.'

Stuart was pleased with the setting of this goal, but knew that his boy tended to obsess about such things. If they didn't come to pass, the disappointment and consequent temper explosions and sulkiness could be extreme.

'Are there other trebles who might sing it?'

'Yes, two, but I'm older than one of them and the other guy is starting to ball-drag.'

'Hamish!' gasped Caroline.

'What's ball-dragging?' asked little Julia.

'Sorry, Mum, I don't know what else to call it – Alex Dickson sounds like Roger. Julia, it's like when Rog goes like this …' Hamish demon-strated the sound of a boy's voice about to become a man's.

The younger brother was already on his way to puberty. He'd begun to demonstrate those secondary sexual characteristics that make the male of the species into men but the adolescent slightly repulsive: wispy hair on the top lip, swollen and sore nipples or 'stonies', the first buds of acne and a not-so-vague whiff of body odour.

Stuart giggled, Roger smiled good-naturedly and Julia laughed with the others. But Caroline felt a small pang as she struggled to accept that her oldest child was approaching his thirteenth birthday.

Three weeks before the end-of-year carol service, Mr Danhauser called Alex Dickson, William Hamilton and Hamish Fraser to the front of the choir gallery, and asked them each to sing the solo. Alex Dickson began first, his first few bars filling the chapel with crystalline clarity. But as he arrived at the lyric 'Mary was that mother mild', the highest note in the verse, his voice snapped and he delivered a ball-drag that made the rest of the choir fall about laughing.

'Shut up, all of you!' Mr Danhauser yelled. 'Anyone who thinks he can do better, come down here!'

Hamish didn't laugh but he was silently delighted.

The choirmaster suspected that young Dickson was too far gone on the path to manhood. 'Alex,' he said gently, 'it's time you went to sing with the altos.'

The rapidly growing red-headed fellow picked up his blazer and slunk off to the back of the gallery.

William Hamilton delivered his audition pitch perfectly. The tone was somewhat harsh and nasal, but he was supremely confident – no matter what the occasion, he would deliver a consistent performance. The choir clapped politely when he'd finished.

Then it was Hamish's turn. The choirmaster had mixed feelings about Hamish. He liked the boy's humour but disliked his air of superiority. His voice had a pleasant tone – almost as good as Dickson's had been and much purer than Hamilton's. But his lack of consistency was a risk.

Mr Danhauser leant over the organ and played middle C.

He counted Hamish in and the boy sang his little lungs out, and finished to loud applause from the choir. Flushed with success, Hamish bowed deeply, the whiff of arrogance becoming a stench as he strode back to the rest of the trebles.

For the next three weeks, Hamish and William Hamilton alternated in the rehearsals. While the former's performances never varied, Hamish was either excellent or diabolical. When he was bad, it was because he'd become complacent and lost concentration. The top Ds in the last two lines were either sharp because he pushed too hard or flat because he neglected to take sufficient air into his lungs.

Two days before the carol service, Mr Danhauser announced that William Hamilton would sing the solo.

When his mother arrived to fetch Hamish that Wednesday afternoon, he was sitting alone on the low stone wall surrounding a small garden blooming with hydrangeas. She knew immediately that her son's dreams had been dashed, and her eyes welled.

'Hello, Hamish!' she forced a tone of cheerfulness as Hamish climbed into the passenger seat.

'Hi, Mum.'

'How was your day?'

'Stupid nerdy schloop William Hamilton is singing the solo on Friday.'

'Oh, Hamish, I'm sorry, that's very disappointing for you – but I suppose there's always next year.'

'No, Mum, there is no *next year*.' He spat out the last words at the one person in the world who would forgive him absolutely anything. '*Next year*, I will not be a treble any more. *Next year*, there will be lots of other trebles. *Next year*, I'll be an invisible alto or tenor.'

Caroline went silent. After an awkward minute, Roger arrived at the car, breathless having just finished an athletics practice (but not yet having had a shower – the sour air coming off him complemented the atmosphere in the car).

'Hello, Rog.' Caroline turned the air conditioning to full and pulled away from the curb.

As Roger chatted happily about how he was looking forward to house athletics, where he'd be competing in the long jump and in the four by one-hundred-metre relay, Hamish stared out of the window, wallowing in self-pity.

At home, Julia and Tina were having tea in the kitchen.

'Sawubona, bafana!' said Tina, cheerful with the warmth of the summer afternoon.

Julia's mouth was covered in crumbs and streaks of Bovril toast.

'You're disgusting,' Hamish snapped, stalking past them both to his room, where he slammed the door.

A few hours later, Stuart returned home to reports from Caroline that their son was in a state of depression and had not been entirely polite or gracious about his disappointment. While Hamish's unpleasantness would be tolerated by his mother, Stuart was an entirely different prospect. He walked into Hamish's room without knocking and found the boy lying on his bed staring at the ceiling.

'Hello, Hamish.'

'Hello, Dad.'

'Hamish, when your mother and I come into the room and speak to you, you will, at the very least, sit up and face us. Better still, you'll stand up! Now get off your bed!'

The boy did as he was bid.

'I believe you are nor going to sing the solo this year.'

'No. That stupid fat boy Hamilton is.' Hamish wrongly assumed that his father would agree that this was an outrage, but Stuart felt a rising anger at the stroppy, ungracious boy who seemed even smaller than normal that evening.

'Hamish, there are going to be countless times in your life when you are disappointed. How you react to disappointment will be a large part of what defines you as a man. I dinna ken if William Hamilton can sing well or nor, and it doesn't matter. He has been selected and you need to accept that with grace – good people delight in the success of others rather than feeling jealous and resentful. Also, you need to put this in perspective – it is one solo, in one carol service. Try to think about the fact that all around you in this country people are experiencing catastrophic sadness.' He paused. 'Think of Reggie and how she lost her mother. That is real disappointment – nor this.' Stuart let the silence fester for a beat. 'Now go and apologise to Mum, Julia and Tina for behaving like a spoilt brat.'

Hamish's face flushed red.

He found Tina in her room, the door open, yellow light spilling out into the last of the twilight.

'Hello, Gogo,' he said, inhaling the kind, familiar smell of her room.

She was knitting on the sofa, the TV on in the corner of the room.

'Hello, mfana,' she said without looking up.

'I'm sorry I was rude to you earlier.'

'It's okay, mfana.' It was clear she wasn't feeling particularly warm to him.

He bade her an awkward goodnight and walked into the garden.

The crickets were calling and the smell of the blooms filled Hamish with calm. He thought about Tina and the hardships of her life – hardships of which he now realised he had no conception. He came to understand that, as a thirteen year old, the irascible foibles of his childhood were not simply going to be forgiven any longer.

The next day at school, he took his place in the trebles and sang within himself, trying desperately not to resent the cherubic figure of William Hamilton, who belted out the solo with standard uniformity. He did, however, notice the slight pallor on his rival's face and saw him blowing his nose during the practice.

The day of the carol service dawned without excitement for Hamish. His mind was occupied with the thought that this was the last day of the academic year and that the following Monday he'd be writing exams – a prospect he dreaded because they required him to sit on his backside for hours on end.

He walked through the archway, over the rough stones of the quadrangle down the corridors, past his Standard Two, Standard Three and Standard Four classrooms, where hundreds of boys his junior were tossing balls, wrestling or unpacking their books. Up the black-slate stairs he climbed and made his way along the top-floor passage to his Standard Five classroom. It suddenly felt like the end of an era; though it was not a period he'd enjoyed, at least it was familiar. The world of the College, with rumours of prefects, bullies and responsibility, was scary.

Halfway through his Maths lesson, during which Mrs Snapplewell tried valiantly to explain a simple geometry problem to Wayne Johnson for the umpteenth time, Hamish was distracted from observing a flock of mynahs fighting on a plane tree outside by a knock at the door. He turned to see Mr Danhauser.

The choirmaster apologised for the interruption and asked if he might talk to Hamish. His heart in his mouth, the boy stood and walked out of the classroom while Wayne Johnson stared slack-jawed at Pythagoras on the blackboard.

'Morning, sir,' said Hamish once they were in the corridor.

'Morning, Hamish,' said the keeper of Hamish's dreams. 'Hamilton is sick – he's not at school and will not be singing tonight. Are you ready to sing the solo?'

The side of Hamish's face tingled. 'Yes, sir, thank you, sir,' he stammered breathlessly, grinning from ear to ear.

'Well, you will need to be much calmer than you are now,' said the slightly alarmed master.

'Yes, sir, I will be, sir.'

The rest of the day passed in a blur. That afternoon Hamish polished his scuffed black shoes to a sheen, made sure his tie was free of cornflake stains, brushed his unruly dark hair and then asked Tina in the politest way he knew how to help him clean a mark from his blazer.

The choir warmed up in the Green Room near the music block. They went through a number of exercises and sang a few of the more difficult sections from the *Navidad Nuestra* before Mr Danhauser led them to the chapel.

It was twilight as Hamish made his way through the school's gardens, the smell of star jasmine hanging thick in the air. On his left, the jacaranda trees fringing the main cricket field exploded purple into the dimming sky; on his right, the stone buildings were draped with sea-green ivy and cascading jasmine.

All around him, parents and boys were walking to the chapel. Hamish and Harry turned through the main archway, walking through a quadrangle and under the bell tower where the College's lion rampant flag fluttered in the evening breeze. Hamish looked into the fishpond and wondered if the enormous goldfish ever felt nervous.

Under the bell tower the congregation peeled off into the rear of the chapel while the choir climbed the stairs past the old armoury, emerging into the gallery suspended above the rear of the nave. Hamish walked to the front, from where he would deliver the solo.

He inhaled the scent of incense and watched as boys and parents filled every available space. He spotted his mother and father talking earnestly just below.

'What could possibly go wrong?' Stuart asked, smiling uneasily. 'If he makes a mistake, well, that's nor a train smash. This is a school carol service, nor the Albert Hall.'

'He'll be inconsolable for weeks – you know that!' Caroline hissed. 'This is a chance for him to fit in and achieve something at school – it will give him a sense of worth here.'

Stuart sighed and then began to giggle.

'What the hell is so funny?'

'I'm just remembering his performance at Jumping Jacks seven years ago.'

'That is precisely why I'm terrified!'

Back in the choir gallery, Mr Danhauser turned to Hamish.

'Are you ready?'

'Yes, sir.' Hamish straightened his tie for the final time.

The lights dimmed and Hamish heard the back doors of the chapel open as the chaplain and his retinue prepared to enter. He heard the clink of the censer as incense dropped onto the coal.

The congregation went silent.

Mr Danhauser nodded to the organist. She played middle C.

The choirmaster looked at Hamish and raised his right hand to count him in. Hamish hummed the note in his head and stepped onto the little teak box from which he was to sing. It was an old box – generations of boy soloists had been standing on it for exactly ninety years.

As it turned out, ninety-one was one too many.

The front panel split upon Hamish opening his mouth.

'Once,' (perfectly pitched) and then in a rapidly ascending glissando, '... AAAAAAH!'

The box gave way, the soloist overbalanced and tipped over the gallery railing, and it was only the lightning reactions of Mr Danhauser and Hamish's sparrow-like physique that saved him from landing headfirst on Father Josiah's pious bald spot.

A collective gasp rose from the congregation as Hamish, flailing, began slipping out of his blazer, the back of which was held fast by Mr Danhauser.

Simphiwe Buthelezi, tenor and first XV fullback, leapt down from the back of the gallery, leant over the railing and grabbed Hamish's left ankle. This had the effect of up-ending him just as Mr Danhauser lost his grip. The blazer emptied onto the pews below, the number of personal effects in the pockets defying their depth. Hamish's concern for his own safety was momentarily arrested as he grabbed for a tiny stuffed mouse his brother had given him years before – possibly the only thing of value he'd not lost within a week of acquiring it. (It lived in his blazer as a comforting reminder of home.)

'Mousie!' he yelled as Buthelezi hauled him back to safety.

The boys of the congregation collapsed into laughter. '*Mousie!*' they guffawed.

Hamish hardly noticed as Mr Danhauser checked him for injuries. But his mother heard, and her tears began to flow as she helped Stuart to pick up the detritus – mints, a broken pen, some coins, a half-eaten sandwich, his diary (with no entries in it), a sharpener and half a ruler.

A spotty-faced youth retrieved Mousie and held it up like a prize. From beside his parents, Roger emerged with the speed of an angry mamba. In one stride he leapt across the nave and up onto the pew where the prize-winner was standing. Before the much larger boy could do anything, Roger had seized the mouse, shoved his brother's tormentor back into his seat and returned to his own place.

'Boys!' There was immediate quiet at the booming voice of Mr Wallace McAdams, the College headmaster.

Hamish had a nasty gash above his right eye from where his head had collected a bolt on the edge of the gallery. With blood running into his eyes and down his face, he insisted that he could sing, but Mr Danhauser directed Buthelezi to take the boy to the boarding house to be cleaned up by the matron.

That year, for the first time in Trinity College history, all the trebles of the choir sang the first verse of 'Once in Royal David's City' – well, all bar the one who was having his forehead dressed.

The Frasers drove home in silence after the service, and Stuart agreed to Caroline's suggestion of burgers and milkshakes for dinner – the sort of meal he detested. The pleasant evening on the verandah and the treat moved Hamish's mood from disappointed anger to nostalgic melancholy. The fact that all the other trebles had performed the first verse did much to dissipate the boy's ire – he'd have been in a mood for weeks if another chorister had performed his solo.

The school year ended with Hamish detesting his exams and under-achieving as expected. Before Christmas, the family went on holiday to Kenton.

One hot morning, they headed down to the beach for an extended stay – never an easy trip due to the number of accoutrements (beach chairs, umbrella, buckets, spades, picnic, towels, books, sun cream, hats …). The parents settled into their holiday reads while Hamish, Roger and Julia began building a beach car, which consisted of a large hole with sand seats.

'Stuart, would you pass me a peach, please,' Caroline said pointedly.

Her husband, who was under the misapprehension that his morning's labours were complete, extracted himself from Robert Ludlum's latest tome, reached across to the cooler box and handed his wife a cold, perfectly ripe cling peach.

'Thanks.'

Stuart held his breath, and then sighed quietly as she replaced her bookmark and set her PD James mystery aside. They would be having a conversation.

'Stuart, do you think Hamish is just a late developer or do you think there's a developmental problem? He's so scrawny compared with Roger and other boys his age.'

'He's fine – he probably won't be the largest boy in the wurld but he'll grow eventually.'

'Why isn't he any good at sport? You were pretty good, and Roger isn't bad.'

'Because he's nor interested, that's why – he doesn't like cricket or soccer, and if you're small and nor very talented, you need to wurk at these things. How much time does Hamish spend practising with a soccer ball or with his cricket bat?'

'None.'

'Precisely – besides which, he rides well. It costs far more than is appropriate but at least that's a sport.'

'Well, yes, but it's hardly doing his image much good, is it?'

'What's image got to do with anything?'

'You know what I mean – he's got one friend at school and Harry's going off to boarding school in Natal next year, so Hamish will be starting in the College with no one … not even Roger.' She sighed, sucking on her peach stone. 'You know I worry about him.'

Stuart snickered.

'What are you laughing at?'

'I just had a flashback to our firstborn dangling from the choir gallery by his ankles.'

PART 2

1990–1994

16

The traditional beginning-of-the-school-year photograph of 1990 saw Julia, now five, prepared for her last year at Jumping Jacks in a smocked dress, sandals and holding a pristine brown suitcase. Roger, gangly and outgrowing his grey shorts, smiled underneath his mop of greasy, dark-blond hair – he'd developed an adolescent aversion to tidying his room, polishing his shoes and washing his person.

Hamish stood to the right of his brother in his new College uniform. His mother had shortened the charcoal pants by at least three inches the night before, and the navy blazer sleeves hung almost to his fingertips. A sense of trepidation could be seen in the oldest Fraser child's smile.

During the trip to school, Stuart pushed an ageing cassette of military music into the Mercedes's sound system, opened all the windows and turned up the volume. 'Rule Britannia' blared as they drove through the rush-hour traffic, with Stuart singing at the top of his lungs, and Hamish crooning too (he didn't know the words so he just mouthed the tune). From the back seat, Roger growled the odd inaccurate note. This had become something of a tradition on the first day of the school year, and Hamish felt inspired while the brass band played.

The car pulled up to the imposing College archway as the final note faded.

Stuart had given up pretending that Hamish would enjoy school. He turned to his smaller son and squeezed Hamish's shoulder. 'Good luck, boy.'

The undersized thirteen year old sighed and opened the door. 'Thanks, Dad. See you later, Rog.'

Hamish walked to the back of the car, opened the boot and took out his new school bag, which contained a new pencil case with new stationery that he'd sworn to keep neat and tidy (a commitment that wouldn't see out the day). He reached up to the boot lid on his tippy-toes and just managed to grasp the short string hanging from the catch that allowed him, with some effort, to pull it shut.

The warm January air was filled with the scent of green oak and plane trees, fresh grass cuttings and flowers sprouting from extensive gardens. The archway's buttresses shone deep green with ivy. Hamish noted the colours and the comforting summer smells and thought about how much he'd rather have been enjoying them in the Inanda garden.

As the car pulled away, he walked under the archway surrounded by young men of the senior years – all substantially larger than he. They pushed and cajoled each other, rekindling relationships that had drifted during the December holidays. Hamish was cowed by the roughness with which they shoved each other into the stone walls.

He moved quickly up through the claustrophobic arch and into the light of the Lion Quadrangle. At the head of the cross-shaped pond, a bronze of the College's lion rampant stood on a plinth; between his front legs, a cub looked out from the protection of his father. Impressive as the piece was, it was a smaller bronze almost hidden in a flowerbed of yellow roses that Hamish paused to consider. There stood David, sword in hand, his right foot on Goliath's recently severed head. Hamish might have taken courage from the piece, but as the Goliaths streamed past, bumping him, he felt more like a fragile worm than a sword-wielding hero.

He flinched out of his reverie as the clock tower struck seven-thirty, and then cast his eyes through the open doors of the chapel, all the way to the rood screen topped with the disturbing image of Christ nailed to the cross.

Quite suddenly, Hamish found himself flying through the air into

160

the chapel. For a split second he thought he may have been caught in some sort of impromptu rapture. He realised it was not so when pain exploded in his right shoulder as it was driven into the worn carpet at the back of the nave. He rolled onto his back in time to hear, 'Watch out, wanker!'

It had been a year since Hamish had seen Nicholas Cullinan and Robert Bosch, and the boys had grown substantially in that time. Robert Bosch was almost unrecognisable, such was the severity of the acne outbreak on his round cheeks.

'You must respect your seniors, doos,' said Cullinan, the great orator.

Hamish couldn't take his eyes off the slick sheen – Cullinan had more oil in his hair than a Wimpy deep fryer.

'What are you looking at, wanker?'

Oddly, to Hamish, this incident was a little like clearing the first jump at a show – his nerves dissipated as his instincts took over and his temper flared. If there was one thing he knew, it was that there was very little these boys could do to him in the confines of a private boys' school.

'I'm looking at your greasy hair,' he replied to Cullinan. Then he turned his gaze to Bosch. 'You look like a pizza.'

The bullies were not expecting this from a junior – especially not such a weedy one. This was their first attempt at intimidation for the year and it wasn't going to plan.

Cullinan grabbed Hamish by his blazer lapels and lifted him clean off the ground.

'Apologise!' he spat.

'No!' the small boy stammered.

'Apologise or you're gonna get hit!'

Hamish surmised that the older boy had clearly not brushed his teeth before coming to school.

'Chips chips chips!' hissed Bosch. 'Pod's coming.'

Cullinan dropped his victim and turned as a teacher walked past the chapel door. The two bullies' legs masked their diminutive victim. The master stopped briefly.

'Cullinan, Bosch, what are you boys doing in there?'

'Praying, sir,' replied Cullinan, grinning stupidly.

'Rubbish,' snapped the teacher as he moved on. 'Get to roll-call or you'll find yourselves on hard labour before the year's even started.'

A moment later, left alone, Hamish rolled onto his back and looked down the nave. Sun streamed through the windows, slicing the dust- and incense-filled air into shafts of pale gold. He considered how pretty the light was compared with the rather horrific figure of Christ's torture. He raised himself, checked that Mousie was still in his inside right pocket and then put his hand into his bag. The pencil case was intact, but it was covered in mayonnaise from his squished sandwich.

'Fuck,' he muttered under his breath. 'Sorry, God.' He bowed briefly to the altar.

Roll-call took place in the Memorial Quadrangle. In the middle of the quad's circular pond was a plinth topped with a bronze of four soldiers in First World War fatigues, standing facing each of the cardinal points, heads bowed and rifle butts resting on the ground. Hamish found the pond disconcerting – struck by the eerie contradiction of the peaceful trickle of water and the ghostly soldiers above.

For Hamish, the time between arriving at school and roll-call, when the official school day began, would become the most awkward part of his five high-school years. Most boys drifted into their social groups before the bell rang at seven-forty, and Hamish found that he had no one to talk to. On this first day, however, he had a task to occupy him: ridding his bag of mayonnaise. He withdrew to a secluded section of the cloisters surrounding the quad and cleaned the mess as best as possible. The bag gave off a vague whiff of stale mayonnaise for the rest of the year.

A few minutes later the bell in the clock tower began to peal and Hamish made his way to the north-western corner of the quad – the designated area for Iverson House. Standing in front of the gathering boys of Iverson were six prefects dressed not in uniform but in blue pin-striped suits. They cast stern looks towards the nervous Form I boys.

'Line up!' yelled the head of house, a massive, neckless fellow by the name of Quentin Allenby.

The Form Is shuffled about in terror while the rest of the house arranged themselves alphabetically in their year groups.

'Form Is! Get in line, alphabetical. Quickly – you think you still on holiday?!' Anton Eisenbaum bellowed. The prefect assigned to the Iverson Form Is was, as far as Hamish could tell, the loudest, most terrifying and thoroughly unpleasant human being ever spawned.

Hamish shuffled to the middle of the stripe. He slotted in next to Robert Gumede – a new boy – on one side and Bernard Fenton on the other.

Eisenbaum went for the most obvious targets first: Basil Anderson and Ryan Henderson, both of whom had reached puberty before they were out of nappies.

'You two think this is some kind of joke!?' Saliva flew from a cavernous mouth not two inches from the startled and spotty visage of Basil Anderson.

Hamish knew that his hitherto miserable morning was about to improve. Anderson was big, and although he wasn't the bluntest pencil in the box, he was no genius.

'No, I didn't hear a joke, sir,' replied Anderson.

'I'm not a sir – what's my name!?'

The new boys were supposed to know the names of all the prefects. Anderson, perhaps thinking of his last dinner, blurted, 'Eisbein ... sir ... um ... sorry, I mean not sir. Just Eisbein.'

Hamish began to giggle. 'Sir Eisbein,' he whispered under his breath. Robert Gumede started to chuckle.

'Eisenbaum! Say it: Eisenbaum!' The prefect's face turned an alarming shade of crimson, which only served to increase Hamish's amusement.

'Sir Eisenbaum ... um ... sorry ... um ...' blubbered Anderson.

'Shuddup!' yelled the prefect. 'Anderson, you better know my name and the name of every prefect in the school by this time tomorrow or you gonna to be in more shit than you'll find in … ah …' Eisenbaum's attempt to come up with a clever simile failed '… in a lot of shit.'

Trinity tradition dictated that when your name was called by your prefect during roll-call, you replied with the Latin *adsum* – I am present. The puce prefect reached into his inside jacket pocket and extracted the list of Form Is. Poor Anderson was at the head of the list and therefore the line.

'Anderson!' he yelled.

'Yes, sir, Eisenbaum, sir … um … no … sorry … just Eisenbaum,' he stammered, sweat glistening on his quivering top lip.

'Anderson! You say ABSOOM – ABSOOM, Anderson. Are you a moron?'

'ABSOOM, sir, Eisenbaum, sir.'

Tears were leaking from Hamish's eyes and he was shaking. Robert Gumede was in a similar state. Alan Barrett was next.

'Barre—' Eisenbaum stormed to the middle of the line and towered over Hamish Fraser and Robert Gumede, who tried desperately to hide their mirth. 'What the hell is so funny, you two?

This was excellent entertainment for those not involved, and all laughter ceased.

Hamish felt like a lead weight had dropped into his lower intestine. His face went cold but began to sweat at the same time, and he made the mistake of looking up – straight into the face of death.

At that moment Robert Gumede – who would spend most of his high school career doing punishments of various kinds due to a chronic inability to cope with authority – chose to speak up.

'I think it's *adsum*, not *absoom*, Sir Eisbein.'

Hamish momentarily overcame his fear – enough to snort once. This set off the whole of Iverson House, who fell about. For the second time that morning, Hamish Fraser found himself suspended from his lapels, legs dangling. He shut his eyes in expectation of a broken nose courtesy of the soon-to-be-selected first XV wing.

From across the quad an upright young man of six feet and two inches walked easily but purposefully towards Iverson House, his navy suit immaculate. The wave in the front of his dark hair – just slightly longer than regulation – indicated a liberal attitude to life and leadership.

The boys went silent.

'Put him down, Eisenbaum,' said David Swart, the head boy. There was no anger in his voice, just quiet authority.

Eisenbaum obeyed immediately. The head boy smiled when he noticed the source of the prefect's ire. Unusually for his exalted designation in the school hierarchy, David Swart sang in the choir and had thus been present during Hamish's death-defying feat at the carol service. He placed his hand on Eisenbaum's shoulder and beckoned Hamish with a flick of his head. 'You carry on with roll-call, Eisie. I'll sort this out.'

A minute later, Hamish Fraser and David Swart were in the Iverson House prefects' room. The older boy turned on the kettle and retrieved two chipped mugs from a shelf crusted with mould, crumbs and something approximating margarine, possibly a century old.

'Tea, Fraser?'

Hamish stared.

'Fraser, would you like some tea? It's not a difficult question.'

'Um, yes, please,' replied the tiniest fellow in Iverson House.

'Three sugars, I assume?'

'Yes, please.'

'Milk?'

'Um ... no, thank you.'

'Good, I'm glad you're still able to speak.' There was silence but for the tinkling of a spoon on crockery. 'There you are.' David Swart handed the mug to Hamish and indicated a grubby old sofa. 'Sit down.'

Hamish took the tea and sat.

'I'm going to tell you something about this school. What you do with what I'm going to tell you, well, that's up to you.'

Hamish sipped his tea. It was delicious.

'Form I is a tough year – you are a small fish in a big pond again and you —' he exhaled loudly as he considered Hamish '— you are the size of a kapenta. Do you know what a kapenta is?'

'No.'

'It's a freshwater fish – but that's not important. Some of the older boys are going to try and dominate and probably bully you because you are small and because you sing in the choir. With the bullies you can either choose to tell a prefect or a master, or you can deal with them yourself. I was about your size in Form I and I found a hard punch to the face was the most effective way to deal with bullies.'

Hamish's half-swallowed mouthful of tea almost escaped his lips at this utterance from the head boy. No one in authority had ever advocated violence as a method of conflict resolution to him.

Swart continued. 'If you thump someone bigger than you, you will have no trouble from teachers. Most bullies are cowards and one punch to the face will normally sort out the problem.' He drained his mug, placed it on the counter next to him and looked at Hamish. His tone changed slightly. 'Anton Eisenbaum is not a bully – he is angry, but he isn't a bully, so I'm going to ask you to treat him with respect as a prefect of this house and Trinity College. Can we agree on that?'

'Yes, Swart,' replied Hamish.

'Good. Are you playing rugby or hockey this year?'

'Um … rugby, I think.'

David Swart nodded. 'Alright then, you had better go to first period – you know where you're going?'

'I think so.'

'Let me know if you have any trouble.'

'Um … okay … thanks.'

'Also, I suggest you go and apologise to Eisenbaum tomorrow before roll-call. He'll be a good oke to have on your side.'

Such was to be the beginning of a brief but powerful mentorship between Hamish and the head boy. David Swart was an anomaly in many ways – a decent sportsman but by no means the best, an excellent academic and phenomenal cellist. In short, the head boy was a budding renaissance man, possessed of that rare human quality that is perhaps best described as 'presence'. Hamish never heard David Swart so much as raise his voice, but equally never saw anyone he couldn't bend to his will. Swart felt no need to impose his exalted position on the younger boys – he treated them with respect and courtesy no matter what their skills on the sports field, in the music rooms, on the stage or in the classroom. There were those that resented him – for being 'too soft' on the younger boys – but they were largely jealous. David Swart was almost universally admired.

The next morning, Hamish resolved he would do as he'd been advised. Before roll-call, his heart in his throat, Hamish walked up to the house, hoping to catch Eisenbaum alone.

The Iverson House common room was on the first floor, accessed from the western side of the Memorial Quadrangle. On the left, as Hamish walked through the door, there was a noticeboard with information of varying importance. To the right was the prefects' room – a section of the house reserved for the blue suits – the place where, quite against any known protocol, David Swart had offered Hamish both tea and a seat.

Behind the closed door, the voices of three or four prefects, Eisenbaum's among them, were castigating someone. Hamish continued down the narrow passage past the bathrooms and the Matric room into the main common room. All four walls were lined with steel lockers, interspersed with wooden cottage-pane windows almost a hundred years old. In the middle of the parquet floor a small, cheap snooker table listed heavily to starboard and a table-tennis table stood – its surface looked as if the first XV had used it for an aggressive scrumming practice. The smell was a mixture of sweaty sports togs, Lifebuoy soap, floor polish and cheap deodorant.

Hamish's locker was halfway along the western wall next to one of the windows, and he would come to spend quite a lot of time there in the late afternoons before choir practice, leaning against the window sill, listening as the noises of the school waned with the evening. Although only one floor up, from the quadrangle the ridge on which the school was built fell away precipitously to the west such that Hamish's vantage was four storeys up. From this lofty perch, he would watch the sun sinking behind the Northcliff Ridge. Below, on the main rugby field, Darren Cockerel, incumbent first XV flyhalf, would be finishing his extra kicking practice. Hamish marvelled at the way the booming sound of each kick would reach him about two seconds after he saw the boot make contact with the abused leather bladder.

Hamish would feel a sense of history in that sill; the way the wood had been worn away in the centre by countless forearms over the course of the twentieth century. He would wonder where those boys had ended up and how they'd experienced the old school. He'd feel an affection for the wood and its history that was at odds with his generally dismissive attitude to his fellow pupils – he had yet to understand that the boys were the school much more than the buildings ever would be.

The sense of nostalgia would spill into thoughts of his own life too. He would play through his memories – squirming at the embarrassing ones, like his adding to the torment of Fatty Campion, and smiling at profound ones, like the night he'd spent at the Ntunjwa homestead.

On that second morning of the Easter term of 1990, Hamish put his tog bag into his locker and took a deep breath. Four boys were playing pool on the snooker table, two were attempting a game of table tennis with a cracked ball and using their hands as bats, and another four were trying to inflict injury on each other with tie flicks. Hamish walked slowly to the prefects' room, where a Form III boy was being interrogated for his suspected involvement in locking Mr Pigglesworth, the ageing groundsman, in the bell tower for the night.

When the door opened, Hamish turned to the noticeboard and pretended to read a withered poster suggesting that doing drugs was a poor life choice. On the bottom left corner, a round blue sticker said, 'No Tolerance for Bullies'. The rest of the board contained house notices: lists of the Form I boys assigned as fags to specific Matrics, and an empty list of volunteers for the house plays.

Finally, the Form III criminal was released. Hamish waited two seconds, turned and then knocked on the open door. The prefects turned to look at the diminutive creature.

'Good morning, Fraser,' Quentin Allenby said without smiling.

'Morning, Allenby. Morning, Roberts. Morning, Nicholson. Morning, Eisenbaum,' said Hamish looking at his shoes.

'What do you want?' asked the head of house.

'Um ... well ... I ... ah ...'

'Come on, Fraser!' blustered Eisenbaum. 'We are having a meeting!'

Hamish shuddered. 'I ... eh ... came to say sorry for yesterday to Eisenbaum ... um ...'

There was a stunned silence.

Hamish considered a stain on the carpet, not knowing if he should actually say he was sorry, or if this was implied by what he'd said already, or if he should wait to be asked to speak. As the silence grew, so the blood drained to his vital organs and he suddenly needed to pee.

Allenby looked at Eisenbaum, mouthed something and tilted his head towards the over-sized blazer standing in the doorway.

'Um, well, yes, good, um, okay, good,' stammered Eisenbaum. 'Well done, Fraser – apology accepted.'

'Thank you,' said Hamish, looking up very briefly, and then disappearing with the speed of a startled rat.

From that day on, whenever Anton Eisenbaum and Hamish Fraser passed each other in the corridors, the former would greet his diminutive junior curtly.

'Fraser.' Eisenbaum would nod his head.

'Eisenbaum,' Hamish would reply.

After this rough start, Hamish slowly settled into the daily routine of College life. His new bag was soiled after a week, his blazer resembled a tramp's coat after a fortnight and his new teachers began the same mournful chorus about his atrocious handwriting, spelling and general tardiness.

The sport he chose to play in the summer term was water polo, largely because, unlike cricket, the matches were only twenty minutes long. Although he was installed in the second of two under-thirteen water-polo sides, Hamish wasn't an entirely ineffective player, because while not fast in the water by any stretch, he was a strong swimmer. The water also reduced the effects of his size deficiency somewhat, and Hamish used the Saturday matches to take out the frustration he built up during the week.

This frustration was contributed to substantially by Nicholas Cullinan and Robert Bosch. If they passed Hamish (or any younger boys) in the corridors, they would shove them into a wall or trip them up. Their favourite with Hamish was to grab his outsized satchel and yank on it with the result that he overbalanced onto his back. Normally they'd leave him to dust himself off and continue to his next class. One day, however, things became a little nastier on account of a new method of torture doing the rounds among the criminally inclined: the wedgie.

The wedgie involved sneaking up behind a victim, reaching into his trousers and then lifting him off the floor by his underpants until the crotch gave way and the garment came free. The torn material would then be held aloft in triumph. Only the very practised and very large could perpetrate the perfect wedgie – it required strength and speed to lift a boy off his feet by his underpants and then shake him sufficiently to tear the pants before he squirmed free. Normally, the wedgie was inexpertly executed: the victim escaped as he felt a hand nearing his backside, or the underpants failed to tear because of a lack of technique or strength on the part of the bully.

It was no surprise that when Nicholas Cullinan and Robert Bosch decided to try their hand at the wedgie, their victim was the smallest boy in the College. Hamish was on his way, late as usual, to his Afrikaans class after break. He detested Afrikaans – he considered his teacher an octogenarian witch for whom a burning at the stake would be too kind a fate. As he descended the steps from Iverson House towards a landing, his sensitive nose picked up the scent of cigarette smoke. He looked up towards the East House entrance just as Cullinan and Bosch emerged from their post-break nicotine fix in a loo cubicle.

Cullinan's eyes lit up and Hamish made to run, but Bosch grabbed his satchel.

'How's about a little wedgie, Fraser? All choir boys like a bit of action on the arse!'

'Fuck you g—' Hamish's breath caught in his throat as pain seared through his body.

'Tear it, man!' said Cullinan coughing and laughing.

'Shit, I'm trying!' Bosch shook Hamish from side to side.

Hamish thought he might split in half and he screamed in agony.

'Drop him! Someone's gonna come and see why this gayboy's screaming like a chick,' said Cullinan.

Hamish's backside slammed into the black-slate landing, winding him.

'Fucken faggot,' said Bosch as they ran down the stairs.

Hamish bit his lip and tried not to cry as his breath returned. It wasn't the pain – that subsided. It was the humiliation combined with an unquenchable rage. He thought about going to find David Swart, but stopped himself. He knew that his housemaster and the head boy would deal with his tormentors immediately. He also knew that unless he dealt with the problem himself, he'd always be a victim.

He resolved to bide his time – reasoning that one day he would grow and exact his revenge.

That Saturday, still smarting from the humiliation of the week and sporting a nasty welt on his undercarriage, Hamish played his first water-polo match. The under-13Bs were the first team to play – at eight in the morning, before the sun had warmed the shaded pool. Hamish took his place among the reserves – three boys who shared the same lack of enthusiasm for freezing their backsides off in a game they cared nothing about.

The coach, Mr Harty, had been a boxer in his day and spoke with a voice like a chainsaw from a punch he'd received to the throat. As the first chukka ended, he growled at Hamish.

'Fraser!'

'Sir?'

'You're up. Harris you take a rest.' The coach turned to Hamish. 'Now, all you have to do is mark that guy there.' He pointed at a medium-sized boy resting with his teammates on the other side of the pool. 'You stick on him and if he gets the ball, I don't care how but you take it away from him! Understand?'

'Yes, sir.'

A player with more knowledge of the game may have taken this instruction to mean 'try to dispossess your opponent legally' – but Hamish had almost no knowledge of the rules.

He dived into the water, surfaced and lined up with his team. The referee's whistle shrilled and Hamish swam with all his might towards the middle of the pool. Once there, he lifted his head and homed in on his opponent.

In the race for the ball, Trevor Masterson of Trinity had been beaten by his opposite number – largely because although he was a fast swimmer, Masterson could not for the life of him swim in a straight line. Indeed, halfway to the middle of the pool, he collided with William van Zyl, who had to be replaced by the second reserve on account of a nasty kick to the left temple.

The winner of the dash to the yellow pill, seeing his mate marked by the human equivalent of a malnourished string-bean, flicked it over to him. Before the larger boy had a chance to think about what he was going to do with the pass, he found himself blinded and sinking. Hamish clambered onto the fellow's shoulders, wrenched the blue skullcap over his eyes and then drove him under the water. The Trinity player made off towards the opposing goal, ball bobbing in front of his arms.

The referee for the day was a twenty-two-year-old Trinity stooge sporting a vicious hangover. Given the earliness of the hour and the paucity of skill on display, Hamish's overzealous execution of his coach's instructions irritated the official thoroughly – he blasted his whistle with alcohol fumes. All players but one stopped and looked to the side of the pool for instruction. Hamish swam on – deafened by fury and competitive zeal. The whistle cut the still morning again but on swam Hamish Fraser, astounded that he'd not yet been dispossessed of the ball and feeling like he might be quite good at water polo.

Three metres from the goal he lifted the ball out of the water with one hand and flung it at the open goalmouth. The pill made a plop as it landed just over the line. Hamish lifted his hands out of the water in triumph. It was only then that he noticed the lack of movement around him, and the shrill blast of the desperate referee.

'Fraser, you idiot, come here! Right now!' Mr Harty bellowed.

'Get out of the pool!' the referee removed the whistle from his mouth for long enough to yell. 'What do you think you're doing? You can't *drown* people in this game!'

Hamish made his way to the side of the pool, face flushed.

From the stands, Stuart sighed heavily as his son climbed from the water in disgrace. Roger howled with laughter.

In five years of high-school water polo, that was the only goal Hamish would ever score.

17

'Did you grab?' asked Johnny Goodenough of Paul Simpson, who was sitting on his desk facing the class.

Most of the boys looked up at the word 'grab' – profoundly romantic slang for French kiss. Paul Simpson's ability with women was legendary and many looked forward to the tales of his 'grabbing' exploits come Monday mornings.

The previous Saturday, Trinity had hosted a social – Hamish's first, since he'd failed to crack an invite to any of the disco birthday parties in the last year of prep school. This had been something of a disappointment, but only the 'cool' boys and 'rebels' made it onto invitation lists. The only 'nerds' or 'co-ords' invited were those with sisters who the host wanted at his party.

Trinity always hosted the first social of the year and it was compulsory for all Form I boys. The official line was that the boys required socialisation with girls after years of single-sex schooling. In actual fact, the Dance Committee needed to raise money to fund the Matric dance, and they expected all the junior boys to spend their pocket money on obscenely marked-up refreshments. A parents' letter detailed the importance for boys to attend so that they might interact with members of the opposite sex in a safe environment. Had any of the girls' parents possessed the slightest knowledge of the College's layout – its innumerable alcoves, nooks, cloisters, quiet passages and secluded gardens – it is likely that Trinity socials would have remained all-male affairs.

Caroline was almost as nervous as Hamish in the days leading up to the social. She feared that her son would be humiliated without a cohort of friends to enjoy the event with. On the Friday afternoon she'd taken him shopping for something appropriate to wear. Hamish wanted a fluorescent-yellow, short-sleeved collared shirt with small black horses printed on it. His mother mercifully persuaded him to go for a branded T-shirt from a surf shop. Then she found him some stone-washed denims. The outfit was completed by his grubby sneakers.

On the Saturday night, it had taken Hamish five minutes to shower and dress himself, and another twenty-five minutes to make an irritating piece of hair at the back of his head lie flat (he eventually cut it off). At seven o'clock, Stuart pulled the car up to the College archway. The stone pillars were strung with garish coloured lights and Hamish could hear the booming bass of music in the distance.

'Good luck tonight, old boy,' Stuart said cheerfully. 'Don't try too hard, see? Just be yourself and enjoy it.'

'Okay, thanks, Dad,' Hamish ball-dragged.

'Have you got your money?'

'Yes, thanks, Dad.' Hamish looked out of the window.

'Off you go then,' encouraged Stuart.

Hamish sighed and climbed out of the car. He waited for his father to drive away before turning to walk across the road, away from the archway and onto the cricket field. It was completely dark in the shadows of the plane trees. Hamish leant up against the stone wall fringing the field and watched. The sound of laughter and the arrival of cars dominated the scene in front of him. Behind, it was silent but for the crickets that had made their home in the verdant turf. Further behind, he could hear the distant hum of the inner-city Saturday night. A dove cooed in one of the trees next to the tuck shop.

Small groups of boys and girls chatted as they passed under the archway. Three girls dressed in denims and tight-fitting tops stopped and pointed at a large young man climbing out of a Jaguar: Justin Hollard, the impossibly good-looking opening bowler of the first XI. They giggled as he nodded nonchalantly in their direction. Hamish noted a few of his classmates arriving on foot – they'd insisted on being dropped near the tuck shop so as not to be seen in adult company. Paul Simpson, Johnny Goodenough and Andrew Marsdorf strode under the archway like they owned the place.

'Do you think Kerry will be here?' asked Johnny.

'Ja, of course,' replied Simpson. 'I phoned her and she said she was coming.'

'You phoned Kerry Fennel …?' Marsdorf's astonishment faded as the boys disappeared into the school. Kerry Fennel was the object of every schoolboy's fantasy – blonde, blue-eyed and sporting a confidence felt at a hundred paces.

Next came Stuart Moses, Mark Gerald and Anthony Faulkenberg, a group of 'nerds' who looked like startled antelope waiting for a leopard to leap at them from the hydrangeas.

It struck Hamish that these boys were bullied as much as he was, although they'd clearly found some solace and probably safety in their companionship. But there was something he disliked about them, and he resented that he was treated in the same way by the movers and shakers.

A few boys arrived alone. Some strode in with confidence but others were tentative; even some of the popular boys seemed affected by the social pressures of the evening. Hamish watched as the captain of the under-15A water-polo side – who had more than once shoved him out of the way in the lunch queue – ducked into a flower bed and spent ten minutes trying to smooth his hair, spraying breath-freshener into his mouth and checking his clothes.

Hamish sank further into the shadows as Nicholas Cullinan and Robert Bosch pulled up in a black BMW 7 series driven by the former's older brother. 'Pump up the Jam' by Technotronic blared as the two boys climbed out of the car in their matching leather jackets and posed for a group of girls. They moved inaccurately to the rhythm and then swaggered through the archway hot on the trail of the startled females.

Eventually, as the lines of people entering the archway dwindled, Hamish emerged from the shadows, crossing the road like a nervous fox. In the quad outside the hall, small groups of young people talked and laughed. Members of the Dance Committee were rounding up juniors, directing them towards a bank of trestle tables to buy refreshments. Hamish looked about furtively, panic rising – he couldn't see a group to which he might attach himself, and he felt deeply exposed standing out in the open. He glanced at his watch – there were two hours until Stuart came to fetch him. As he was about to turn around and return to the shadows, someone slapped him on the back.

It was James MacDonald – a year older than Hamish and an old family friend.

'Hamish Fraser!' James said, rushing past with a bevy of young girls and his friend Matthew Evans. 'Don't just stand there, come and dance!'

He tugged Hamish's sleeve and the smaller boy found himself dragged along. Half a minute later he was in the hall with lights flashing as 'I Just Can't Get Enough' by Depeche Mode was replaced by the driving guitars of The Doors' 'Roadhouse Blues', and the group started leaping up and down like head-banging Maasai. Two of the girls, both dressed in designer torn denims, flung their long hair around in time with the rhythm. The strobing spotlights froze them at intervals, backlighting them with ethereal, full-body halos.

The music worked its magic and Hamish joined in, throwing his head back and forth as the song consumed him. Quite suddenly, he felt happy.

As The Doors segued into REM's 'Stand', James and the others stopped dancing and made for the door. Hamish followed, noticing Bosch and Cullinan lurking in a corner emptying tot packs into their Coke cans. James led the group to the middle of the quad.

'Geez, what awesome songs!' said Hamish, out of breath and exhilarated.

'We could see you enjoyed them!' replied one of the girls, winking at her friends. A giggle rippled through the group.

'Let's go back for more!' ball-dragged Hamish with a grin.

'This is Hamish, guys,' said James. 'Nah, let's take it easy for a little while.'

There was a slightly awkward silence.

'Oh, ja, okay, cool,' said Hamish, his English lilt making his attempt at nonchalance sound ridiculous.

Another snigger rippled and Hamish's eyes darted over the faces of the group as Anthony Dickson, the joker in James's class, arrived.

'You will not believe what I've just seen!' he said.

Everyone turned to the new arrival and Hamish found himself on the periphery.

'Billy Burden just grabbed Alice Wagenburger – you know that huge chick with the braces?'

'Fuck off!' exclaimed James's friend Matthew. 'You must be joking!'

'She had him pressed up against the door of the Green Room!'

'What were you doing there?' asked Hamish loudly in a vain attempt to include himself.

Dickson frowned. 'Who are you?'

Hamish's face flushed. 'Um … I …'

But Dickson continued with his story, point made. 'I told Burden he'd better give me his smokes and tot packs or I'll tell everyone about Alice.' He laughed. 'She ran off crying or something and Burds handed this over.' He opened the lapel of his denim jacket slightly to reveal a string of whisky tot packs and a box of cigarettes. 'Who's in?'

'Yes, please,' said one of the girls.

With that, the group departed to enjoy their contraband, leaving Hamish standing alone in the middle of the quad. He wished he was at home – he looked at his watch, still an hour and a half till pick-up. He wandered over to the drinks' trestle. No one tried to cajole him into buying anything – he felt utterly invisible as he paid for a Lemon Twist and found himself walking almost unconsciously through the quad towards the archway and the safety of the crickets and the plane trees.

The only person he saw on his way was Alice Wagenburger. She was sitting on the steps leading to a rose garden under the bell tower, her head in her hands. Loud phlegmy sobs emanated. Hamish paused and looked at the devastated girl.

'I'm sorry,' he said.

She looked up. Her wildly amateurish and overzealous application of make-up had run all over her large cheeks and mixed with enthusiastic acne.

'Are you okay?' he asked.

She considered the miniscule boy. 'Just leave me alone,' she snapped. 'Just fuck off.'

Hamish felt no anger for the helpless girl, only a shame he couldn't understand.

He wandered out of the archway and back into the shadows. There, he sat on the grass beneath the low wall with his drink. He missed Roger and Julia and his mum and dad. He felt ashamed about missing them and frustrated that he'd been unable to ingratiate himself to the dancing group. Tears ran down his cheeks and onto the grass as the half-moon appeared from behind some gently floating clouds.

A little while later, he saw Justin Hollard leading a girl onto the field, and strained to hear their conversation.

'This is where I spend my Saturdays,' Justin was saying.

'Show me the pitch.' The girl took his hand and they walked out onto the field, the moon and the light from the city casting a muted, sage light over them. Hamish watched them embrace in the middle of the pitch. He heard her laugh – such a cheerful sound it made him smile through his tears.

He sat there until Stuart arrived to fetch him.

'How was it?' the father asked as the son leapt into the passenger seat of the Mercedes.

'It was fun, thanks,' lied Hamish, looking out of the window as the car pulled away, hoping desperately that his father wouldn't see that he'd been crying.

'Did you meet any nice gurls?'

'Yes, a few,' Hamish replied, thinking about the ones he'd briefly danced with.

'Well, that's good! What were their names?'

There was an awkward pause.

'I don't know!' Hamish snapped.

'But didn't you introduce yourself?'

'It's not like when you were young.' Hamish realised he was shouting and took a deep breath. 'We just dance in groups and no one really talks to anyone.'

'Oh,' said Stuart.

Back in the Maths classroom that Monday morning, the boys were all eager to know if Simpson had grabbed Kerry Fennel. In addition to being the most stunning girl in all of creation, she was in her second year of high school and therefore normally courted by much older boys. Simpson felt nothing for this convention.

Before he could answer the question, Philip Cooper reminded every-one, 'She's going out with Madman Jones in Form IV!' and an excited murmur fizzed through the room.

'Not any more,' said Simpson.

'So you *did* grab her!' Andrew Marsdorf idolised Simpson.

'Well, let's just say that we weren't praying in the crypt at ten o'clock on Saturday night.'

Admiring laughter rippled through the room.

'I grabbed Angie MacNamara in the Prep bio lab,' added Dylan Crane, an oafish boy with a brush cut and substantial overbite.

'Angie MacNamara is so gross, she was probably made in a bio lab – like Frankincense.' This from Marsdorf again.

Louder laughter filled the class.

'That's Franken*stein*, arsehole,' quipped Simpson, 'but she is a bit green.'

Hamish, not finding any of it particularly amusing, laughed loudly regardless. As stories of other conquests went around the class, he became more and more desperate to join in. When it emerged that even Stuart Moses had managed a grab among the clivias next to the amphitheatre, Hamish could hold it in no longer.

'I grabbed a girl too!' he said as silence fell.

All heads turned to look at him.

'You weren't even at the social, were you?' Marsdorf threw a knowing glance at Simpson.

'Yes, I was,' Hamish snapped.

'Come on, Fraser, who did you grab?' groaned Crane.

Hamish flushed. 'A girl called Amy,' he said. 'She's two years older than me!'

Marsdorf smelt a fib. 'Amy who? I don't know any Amy.'

'Amy Patrick,' he stammered frantically. 'Anyway, it doesn't matter.' He pretended to become suddenly engrossed in his Maths textbook.

'I don't believe you, Fraser,' laughed Marsdorf. 'Where did you grab this Amy Patrick?'

Hamish felt eyes boring into him. 'I grabbed her against an oak tree at the stables.'

'Where?' Philip Cooper was hysterical.

'At the *stables* with his *pony*!' whooped Crane as the few giggles turned into twenty-two full-bellied laughs.

Hamish felt nauseous. He leapt out of his seat and ran for the door, bumping into Mrs Biden, the Maths teacher. Her armload of books went flying, a large textbook catching her on the end of her nose.

'Fraser!' she shouted. 'What the hell are you doing?!' She lifted her hand to her bruised snout. 'For godsakes – have an hour of hard labour! Now go and sit down.'

The contrast between his social standing at school and the stables was stark.

A year earlier, after much cajoling from Caroline and Annabelle, Stuart had agreed to the capital expenditure required to purchase Hamish a horse of his own, and Timothy (Amy's old pony) had joined the Fraser family. Over the course of twelve months, Hamish had ridden his pony through the grades, and as he started his high-school career they'd been promoted into children's A grades.

There was one other A-grade children's rider at the Inanda Club. Jane Emmerson was hugely talented and ambitious. She was also, in Hamish's mind, deeply attractive.

The Emmerson family lived in palatial opulence on a three-acre spread in Bryanston that made the Fraser's Inanda schloss look like a caravan. On the occasion of her thirteenth birthday – two weeks after the mortifying social – Jane invited her friends from the stables for a braai and a sleepover. The five partygoers were in their first years of high school, but for Raymond Serrao and Angela Smythe, who were a year younger. Raymond and Hamish had become relatively good friends at the stables – the former saw his riding very much as a hobby, so there was no competition, which suited Hamish's fragile ego. Hamish had found that he could be more natural around these peers, who respected his skills as a horseman.

The rivalry between Hamish and Jane was, however, intense. She owned two top-class ponies, rode five times a week and competed in every possible show. The extra practice and dedication showed in her results, and Hamish seldom beat her. She was also utterly reckless with her own safety and took chances that many other competitors wouldn't dare.

Hamish's only source of dissatisfaction with the horse crowd was the lack of romantic interest demonstrated by Jane. After Amy had kissed him in the shade of the old oak tree some three years previously, Hamish, in typical underestimation of the effort required to achieve his goals, had assumed that the mystery of women was solved. To his great surprise (but no one else's), he had not had his way with any girl since.

Jane flirted just enough to keep him interested but was constantly courted by older boys. She enjoyed Hamish's sarcastic wit – especially when it was directed at people for whom they shared a mutual disdain. When her party came about, Hamish became determined to rectify the paucity of feminine affection in his life: this was the night he would act on his crush.

He thought long and hard about what to buy Jane for her birthday, but in the end he had to ask Caroline for advice.

'Mum,' he said, red-faced and fidgeting as his mother arranged flowers in the kitchen.

'Yes, darling?' Caroline snipped a rose stem and settled it into an enormous glass vase.

'Mum, I need to get a present for Jane …'

Caroline had watched her son talking to the sassy girl often enough to know he was destined for disappointment.

'Well, what do you want to say with the gift?'

'What do you mean?'

'Do you want to tell her you like her, or just give her something nice that she can use?' She continued arranging the blooms.

'Um, I think I want to give her something nice …' He opened the fridge, took out a juice box, replaced it and then closed the fridge.

Caroline placed the last piece of baby's breath into the vase and turned around.

'Hamish, you need to be careful of this girl – she's probably too old for you.'

The boy, astounded that his secret was out but at the same time relieved, puffed out his chest in defiance. 'Why? I'm the same age as her.'

'Yes, but girls grow up faster than boys and she's probably attracting the attentions of bigge— … um … older boys.'

'Hmph, we'll see about that.'

'Okay,' soothed Caroline, 'well then I suggest you get her something nice but not over the top – not something that's going to scream that you have romantic inclinations.'

'How about a necklace?' Hamish looked hopeful.

Caroline rolled her eyes. 'That's exactly what you should *not* get her. Besides, anything worth wearing will cost more than you have and more than I'm willing to give you.'

'What then?'

'We need to go and get you a new numnah tomorrow, so how about you choose her a nice tie pin that she can wear at shows.' Caroline picked up the vase and moved towards the kitchen door. 'That way, it will be something pretty, but not very expensive and it's also useful to her.'

Hamish followed his mother through to the hall, where she placed the vase on an antique rosewood table. Understanding dawned.

'I see what you mean,' he replied. 'Good idea.'

A brass tie pin was duly presented that Saturday evening – beautifully wrapped by Caroline after Hamish had attempted to leave the house with a box looking as if it'd been assaulted by a rabid rat. The re-wrapping had taken place while the agitated boy watched over his mother's shoulder, unusually concerned with being on time.

Thirty minutes later, Jane, Jennifer Carmichael and Hamish were sitting on the paving next to the pool, their feet resting on a mosaicked martini step while Angela, Susan Bentlage and Raymond horsed about pushing each other off an inflatable lilo. The girls were growing into young women, and this was made all the more obvious by their bikinis. Since that golden morning when Hamish had met Reggie in the walnut tree at Jumping Jacks, he'd been affected and fascinated by the feminine. Now, with the addition of adolescent hormones (a slow drip rather than a gush, it must be said), the attraction was taking on a more carnal nature.

Jane was blonde and green-eyed with a button nose. She was wearing a bright-green bikini and her shoulder-length hair was tied up in a loose ponytail that left strands hanging down her long neck. She flicked back her head and laughed as the massively muscled Susan came up under the lilo and propelled both Raymond and Angela into the water with a mighty splash.

Hamish stared at where Jane's neckline joined her shoulders, the light of the setting sun catching the sparse down on her smooth skin. Smoke from Mr Emmerson's braai drifted over the pool, and Hamish couldn't imagine a place he'd rather be.

Jennifer, dark-haired and brooding, noticed the stare her friend was receiving. She raised an eyebrow at Hamish.

'How's Ricky?' she asked Jane.

Hamish's hackles rose immediately.

'He's cool, I guess,' replied Jane sipping her drink. 'I saw him last night.'

'You *saw* him last night?' asked Hamish. 'As in you looked at him?'

'Well, he was at the Italian Club so, yes, I saw him.'

'I'd imagine you'd have heard him before you saw him,' said Hamish. 'I get a headache just thinking about his voice.'

'Who's Ricky?' Raymond arrived at the side of the pool.

'You mean you don't know Ricky Flanagan?' Hamish raised his voice. '*The* Ricky Flanagan? Where have you been, Raymond – hiding under a rock? Well, let me explain to you before one of these ladies tells you something that isn't true about the great R Flanagan.' Hamish sipped his Coke, pausing for effect.

The twilight closed slightly.

'R Flanagan is possibly the foulest human being in all the land – and would you like to know why?'

'Yes, please,' replied Raymond, happy to play sidekick. They enjoyed it when Hamish entertained them like this.

'Well, he is a main man about town – tipped to be the junior champion this year. But there are two things you must realise about him, Raymond. The first is that he has a case of acne that makes him look like the victim of an aggressive scabies infection.'

The audience was laughing now.

'The second thing is that R Flanagan smells odd. To me, it seems as if he has not bothered to wash his feet properly and then applied talcum powder to hide the stink.'

'He does smell a bit cheesy,' agreed Jennifer, smiling.

'Hmm,' said Jane, miffed that she should be associated with a boy thus described.

'The worst thing about him, however, is his voice. When he speaks, it's like listening to Satan with laryngitis. His voice has the quality of a sick chainsaw, and if he's within a hundred metres when he opens his mouth, you immediately get a migraine.'

'Oh rubbish, it's not that bad,' said Jane.

'It is so! He walked past me at the Summer Classic last year shouting something at his friend about how great he is, and my vision immediately blurred. I had to go and have a lie-down in the ambulance!'

A red-eyed dove cooed from a row of cypress flanking the pool. Its call mingled with the giggles of the happy teens as Jane's mother called from the verandah table.

'Come on, kids, dinner's ready!'

'We're not kids,' snapped her daughter.

'No, of course not, Jane dear – please come and have dinner anyway.'

The recently designated young adults enjoyed a sumptuous meal, waited on by Dorcas and Francina, who moved silently around the table clearing plates and replacing platters of braai meat, salad, garlic bread, potato bake, ice cream, malva pudding and custard. At the end of the meal, they all sang happy birthday and tried valiantly to find room for a piece of Jane's chocolate birthday cake.

Then it was time for gifts. Jane received an assortment of horsey things from her friends. She opened Hamish's last.

'Did you wrap this?' she asked of the perfectly covered box.

Hamish grinned. 'I may have had some help,' he admitted.

Jane carefully removed the golden ribbon and then unwrapped the white box without tearing the paper. She pulled off the lid to reveal a brass tie-pin with a horseshoe clasp nestled in yellow cotton wool. The effect of the gift on its recipient was as Caroline predicted. Jane was touched and understood its subtle meaning.

'Thank you, Hamish,' she said, 'it's beautiful.'

The boy turned a shade of pomegranate.

Mr and Mrs Emmerson were then banished from their sitting room, which was turned into a makeshift dormitory-cum-cinema. The party-goers moved the furniture to the sides and set mattresses and blankets on the carpet in preparation for a video – *A Nightmare on Elm Street*, de rigueur for these sorts of occasions.

By the time he returned from cleaning his teeth in the bathroom, everyone was waiting to start the terrifying, two to twenty-one-rated film. Thinking that being in the dark and covered with blankets might precipitate a physical interaction, Hamish was determined to engineer himself a place next to Jane and was delighted when she patted her mattress as the lights went out.

'Come sit.' She smiled.

He slipped under the blankets next to her, their legs touching. Hamish's evening was going perfectly according to plan. Across the darkened room, it was clear that Raymond's night was also taking a turn for the romantic: he'd nonchalantly slipped an arm over Angela's shoulder and she was snuggling into the embrace. How in the hell, thought Hamish, had Raymond managed to know when and how to do that? It seemed like the most natural thing in the world, but a charging herd of tyrannosaurs couldn't have convinced Hamish to attempt the same with Jane.

For a few hours, the group chatted and laughed and barely watched the film before they began drifting off to their dreams. Hamish, however, lay awake, hoping desperately that Jane would reach across and slip her fingers between his. He made sure his palm was ready next to her should she decide to take that initiative, and shifted every so often so she'd know he was awake. Eventually, her breathing became regular and deep. The last thing he heard before he fell into an uneasy doze were the aquatic noises emanating from Raymond and Angela.

The next day was Sunday, 11 February 1990. Hamish woke up feeling dejected, his mouth dry. Light streamed in through the open curtains and a delicious smell of cooking bacon filled the house. He turned onto his side to look at Jane. She was lying peacefully on her front, her left arm cradling her head. Her full, taut lips were very slightly parted and Hamish longed to lean over and kiss them. She shifted slightly and Hamish quickly rolled over. It was then that he realised he had dribbled voluminously onto the pillow next to him. He felt a sudden and over-whelming sense of self-revulsion.

He slowly sat, turned over the pillow and headed for the bathroom to drink some water, clean his teeth and wash his face. Often when he drank water from a tap, he thought of carrying those heavy containers up from the river with Ayanda, a memory that helped him to put things in perspective.

From the bathroom he didn't really know what to do. He could hear Mr and Mrs Emmerson chatting in the main bedroom, but didn't think wandering in and saying good morning was quite slumber-party eti-quette, so he drifted through to the kitchen, where he found Dorcas and Francina frying bacon, mixing scrambled eggs, slicing tomatoes and mushrooms, brewing coffee and chatting animatedly.

'Sanibona, bomama,' he greeted.

They turned with surprise.

'Sawubona, nkosana,' replied Dorcas, the shorter of the two. 'Ufun' ikhofi?' This was a step too far for Hamish's Zulu, so Dorcas asked him again in English. Hamish didn't drink coffee but it smelt so delicious that he accepted a cup and sat at the kitchen counter on a cane barstool. The kitchen was very different from the one at home – ultra-modern, from what he could tell, with melamine counters and a dazzling range of brand-new appliances.

'You sleep well?' asked Dorcas.

'Yes, thank you,' smiled Hamish. 'And you?'

'Good, good,' replied Francina. Conversation flagged until Hamish remembered that Tina loved to go to church on Sundays.

'Are you going to church today?' he asked.

'Today church?' replied Dorcas wiping her hands on her apron. 'No, not today, nkosana. Today we are watching TV in the afternoon.'

'Oh,' said Hamish. 'Is there a good story on?'

Dorcas and Francina's eyes met briefly.

'No, nkosana, there is no story today. Today Nelson Mandela is coming out from the jail.'

Hamish remembered hearing about this on the news. Suddenly the excited atmosphere in the kitchen made sense and the boy realised it had nothing to do with serving breakfast to the Emmersons or their guests, hitherto sprawled about on the living-room floor.

'It's great that he's going to be released,' said Hamish lamely. 'South Africa will be good now without the National Party.' This was the extent of his political commentary – not that he was shy to express an opinion based on nothing but wild hearsay. 'The ANC will be a great government. I'll vote for them when I'm allowed to vote.'

Francina looked surprised. 'You know the ANC?' she asked, removing the bacon from the oven, where it had been crisping. She placed it on some kitchen towel.

'Well ... um ... I ... eh ... know who they are ...'

He remembered an incident from three or so years previously: he'd arrived home from school armed with a joke. As Stuart was fetching a light bulb from a cupboard in the kitchen, Hamish had wandered in.

'Dad, did you hear about the dyslexic terrorist?'

Stuart retrieved the sixty-watt bayonet from the stock, grateful for his wife's superb ability to maintain a supply of household spares. He turned to his son and raised an eyebrow.

'No, I didn't.'

Hamish grinned as he delivered the punch line. 'He went to work for the CNA.'

The boy had expected his father to be most impressed by the topical joke's sophistication.

Stuart had placed the bulb on the counter next to him. 'Hamish, you must not believe everything you hear at school, especially from your frie— ... um ... peers. There is a saying that goes "One man's terrorist is another man's freedom fighter."' Stuart saw his son's eyes glazing over. 'It all depends on one's perspective.'

Back in the Emmersons' kitchen, the lady of the house arrived in a cotton dressing gown.

'Morning, ladies,' she greeted and then she saw Hamish. 'Oh, hello, Hamish – you're up early.' (It was eight-thirty.)

'Good morning, Mrs Emmerson,' Hamish replied standing up from the stool.

'Now, Francina, please make sure that you mop up that extra bacon fat – not like last time.'

Later that day, all five Frasers, along with about twenty million other South Africans, sat glued to their television. Hamish noticed two things from the afternoon.

The first was that an industrious cameraman with an eye for detail spotted a man in the crowd – an enormous gathering of people dancing and chanting in the Cape summer heat. The man was sweating, dressed in rags – his trousers much too short for him, his shoes with uppers that had long since detached from the soles. He had found a tap outside the Victor Verster prison from which to slake his thirst. Hamish remembered it because as the image appeared on screen, he himself was sipping Coke from a glass filled with ice.

The second was that, eventually, the man who would lead South Africa into its uncertain future emerged from the prison dressed in a sombre suit, his wife, Winnie, holding his left hand.

'He looks like a friendly grandfather, not a terrorist,' observed Hamish.

Winnie Mandela then lifted her left fist into the air.

'Oh!' exclaimed Caroline, slightly alarmed. 'She's doing Black Power!'

18

On the first day of the Winter Term, 1990, Hamish followed the now-familiar path from the archway to the Memorial Quad, distracted by a wintry chill and the fact that he'd left his jersey at home. In what was becoming a regular occurrence, once under the bell tower, he found himself flying. This time, his right shoulder collected the wooden door of the side chapel.

He turned to face Nicholas Cullinan and Robert Bosch, knowing this would be a short episode because there were too many people around for extensive torture or a wedgie.

'Is little choir boy going to play mofstok?' Bosch sneered as Cullinan held Hamish's face up against the door.

The smaller boy gritted his teeth, determined to ignore them.

'Fucken A he is,' Cullinan hissed. 'The choir boys are all faggots – this one will also play moffie stokkies!' He gave Hamish one last shove into the door and the two of them departed as Mr Danhauser walked by on his way to the choir gallery.

'Hello, Hamish,' said the music director. 'How was your holiday?'

'Good, thank you, sir. And yours?'

'It was a good break – see you at rehearsal.' The master departed with a smile.

It was in this term that Hamish had to choose a winter sport, and there were two options: rugby or hockey. Hamish had already chosen to play rugby – it was what Stuart had played at school and university. He reasoned that hockey was like a mixture between soccer and cricket, neither of which he had any aptitude for. He also found the thought of hard balls, propelled by wood and aimed in his direction, somewhat terrifying.

In the Memorial Quadrangle, David Swart was sitting on the concrete rim of the central pond, watching the boys arrive. The head boy called Hamish over.

'Fraser, good morning. How's it going?'

'Hello, Swart,' replied Hamish with a smile.

A rapport had developed between the two during the first term. They both sang in the choir and when there was late choir practice, they were often the only ones in the house come late afternoon. Normally, Swart would be reading in the prefects' room when Hamish returned from his sports practice or from doing his homework in the library.

On one occasion, the head boy had found Hamish staring out of the western window next to his locker, watching a chopper land on the roof of the nearby hospital.

'Some poor victim of the roads,' the head boy guessed. 'You hungry?'

'Um … yes,' replied Hamish, whose school days seemed a time of eternal famine.

'Me too. There's some bread left over in the prefects' room. If you toast it, we can share it.'

Prefects, as a rule, did not invite Form Is into the hallowed space of the prefects' room unless it was to fag. Hamish followed his senior, baulking slightly as he stepped through the doorway. He wandered over to a grubby Tupperware, where two slices of semi-brown foam were masquerading as bread.

'Shall I check if there's a bit more in the Matric common room?' Hamish suggested.

'Sure,' replied Swart re-opening his copy of *Tess of the d'Urbervilles*. 'But don't get caught keiffing their bread.'

Hamish grinned and ran lightly down the short corridor to the

Matric common room. It was mercifully empty, and he found another Tupperware containing two more slices and a smidgen of yellow spread of indeterminate providence. He lifted both.

'Thanks,' said Swart as Hamish proffered the refreshments. 'Have a seat in here if you like.'

Hamish sat down gingerly on one of the brown sofas. The silence in the prefects' room was just becoming awkward when the older boy closed his book.

'So, are you playing rugby next term?'

'Yes, no mofstok for me!' Hamish assumed that his use of the term he'd just learnt would generate a smile, but David Swart blanched.

'I don't think you should call hockey that – some of the toughest sportsmen in the school play hockey.'

'Oh.'

'You know what a moffie is, right?'

'Ja, it's a gay,' replied Hamish.

'Yes – but it's a pretty nasty way of describing a gay.'

'Oh.' For an awkward second Hamish stared into his black tea. 'In Divinity the other day, Father Josiah said that being a gay is a sin.'

Swart's eyes rolled ever so slightly heavenward and he sipped his tea thoughtfully. 'He's told us all that. What do you think?'

'I dunno. It doesn't seem natural really – I'm not gay.' Hamish reassured the head boy.

In a way that was entirely conversational, as though he was talking to an old friend, Swart said, 'The kindest dude I know is my uncle. He's gay – he told me about a year ago. I don't believe he's a sinner. He's had a shit life because of it. Reckons if there was one thing he could have changed, it would be that.'

Hamish was fascinated – mainly because the older boy was taking him into his confidence.

'I come from an Afrikaans family – very conservative on my mother's side. They don't like blacks, Jews, Indians, coloureds or Brits – shit, they'd really hate your accent.' He chuckled. 'But the thing they hate most of all is homosexuals. They go on and on about how unnatural it is and how gays are all going to hell. Anyway, old Uncle Koos is my mother's brother, and he reckons he's as queer as an eleven-rand note.' David Swart drained his tea. 'Good tea, thanks. Koos didn't choose to be gay so how can it be unnatural?'

Hamish was stumped.

'Anyway,' Swart continued, 'it got me thinking – even if it was a choice, who's to say that it's a wrong choice if he's not harming anyone? Koos spends his life fixing motorbikes and listening to Bob Dylan records – never hurt anything in his life.'

'God,' replied Hamish warming to the conversation. 'Father Josiah says the Bible says it's wrong and this is a church school, so surely he must be right.'

'Ja, but the Bible also says we should kill gay people.'

'But times change,' replied Hamish.

'I'm not sure that you can pick and choose. Anyway, I'm not trying to convince you – just think about not using the word "moffie".' David Swart looked at his watch. 'Oh shit, we gonna be late – it's five o'clock.'

The two of them leapt up and ran. Hamish tried to keep up as the bigger boy took two stairs at a time. They emerged into the Memorial Quadrangle, the late summer casting golden beams through the western arches. Together, they tore across the uneven paving, under the trees towards the chapel. Hamish felt happy for the first time since he'd started in the College and wished that there had been a few other boys around to see him in company with the head boy running to choir practice.

At break time on the first day of the winter term, Hamish reported to the Geography teacher's room. It was here that the Form Is who'd selected rugby would add their names to the list.

'You gonna play rugby?' asked Basil Anderson.

'No, I'm here for pottery club – am I in the wrong place?' replied

Hamish, reading the derisive look on Basil Anderson's face.

The burly fellow snorted as Hamish appended his name to the list of rugby players.

'The rest of the co-ords are doing hockey.' Anderson played to a small audience of boys who would almost certainly make up the under-13A team. 'De Ville's gonna play hockey, so is Moses.'

David de Ville had possibly the largest intellect Trinity College had ever enjoyed educating. He was one of those outrageously bright boys who won mathematics Olympiads and destroyed chess opponents by simply looking at the board. His hand-eye co-ordination, however, was so poor that Hamish felt like an international-quality slip fielder in the genius's company. He also ran as if lead weights were attached to his heels. Instead of lifting onto his toes like most people, he ran on the back of his feet and then leant forward in order to avoid tipping over backwards, arms flapping behind him like a penguin's flippers.

Hamish glared at Basil Anderson. 'And de Ville will probably go on to be a rocket scientist, but I'm not following what that has to do with my choice to play rugby.'

'Sit down, lads, and be quiet!' came a booming adult voice as the Geography teacher entered his classroom. Mr van Zyl was a man who taught Geography so that he could coach rugby. (He did not coach rugby because he was a teacher.) He slammed his hand on the desk and looked around at his new recruits. 'Now, playing rugby is a serious choice, lads – it's a dangerous game for warriors. Are you all young warriors?'

'Yes, sir!' the rest of the boys shouted.

Hamish sighed – he detested this sort of rah rah.

'I can't hear you! Are you all warriors!?' the master bellowed.

'YES, SIR!'

'There is time to back out now. For those of you who still don't know what you want to play, here's a bit of advice. If you want to avoid being hurt, then hockey is probably for you. Often the guys who aren't very good at sport play hockey.'

This assertion, as far as Hamish could see, was ridiculous.

'Mofstok,' said Basil Anderson under his breath and the coach smiled.

'Sir?' Hamish raised his hand.

'Yes – what is your name?' The coach's eyes revealed disdain for such a weedy rugby player.

'My name is Fraser, sir.'

'What is your question, Fraser?'

'Well, sir, I'm a bit confused. I'm told that the guys who have no co-ord play hockey, but surely the chances of being injured on a field of twenty-two boys armed with sticks and no co-ordination are greater than the chances of being hurt while lurking on the wing for a junior rugby team?'

Silence.

Mr van Zyl made a mental note to send the cheeky boy straight to the under-13Ds.

'Fraser, if I ever see you or anyone else lurking on the wing and not pulling your weight, I'll make sure that you go and play mof— ... hockey! Now shuddup!'

There were no trials for the under-13s. Those thought to be good sportsmen were immediately selected to the A squad and the flotsam assembled on what was known as the Faraway Field later that afternoon. The field was tucked away at the bottom of the school grounds, its players' lowly status accentuated by the half-length posts at each end.

Stuart had suggested that Hamish learn to play scrum half because it was the position often occupied by the smallest player in the team. Hamish had no idea what a scrum half was and had actually never held a rugby ball. The moment, however, he touched the scuffed leather bladder, he fell in love.

His coach was an irascible Irish Chemistry teacher by the name of Mr Smythe.

'Fraser,' boomed the coach, 'I want ya to smell dat ball!'

'Sir?'

'Go on, smell it! Tell me what ya tink!'

The other members of the squad looked at Hamish in his oversized maroon jersey, the hem hanging below the line of his shorts. He put his nose to the ball and inhaled – a smile spread across his face. The ball was old – years old. It was rounder than a rugby ball should be from years of re-inflation – the under-13C and D squad received only hand-me-downs from other teams. Not for them the brand-new Super Springbok balls that the As and Bs were using. Hamish smelt history in that ball.

'It smells like grass and soil and leather, sir.'

'Ah, yes, good! What else? Smell it again, boy!'

The other boys began to giggle.

'Sweat, sir? It smells like sweat as well.'

'Dat's right!' Mr Smythe turned to the rest of the squad. 'You guys are probably tinking dat you're down here on de bottom field because you'll have no chance of making de first fifteen one day! Well, let me tell ya someting. If ya sweat over dat ball as hard as ya can, any one of ya can play in de first fifteen. It'll just take some time. You understand?'

'Yes, sir!' A chorus from the lowest-ranked rugby players at Trinity College.

'One more ting: for dose of ya who don't want to play for de first fifteen, dat's okay, but you're all going to try as hard as you can! Is dat clear?'

'Yes, sir!'

With that, the boys were dispatched to warm up with two laps of the field.

Mr Smythe quickly noticed that the eloquent but weedy boy had no idea how to pass a ball but was relatively fast. Hamish thus found himself out on the left wing for the under-13D team.

Now, it must be understood that for the ball to ever reach the wing in the under-13Ds, countless forces in the universe have to pull together at the same time – the chances of which are about as great as life spontaneously arising from the primordial soup. The left wing, therefore, spends a lot of time running up and down waiting for the ball, which seldom

197

makes it past the inside centre before being dropped.

On the night after his first practice, Hamish demanded that he be given a rugby ball so that he could practise in the garden. For the next five years, the first part of Stuart's evenings required that he pass and receive a rugby ball from his eldest son until darkness made it too difficult to see. Over the years, Hamish's ability to pass improved steadily until, by his final year in the College, he could throw long passes both ways and kick with a relative degree of accuracy.

By default, so could his father and sister.

The under-13Ds lost their first four games of the season. In those four games, on the wing, Hamish received the ball four times – he dropped it twice and the other two times was driven into touch by opposition loose forwards who couldn't believe the negligible mass of the Trinity left wing.

When the fifth match, against King James, came along, nobody expected them to win. In fact, no one other than Mr Smythe thought about the under-13Ds at all – not even the members of the team. Bar one. Hamish Fraser thought about three things during the winter months of 1990: rugby, riding and Jane (but not always in that order). He dreamt about scything down the wing like he'd watched Anton Eisenbaum doing for the first XV. He fantasised about kissing Jane Emmerson in a variety of situations, most of which had them meeting in dark corners by chance (in the tack room during a rainstorm, for example). He thought about galloping through the finish poles at the Children's Festival just a fraction of a second ahead of her and then consoling her afterwards.

The fifth match was an enormous affair. King James was a huge government school that had twice as many pupils as Trinity, most of whom were conditioned into believing that if there was one thing more important than God, it was rugby. The last time the Trinity first XV had beaten King James was so far in the dim mists of history that no one alive could remember it.

The Friday before the match, Hamish was on fagging duty in the prefects' common room. He made his way there at the beginning of break and waited to be called in to make toast and tea for the prefects. When the door opened, there was only one prefect in the room: Anton Eisenbaum.

'Morning, Eisenbaum,' said Hamish staring at his feet.

'Morning, Fraser. Two pieces of toast and a coffee with three sugars.'

'Coming up,' replied Hamish scuttling into the room.

Eisenbaum returned to a chair and resumed polishing his rugby boots. Hamish wondered why he had not been instructed to do this menial task.

'Fraser,' Eisenbaum said, as if reading Hamish's mind, 'you know why I polish my boots before each rugby match?'

Hamish assumed it was for the girls from sister schools who arrived in droves on Saturday afternoons to watch the first XV. He thought better of saying this.

'No, Eisenbaum, I don't know.' The toast popped up and Hamish began to butter it, hoping to extract himself as soon as humanly possible.

'Two reasons,' Eisenbaum began without looking up. 'The first is that I respect Trinity and our traditions – polishing my boots shows the jersey my respect. The second is focus. I use this time to get my mind right for the game. I go through the moves in my head. Focus, Fraser, fuggen focus.' He finished the boots and slipped them neatly into a special shoe bag and then looked up as Hamish handed him a plate and mug. 'Thanks.'

Hamish turned to leave.

'Where you going?'

'Um ... sorry ... what else do you need?' asked Hamish.

'I don't need anything, but I haven't finished fuggen talking to you. Wait to be dismissed.' Eisenbaum bit into the toast and slurped the coffee, and then he said something that nearly felled Hamish: 'I've watched a few of your games this year.'

'You've watched the under-13Ds?' Hamish was incredulous that a member of the first XV had made the effort to arrive for the first match of the day – that of the school's lowliest and most unsuccessful team.

Eisenbaum looked up sharply. 'Don't fuggen interrupt me!'

'Sorry.'

'Your problem is you lack focus. You stand around on the wing wait-ing for the ball to come your way and if it doesn't, you just kind of check out the fuggen weather or scratch your balls.' He slurped again, and shovelled half a slice of toast into his mouth. 'You like rugby, right? I've seen you walk around with a ball everywhere.'

'Yes, I really like rugby a lot.'

'Well then, you need to fuggen focus! You're a wing at the moment but you should be a scrum half – you not big enough to play wing. Doesn't matter. If you on the wing, you must go looking for the ball. You know that in the under-13Ds there's fuggall chance the ball's going to make it to the wings. Okes don't have the skills to pass or catch. So you must go find the fuggen ball. Know what I mean?'

'I think so.'

'You don't sound like you know. I mean that unless you have a set move or you're defending, you don't have to be on your wing. You can just arrive in the middle of the backs, catch the ball and fuggen charge into the opposition.'

The last bit was delivered with a wistful look. Anton Eisenbaum was the top try-scorer for the first XV that year. He was tall and very fast, but Hamish imagined it was the look on his face that must have terrified the opposition: when he ran with the ball, Anton Eisenbaum looked like a murderous demon.

'Now you can go. Good luck tomorrow.'

Hamish turned to leave.

'And make sure you polish your fuggen boots – get your mind right.'

'Yes, Eisenbaum.'

The away game against King James was on a typical highveld winter morning – crisp and cold. Hamish woke early and dressed himself in his maroon jersey and white shorts (which normally remained white for the duration of the game). Then he went out to the laundry, where he retrieved a Tupperware of polishes and brushes.

The top half of Tina's stable door was open, the weak winter rays drifting through and making a warm patch on her sofa. She was sitting in the sun with a tin mug of steaming tea.

'Sawubona, Gogo,' he greeted, opening the bottom door and walking in.

Tina smiled. 'Sawubona, mfana.'

Hamish sat down on the floor and began an ineffectual job of polishing his boots.

'Hamish, why you don't take off the mud first?' Tina asked.

'Oh, I don't think I have time.'

'You must make time – go out quickly and hit them on the bricks outside,' she instructed firmly, frustrated once again at his poor planning.

With her coaxing and cajoling, Hamish's boots were shining just as his father appeared in the kitchen door.

'Go quick!' Tina smiled. 'I can put the polish away.'

At King James, the under-13Ds would, as always, be playing first, which meant they'd have to break the film of frost that covered the field. Hamish warmed up in the frigid air with the rest of the team, all determined not to take off their tracksuits until the very last minute.

A problem revealed itself as the boys ran their two warm-up laps. Andrew Wilkinson, the fly half for the match, was absent. In any other team, it would have been a disaster to have the pivot in the backs missing, but the skill levels of the under-13D boys were similarly dire, so it wasn't particularly hard to replace him.

Hamish, being the boy who took rugby most seriously, noticed the absence immediately. He broke from the rest of the group and trotted over to Mr Smythe. The coach's passionate red moustache glistened in the early sunshine.

'What is it, Fraser? Don't tell me you're sick or someting?'

'No, sir, not me, but I think Wilkinson is sick, sir – he's not here.'

'Oh, jaysus,' exclaimed the Irishman. 'What de fe— … What are we gonna do now?' He turned and looked at the team running around the field. Then at Hamish. 'You know all de moves, right? De skip one, de switch and de double dummy?'

The boy looked at him, realisation dawning. 'Yes, sir.'

'Good, well, you been practising. I seen ya. You be de outside half today. We'll put dat fellow Hing on de wing.'

'Yes, sir.' Hamish beamed.

'You'll have to kick for de posts as well, you know dat?'

'If we score a try – yes, sir, I'll try.'

'*If* we score a try? *If* we score a try? Fraser, you best make sure we score more dan one try!'

A few minutes later, Hamish was standing in the centre of the field, a new match ball in his hands (King James took rugby so seriously that even the under-13Ds used a new ball for matches). The leather was hard and shiny. Hamish put his nose to it – it smelt a bit like his saddle. He dug his heel into the halfway line to make a little divot and placed the ball, end up, into it. Then he took three deliberate steps back. His forwards were lined up to his left. Ten metres in front of them the large King James forwards waited in their menacing red jerseys – to a boy, at least five kilograms heavier than their private-school counterparts.

Hamish looked to the side of the field. His father was standing with a few other dads. At the halfway line, next to his coach and dressed in his normal school uniform with just a white scarf designating his membership of the first XV, was the glowering figure of Anton Eisenbaum.

'Focus, Fraser, focus!' Eisenbaum yelled at the new fly half.

The referee blew the whistle and Hamish kicked off into the arms of the waiting King James forwards. The teams tore into each other with a gusto that belied their lowly stations and skill levels. Hamish acquitted himself relatively well in the fly-half channel – he took the ball running, didn't drop it and shovelled it on to his centres with relative success. Mr

Smythe and Anton Eisenbaum bellowed instructions and encouragement from the sidelines, which inspired the fathers to voice their own fevered enthusiasm for their boys.

The under-13Ds were not a team used to playing with a vociferous group of spectators, and it made a difference: quite against expectation, the half-time score was four all with one try apiece. (Both Hamish and his opposite number had hopelessly missed their conversion kicks. In the former's case, he could just kick a ball over the cross bar from the centre of the twenty-two metre line – any further or any additional angle made a successful kick unfeasible.)

The King James coach was staring down the barrel of an embarrassing defeat to Trinity – there was no greater ignominy for the rugby players and coaches of the proud old government school. He stormed onto the field as his boys ate their oranges and berated them loudly for their lack of effort. Then he began to whisper, pointing out that there would be an outrageous mismatch in the fly-half channel if they used their big locks to run at the Trinity pipsqueak.

On the other side, Mr Smythe, who would have considered a twenty-point deficit at half time a success, and the now-frenzied Eisenbaum were giving their half-time speeches.

'Well done, boys!' said the coach. 'But dis game is not over yet! You boys are on de verge of history here – you must not give up now.'

'Come on, okes!' yelled the prefect. 'You gotta fuggen focus – put these guys away now.' He slapped his pocket with the College's lion rampant badge. 'You play for this and you play for each other!'

The second half began and for some time Trinity maintained possession. Eventually, however, the red jerseys turned the ball over, allowing the new King James game plan to be effected. Their scrum half flipped it to a monstrous redhead, who built up a head of steam and homed in on Hamish Fraser, ball tucked firmly under a not insubstantial left arm.

As Hamish realised that he was the monster's target, his face registered alarm. He gathered himself into a crouch as Mr Smythe had taught him and prepared to tackle. The redhead, quite against the spirit at this level of rugby, led with his meaty right forearm, collecting Hamish's forehead and knocking him over backwards. The smaller boy grabbed desperately at the fat limbs as they stomped over his thighs, stomach and chest, but to no avail. The massive lock tripped slightly, righted himself and charged for the try line, dotting down close to the right-hand touchline.

Hamish Fraser now knew that he was in a rugby match. The 'medics' – a few boys with either a vague interest in sports injuries or a macabre desire to see human trauma – ran onto the field with a polystyrene box of ice and a water bottle.

First on the scene, however, was Robert Gumede, the best player in the under-13D team by a country mile – when he put his mind to it. He was short, but fast and strong, and could quite possibly have played for the A side but for his chronic dislike of authority. On that day he was playing eighth man and had thus far not troubled himself to break a sweat.

Gumede pulled Hamish to his feet. 'You okay?' he asked, his eyes blazing with anger.

'I think so.'

'That's not fair – you can't bash someone in the face like that.'

The fly half missed his conversion and so, with fifteen minutes to play, Trinity was eight to four down. Moments later, the same move was repeated. The huge redhead thundered towards Hamish. As he was about to make contact with the smallest boy on the field, something like an enraged black leopard flew into him.

In a horizontal dive, Robert Gumede's shoulder drove into the monstrous child below his rib cage. The ball spilt forward and the redhead hit the ground with a tremendous thud. The referee blew his whistle for a knock-on. Play stopped and the sound of wheezing mingled with groans as the prone boy's breath came back. A minute later, he was helped from the field by the 'medics' and his coach.

Gumede had wrested control of this game and he was going to finish it.

With just two minutes to go, there was a Trinity line-out on the halfway line. Gumede separated himself from the pack of forwards and placed himself at inside centre.

'Gumede, what you doing here?' Bruce Templeton, the under-13D inside centre complained. 'I'm the inside centre, man, get out the way!'

The eighth man ignored him. 'Fraser, when you get that ball, you pass to me okay?' Gumede instructed.

Hamish thought this an excellent idea.

The line-out was a complete lottery but somehow the Trinity locks managed to win the ball. The scrum half lobbed it to Hamish as Gumede, five metres behind, began to sprint.

'Now! Give it to me now, Fraser!'

Hamish caught the pass and popped it neatly to his right just as the number eight flew past. Gumede ran over the top of the combined efforts of the King James centres and dived under the posts to score, levelling the points at eight all with the conversion to come.

'Can your boy kick it over from dere?' Mr Smythe asked Stuart as Hamish lined up the kick.

'I really don't know,' replied Stuart, chewing his fingernails.

'Fraser!' Anton Eisenbaum's blood pressure was way too high for someone his age. 'Focus, man! Focus,' he boomed.

Hamish looked at the ball and then to the posts just fifteen metres in front of him.

'Watch the ball, please just watch the ball,' Stuart whispered under his breath.

Hamish ran forward and swung his spindly right leg.

The ball left the ground wobbling mightily and gained height. Almost as quickly, it began to fall. There was a collective hush from the parents, the coaches and all thirty players on the field. No one noticed Hamish overbalancing and falling onto his backside, the position from which he watched the fate of the beautiful oval.

After what felt like a decade, the ball reached the poles, landing on the cross bar and bouncing straight up.

There was an audible sucking in of air from spectators and players.

The ball dropped onto the cross bar a second time and then fell towards the waiting arms of the King James boys – behind the try line.

The final whistle blew to the cheering of the Trinity under-13D team. On the side of the field, Anton Eisenbaum let out a roar that would have shamed a lion. Mr Smythe, overcome with Irish emotion, flung his arms around Stuart.

'We fekken won!' he said. 'Can you fekken believe it?!'

Hamish just sat there. He had no desire to move from where he was for the rest of his days. He breathed in the crisp winter air and the smell of the dry turf and turned his face to the sun. Then he smiled.

The following Thursday, assembly was held in the amphitheatre. Mr McAdams, the headmaster, was a tall and lanky man in his early sixties. He was also a Trinity Old Boy and one-time first XV wing. His weekly announcement of the rugby results meant a lot to him.

'Results of the rugby against King James,' he began, perusing the list in front of him. 'First XV lost 58–3. Seconds lost 45–20. Thirds lost 16–12. Fourths lost 23–0. Fifths lost 86–nil.'

There were a few giggles.

'Under-15A lost 42–4. Under-15B lost 23–6. Under-15C lost 31–4. Under-15D lost 33–nil. Under-14A lost 23–10. Under-14B lost 34–9. Under-14C lost 23–18.'

The headmaster cleared his throat. 'U14D lost 104–nil.'

Spontaneous laughter rose from the boys.

'I'm not sure what's funny, boys!' boomed Mr McAdams.

The laughter died.

'Under-13A lost 56–10. Under-13B lost 25–8. Under-13C lost 32–12.' He stared down at his page and then up at the assembled boys, most of whom assumed the list of shame was complete and readied themselves to be dismissed.

Mr McAdams's jaw clenched and relaxed as a tear formed in his left eye.

'Could the members of the under-13D team stand up, please.'

From their houses in different places around the amphitheatre, the fifteen boys of the under-13D stood up. The school went quiet.

'Under-13D —' the headmaster paused, bit his lip, wiped his eye and swallowed '— won 10–8.'

The school erupted into wild applause and cheering. Next to the headmaster, whose cheeks were wet, David Swart clapped and laughed.

Hamish beamed as hands from all around patted him on the back. Although this would be his one and only school sporting triumph, he would never forget the euphoric feeling of being part of something that made people happy.

19

With the passing of his fourteenth birthday in October 1990, Hamish became a junior rider. This meant that he could no longer ride his pony, Timothy, and had to enlist the services of a horse. Timothy was duly sold to a promising young rider at the Inanda Club.

Earlier in the year, Stuart had made a calculated gamble and taken a job with a new construction company: he wanted a challenge and there were promises of share options and gargantuan bonuses. A few months after he began, however, it became apparent that the business was in dire straits. The managing director was arrested for fraud and Stuart, along with a few others, set about rebuilding.

The upshot was that Stuart found himself slightly skint as his oldest son turned fourteen, what with three children at private schools, an ageing Inanda home on an acre property and a holiday house in Kenton. Paying for a horse's stabling, shoes, feed and endless vet's visits began to fall off as a financial priority.

So it was that Hamish's steed was downgraded. Timothy was a top-class pony and Annabelle managed to sell him for substantially more than Stuart had paid for him, but his replacement did not come with quite the same pedigree.

'Well, for that sort of price,' said Annabelle, 'Sports Vision is probably the best we can do.'

Hamish, Annabelle, Stuart and Caroline were sitting under the vine-covered pergola outside the stable office. Hamish had just taken a sip of juice from a box and at the mention of the horse, he ejected it involuntarily. Mercifully it missed his short-tempered teacher.

'Sports Vision?' said Hamish, incredulous.

Annabelle was not above yelling at her pupils in front of their parents.

'Yes, Sports Vision, you little brat. Have you got a better idea? Have you suddenly become an expert judge of horse flesh?!'

Hamish went crimson, his ears stinging because he knew what was coming next.

'Hamish, you can be the foulest child sometimes,' said Stuart. 'Apologise now or we will get up and never come back. I cannot believe that at fourteen you still behave like a bratty three year old. It's so disappointing.'

'Embarrassing,' agreed his mother, who was feeling the strain of the financial pinch.

The boy squirmed. 'I'm sorry, Annabelle.'

She grunted in disgust. There followed an awkward few minutes where the adults, despite their love for the boy, allowed their mutual frustration with him to dissipate.

'I'm sorry, Mum and Dad. I'm really grateful that I can ride. And I'm sure Sports Vision will be a good horse for me.'

'Well, let's go and have a look at him,' sighed Stuart, and the slightly mollified party made its way to a stable at the end of the row, five doors down from Timothy's.

The pony's ecstatic new owner was shovelling carrots at Timothy, who gave no obvious indication that he recognised his previous providers. Hamish felt slightly betrayed. The new horse's head was not out of his stable, so the Frasers looked in over the bottom door, their eyes unaccustomed to the darkness.

They reversed at a tremendous speed as a shape launched itself towards them. Caroline overbalanced and sprawled on the concrete paving. Stuart tripped over his beloved, his open palm landing in a steaming pile of Sports Vision's dung. (In the four years that Hamish owned the horse, he never once saw him make a deposit inside his stable.)

Hamish ducked and then looked up. A chestnut head with a white blaze down its length, ears pinned back, emerged over the top of the stable door, bared teeth first. Caroline and Stuart crawled from harm's way and stood up, the mother's knees gashed and her normal poise destroyed.

'He can be a little … difficult in his box,' said Annabelle hopefully.

'A little *difficult*?' Stuart wiped his hand on the grass outside the stable. 'He's bloody savage!'

'Colin,' Annabelle summoned the groom from where he was refilling a bucket, 'bring a halter over here and take Sports Vision out of his box.'

Hamish watched fascinated as the horse, which had since retreated into the darkness, emerged again with the speed of a striking puff adder as Colin arrived with a halter. Colin just slapped the muzzle gently and, in a second, the halter was on and the bottom door open.

The horse immediately deposited another enormous pile where Stuart had fallen.

'Bloody animal's got constipation, maybe that's why he such a bugger,' the father observed.

From the description of how Sports Vision introduced himself to the Frasers, one might expect that he was the size of a charger, coat shining over ripples of taut muscle. Well, Sports Vision was indeed a vision, but not of the sort that dreams are made. The animal was barely regulation size for a horse, his red chestnut coat without lustre. It had been a long time since he'd had a private owner, largely because of his generally poor attitude and, while not neglected, Sports Vision lacked any sort of muscle tone, with the result that he appeared much older than his sixteen years – he was almost exactly two years older than Hamish.

The boy stared, imagining the laughs that would be cast his way at shows. His father felt perhaps he'd been a bit harsh about his son's initial reaction to the beast.

'He's nor much to look at, is he?' Stuart said.

Annabelle, seeing a potential sale going bad, stepped in. 'Not at the moment, but with some schooling he'll put on muscle. We'll feed him up now that he'll be ridden three times a week, and that will make him look healthier. As for his character ... it'll be good for Hamish to learn to cope with him.'

'Good for him? More like fatal,' muttered Stuart.

'Come and take him,' Colin said to the diminutive fourteen-year-old. 'He can't bite outside the stable.' By which he meant Sports Vision was unlikely to use his teeth outside.

Hamish walked over and took the lead from the groom. The horse by this stage was nibbling on a tussock, ignoring the attentions of the humans. Hamish reached up and patted him gently on the neck. The horse's skin flicked, and as the boy turned to give a thumbs-up to the adults, Sports Vision lifted his head and bit Hamish on the back of his right shoulder.

Hamish dropped the halter lead and yelled. The horses in the paddock nearby started at the noise, grooms came charging out of stables and riders in earshot came running. Annabelle, Stuart, Colin and Caroline launched at the now bleeding boy, a flock of doves scattering from the syringa tree above their heads. The only organism that did not react was Sports Vision – he carried on eating, albeit with a piece of turquoise shirt material hanging from the left side of his mouth.

Twenty minutes later, his bleeding shoulder bandaged, Hamish walked up to the mounting block where Colin was standing with the horse, who was saddled and looking for all the world like the most docile equid in the yard. Hamish mounted quickly – he was afraid of no horse once he was on its back. He knew it was now that their relationship would have to be established.

Hamish gathered the reins and gave his new steed a sharp kick in the ribs. The animal grunted, pinned back his ears and kicked out with an irritated back hoof. Hamish tapped him sharply on the backside with his crop. Sports Vision snorted and as he kicked out again, Hamish slapped him harder. The horse walked forward.

'Good boy,' whispered Hamish smiling at this small victory.

The deal was sealed an hour later, and Hamish became the new owner of the cheapest and most bad-tempered horse at the Inanda Equestrian Club.

'I suppose we might be able to recoup the cost at the dog-food cannery,' said Stuart as they drove out of the yard.

Sports Vision and Hamish's first show took place just a week later. It was a training show and Hamish was entered in the last two classes. The venue was a long way out of town at the Inanda Country Base, and a group of nine riders and ten horses set off on the warm Sunday in late October.

One of the adult riders was Toby St Claire, who'd imported a massive, dapple-grey Hanoverian mare from Namibia as a fiftieth birthday present to himself, or, more likely, to launder some of his ill-derived booty. Toby's ability on horseback was vastly beneath the price and potential of his mount – they were competing in the first two classes over fences barely in excess of two feet. The other adult rider was Alice Monahan, a neurotic forty year old who'd been competing in the first two classes of the day since she'd started riding some six years previously.

Jane Emmerson's two magnificent ponies had been replaced with two equally impressive horses: dark bay geldings purchased from a rider who'd successfully competed with them in the adult A grades. As the animals were led from the horse truck, the contrast between the Hanoverian, Jane's horses and Sports Vision could not have been more stark. The former three shone in the early sun, heads held high, sniffing the air.

Sports Vision and Hamish emerged last. The moth-eaten chestnut, whose coat showed no signs of shedding its winter layers, stumbled out of the trailer with his nose to the ground. His keen eye spotted an unattended bunch of carrots on an upturned bucket. He surged towards the unguarded treats, yanking Hamish off his feet.

'Come here, you bloody stupid animal!' Hamish yelled, jerking the halter rope with all his might.

Shocked by this outburst, Sports Vision ceased his carrot charge.

'Hamish!' exclaimed Alice as her docile liver chestnut shied very slightly. 'Please, you're startling Betty!'

This only served to irritate Hamish. He began to feel the awful inadequacy that surrounded him at school. It was not a feeling he'd ever experienced during his equestrian pursuits. He had the worst-looking horse there and the vile creature had just dragged him through the mud. It was embarrassing.

'Alice, please,' he snarled. 'That nag of yours is so decrepit a bomb wouldn't startle her – or you for that matter.'

He regretted his words instantly. Alice was extremely sensitive. She took her shows very seriously, despite having languished in the novice classes for over half a decade. At these training shows, most competitors dressed casually; Alice dressed as though she was about to compete in an Olympic show-jumping event, with her greying hair tucked into a hairnet, her hat fastened to the top of her head, wearing a beautifully tailored tweed jacket, white jodhpurs and silk riding shirt fastened with a gold tie pin.

At Hamish's outburst, her eyes welled up, bottom lip aquiver.

'Geez, Hamish, you're such a shit sometimes.' Jane turned away in disgust. That really stung. Up to that point, Hamish had still harboured a vague hope of romance with Jane, but as she showed him her back, he knew it was never going to happen. She walked off, leading one of her two prancing steeds.

Hamish followed behind the group to a huge willow tree where the grooms had hung hay nets in the branches and set their upturned buckets in the shade against the trunk to sit on. The riders handed over their mounts and departed to check the order of events at the judges' box and pick up some bacon-and-egg sandwiches.

'Hamish?' said Colin as Hamish handed over Sports Vision.

'Ja,' said the pathetically morose teenager.

'This horse is a good horse. You will see – he's like you. Angry all the time but he's strong!'

Hamish smiled. 'Thanks, Colin, maybe you're right.'

'Not maybe. I'm right.' The groom laid a tender hand on the chestnut's forehead. The horse breathed out in greeting.

Toby hung back from the rest, most of whom were trying to comfort Alice, whose overzealous application of make-up was combining with her tears such that it looked as if her face was melting off her skull.

He waited for Hamish to catch up with him. 'You know, my boy,' he said, 'you go a pick your enemies. You're a brigh kid, but you can be a real bastard sometimes.' He paused to take a swig from a silver hip flask and then offered it to Hamish.

'Um … no thanks,' said Hamish.

'You sure? I's a Macallan eigheen year old.'

'It's eight in the morning!'

'You see? Tha's wha I'm talkin about … you're all uptigh. Look at me, I'm a small guy like you but I done alrigh. Tha's cos I know ow to pick me battles and I don' give a shi wha anyone finks. Old Alice, well, she's no one's enemy bu her own, much the same as you.' He offered the flask to Hamish again. 'Go on, loosen up a bit and go make friends with Alice.'

Hamish took the flask, sniffed the contents and took a tiny sip. His face contorted in disgust as the fiery liquid burned down his throat and Toby roared with laughter.

Hamish found Alice emerging from the lady's cloakroom (a shed with an aged and stained throne in it). He felt dreadful when he saw her dishevelled state.

'Alice, I'm so sorry. I didn't mean what I said.'

She stared at the boy. 'You really hurt my feelings and Betty's,' she sniffed.

Hamish gritted his teeth. 'I'm sorry I hurt Betty too,' he croaked.

'Are you really?'

'I promise,' he lied. While he felt no remorse for the horse, he did not want to continue as a disfavoured member of the group.

'Well, okay then,' she said.

Hamish held his breath – if she'd asked him to go and apologise to the horse, it would have been a bridge too far.

Feeling rather depressed, he went off in search of a bacon-and-egg roll. His stable-mates had already bought theirs and found a place to sit on the arena's grass bank. He took his breakfast and walked onto the cross-country course. The Inanda Country Base boasted enormous grounds with huge swathes of natural highveld vegetation.

The dry grass had burnt at the end of spring and the blackened tufts, topped with a first hint of green, crunched under foot. Each step sent up little puffs of charcoal-scented dust, which mingled with the fragrance of new leaves drawn by the first rains from the blackened earth. After ten minutes or so, Hamish found himself up on a ridge north of the arena. The sound of the show's announcements floated up on a breeze and then away again. He sat on a rock, took his roll out of its paper packet and savoured the flavour of the butter, bacon, fried egg and fresh bread.

For a few moments he forgot entirely about the show. On an adjacent rock a lizard, about three inches long with chocolate-coloured skin and a dun stripe down each flank, emerged from under a small overhang. The little reptile lifted its belly off the cool stone and turned its back to the sun, slowly turning its head from side to side as if giving consideration to an intellectual conundrum. Its tongue flicked out every few seconds to test the air. Hamish felt a sense of kinship and gratitude that it had chosen to share the moment with him.

At the base of the lizard's rock, a line of ants emerged from their nest in the soil, and the sound of grassland birdsong drifted through the morning. Hamish sat perfectly still, instinctively aware that human movement would break the spell that had formed around him. The only thing he allowed himself to do was inhale the smell of earth and new wild grass warming in the sun.

After about ten minutes, the lizard, sufficiently warm, scuttled off in search of a meal and Hamish raised himself from the cool surface of the rock. He walked slowly back towards the arena, feeling a deep sense of peace. He found his way to the rest of the crew just in time to see Alice entering the arena on Betty – he had to hand it to her, she and her horse were immaculately turned out.

'Where'd you go off to?' asked Raymond.

'Just to eat a roll,' Hamish replied.

The bell sounded and Alice began. They achieved a clear round over the jumps, but Alice rode the horse so slowly that they incurred time penalties – a remarkable achievement at this level of show-jumping. Despite this, she was ecstatic when she returned to the waiting group.

'After all the *stress* of this morning, I can't believe Betty jumped so *well*. I only finished plaiting her mane a *few minutes* before warm-up and then, and then, well, there were other *people* in the warm-up arena and you know how Betty would really rather be in the warm-up arena *alone*. I had to go and …'

Hamish lay back in the grass and looked up at the sky.

The first and second classes took the best part of four hours to finish. By the time class three came about, Hamish was thoroughly bored. He was number twenty-five of thirty riders. Jane was first to ride and she cleared the fences with consummate ease and elegance. Ten horses before his turn, Hamish went to warm up. Sports Vision had been snoozing on his feet for most of the day, so he was stiff and not overly excited at the prospect of a Sunday-afternoon jump.

In the warm-up arena there was a bit of a scrum – horses and riders trotting and cantering about in all directions, one or two attempting the warm-up jumps and the air clogged with dust. Sports Vision was not a horse given to great affection for his conspecifics, and the swirling mass irritated him. He trotted around with his ears flat back, which did little to improve his less-than-impressive physique. Hamish found space to canter a few circles and then turned his horse to the warm-up jump.

He came around the corner with five strides to the fence. Normally he was good at judging the distance between himself and the jump and then adjusting the horse's stride accordingly. Today, he just couldn't quite see his stride. There wasn't time or space in the warm-up arena to rectify the problem.

The marshal at the gate called his name with a megaphone. 'Are you Hamish Fraser?' said the long-suffering volunteer, who'd been standing in the sun for hours.

'Yes, ma'am,' replied Hamish.

'In you go,' she said, lifting the boom.

Sports Vision wandered into the arena without enthusiasm. Hamish steered him around the perimeter as the object of his desire completed another immaculate round on her second horse. He thought how beautiful she looked today in her tight-fitting red polo shirt and cream jodhpurs.

Hamish and Sports Vision didn't start well. As the bell went for their round, Hamish gathered the reins, sat deep into the saddle and gave the aid to canter. The ill-tempered beast failed to follow the relatively simple instruction; instead, he began a trot that became increasingly extended. Hamish felt his face redden with embarrassment as he desperately tried to achieve a canter while his horse just trotted faster and faster. When he hauled on the reins, Sports Vision pushed out his head and opened his mouth like a donkey about to bray. It wasn't pretty.

Hamish reapplied the canter aid, combining it with a sharp smack from his crop. This had the desired effect and they headed through the start poles towards the first jump, a small spread. Hamish completely misjudged his stride and planted the horse almost under the fence. Mercifully, Sports Vision rectified his rider's mistake. They cleared the next two fences without too much trouble and then approached a combination: two jumps set a stride apart. Hamish miscalculated the distance again and lengthened Sports Vision's stride. They arrived at the fence half a stride too soon and the horse took off. Hamish wasn't expecting the jump and instead of folding forwards with the movement, he fell backward.

He may well have recovered had it not been for the second jump in

217

the combination.

Sports Vision landed, took one extended stride and took off again. The rider, already unseated, had no chance – he flew up and over the horse's rump.

There was a gasp and then a groan from the spectators as Hamish's head hit the ground and his body folded over his neck at a horribly unnatural angle.

People began running from all corners. First on the scene was Toby – full of concern, but absolutely clueless about what to do with the unmoving boy.

'Amish, Amish – can you ear me? Oh, Christ!' He reached for Hamish's shoulder and shook it gently. 'Amish?'

'I'm not sure we should move him,' suggested Raymond.

'I'm just tryin to check e's alive!' snapped Toby.

'I think he's breathing,' said Jennifer.

Raymond knelt next to Hamish's head. 'Hamish, old buddy, old pal.'

At last, the boy stirred, rolled onto his back and opened his eyes. He blinked up at the bright sky and the faces staring down at him.

'Amish, can you si up, boy?' asked Toby.

Hamish groaned, a wave of nausea turning him roughly the same shade as the turf he was lying on. He slowly raised himself to a sitting position and brought his knees up underneath him.

Finally a medic, who had completed as much exercise as Toby had medical training, wobbled onto the scene, stuffing the last of a hamburger into his cavernous mouth. The fellow had been at the show since seven o'clock, and his only action had been to remove a splinter from a child's finger; he wasn't about to pass up a real disaster.

'Stand aside, give the patient space,' he instructed. Hamish registered with displeasure that he'd just been referred to as 'the patient'. 'Don't move him – there could be a spinal injury and permanent paralysis!'

'You're about five minutes late with tha instruction, fatso,' said Toby.

'I'm fine,' Hamish rasped, standing. 'Where's my horse?'

No one had thought much about Sports Vision. The belligerent steed was about twenty metres away – grazing peacefully on the manicured arena turf. The fallen rider began an unsteady totter towards his mount.

'You can't move!' blustered the medic.

'Apparently,' Hamish turned, coughed and snarled, 'I can.'

Raymond detached himself from the onlookers and walked next to Hamish, thinking better than to try and help him. He held Sports Vision as Hamish remounted. The pair had long-since been eliminated from the class, but Hamish was determined to at least ride from the arena – if just to restore a modicum of dignity.

As he dismounted in front of Colin a few minutes later, Hamish shook his head. 'I don't think this horse likes me,' he said, smiling weakly.

'You will see,' said Colin. 'You don't look good – go and sit down. You must drink Coke.'

'Okay,' said Hamish, feeling woozy. He made his way back to the grass bank, where Toby presented him with a Coke.

'Shanks,' said Hamish.

'Wha?' Toby asked.

'I sh … sh …' The boy blinked and tried again. 'I said … sh … thanks.' Hamish's vision began to swim. He flopped forward and vomited.

A few minutes later, still unable to utter a complete sentence, he was in Toby's Jaguar, driving for hospital. Every ten minutes, the car stopped for Hamish to lean out of the passenger door and vomit. Toby used the Jaguar's car phone to call Stuart and Caroline, who raced to meet them at the Sandton Clinic.

The mother was in a predictable state, swearing blind that she'd never let her son out of her sight again and berating herself for being a poor parent. By the time they arrived, Hamish had been assessed by a doctor, who had diagnosed a concussion.

'We'll keep him here for a few hours but I don't think he needs to stay overnight,' he told the concerned parents. 'He can speak again – it's not uncommon for a concussion to result in drunken speech and even memory loss.'

'Oh, my poor baby!' groaned Caroline.

'Will there be any lasting effects?' Stuart asked with a furrowed brow.

'No, I shouldn't think so – he's going to have a horrible headache for the rest of the day and he'll feel a bit groggy as the bruise on his brain heals.'

'Bruise on his brain?' wailed the mother.

'Yes, that's what a concussion is – but he'll be fine,' reassured the sympathetic doctor.

Hamish spent the rest of the afternoon and most of the night alternately being sick and then lying on his bed with a pounding head. As he lay there, he thought about how he'd always imagined an injury like this – a broken limb or a concussion – to be a mark of pride. He'd fantasied about arriving at the stables sporting a black eye or a plaster cast on his arm.

'Oh, Hamish,' said Jane in the boy's imagination. 'You're hurt!'

'Oh, it was just a rugby match,' he replied nonchalantly.

In his mind, she would find out that the wound had been inflicted during a heroic, try-saving tackle of a much larger boy. Her eyes would then betray a long-hidden admiration. She'd tuck a lock of blonde hair behind her diamond-bejewelled ear and reach out to squeeze his hand.

Back in reality, he'd gladly have sacrificed ever seeing Jane again for a cessation of the agony in his skull. When it eventually did recede, the only thing he felt was shame. He'd almost wiped himself out in a lowly training show – and simply because he'd been riding badly. Jane had comfortably won both classes while moth-eaten Sports Vision had munched hay from the sidelines, his rider back home in a foetal position.

Hamish almost told his mother that he was finished with riding, but he returned to the stables five days later. Normally he looked forward to his shared Friday-afternoon lesson with Jane, but a cloud of depression hung over his head as he wondered how he would face her.

Jane was already at the clubhouse when he and Caroline arrived.

'Hamish!' exclaimed Annabelle. 'Are you okay?'

'I'm fine, thanks,' he replied quickly. 'Hi, Jane.'

'Hello, Hamish, how's your head?' Her tone was kind but tinged with condescension.

'It's fine, thank you,' he ball-dragged.

Hamish had heard it said that you have to reach rock bottom before you can come up again. For him, that ball-drag blasted a new hole in the bottom of the rock. Jane turned her head away.

The afternoon light filtered through the syringa leaves as he walked to Sports Vision's stable. The trees were in flower, and for the first time he noticed how much he loved the fragrance of the blossoms. At the old oak tree where Amy had kissed him, he paused briefly to run his hand over the rough bark. The semblance of a smile returned to his face.

Outside Sports Vision's stable, Colin was sitting on a log repairing a hay net, a newspaper cigarette hanging from his lips. He looked up as Hamish approached.

'Ah, you are back!' he said, sounding surprised. The grooms gave even money on the petulant boy returning to ride.

'Yes, I'm back.' Hamish sat down on the log, the buzzing of bees filling their air in the blossoms above.

Sports Vision poked his head out of his stable door and gave an almost imperceptible grunt, his ears pointed forward.

'He knows you!' said Colin.

The boy smiled.

20

Early in 1991, in Hamish's second College year, a school bus service was instituted. The nearest stop was just a block from the Fraser home and, for Caroline, removed the nightmare associated with scheduling the retrieval of her boys from school.

In the afternoons, Hamish and Roger would simply select the most convenient bus. This was where the joy of the bus ended for the older brother. To start with, he hated the smell. The bus stop at school was under a line of jacaranda trees that in early summer looked lovely with their purple blooms, but when the flowers drifted to the ground, they gathered in piles, mixed with summer rain and rotted, their stench mixing with the bus's acrid diesel fumes. That was on the outside. Inside, the air was turned fetid by sixty adolescent boys and young men, many of whom had just completed playing sport and some of whom just boasted extremely poor personal hygiene. It was worse on rainy days when the windows were closed.

Mostly, Hamish also disliked the social conventions of bus travel: the older you were, the further back you were allowed to sit. The honour of occupying the bench seat at the rear went to the Matrics. (Hamish couldn't figure out quite why sitting in the back should be considered such a privilege because, technically, the rear of the bus arrived marginally later than the front.) The hierarchy was blurred further forward, but no one could say exactly where the cut-off points were. For the younger commuter, unless you sat very close to the front, the chances of being turfed out of your seat were high.

In Form II, seating on the bus was a lottery. The Prep pupils sat right in the front, and even the bravest College bullies were afraid of dishing out abuse to them, because the punishment for such an offence was swift and severe. Marlon Brown, aged seventeen, had slapped a Prep boy in the tuck-shop line and found himself looking for another school that very afternoon.

The Form Is and IIs were easier prey because they were less inclined to rat on their tormentors.

'Hey, Goodenough, what you doing sitting all the way back here?' Roland Schoeman (Matric) asked one afternoon of Johnny Goodenough (Form II).

The younger boy was in no-man's land, six rows from the back seat on a full bus, sitting on a two-seater next to a Form III.

'Ah, come on, Schoeman, there's no seats up front,' Goodenough entreated.

'That's not my problem, Goodenough. Bugger off.'

'Ag, come on, man!' The younger boy complained, picking up his bag and moving a few seats forward, where he displaced the aggression by repeating the eviction process on a Form I.

In the time-honoured manner of social primates through evolution, whenever there was a chance to consolidate positions on the hierarchy, the boys used it. In that confined and malodorous space, there was nowhere to hide and no safe place to extract to. It was a calculated risk to try to assert yourself in the bus – if you failed, you dropped in the estimation of the other boys and fell down a few social rungs.

In the case of Matrics shifting Form Is, it was easy: there was a substantial difference in size. Things became a little less clear with, for example, a Form II and a Form III: a big Form II could outweigh a small Form III.

In an interaction such as that between Johnny Goodenough and the much larger Roland Schoeman, the former made only a half-hearted attempt to save face. No one expected him to put up genuine resistance, so the interaction remained verbal. However, when verbal requests were refused and the boys were closer in age, things became interesting. By way of example, the interaction of Alan Jones (AJ), Form III and wannabe rebel, interacting with Johnny Goodenough (JG), large Form II and confident 'cool kid':

AJ: Get out, I want that seat.

JG: No, I'm not moving.

AJ would be faced with the choice to capitulate or to escalate. If he chose the former, he would lose some face, but not many would notice. Escalating would mean the development of an audience.

AJ: I'll smack you, you little shit. Now move.

Now commuters would be distracted from their conversations, nose-pickings and musings – there was entertainment to be had.

JG would have to decide whether or not to call AJ – was he bluffing or was there a real chance of being thumped? Likewise, AJ would have to decide if he was prepared to actually engage the younger boy physically. Sometimes, a plucky Form I would refuse to vacate his seat and would then be bodily lifted and tossed out. If the boys were closer in size (as in this example), then the larger would find himself in a precarious position: if he failed to extract the errant junior, his shame would be substantial, he'd have to go and sit somewhere else, and his social standing would be almost irrevocably diminished. It was something of a no-win situation for the bigger boy, because if it turned into a fight and the smaller boy gave a good account of himself – especially if he was a popular fellow – then public sentiment would turn to the underdog.

In the five years that Roger used the bus, he never once had a physical altercation. As a junior, he always correctly gauged the right place to sit. As a senior, his demeanour was generally so pleasant that if junior boys were out of place, they just moved of their own accord. Hamish's career on the bus, on the other hand, was a litany of conflicts.

The logic of the senior boys sitting in the back as some sort of divine right was utterly absurd to Hamish, and he normally just sat on the first seat he could find. If it was an early bus and there were a lot of Prep boys going home, he'd move to the middle in order to find some peace and quiet. The Prep boys were almost universally enthused by the bus – possibly due to the little yellow packets of sherbet the tuck shop sold for five cents a pop. The excitable fellows would charge about at the front of the vehicle, mouths red from the vile sweet, leaving little piles of sticky white powder on the seats, the floors and each other. Combined with moisture from muddy feet, spilt juice, sweat or saliva, the sherbet turned crimson and sticky. So Hamish tried to sit behind the Prep boys.

He was, however, often the target of verbal assaults from seniors who thought such a small fellow belonged further forward. He normally just stared at the aggressors without saying anything at all. Most of the time, they moved further to the back and sat down.

Unsurprisingly, much of his trouble came from Nicholas Cullinan and Robert Bosch. Hamish was normally on a later bus than his nemeses because of his singing in the choir and recently starting guitar lessons but, inevitably, conditions conspired to create a showdown.

Form II was Hamish's least favourite year at school to date. Academically, nothing had changed, but worse still, he had failed to arrive at puberty. It was increasingly embarrassing to change for swimming, and he had to withdraw to a loo cubicle, emerging with a towel around his waist while the bigger boys wandered about proudly displaying their manhoods. In the choir, he continued to sing with the unbroken-voice altos – the only Form II and one of only six blue blazers in a sea of grey Prep colours. Gone were the soaring treble lines of melody, and he longed to be driving the harmony in the basses, rather than filling it anonymously at alto. The rugby season had been unremarkable, but for the fact that he had converted himself into a scrum half for the under-14D team and had played a few games for the C side. His many frustrations had resulted in a lot of time spent apologising to his family and horse for frequent losses of temper.

The day Nicholas Cullinan decided he would like to sit where Hamish had placed himself on the bus was a Monday in November. There was a year of pent-up frustration boiling in Hamish and, perhaps, an increase of pubescent testosterone in his endocrine system.

The four o'clock bus was unusually empty as Hamish made his way to a three-seater – making sure there were six rows of seating behind him. As he waited for the bus to fill, he stretched out on the seat, his back to the window, and promptly fell asleep. In the seat behind him, Nicholas Cullinan sat down with two of his friends, while Hamish remained alone on his three-seater. It took about five minutes for Cullinan to register that Hamish was sitting more comfortably than he was.

'Hey, Fraser,' he began. 'Get off this seat; I wanna sit here.'

Hamish looked up at the glowering face, the greasy dark fringe hanging over the bigger boy's right eye. He knew one thing for certain that afternoon: no matter what, Hamish Fraser was going to remain where he was until his stop. Still, he moved his legs off the bench so that he only occupied the third closest to the window.

'You're welcome to sit here,' he said, and turned to look out as the bus pulled off.

Now it was Cullinan's move – he could just sit down and leave it, and no one would have paid much attention. Cullinan chose to escalate.

'I want the three-seater. You fuck off and find somewhere else to sit.'

An audience was duly formed.

'Make him move; make him show you respect!' urged Kevin Webster, also a year Hamish's senior.

'I'm not moving,' said Hamish. 'You're welcome to come and sit here, or you can stay where you are, but I'm not moving. I got here first.'

'I'm your fucken senior! You have to respect me – now move or you gonna get hit!'

The die had been cast – there was no way for Cullinan to back down now. The whole bus was watching and Webster's constant refrain 'Make him show you respect!' tinged with mocking, wasn't so much an encouragement as a taunt.

Nicholas Cullinan was not going to be made a fool of.

'I'm gonna give you one more chance and then you gonna get fucken hurt,' he hissed.

Hamish's heart rate escalated. He was afraid, but far more than that, he was angry.

'Fuck you, Cullinan,' he snarled, seething. His hands gripped around the bar on the seat in front of him as he braced for impact.

Cullinan opened the exchange with a hard slap to the back of Hamish's head.

Next, two powerful hands gripped the back of his collar and wrenched upwards. The knuckles ground into the back of Hamish's skull as his backside came off the seat. Still he gripped the seat in front – his hands unusually strong from years of holding reins – jamming his shins underneath it, immovable. Cullinan jerked and wrenched until the collar of Hamish's shirt gave way. He released the ruined garment, red-faced with exertion and embarrassment.

'Fuck man, Jesus! Make him show you respect,' taunted Webster.

The next attack came from side on. Cullinan flew at the smaller boy, smashing his shoulder into his victim's puny left bicep and driving him into the side of the bus. The wind left Hamish's body with an audible groan. Again and again the bully pummelled his victim against the window until sweat poured down his forehead.

Hamish's breath returned in ragged gasps.

The whole bus was watching now, and Kevin Webster continued his gormless chorus: 'Make him show you respect, for fuck sakes, man – he's a faggot choir boy!'

If there had been some Matrics on the bus that day, they may have intervened, but Nicholas Cullinan was from the most senior cohort and none of his classmates was prepared to tell him to back off.

The bully came again from the side. One hand lunged at Hamish's ruined shirt lapel, an unkempt nail breaking the skin of his cheek. Cullinan wrenched at the shirt while his other hand tore at the bird-like wrist attached to the seat in front. Hamish knew that if he lost his grip, he'd be on the floor in the aisle in less than a second. He squirmed, using his whole body to force the hand on his lapel to lose its grip. He then jammed his body against the arm holding his wrist, which bent it unnaturally, forcing Cullinan to let go. Two more blows slammed onto the back of his head.

Panting like rabid pit bull, Nicholas Cullinan finally retreated to the seat from whence he'd come. His friends moved over in disgust.

The bus was completely silent but for the panting of the bully and his victim.

'I can't believe you let that fucken faggot stay there,' chirped Webster eventually.

Nicholas Cullinan stared ahead.

It was only then, as the adrenaline ebbed, that pain began to register in various parts of Hamish's body. His shins sported raw patches over the bone where they'd rubbed against the metal frame of the seat in front. Stabbing pain shot through his ribs every time he inhaled, and blood trickled down his face and onto his neck. He rode the rest of the way looking out of the window, two spaces still empty next to him.

When, twenty minutes later, the bus stopped at the junction of Central Road and Third Avenue, Inanda, Hamish drew himself to his full five feet and two inches, lifted his bag from the floor and puffed out his almost concave chest. The bus went quiet as he walked down the passage, the left side of his face bleeding onto his ruined collar. All eyes were on him and there was no mocking in the looks. Perhaps there was even admiration.

Stepping down onto the pavement, he sucked in the fresh air. Pain surged in his left side. The door hissed shut. Faces looked down at him as the engine roared and the bus began to edge forward. As the face of Kevin Webster drew level, Hamish raised his middle finger.

'Fuck you,' he mouthed at the bigger boy, who stared in astonishment.

A block from home, Hamish looked up to see clouds floating overhead in the summer sky. A red-eyed dove called from the suburban forest.

A few minutes later Tina's voice came over the intercom on the Fraser driveway and the gate slid open. In the kitchen, Caroline and Tina were making a shopping list. They both turned and gawked as he came through the door.

'Hamish, what happened?' Caroline wailed.

Tina immediately moved to calm the situation. 'He's okay, Mummy.'

To his great surprise, Hamish managed to hold it together and even managed a small joke.

'I had a little altercation on the bus,' he said, feeling rather proud of himself.

'Who did this to you?!' Caroline was becoming slightly hysterical.

'That arse, Nicholas Cullinan.'

'I'll bloody kill him,' she yelled. 'Why ... why did he attack you?'

'He wanted the seat I was sitting on ... Doesn't matter; it's okay now. Let me go and put my things down.'

He dumped his stuff in a pile on his bedroom floor and then wandered into Julia's room, where he found his sister doing her spelling homework. As she turned to greet him, tears sprang from his eyes.

'What's wrong, Hamish?' frowned the eight year old. 'What happened to your face?'

Her brother just shook his head as tears rolled down his cheeks. She climbed off her chair and threw her arms around him, which doubled the water works.

'Nothing, don't worry,' Hamish sniffed. 'I just had a bit of trouble at school.'

'Come, we must go and see Mummy, and you must have some nice toast and hot chocolate.' It was exactly what he felt like.

The next day, when the Mercedes stopped outside the College, Stuart turned to his son.

'Are you alright this morning?'

'I'm fine, Dad.'

Hamish Fraser walked through the school archway and passed the statue of David feeling a bit taller than he had the previous day. Roger remained close.

The first person they came across as they emerged into the Memorial Quadrangle was Kevin Webster, who was reading the noticeboard with a friend. He turned as the Frasers walked past. Hamish stopped, looked him in the eye and then, in a distinctively ill-considered manner, imitated the chorus from the previous day.

'Make him show you respect,' he said. 'You fucking dumb prick.'

'Hamish,' sighed Roger.

Kevin Webster's beady eyes swelled. 'Fraser, I swear I'll —'

'Fraser!' The headmaster emerged from his office next to the noticeboard.

'Morning, sir,' the boys said in unison.

'Fraser, that language is not what I'd describe as gentlemanly,' said the headmaster.

'No, sir.'

'Well, you can think about it while doing two hours of hard labour on Friday afternoon. Come and get your slip at break time and do not forget.'

'Yes, sir.'

So it was that, instead of riding Sports Vision that Friday afternoon, Hamish cleaned out the bilges in the biology laboratories. A fine consolation was the company of Robert Gumede, who, for his myriad indiscretions, spent every Friday afternoon doing hard labour.

'Why are you here?' asked Hamish as he dipped a small bucket into the collection tank to decant a vile green gunge.

'Because this is the lot of the black man,' Gumede replied.

'No, Gumeedee,' growled Mr Harty, who was supervising. 'You are here because you told Miss de Stanislao that she is a foxy lady.'

Hamish laughed.

'I spoke the truth,' the seasoned felon replied. He sat back on his haunches. 'You can't deny it, sir, can you?'

Mr Harty stifled a laugh. Like most staff, he found Gumede frustrating and amusing in equal measure. 'Shut up, Gumeedee, and get on with your labour.'

The stocky boy set lazily to his task. 'And you, Fraser? What did you do?'

'I called Kevin Webster a prick in front of old McAdams,' whispered Hamish.

'You called Kevin Webster a prick?' repeated Gumede loudly. He turned to Mr Harty. 'Both of us, sir – punished for telling the truth. This is not what I expected from my education at this supposedly fine institution.'

Mr Harty hid his grin in the pages of his book.

21

At the end of Form II, Hamish had to choose the six subjects that he would take through to the end of school. Three were compulsory – English, Afrikaans and Maths. Then he had to select Physical Science or Biology (or both). The other two could come from History, Geography, Art, Music, Zulu, French or Latin. Hamish picked Zulu as one and then, to everyone's surprise, added Music to the list.

On the day of the choosing, he walked down to the Music Department to plead his case with Mr Danhauser.

'You gave up on music theory a year ago,' said the director. 'Why do you suddenly want to take it up again?'

'Well, sir, I guess I'm growing up,' replied the boy.

As far as Mr Danhauser could tell, Hamish was doing very little growing at all. 'No,' said the master. 'I think you just don't like the other options.'

Hamish remained silent for a few seconds. 'You're right sir, I don't much like the other subjects – but I'm pretty sure I could do this.'

'You've been playing the guitar for about a year. The other five boys doing Music have been playing their instruments for more than five years each – two of them since they were four years old.'

But Hamish was a natural musician – he had a good ear and feel for music. He might not win any competitions by the time his Matric practical came along, thought the teacher, but he would pass.

'Alright,' Mr Danhauser said at last, 'but I reserve the right to ask you to change come June next year if I think you're not going to make it – I'm not worried about the theory side of things, but you are far behind from a practical point of view. Mastering an instrument takes years of muscle memory and you don't have that, which means you are going to have to play for at least an hour a day.'

'No problem, sir,' said Hamish smiling.

It was not the option of Music that was Hamish's most inspired choice, however – that was Zulu. Of the seven boys who opted for the language, only two were white. The other paleface, Simon Johnson, was a goal-orientated young man who'd known from very early on that he wanted to be a doctor. He had done his research, and the gatekeepers of the medical faculties he'd canvassed had suggested he study an African language to enhance his chances.

Of the black boys in the class, only Robert Gumede was a mother-tongue Zulu speaker. Peace Nkuna's parents were both Shangane, Albert Masina was from Swaziland, Andile Pondo had a Xhosa mother and a Sotho-speaking father, and John Radatso spoke Pedi at home. All could speak Zulu to a greater or lesser extent – the Zulu spoken in the townships mixed English, a smattering of Afrikaans and a whole lot of area-specific slang. Barring Gumede, however, none of the other boys had ever written the language and they didn't possess the depths and complexity of the rural idiom.

Zulu at Trinity was delivered at third-language level, which meant that despite the fact that none of the black boys (except Gumede) was ever going to be confused with a rural Zulu, they would all achieve As with but the smallest application.

Hamish chose the language for a few reasons. Firstly, he'd been able to greet people in Zulu since the age of four, but his skills had stalled there. He had supposedly been learning Zulu in the classroom for four years, but every year it was the same lessons – again and again. He so vividly remembered sitting around the Ntunjwa fire, completely oblivi-ous of the Xhosa conversation until it was translated for him. The look on Tina's face was one of perpetual disappointment whenever she attempted more than just to greet him.

Secondly, the young Fraser was becoming more politically aware, but not because of any concerted effort on his part. He avoided reading anything in the newspaper other than the rugby reports (which he scrutinised in two broadsheets every day without fail). He read no books on politics or history, and his knowledge of South Africa's past came from prep-school lessons that had focused almost entirely on the trials and tribulations of the Boers fighting natives who objected to their land-grabbing ways. He had gleaned from one of the tunes in Stuart's collection of military music some background about the Zulu victory at Isandlwana. The idea of the Zulu underdogs armed with nothing but spears beating the British armed with rifles gave the Zulus, to Hamish's mind, a tremendously noble bearing.

Caroline and Stuart watched the news every evening, and that meant by default that Hamish, Roger and Julia did the same if they didn't fancy doing their homework (which, in Hamish's case, was always). While Hamish did not enquire hugely into the machinations of the interim government of national unity or the conferences that would eventually draw up the South African Constitution, he couldn't help absorbing something of the country's troubled past and turbulent present. From his parents he'd learnt a strong sense of right and wrong, while his position as a perpetual underdog (often by his own design) had made him sensitive to the world's injustices. The young Hamish was savvy enough to realise that learning a local language would make navigating the so-called 'New South Africa' a little bit easier.

So it was that the seven boys of the Form III Zulu class gathered in the classroom on the second day of 1992's Easter term to wait for their teacher, who, when she arrived, presented something of a surprise. In all their years at school, not one of the boys had ever been taught by a black teacher. Miss Vuyelwa Mkhize, aged just twenty-three, wafted into the classroom looking for all the world like she'd been teaching teenage boys all her life. This, as it turned out, was her very first lesson.

Hamish was mesmerised by his new teacher – mainly of course because she was black.

That first day, Miss Mkhize was clothed in a purple dress that flared at the knees and was tied at the waist with a bright-yellow belt. On her head, she wore a multicoloured headband above which her hair pointed skyward.

The boys went quiet. Well, six of them did.

'Sawubona, Tisha,' Gumede said, slowly giving her his toothiest grin.

She placed a basket of stationery and books on the desk and looked up at the boy who had greeted her. Then she took a piece of paper slowly from the basket and perused the list on it.

'You must be Robert Gumede.' She chose to address the boy in English.

'Yebo,' he said with a cheeky twitch of his eyebrows. 'My reputation clearly precedes me.'

'No,' she replied, 'it's your accent. From this list of names it seems to me that you are the only mother-tongue Zulu in this classroom.'

'Quite possibly descended from Shaka himself,' said Gumede.

'There is no record of Shaka having sired children,' she said quietly. 'But, yes, your reputation does precede you. I have a stack of hard-labour forms here with your name already filled in, so I suggest you keep quiet for now.'

By the end of the lesson, Hamish knew that his Zulu was about to improve.

'You two boys,' she addressed Hamish and Simon Johnson, 'if you want to learn isiZulu, you are going to have to practise. These lessons will give you the tools to go and learn the language, but you will not become fluent by sitting in this room. You must listen to Zulu radio, talk to your maids and housekeepers. The cashiers at the shop. The bus driver. The workers in the gardens here at school and the people that serve you lunch.'

'Ma'am,' asked Hamish, 'what if they aren't Zulus?'

'Are you Hamish or Simon?'

'Can't you tell from his accent, ma'am?' asked Robert Gumede faster than Hamish could take a breath.

She pulled a hard-labour slip from her basket, signed it and handed it to Gumede. 'No, I can't.' She looked at Hamish.

'I'm Hamish Fraser, ma'am.'

'Hamish, you will struggle to find a black person in South Africa who does not speak some Zulu.'

Hamish took this advice to heart. From that day on, every black South African he spoke to (barring the boys in his class, who spoke to each other in English) was harassed with appalling Zulu grammar and vocabulary. Hamish's main teachers became Tina at home and Colin at the stables, neither of whom was Zulu (Tina spoke Sotho at home, while Colin's home language in Zimbabwe was Ndebele). But over the course of the next three years, Hamish absorbed sufficient Zulu to make himself conversationally understood (fluent would be an exaggeration).

In the classroom, each sentence in his rudimentary literature text had to be painfully dissected using a dictionary and grammar manual. The black boys were thoroughly bored, and chatted among themselves as Miss Mkhize's patience was tested by Hamish and Johnson. Slowly, however, Hamish's vocabulary began to swell and his oral examinations started to reflect the effort he was bringing to practising.

One late afternoon that winter, Hamish was sitting on the log outside Sports Vision's stable, leaning against the whitewashed wall listening to the gentle sound of the horses pulling hay from their nets. As the grooms drifted off to their quarters, Hamish watched the eastern sky turn from winter blue to indigo, a few brave stars shining through Johannesburg's smog. Soon, the scent of wood and coal fires started to drift over the stable yard as the last of the red-eyed doves cooed above him in the ever-green cypress trees.

As dusk faded, Hamish wandered up to the clubhouse. Unusually, Angela Smythe was waiting for her mother, a nurse, to come and collect her. The parent arrived as Hamish retrieved his bicycle from the clubhouse.

'Hello, Mrs Smythe,' greeted Hamish.

'Hello, Hamish,' said the austere woman, who'd clearly experienced a very tiring day.

At that moment, a great wailing sounded from the car park.

'Oh God, they must be fighting again,' said Angela's mother.

'But that's a woman,' said Hamish.

'Their women fight as well,' she snapped as the wailing became louder.

'Should we go and see what's going on?' asked Hamish.

'Sounds like it's coming from the groom's compound. That's a very dangerous place – those guys drink and fight. It's part of their culture,' said Mrs Smythe.

The wailing ceased and the white people sighed with relief.

'Whose culture?' asked Hamish, slightly sardonically. 'The grooms' culture?'

'No, Hamish,' snapped the testy mother, 'not grooms. You know ...' She paused and then whispered, 'Blacks.'

The wailing began again.

'But that's not in the compound,' said Hamish. 'That's coming from the car park.'

The need to decide what to do next was negated by the arrival of Colin, who ran up to the clubhouse in great distress. The man looked at Mrs Smythe, who was still in her nurse's uniform.

'My wife!' he gasped. 'Come quickly please, to help.'

Mrs Smythe may have been born of Jurassic attitudes to the darker races, but she was also a superbly trained medic. 'Show me,' she ordered.

Angela and Hamish followed the two adults towards the source of the wailing. There, in the dust at the edge of the car park, where only Mrs Smythe's ageing BMW waited, lay a figure. The light was too poor to make out her features until they were all close by. As the noise from the prostate woman became louder, Mrs Smythe knelt over her and quickly assessed that the woman was almost certainly in labour.

'Go to Annabelle's house and phone for an ambulance,' she ordered no one in particular.

Colin ran.

With the onset of another contraction, Colin's wife grabbed Mrs Smythe's hand and squeezed. 'Umntwana uyeza,' she said, wide-eyed with terror.

'What?' asked Mrs Smythe.

Hamish suddenly realised that he understood. 'She says the baby's coming,' he stammered.

Mrs Smythe stared at him in astonishment. 'You speak this language?'

'Well, no – a little – not well.'

'Tell her I am a nurse and I will help her,' snapped Mrs Smythe.

Hamish fought for the words, beyond delighted to be of some assistance in the emergency. 'Umama uthi uzokusiza – ungunesi.'

The mother-to-be relaxed. Mrs Smythe extracted her hand from the woman's.

'Angela, hold her hand and don't let go,' she instructed her daughter while moving around to examine the birth canal. 'Hamish, ask her what her name is,' she instructed.

Hamish did this and the woman answered that her name was Thandekile.

'Hamish, while I look after Thandeekeelee, go to the compound and get some blankets. Also, we need a torch.'

Hamish had never been to the grooms' quarters. In the darkness, he charged across the car park towards the lights that twinkled through a small copse of trees. Ten rooms, no more than three-by-three metres each, surrounded a central courtyard of dirt. There was a fire in the middle, and the grooms were sitting around it on stools inexpertly nailed together from bits of packing crates and other salvaged offcuts. The men leapt to their feet when Hamish arrived – a white person appearing at night meant something big was afoot.

'Sanibonani,' Hamish greeted, feeling as much of a Zulu as Shaka by that stage. 'Ngicela …' he paused, realising he had no clue what a blanket or a torch were in Zulu. 'Um, ngicela amablankets and a torch. Colin's wife is having a baby.'

Elvis ran into his room and emerged with two old blankets and a torch. Hamish grabbed them and charged back to the car park. One blanket went under Thandekile's head and the other covered her torso – the night was cold.

Mrs Smythe was kneeling between Thandekile's knees. 'Give me the torch,' she said, holding out her hand.

Hamish did as instructed and Mrs Smythe pushed the switch forward. The beam it produced was about as bright as that of a dim candle – but it revealed all that Mrs Smythe needed to see. She reached under the blanket and put her hand on Thandekile's belly where she felt around for a while.

'This baby is coming right now,' she said, a hint of excitement in her voice.

'What, here … in the car park?' Hamish was astonished. 'Shall I ask her to hold it in?' Hamish didn't think he had the vocabulary to make this request, but he was willing to try.

'Don't be bloody ridiculous!' Mrs Smythe snapped. 'She can't hold it in!'

'Okay,' he said. 'What can I do?'

'Are you squeamish?'

'No, not at all.'

'Come over here and hold the torch.'

Hamish took a deep breath and shuffled around to where Mrs Smythe was kneeling. He took the torch and squatted on his haunches.

'Tell her we are going to deliver this baby and that it will be alright – I've done this many times.'

'I, um … I don't know how to say that,' Hamish admitted.

'Okay. Do you know the word for push?'

Hamish searched his mind. 'Sunduza.'

'Can you tell her when it's sore, she must push?' the nurse asked.

Hamish turned to Thandekile. 'Unesi uthi uma ubuhlungu, uyasunduza.'

The patient wheezed an acknowledgement.

'Now shine the torch between her legs,' ordered the nurse as the next contraction racked Thandekile's body. 'Soondooza!' yelled Mrs Smythe and Thandekile did as instructed.

Hamish stared dumbfounded as the baby's head emerged. He only began to feel awkward at his position when Colin and Annabelle arrived a minute later.

'The baby is nearly out,' the nurse told the new arrivals.

Thandekile groaned in agony.

'Soondooza!' encouraged Mrs Smythe.

Thandekile gave one final push and Hamish watched as the nurse, with surprising force, cupped the baby's head in her hands and pulled the shoulders out into the open. Suddenly, the infant was free, attached to its mother only by the bloody umbilical cord.

There was no sound.

Mrs Smythe, now covered in mucus and blood, turned the baby onto its side, opened its tiny mouth, slipped her pinky finger into it and pulled out a lump of mucus. Then she gave it a sharp tap on the backside.

The chilly evening filled with the yowl of a newborn human being, and the nurse looked up at Colin.

'It's a boy, Colin.' She smiled. 'And he looks very healthy.'

'Ingane yakho, ingumfana,' Hamish said to Thandekile, who smiled through her exhaustion.

The ambulance arrived a few minutes later.

Hamish, despite the winter's night, cycled home feeling warm as toast. 'Sunduza,' he said to himself with each push of the pedals.

22

Of Hamish Fraser's twenty milk chompers, only four fell out of their own volition. The rest were removed by a very patient (and subsequently quite well-off) dentist. There were so many abscesses, extractions and cavities in Hamish's mouth that he dreaded his visits to the dentist with a fear that he imagined soldiers at the Somme felt just before they went over the top. Many of the problems stemmed from the fact that human milk teeth are simply not designed to last the amount of time they were required to in Hamish's mouth.

Just before his sixteenth birthday, Hamish received a 'gift' from his parents. It began with a trip to the Rosebank Clinic and a meeting with a maxillofacial surgeon, who showed Caroline and Hamish the extent of their boy's orthodontic problems with an X-ray: Hamish's top-right canine was inconveniently poised to erupt in the middle of his palate.

So it was that Hamish was placed under general anaesthetic, waking an hour or so later with a gaping hole in his palate from which the tip of the errant canine protruded. The tooth would slowly emerge with the aid of an implanted plastic track. Another visit to the dentist resulted in the removal of four permanent molars, after it was decided that Hamish's mouth would forever be too small for the number of teeth nature had intended.

Many of Hamish's peers had received their braces around the age of thirteen and were now enjoying the fruits of their painful orthodontic journeys. Aged sixteen and one week, Hamish spent an extended morning away from school having an intimidating amount of metal cemented and then wired to his teeth. A wire attached the delinquent canine to its colleagues, drawing it very slowly forward over the course of the next year. To complete the joy, Hamish received a head gear that had to be worn every night for twelve months to correct an overbite he had never noticed. When Stuart woke Hamish in the mornings, the boy looked and felt like a victim of an ancient torture technique.

Along with the braces, the first flushes of teenage acne were appearing on Hamish's face, as were some sparse hairs on his upper lip. After Hamish's Form III exams, the Frasers departed for their annual Christmas holidays on the Eastern Cape coast, where the fresh sea air, rather than cleaning out his pores, seemed to greatly enthuse the spots. These remained on the family's return to Johannesburg.

Early in 1993, his second to last year in high school, it was decided that Hamish should be made partially financially responsible for his affairs: with a small allowance he would have to budget for his own clothes, entertainment and matters of personal hygiene. He chose to forgo the services of his hitherto hairdresser, a highly skilled but extremely expensive woman who plied her trade at a swanky salon for the well-to-do. His father recommended a Greek barber a few blocks from home.

Aristotle spoke no discernible language as far as Hamish could tell, but he was fast and, more importantly, he was cheap. Another advantage were the girly magazines that littered the waiting area – had Hamish not felt too shy to touch them. He would glance furtively at the covers and then check if anyone had observed his lust.

His first visit to Aristotle's was on a Friday in early January.

'Good afternoon,' said Hamish, as the previous client departed.

Aristotle grunted and gestured wordlessly to the barber's chair. He wrapped a clean apron around Hamish's neck and tied it firmly at the back.

'Is long …' he commented, picking up strands of Hamish's thick, dark hair.

'Well, yes, but just a short back and sides and a little off the top,' said Hamish.

There was another grunt and Aristotle reached for his shaver. The lights dimmed slightly as the machine came to life.

Ten minutes later, Aristotle had certainly achieved a short back and sides. He had failed, however, to 'take a little off the top'. The crown was covered with less than an inch. With his lengthening face and high forehead, Hamish resembled a caricature from the Simpsons (although not quite as yellow). What he saw as he examined himself in the mirror on his return home – unattractive eruptions of stringy top-lip hair (unshaveable because of the acne), a mouth full of metal and his high forehead exposed and blotchy – made him feel like wearing a bag over his head. He had no way of knowing that the weekend to come would be precisely when he wanted to look and feel confident in his own skin.

On Sunday morning, Hamish woke early for a show. (He didn't struggle to wake up early on Sunday mornings because he seldom went anywhere on Saturday evenings.)

A positive aspect of Hamish's life was the relationship he'd developed with Sports Vision. Mutual and often violent disdain had warmed to tolerance and eventually affection. The horse would neigh loudly at the sound of Hamish's voice, and after their lessons the animal would rest his head against Hamish's chest and nod off until Colin brought his supper. As a pair, though, their performances in the arena were as erratic as their moods. If Sports Vision felt like it, he jumped like a champion. If Hamish was slightly off his game, the horse was prone to stopping at jumps without reason, often sending Hamish flying over his head.

This show was at the Transvaal Horse Society and Hamish was the only competitor from the Inanda Club – Jane Emmerson and her family had long since emigrated to Australia. That morning, while the spotty-faced youth slouched off to warm up, Caroline found a place under a bottlebrush tree on the side of the arena, bought bacon-and-egg rolls and collected a programme in which she found her son's name and his class. Hamish and Sports Vision were slowly progressing through the C grades.

Up on horseback, with his hat over his awful haircut, Hamish felt he looked a little less offensive. Sports Vision, in contrast, was looking better than he had for years. Through Colin's efforts, the little chestnut's coat was short and brushed to a shine, but the most impressive part was the muscle tone he had developed. Hamish had spent many disciplined hours patiently schooling in the dressage arena and then galloping up and down the polo ground for fitness. Quite to the amazement of all who knew him, Sports Vision was now turning heads (when he wasn't lunging at human or equid with bared teeth).

As they trotted around the warm-up arena, a voice on the PA system made Hamish swing his head towards the main arena and gasp.

'That was the bell for number eighteen, My Fair Lady ridden by Rebecca Fine.'

It wasn't a name he'd heard for a very long time. Memories exploded as he trotted to the arena fence to see if his ears had deceived him. The horse was a grey mare of about sixteen hands jumping at the far end of the arena, but he couldn't make out the rider's face beneath her helmet.

The pair cleared an oxer and then turned for a related distance that would take them past Hamish. On landing, the rider's head faced the ground with the momentum, but as they rounded the corner right in front of Hamish, she sat up to look for the next obstacle.

His breath caught in his throat. There was no mistaking her – even after seven years.

Reggie.

'Hamish!' shouted Annabelle on her way to help him warm up. 'What the hell are you doing – have you jumped yet?'

'No, I haven't, sorry, I —'

'Well, hurry up!' She stalked off.

As they cleared the first warm-up fence, Hamish heard the announcer's voice again.

'A very neat clear round from My Fair Lady and Rebecca Fine. Next to jump we have ...'

'Hamish!' yelled Annabelle again. 'What's wrong with you today? Concentrate – I'm not here for my health!'

As Hamish circled around to approach the warm-up jump again, Reggie rode down the track between the two arenas. She took off her hat, but didn't glance at the unimposing combination of spindly boy and small horse. Hamish wanted to scream her name.

He and Sports Vision jumped a clear round and trotted back to where Colin was seated on an upturned bucket in the shade of a spindly acacia.

'Colin, you won't believe what just happened!' he began, desperate to share his enthusiasm. 'Reggie's here!' This was ridiculous, he realised – how would Colin know who Reggie was.

'Ah, yes.' Colin's face betrayed him.

Hamish ran up to where his mother was sitting with her knitting. 'Did you see her?'

'Well ridden, that was a good start. Did I see whom?'

'*Reggie*! She's *here*. She's riding a horse called My Fair Girl or something!' Hamish grinned, which was unfortunate, because the inside of his lips drew over his braces and cut into them. A trickle of blood formed on either side of his incisors.

Caroline, always at the ready, produced a tissue.

'Now calm down,' she said. 'You're bleeding. Are you sure it was her?'

'Yes!' He tore off his tweed jacket, slung it over his camp chair and began rifling through his mother's bag. 'Where's your programme?'

'Hamish, please! Calm down and breathe – you're getting over-excited.'

'Here it is!' He wrenched the pages from the bag and frantically rifled through them to the C-grade classes. 'There!' he pointed at the name and showed it to his mother. 'It's her – I promise it's her!'

'That says Rebecca Fine, not Regina,' observed Caroline.

'That's her second name!'

Annabelle arrived with a coffee she'd just bought. At a startling volume and speed, Hamish told Annabelle the story.

'You need to calm down,' she said quietly, her left eyebrow rising. 'You're going to have a heart attack. Have you even thought about planning your jump-off track?'

'No, but —'

'Hamish!' Annabelle snapped. 'Sit down and listen to me.'

The gibbering boy obeyed.

'Two things. Firstly, you are here to ride. It's cost your folks' money and my time for you to be here. You owe it to us and yourself to concentrate and ride to the best of your ability.' She paused and then smiled. 'Secondly, you are being uncool in the extreme – this kind of behaviour would make any girl think you belong in a loony bin. If you want to impress her, ride well.' She considered for a moment that even the coolest demeanour wouldn't overcome his bizarre haircut, bleeding lips, spotty face and the grease stain on his shirt.

Somewhat calmer, Hamish set to working out a route for the jump-off, but his eye kept flitting to the pockets of spectators and riders camped around the arena.

As he rode into the arena, the final competitor in the class, My Fair Lady and Rebecca Fine were lying in second place. Sensing his rider's extra energy, Sports Vision arched his neck and began to prance as the bell went for Hamish's round. The two of them flew through the start poles at a terrific rate and recklessly completed the course. The choice as they came into the final fence was to cut in front of another jump, leaving just two and a half strides to the wide oxer, or play safe and go around. Hamish, quite against character, took the gamble.

There was a collective gasp from the small crowd as the little horse made the corner with just two strides to spare.

'Come on, boy!' Hamish shouted.

Sports Vision took two long strides and leapt, but the take-off point was too far from the fence and his back-left hoof clipped the rear pole. It fell to the ground as they galloped through the finish line, well in front of the next closest time, but with four faults for the pole.

Despite this minor mishap, they placed fourth.

While Hamish was flying around the course, Reggie had approached the entrance to the arena in preparation for the prize-giving.

'Last to go in this C-grade Welcome Stakes is Sports Vision, ridden by Hamish Fraser,' came the announcement over the loudspeakers.

Reggie dropped the buckle she'd been tightening and looked up.

'Excuse me, but who's that rider?' she asked the marshal at the boom.

'That's, um ...' The woman consulted her programme. 'Hamish Fraser and Sports Vision.'

'Hamish Fraser?'

'That's what I said.'

After his round, Hamish waited for the prize-giving at the far end of the arena in front of the judge's box. He watched, his heart in his throat, as the other three placed competitors arrived. They came in order, the winner followed by Reggie and then the third-placed pair.

Hamish fastened the top button of his jacket to cover the grease stain on his shirt, his face flushed. As My Fair Lady approached, he pretended to make an adjustment to his stirrups.

'Hamish?' Reggie said.

The hair stood on the back of his neck and every piece of skin began to tingle. He forced his eyes upwards to meet hers.

'Hello.' He swallowed.

Her large, bright eyes were almost navy. Her lips were fuller than he remembered, the sides turned up in a smile – the top one a little longer than the bottom. She had a round, strong chin and high cheekbones.

'It's been, like, seven years, right?' she asked.

'Yes, it's been about seven years.' His voice boyish.

Then she smiled and he noticed that her bottom teeth were

ever-so-slightly skew.

Hamish, in his anxiety, had failed to notice Sports Vision blowing into My Fair Lady's nose in greeting. Suddenly, the little chestnut flattened his ears and made to bite the grey mare, who started backwards.

Hamish slapped the horse over his ears and tugged on the right rein.

'He's not very friendly, is he!' Reggie said without anger.

'He's a bit of a bastard actually,' agreed Hamish.

'We'd better go and line up,' she said. 'They're waiting.'

After the lap of honour accompanied by (in Hamish's opinion) a horrendously popped-up version of the 'Hallelujah' chorus, the riders left the arena.

Reggie waited for Hamish outside.

'Where are you sitting?' she asked and he pointed.

'Just over there. My mum is here – she'll be so happy to see you.'

Reggie returned the mare to her groom and then walked over to join Caroline and Hamish, who were sitting under the bottlebrush tree.

'Here she comes,' Hamish said to his mother, paling. Reggie had removed her hat and shaken out her almost-black hair, which fell both sides of her shoulders. The curls had released somewhat over the years, but it still looked wild.

Caroline put down her knitting. 'Reggie!'

'Hello, Caroline!' Tears brimmed in the girl's eyes and she threw her arms around Hamish's mother.

Finally, Caroline and Reggie released each other and the girl turned to the boy.

'Well, you'd better give me a hug too,' she said, wiping her eyes.

Hamish was rooted to the spot. Then he took a step forward. She closed the distance and put her arms around his shoulders. Although they were the same height, Hamish was standing below her on the bank and his failure to move forward meant that the top of his head came up to the bridge of her nose. Desperate not to show his catastrophic haircut, he still had his helmet on. The embrace was therefore clumsy and emasculating – he had to put his arms round her waist as she enveloped him in what felt like a motherly way.

The embarrassment wasn't strong enough for him to fail to appreciate the curve of her narrow waist and strangely taut back muscles. He inhaled and her scent threw him back to their very first meeting in the walnut tree some twelve years previously.

Annabelle watched the interaction with amusement and concern. She'd grown to love and understand Hamish over the ten years she'd known him. She believed the plaster needed to be pulled off quickly: as the two teenagers let go of each other, Annabelle grabbed the boy's helmet and pulled it off.

'Come on, Hamish,' she said. 'Say hello properly.'

'So that's why you're wearing your hat,' Reggie laughed.

'Yes,' sighed Hamish. 'I was attacked by a combine harvester yesterday.'

For an hour before the next class, Caroline, Hamish and Reggie talked non-stop, and by the time the contestants had to walk the course for the next class, there'd been laughter and quite a few tears as the events of the intervening seven years flowed between them.

Reggie was still living in Observatory with her grandparents and being schooled at a Jewish school in Linksfield. She rode at a yard in Benoni and had only just recently been granted permission to begin competitive show jumping because of a string of excellent academic results. Her father remained at the university and hugely active in the ANC. He still lived in the Orange Grove house, but, Reggie lamented, the garden was now either a dustbowl in winter or a tangle of weeds in summer, and she refused to see him there because it sullied the beautiful memories of the home her mother had created. In fact, she avoided seeing him whenever possible – a situation that suited him well. Albert hated the fact that she rode horses, because it was elitist. He continued to be disgusted by the life of luxury his parents and daughter enjoyed.

'Are your grandparents here?' Hamish asked.

'My grandmother – the Batbitch – comes religiously to all my shows,' Reggie replied. 'She is very, eh … goal-orientated. If I don't place in both classes, she lets me know how disappointed she is.'

Caroline bit her tongue. Hamish didn't.

'What a cow!' he said.

'Hamish!' snapped Caroline.

'It is what it is.' Reggie smiled wanly, her enormous eyes glassing. 'At least I get to ride. Anyway, I'm going to be in trouble when I get back now – especially if I tell her I've been lurking here with the Frasers!'

'You think she still won't like us?' asked Caroline.

'She doesn't like anything that reminds me or them of my mother – but they also don't like gentiles much. That's why I'm not Regina any more – they insist that I'm called Rebecca, which is the name every woman in the family has had for God knows how long.'

'I can still call you Reggie though, right?' asked Hamish.

'Of course – you *must*! Anyway, it was very special to see you both again. I won't tell Batbitch I've seen you – she might not allow me to come to shows out north again.'

'Won't they hear my name being announced?' asked Hamish, wondering how hard it would be to change his identity.

'No, Batbitch doesn't like the dust of the arena, so she sits a long way off and I'm actually not sure she'd remember you by name. Just don't go beating me too often, or there could be trouble.'

Hamish desperately wanted to ask for her phone number, but the words stuck in his throat.

Caroline came to his rescue. She took a notebook and pen from her bag, scribbled their home phone number on the first page and tore it out. 'Reggie, you know you can call us any time – if you're ever in trouble or feel like a chat, just call.'

Reggie smiled. 'Thank you, Caroline.'

Hamish stood up. 'Bye, Reg – phone sometime soon,' he croaked as nerves consumed him.

Reggie hugged Caroline, then flicked her hair over her right shoulder, and embraced Hamish (this time on level ground).

'It's lovely to see you again, old friend,' she said.

Hamish sniffed the subtle fragrance of jasmine in her hair. He never wanted to let go and made sure not to until she did.

He watched her walking away, the cream jodhpurs accentuating the curve of her teenage hips and strong legs. 'Old friend'– words that would consume him for the rest of the week.

Hamish and Sports Vision won the next class comfortably, but by then Reggie had left. Her mare knocked a pole in the first round, so she and My Fair Lady had departed post-haste with a thoroughly irritated grandmother.

Hamish did not stray far from the telephone for the next seven days, by the end of which he'd given up hope. A fortnight later he no longer noticed its ringing. A week after that, he and Roger were in the middle of a tennis game (in which Roger was giving his 'big' brother a hiding) when Julia came skipping out of the back door.

'Hamish!' she screeched as he was lining up a tremendous forearm.

He swung and connected the ball with the top of his racket frame. The yellow orb rocketed over the court fence into the neighbour's property.

'Oh, for fuck sakes!' shouted someone from next door – it was the seventh time Hamish had disturbed their Sunday-afternoon braai.

'Hamish, phone for you!' yelled his sister disappearing back inside.

Hamish dropped his abused racquet and ran. He tried to hurdle the court fence, but his back leg snagged and he slammed into the grass the other side, rolled once and was back on his feet in one fluid movement – ignorant of the bleeding graze on his knee. He tore around the side of the house and over the verandah, where Stuart had nodded off reading the *Sunday Times*.

'Hello,' Hamish panted into the phone.

There was a brief silence the other side.

'Howzit.' A male voice, then laughter. 'You thought it was a girl!' said Raymond.

'Hello, Ray,' sighed Hamish.

'Don't worry, I won't keep you.' His good-natured stable friend was still laughing. 'I just wanted to know if you gonna come to my birthday next week. We're having a party at my place – well, my folks' place, obviously.'

'Well, unless this girl phones and asks me on a date, I'll definitely be there.'

'China, you know that's not how it works,' said the younger and more skilful courter of women. 'Why not just give her a bell and ask her out? Bring her to my party.'

'It's complicated.' Hamish gave a brief summary of the situation. 'I don't even have her number.'

'Sure, but you're hardly brave when it comes to chasing pretty ladies. Jissus, Jane left for Australia thinking you wanted to be her brother.'

'Jane never liked me that way,' complained Hamish.

'Yes, she did!' howled Raymond. 'A few years ago she had a lank *huge* crush on you – everyone knew, except you. Obviously.'

'Shit.'

'Yup. Anyway, I need to invite some other okes and ladies. I hope whatshername calls you – I'll check you next week Saturday. Six o'clock – all you need to bring is a huge present for me.' He rang off.

Hamish wandered back outside to complete his tennis drubbing, which was all the more severe because Roger had just been harangued by the neighbour.

Later that evening Hamish was trying and failing to bring his mind to bear on an Afrikaans essay while the rest of the family watched the M-NET movie. At about half-past eight the phone rang. He looked up briefly, but his name wasn't called so his eyes returned to the page, which still contained only his name, the date and the heading: 'Die karakter van Saul Barnard'.

Ek gee nie 'n kak nie vir die karakter van Saul fokken Barnard, he wrote on the page and then crumpled it up.

'Hamish?' His mother walked into his bedroom. 'Reggie's on the phone for you.'

Hamish went cold and hot. As he walked through the family room to the study where the phone lived, Julia whooped, 'Oooooo, it's Reggie on the phone, Hamish, ooooooh!'

'Shut up, Julia!' he spat. 'Hello?' he said into the phone.

'Hello, Hamish,' said a sad voice. 'How's it going, old pal?'

A spike through his guts.

'It's going fine, thanks … old … pal.' He said with emphasis. 'You don't sound so happy.'

An hour later, Stuart stepped into the study to tell his son it was time to ring off. Through laughter and tears, Hamish and Reggie had rehashed the depth of every mutual memory.

As he lay in his bed later that evening, his Afrikaans essay not even begun, Hamish felt uncomfortable. He was infatuated by Reggie, but no matter how much he played over their conversation, he could find no indication that she felt the same – she kept calling him 'old pal' or 'oldest friend'. His analysis of the call led him to believe that she had phoned to remember her mother and the happy times of a period in her life that was filled with love and safety. He had no idea when or even if he'd hear from her again. She'd refused to give him her grandparents' number. The only reason she'd managed to phone at all was because they'd gone out for the evening.

There was so much that he wanted to know. Top of that list was whether she had a boyfriend, but every question he'd asked about her current life had been deftly deflected.

23

Iolanthe – a Gilbert and Sullivan musical.

Auditions at 14h00 on Tuesday in the Green Room. The boys of the College will combine with the girls of Brighton College to continue the fine tradition of Gilbert and Sullivan musicals at Trinity.

The notice was pinned on all the house boards. Hamish felt a flutter of delight as he walked into the common room on the first day of his Matric year. He remembered little of the tasks of his life unless they were committed to paper, and then he had to remember to look at his list, and then he had to remember where his diary was. There were, however, some things Hamish never forgot: rugby practice, riding lessons, concerts and play auditions.

That Wednesday afternoon, Hamish was the first to arrive in the Green Room. Mr Danhauser, who was in charge of the music side of the play, was playing a Beethoven piano sonata as he waited for the prospective thespians. He ceased his practice as Hamish entered and smiled somewhat mournfully.

'Hello, Hamish.'

'Hello, sir. You don't look very happy, sir,' observed Hamish. There was a level of informality between the master and the six boys who took

Music as a subject.

Mr Danhauser was a man who loved Beethoven, Tchaikovsky, Bartok, Stravinsky and Bach. He enjoyed rock and some pop.

'I hate Gilbert and Sullivan,' he confessed quietly. 'It's too much for my Afrikaner blood.' His fingers played the first few bars of the opening chorus for the fairies. 'Plinky plinky plinky,' he sang in a high falsetto.

Hamish laughed. 'But there'll be girls, sir!'

'That is the biggest problem of all!' Mr Danhauser moaned. 'In about ten minutes, every tone-deaf brute in this school is going to come through that door – suddenly interested in becoming an opera star.' He sighed dramatically. 'Then I'm going to have to get them to concentrate enough to sing in four parts while their hormones are telling them to do God-knows-what to the female members of the cast.'

Traditionally, the female parts in Trinity Gilbert and Sullivan pro-ductions had been performed by boys with unbroken voices. Now, for the first time, actual females would be performing the soprano and alto parts – which had resulted in a hitherto unseen enthusiasm for Gilbert and Sullivan, and serious competition for places in the cast.

'The girls aren't coming today are they, sir?' Hamish was alarmed.

'Good God, no.' Mr Danhauser shook his head in disgust. 'Can you imagine trying to make the boys sing while they gawk at the poor girls like a bunch of slavering jackals? No, we will audition them separately.'

'Can I do my audition now?'

Mr Danhauser played a note. 'Sing this,' he said sarcastically. 'For most of the Philistines, that's all I can hope for.'

Hamish frowned. 'Is that all?'

The teacher took a copy of the music from the top of the piano, opened it and handed it to Hamish. 'See if you can read this – a half-musical monkey could manage.'

Hamish sang the part well enough.

'That's fine,' said Mr Danhauser. 'Some notes are a bit high for you, so we'll have to do a bit of work on them, but this is the right part for you.'

'What part is it, sir?'

At that point, other boys began drifting into the room.

'Watch the noticeboard over the course of the week. You can go now.'

Hamish, thus dismissed, slipped out through a side door leading to the stage as a shove of young men made their way in through the main door – most of them hadn't seen the inside of the Green Room since their prep-school days.

The cacophony of young men's voices faded as Hamish clicked the door closed. The backstage area had a unique smell that made him feel tremendously excited. He walked into the middle of the stage and looked out.

The parquet floor of the hall had been polished during the Christmas holidays and reflected the afternoon light streaming through the windows. The walls were panelled with wooden honour boards – academic geniuses and head boys' names immortalised in golden engraving. Hamish knew that he would never feature, but that the Fraser name would appear courtesy of his brother's brain at least.

Hamish climbed a ladder fixed to the wall stage right, the rungs ancient and worn in the middle by countless hands and feet. The ladder led through a narrow hole in the concrete mezzanine ledge from which the curtains were operated. Hamish paused on the ledge and laughed as he remembered the opening night of the previous year's play.

Operation of the red-velvet curtain had been the preserve of Stuart Moses, who had jealously guarded his domain. At the appropriate time, Moses would climb off the mezzanine onto the curtain's counterweight. The curtain would rise as he plummeted to ground level, holding on to the rope for dear life. Mr Morris (backstage manager) had formally retired young Moses when the opening night of *The Merchant of Venice* had ended before it began: the groundsman and his maintenance team had spent the best part of two hours trying to extract Stuart Moses from the gap between the ledge and the wall after puberty had made him too large for the job.

From the mezzanine, Hamish climbed a ladder angled up to a narrow catwalk suspended directly above the stage. In Form II, he'd been lowered from here on a swing for his performance as the Teen Angel in *Grease*. Rapturous applause had followed as the girls' chorus carried him off in his white-satin suit.

In the middle of the catwalk was another vertical ladder. Hamish climbed it and walked gingerly along a thin ledge to a platform about two storeys above the main stage. Two windows – one facing west and the other north – opened out onto the red tiles of the roof. The northern window looked through the foliage of the massive oak trees surrounding the prep-school playing fields. Hamish loved the eye-level view of the foliage – like a wilderness suspended above the mayhem of the city.

Over the years, industrious backstage crews had furnished the platform with old cushions and chairs. Stuart Moses and his ilk had even managed to install a kettle and secret stash of coffee, biscuits, cigarettes and a bottle of First Watch whisky. This was the refuge where the backstage boys cosseted themselves for a smoke and a drink while the rest of the school roared inanely for the first XV – the sort of space a few masters knew about but left alone out of sympathy for the harmlessness of the Stuart Moseses of the world.

Sitting on the west-facing window sill, Hamish found himself reminiscing about his experiences on the stage. He'd won a cameo award for his performance in *Raiders of the Lost Aardvark*, the house play in Form I. In the house music competition when he was in Form IV, Iverson had performed *The Lion Sleeps Tonight* and Hamish had delivered a comic performance dressed as a lion, his high falsetto rendition of the chorus causing apoplectic laughter.

Offstage, he remained desperately shy with strangers and unable to look women in the eye. He hated meeting new people. When he stepped onto the stage, however, the audience invisible behind the blinding lights, he had a confidence that made him feel like a totally different person. He felt not one flutter of fear and he hated leaving the stage. Trinity plays normally enjoyed a five-day run, and Hamish felt bereft for weeks after they ended.

His time on the stage hadn't always been a triumph though. Every year there was a fund-raising event for the Matric dance called Mr Trinity – a glorified fashion show attended by hordes of young women who came to laugh, shout and, every so often, swoon. There were two competitions in Mr Trinity – one for the Form Is and IIs, and one for the Form IIIs and up. Hamish had entered every year. In Form I, he'd thought he might have a chance – the girls at the stables had said he was cute but they hadn't added that he was cute for a ten year old, not a young teenager.

Each competitor had to arrive on stage three times: in school uniform, in sports kit and in formal wear. Displaying a continued and chronic lack of social understanding, Hamish had chosen riding as his sport. For originality and courage, he could not have been faulted, but for an understanding of fashion and young women, he could only have been further from the mark if he'd chosen ballet.

There was polite applause when he'd arrived in his uniform, Madonna's 'Vogue' blasting over the PA system. But when Hamish Fraser – all five feet and one inch – arrived for the sports section mounted on a hobby horse in his skin-tight jodhpurs, boots, spurs, tweed jacket and giant riding helmet complete with full head harness, the audience was stunned into a silence so complete that the DJ turned off the music thinking that an emergency announcement was about to be made. Hamish cantered to the front of the stage and back, his footfalls on the wooden panels the only sound.

At the back of the hall, in the gallery for the parents waiting to take their children home, tears of laughter, sadness and frustration ran down Stuart's face.

Next to him, Johnny Goodenough's father whispered, 'The boy's got balls, I'll give him that.'

Hamish himself was flabbergasted not to have made it into the final round, even after the debacle of the formal section, in which he'd worn a rather-too-shiny dinner jacket. He'd left his shoes behind and thus borrowed some from James MacDonald – four sizes too big for him. When he tripped over his own feet halfway down the ramp, the audience had exploded into laughter. To his credit, Hamish had stood up, removed the shoes and bowed deeply, which had endeared him somewhat.

In four attempts at Mr Trinity, Hamish had never made it into the final ten. In Form I, Paul Simpson had won the junior competition. Later in their Matric year, Simpson, the head boy, would enter again, walking away with a second victory – sporting the body of Adonis and a jaw squarer than Superman's. Hamish would win a prize for the most consistent entrant.

The sound of Stuart Moses yelling at his junior backstage crew in the wings below snapped Hamish out of his reverie, and he climbed back down to ground level, escaping unnoticed through a side entrance.

At break a week later, an unusually large crowd of all ages gathered at the music noticeboard to see if their names were on the cast list. Hamish stood behind the group, watching the good and great of the College, many making their first-ever visits to the Music section.

'Oh, come on, man!' moaned Wayne Johnson, superb sportsman but appalling singer. 'That gayboy Music teacher's always hated me!'

Paul Simpson was at the front of the line being slapped on the back by his sidekick, Andrew Marsdorf. Simpson had grown to a height of six feet and two inches, his dark hair was perfectly in place all the time, and he had the easy manner of someone without a trouble in the world. His elevation to the position of head boy had been as inevitable as the rising sun.

In theory, the prefect body was constituted by a voting process. (Hamish Fraser had received two votes – one from Roger and one from himself.) In reality, the staff used the votes as a vague guideline. There were only two people in the world – Hamish and his mother – who'd been surprised when his name hadn't been read out by Mr McAdams at the announcement assembly.

Hamish had had a chance to prove his leadership qualities as director of Iverson in the previous year's house music competition. It had taken all of one practice for the house choir to mutiny. Salim Naidoo, two years younger than Hamish, had led a deputation of disgruntled boys to the housemaster's office and told him, in no uncertain terms, that while they cared deeply for the reputation of Iverson House, they were unable to continue under the abusive and dictatorial baton of Hamish Fraser.

The conductor was duly summoned to face his detractors.

'Fraser, I'm hearing some pretty disturbing things here,' began Mr Huddle. 'Naidoo, please repeat what you said to me.'

'Well, sir, Fraser called us names and said mean things,' began Naidoo.

'Yes, yes, you've said all that – what did he say?'

'I was a bit late, sir – because I had an extra-Maths lesson. When I arrived for the rehearsal, Fraser said, "You, Naidoo, are a portly and imbecilic disgrace to Iverson House." I had to go and look up "portly", sir, and it means fat, sir.'

'Did you say this to Naidoo, Fraser?'

'Well … eh … yes, sir, I did …' Hamish stammered, 'but he *was* late!'

'That has nothing to do with his intelligence or mass!' The housemaster was testy. 'Piper says you called him a "grubby little wastrel".'

'And he said I look like I'm sucking an orange all the time,' complained Jamie Piper, a Form I boy with a gum line proceeding with such alacrity that his teeth were barely visible.

'He also said we sound like a bunch of tone-deaf chainsaws,' concluded Naidoo.

'Sir, they sound terrible!' complained Hamish.

'Shut up, Fraser!' yelled Mr Huddle. He turned to the motley crew of Iverson House musicians. 'Thank you, boys, you may go.'

They all turned to leave.

'Not you, Fraser!'

Hamish waited for his choir to depart.

'Fraser, you are an anomaly.' The housemaster leant back on his chair, the bridge of his nose clasped between thumb and forefinger.

Hamish considered the avocado-green carpet and thought how his mother would never have allowed such an abomination in her home.

The teacher sighed and sat forward. 'Presumably you want to amount to something in this life. God knows you're involved in enough activities at this school – probably to avoid actual academics. I've yet to meet a teacher who thinks you're performing to anything like what your IQ says you should be. Do you want to be a prefect next year?'

Hamish looked startled. 'Of course, sir!'

'Fraser, I would like you to cast your mind back to your Form I year and ask yourself if David Swart would have ever referred to anyone – let alone someone he was hoping might vote for him to be a prefect – as a wastrel sucking an orange peel?'

'Well, sir, I …'

'Shut up, Fraser – that was entirely rhetorical.' Mr Huddle frowned at the skinny Form IV, whose braces carried the remnants of his breakfast. 'Fraser, I realise your time here hasn't been the easiest. Try and remember that it is probably the same for many of the boys younger than you.'

'Yes, sir.'

'Now take this and go away.' The housemaster proffered a slip for the Friday session of hard labour.

Hamish took the words from Mr Huddle to heart and managed to coax a reasonable performance from the Iverson House choir, but Naidoo, Piper and all the others remained scarred by their initial trials with Hamish. Come voting day, his name was very far from their minds – perhaps fearing dictatorial consequences should angry Fraser be granted the honour of a blue pin-striped prefects' suit.

At the Music noticeboard, a few Form IIIs shoved some Form Is out of the way in their quest to see if they too would be part of the Peers chorus, oblivious to Hamish – two years their senior.

There were two names of interest to Hamish on the cast list.

Robert Gumede was appended to the part of the Lord Chancellor, comic baritone. As far as Hamish was concerned, Gumede was the greatest comedian Trinity had ever schooled. Hamish was also fairly sure he'd never heard the fellow sing a note, baritone or otherwise.

Looking further down the list, Hamish's heart leapt slightly as he saw his name next to the part of Strephon, an Arcadian Shepherd – also baritone.

The first rehearsal was set for the following Tuesday evening. Much to the disgust of the male cast, the first fortnight of practice was going to be an all-male affair. Mr Danhauser and Mr McAdams, who was to be the director, agreed that the music needed to be thoroughly learnt by the boys before they introduced oestrogen to the situation. The lead roles had extra rehearsals to learn their solos and Hamish set himself to the task with great gusto.

For Mr Danhauser, those first rehearsals were a trial. About half of the thirty boys in the men's chorus were choristers used to singing in parts. The lack of singing experience was nevertheless a small part of Mr Danhauser's troubles. In 1994, at an all-boys school, the terms 'faggot', 'moffie', 'gayboy', 'pooftah', 'queer' and myriad others were often applied to members of the choir or orchestra, and the rumour mill was quick to apply such to Mr Danhauser, as an unmarried Music master. Hamish himself was not above using these insulting epithets; he thought, like most of the school and despite his conversation with David Swart five years previously, that homosexuality was a sin, or at the very least not a good idea.

On the other hand, Mr Danhauser was Hamish's favourite teacher by a country mile – enough for Hamish to pray in chapel on Wednesdays that if Mr Danhauser was gay, then might God make him less so.

Mr Danhauser was entirely used to facing a sea of covertly hostile faces. Any chorus member who felt he might misbehave at rehearsals because of some perceived 'homosexual weakness' on the part of the choirmaster was to be thoroughly disabused of the notion by the end of the first practice.

Mr Danhauser stood at six feet and one inch. He wasn't muscled but was blessed of a naturally slim physique that, had he taken an interest in it, would have gained condition quickly. Such vanities did not bother him, however. He had a full head of slowly greying hair that was parted on the left and always neat. His smile was infectious, because when he was genuinely amused, his whole face joined his mouth in an expression of joy. He also had a vicious temper set off by a short fuse.

Dylan Crane made the first mistake.

The male cast filed in ones and twos into the Green Room for their first rehearsal. They were largely senior boys, because there were no unbroken voice parts. The fifteen tenors consisted of four actual tenors from the choir, five altos and a few surprisingly good non-choir members. The basses were all Form IVs and Matrics.

'Good evening,' said Mr Danhauser, walking around to the front of the piano.

The boys, seated on ancient wooden benches, stared up at him as he gave a pile of music to a young tenor and asked him to hand the scores around.

'Many of you will not have sung in parts before and, much like in sports, you need to warm up your voices before you can sing properly.' He sang the first exercise. 'Me me me me me, ma ma ma ma ma, mo mo mo mo mo.' Then he played a chord and, led by the choir boys in their ranks, the male cast began to sing their warm-up.

All except Dylan Crane, who found the whole thing rather ridiculous.

'How would this fag know about sports practice?' He whispered to Bradford York behind his music.

Mr Danhauser stopped playing. He stood up from the piano and pointed at Dylan Crane.

'What is your name?'

'Crane,' mumbled the teenager with practised, oafish insolence.

'Speak up,' snapped Mr Danhauser, the corners of his mouth turning down.

Eager faces looked on – all the boys had seen teachers bested by class-mates with quick, cheeky wits, their insolence dissolving the class into ripples of laughter.

'Crane,' said the boy, undeterred. 'Dylan Crane.'

'Why are you here, Crane?' Mr Danhauser raised his voice.

The boy shrugged his shoulders.

'Does that mean you don't know?'

Dumb insolence.

The choirmaster's temper snapped. 'You will speak to me when I ask you a question!' he roared, smashing his hand down on the piano lid. A clay vase of nasturtiums leapt up and then shattered on the floor.

Crane's eyes widened.

'WHY ARE YOU HERE?!' bellowed the choirmaster.

'To be in the play, I guess,' the boy mumbled.

Mr Danhauser launched himself across the room, his face stopping inches from the teenager's. Crane's head smacked into the sill behind him as he tried to avoid the teacher.

'If you have to GUESS why you are here, then I don't want you here!' Saliva flecked Crane's startled face. 'You can go and GUESS somewhere else. Get your arrogant foulness out of here and don't you dare come back.' The teacher remained with his face precisely where it was until Crane had no choice but to wriggle out from under Mr Danhauser's nose.

Thus ended Dylan Crane's brief foray into the world of operetta.

Mr Danhauser returned to the piano and straightened his tie. 'Would anyone else like to say anything?'

'Yoh!' said Robert Gumede, who was reclining in a chair near the back of the room. 'Not after that, sir. I think we'll just sing, if you don't mind.'

Mr Danhauser's face cracked a slight smile and the rehearsal continued without incident.

An hour later, Mr McAdams arrived to check on progress. He cast his eye around the room as the boys groaned through the first Peers' chorus.

'Where is Crane?' he asked as they burped the last note.

'He's guessing, sir,' said Robert Gumede, quick as a flash.

264

'What? What's he guessing?'

'That was the very question Mr Danhauser posed to Crane, sir, and the answer was unsatisfactory.'

After two weeks, Mr McAdams finally announced a combined rehearsal, along with a stern warning.

'You will all behave like gentlemen next week,' he began. 'The girls are going to be much more nervous than you boys – coming here will be intimidating for them.'

Hamish thought this a strange pronouncement. Terrified at the thought of singing in front of girls, he considered that if they were more nervous than he, they must be virtually catatonic.

'I expect you to act with chivalry, boys – as gentlemen to ladies.' He said the word 'ladies' with an exaggerated 'a', a wistful look glazing his eyes. 'You must remember to stand when the laaydees come into the room. Make sure they always have somewhere to sit and speak to them in a soothing manner – a laaydee loves to be soothed.'

The great day finally arrived. For the first time in most of their lives, the male cast was on time to a man – but for Hamish Fraser, who was delayed by a riding lesson. He walked into the hall ten minutes late, just as Mr McAdams launched into an in-depth treatise on the traditions of Gilbert and Sullivan. Mr Danhauser sat at the piano looking like he'd sooner be subjected to the rack than hear about the supposed virtues of Messrs G and S. So it was that the girls and boys were primed for a distraction.

Fraser provided it.

He opened the creaky hall door and strode in wearing a grubby pair of jodhpurs, spurs still fixed to his ankles. All eyes turned.

Mr McAdams turned to the latecomer.

'Fraser! What the hell are you wearing? This is not a ballet, boy – it's an operetta!'

The cast sniggered.

'They're my jodhpurs, sir,' said Hamish.

The sniggers turned to laughter.

'Your jodhpurs?' McAdams stared. 'Your *jodhpurs*? Have you taken to riding your horse to school? Is he tied up outside?'

Hamish opened his mouth to answer.

'Not a word!' snapped the headmaster. 'There are no horses in G and S, so make sure you don't pitch up looking like a jockey again.'

'I'm not a jockey, sir. I'm a show jumper,' replied Hamish as he scuttled to the stage and sat down next to Robert Gumede.

The boys and girls roared.

'Fraser, you sure know how to make an entrance,' Gumede whispered, shaking his head.

'Right, now that Muis Roberts has joined us, we can continue ...' Mr McAdams resumed his speech. When his lengthy history of G and S at Trinity was complete, he picked up a leather-bound notebook and fountain pen. 'Let us go through the plot of this great story and the players,' he said with great excitement. 'When your name is called, please stand up so that the rest of the cast can see who you are.'

As Mr McAdams droned on, Hamish's concentration drifted towards the line of females sitting on the stage. The first girl he noticed was a waif with lank, mousy hair, hunched shoulders and a severe case of freckles. Hamish thought she looked like a frightened rabbit. The next one to catch his eye, and that of many others, was a young woman leaning back on her hands. Angelica Constable would be playing the part of Celia – a fairy. Her shapely legs were covered in black tights, her high-arched feet in red dancing shoes. She wore a pale-blue T-shirt and the way she sat accentuated her extravagant bust. Her red lips were slightly parted below a thin, small nose and wide hazel eyes, her hair a mass of strawberry-blonde curls that reached down to the stage behind her. As Hamish stared at the apparition, he heard his name.

'Hamish Fraser – or Muis Roberts, the jockey over there – will be playing the part of Strephon, the Arcadian Shepherd. Stand up, Fraser.'

Hamish did as he was bid. He had failed to actually read the story or the plot of the comic opera, and while he had made a concerted effort to learn the music, he had no idea how the cast tied together. Mr McAdams's next words were therefore something of a surprise.

'Strephon is the son of Iolanthe and the Lord Chancellor – he is, consequently, half man and half fairy.'

'We can see which half is fairy!' blurted one of the older girls, and the rest of the cast laughed at him once again.

His humiliation thus complete, the rehearsal continued.

Eventually, some actual acting did happen. Iolanthe, Strephon's mother, played by a girl with a balletic disposition and kind smile, was sitting in a bucolic meadow as her son entered for his opening number. Frolicking across the stage in his jodhpurs, Hamish made his entrance from stage right, playing a make-believe flute.

The audience of cast members' giggling ceased as Strephon began to sing.

At seventeen-and-a-half years old, Hamish stood at five feet and five inches. Acne (not appalling, but unattractive) flecked his cheeks and his dark hair was unruly. But his voice had finally broken and the rich baritone that emanated from his bird-like frame was incongruous. The audience watched, captivated briefly by the straight-backed and powerful confidence with which Hamish embraced his effeminate role – a confidence that was entirely absent when he wasn't performing.

'Good morrow, good mother!' he boomed.

For the next rehearsal, the cast was split into two groups: the lead parts went through their scenes with Mr McAdams on the stage, while the rapidly ageing Mr Danhauser took the chorus to the Green Room, where he set to banging the piano until every note was engraved into the brains of the peers and fairies.

It was during that Thursday night that Hamish was introduced to the woman who was to play Phyllis, and with whom he would have to feign a mutual love. On sighting her, Hamish knew this would require a Tony Award-winning performance.

In the scene, Phyllis emerges from stage left blowing on a flageolet and dancing lightly over to where her betrothed stares wistfully into the golden light, contemplating a life of marital bliss. So soft is her entrance that Strephon is not supposed to notice her until she begins singing.

This, with the best acting in the world, was impossible because Natalie Smith thundered onto the stage with all the grace of an enraged bison, shaking the very foundations of the old school hall. Her massive lungs forced air into her flageolet at such a pressure that half the dogs in Northcliff set to mournful howling. She came to a halt in front of Hamish, a full two inches taller and at least a stone heavier, and adopted a pose resembling Wayne Johnson just before he smashed an opponent to the ground in a rugby match.

There she stood, dressed in tight-fitting black running shorts, her legs set wide apart like two pillars that even Sampson would have failed to shift. Bulging quadriceps exited the shorts and almost enveloped her kneecaps. Hockey socks rested around a set of elephantine ankles only marginally narrower than the powerful calf muscles above. Affixed to the size-nine feet was a pair of hockey boots. Much like Hamish's, Natalie Smith's teeth were covered in steel. She had, however, failed to remove her supper from them, and Hamish wondered if his betrothed was perhaps still mid-meal.

At her approach, Hamish took a step backwards and lifted his arms reflexively in defence. As she bared her chompers in preparation for her first line, Hamish's first attempt at demonstrating lust failed.

'Fraser!' yelled Mr McAdams from his seat in the front row. 'What are you doing, boy? Stop backing away like a startled puppy. She won't bite!'

'Don't believe him, Fraser,' hissed Gumede from the wings just behind Hamish. 'She's going to eat you.'

Natalie Smith, thankfully, did not hear this as she stomped back to the wings for a second go.

'A little less blasting on that whistle, I think, Natalie,' suggested Mr

McAdams. 'In fact, this time just pretend to play it.'

The second time round, Hamish held it together marginally better – until Gumede whispered, 'Yoh, she's hungry for you,' which made Hamish start to giggle.

'Fraser! What is so bloody funny?' yelled Mr McAdams, thoroughly irritated.

'Sorry, sir. Nothing, sir,' replied Hamish.

The headmaster stalked up to the stage in time to see Gumede disappear behind a curtain. He needed no further evidence.

'Goomeedee!' he yelled. 'You and Fraser can enjoy two hours of hard labour on Friday – see how funny you find that!'

On the third attempt, it became apparent why it was that the least fairy-like member of the female (or male) cast had been chosen to play the part of Phyllis, the most difficult female singing roll. Hamish's tight-jawed expression went slack as the first note escaped Natalie Smith's cavernous buccal cavity. The voice of a La Scala-quality soprano blasted the hair on his forehead backwards.

Hamish looked forward to the thrice-weekly rehearsals as much as he looked forward to rugby practices. They began with supper in the dining hall – the quality of which had nothing to do with Hamish's enjoyment. Mr Aaron, the Trinity caterer, produced more sweat during an afternoon cooking session than a herd of horses galloping the Durban July. This he dripped liberally into the serving trays of rubbery beef, frozen vegetables and semi-mashed potatoes, which were slopped onto plates with the care one might devote to the disposal of sewage. While the quality of the food belied the august school's reputation, the company at supper was excellent.

Hamish made sure to sit near Robert Gumede, because all the interesting girls in the play, including the divine Angelica Constable, found themselves drawn into the confident young man's ambit. The atmosphere was accepting, and the cast an eclectic mix that allowed the half-man, half-fairy to add the odd off-the-wall comment without causing offence.

Hamish seldom lingered at the table, preferring to arrive in the hall while it was still quiet. He loved the smell of the stage – the paint, the old curtains, the dusty gangways and balconies, the rough, unplastered stone walls and the bits of old props left from countless productions. While he had no real love for G and S, Hamish appreciated the sense of history – even if it wasn't particularly relevant to the lives of the boys and girls performing it.

Being around the girls of the cast also filled him with a sense of delight, though he seldom managed to hold anything but the most perfunctory conversation with any of them. He was, like all of the other boys, fascinated by the figure of Angelica Constable, who knew full well her effect. Initially, Hamish couldn't figure out why she hadn't been cast as Phyllis – he'd have had no trouble at all pretending to be in love with her. But her voice was thin, nasal and raspy, and she'd probably have been better off saying her words than attempting to sing them.

Eight weeks into the rehearsals, the play was beginning to take shape. Everybody had a vague understanding of where to be and when, and the music was coming along relatively well – the chorus of young men tended to bellow out the bass part and ignore the tenor bits, but there was still time to rectify that.

There were seldom more than three staff members at rehearsal, and all were fully occupied. Mr McAdams directed, Mr Danhauser banged on the piano in a state of frustrated disgust and paid little heed to the cast not directly involved in each scene on stage, and the backstage-manager Mr Morris's sixty-a-day nicotine habit necessitated his absence from the building on a more or less permanent basis.

Commotions behind the wings often had Mr McAdams frothing at the mouth, his thin white hair aquiver. Sometimes it was Stuart Moses berating a naughty junior for trying to leap onto the curtain counterweight. Once, Alan Samuels detached the Arcadian backdrop from its moorings while hiding from Mr Morris, whose lighter he had secretly modified (causing the master a nasty singed eyebrow). The massive curtain rod gave Samuels a concussion for his troubles.

It was also entirely common for two cast members to be caught in a clinch.

For the cast, the absence of authority was most utilised for illicit liaison – the main reason most had auditioned in the first place. Couples melted into darkened bunkers, galleries and attics using myriad hatches and ladders.

'Busted, Masterson, you scaly oke!' yelled Albert Masina from the orchestra pit one Tuesday evening as Robert Gumede was delivering a brilliant rendition of the Lord Chancellor's insomnia song. Masina had spotted Mark Masterson with Melissa Flamond (both aged sixteen).

'Oh, for godsakes!' yelled Mr McAdams. 'What the hell is going on under there?' He stormed to the edge of the pit and glared into it. 'Masterson, leave that poor girl alone, you depraved villain. Have an hour of hard labour on Friday! And you, Masina, are a beastly voyeur. You can have two hours.'

Hamish fantasised about being caught in a clinch with one of the fairies, and had on more than one occasion fantasised about being cosied up with Angelica Constable in the privacy of the platform above the stage. But thus far no girl had shown the slightest interest, apart from Natalie Smith, who'd winked at him, which made him careful never to be cornered.

One evening Hamish was onstage practising the final scene with Natalie. They were holding hands and singing their final number, Natalie's magnificent soprano intermingling with flying bits of saliva and orthodontic jetsam, when there was a commotion from the top platform – a startled yelp rather than the usual good-natured cackling that normally accompanied a 'busting'. Then a gasp – feminine. The noise was loud enough to arrest the performance and cause the orchestra to cease.

'What in the blazes is going on up there?' Mr McAdams, in something of a panic about the imminent opening night, bellowed from the audience.

Hamish looked up, but was blinded by the suspended lights. Loud scuffling emanated from behind the glare. Feet and hands grasped and slipped on ladders. By the time the headmaster had made it onto the stage, all was quiet.

Mr McAdams lost his patience. 'From now on, all of you – boys and girls – will sit in the audience for the duration of rehearsals. You will only move between the stage and where I can see you!'

One by one the cast filed out sullenly from behind the wings and sat down on the beaten-up chairs in the hall. A few of them were whispering excitedly.

'Please continue, Mr Danhauser,' Mr McAdams instructed the Music director, who was standing with furrowed brow and poised baton.

The orchestra took up their instruments and began afresh. With Herculean effort, Hamish re-enacted his love for Natalie.

Saucy news took very little time to spread.

The next day, the Frasers arrived at school at the normal time and Hamish made his way to the Memorial Quadrangle. As was his normal routine, he placed his bag as close to the choir gallery as possible so as to retrieve it quickly after assembly, after which he would peruse the notice boards. During the rugby season, this served the purpose of revealing the coming Saturday's team sheets; out of rugby season, it was simply something to do rather than find someone to talk to. Over the course of four-and-a-bit years, Hamish had perfected the art of looking busy so as not to appear friendless.

That day, he arrived with five minutes to spare before the bell. A knot of Matric and Form IV boys in the *Iolanthe* cast, clearly in something of a flutter, was gathered in the corner of the quad. Hamish had gained some status among these boys because of his lead role so he wandered over to see what the fuss was about. In the middle of the ten or so boys sat Andrew Marsdorf, speaking in conspiratorial tones.

'... then I climbed up that ladder – I was gonna have a quick smoke on the platform while Fraser and that ogre chick did their thing.' He looked up to see Hamish observing from behind the group. 'And I could hear there was someone up there already.' He paused and lowered his voice as a breeze blew through the cloisters and sent a few leaves into a flurry. 'Two people actually – a guy and a chick. And they were obviously not doing their Maths homework.'

There were a few giggles.

'So I kept climbing really quietly – knowing I was going to bust some oke giving it to some slut.'

The boys leant in unconsciously.

'And I wasn't wrong. I stuck my head over the ladder. "Busted!" I said and flicked the light switch.' He whistled and shook his head. 'You okes won't fucken believe who it was!'

'Who?' demanded an impatient Form IV.

'It was Angelica Constable,' Marsdorf said.

A ripple of appreciation and envy ran through the group. All of them longed to be caught in flagrante delicto with Angelica Constable – grabbing her would make a boy an instant legend.

'And you know who she was with?'

The boys all held their breaths in anticipation, wondering if they were perhaps standing next to the soon-to-be-crowned legend. Marsdorf shook his head.

'It was Robert Goo-fucken-meedee.'

'Fuck!' said Jerry Preston. 'Angelica with a zot!'

Incredulity echoed through the knot. Suitably convinced that his story had shocked, Marsdorf continued.

'And it's not like he tied her down or anything. He was sitting on that fucked-up old couch and she was sitting on his lap – he had his hands up her fucken shirt!'

'What a slut,' said Neil Long to nods of agreement, the sentiment in the group now edged with malice.

It would be too strong to suggest that Hamish had forged a friendship with Gumede over the years. He had tried, in his way, but was fairly convinced that Gumede, like most of the boys in his class, didn't care much for him. Regardless, Hamish admired Gumede for his obvious intelligence, talent and inability to give two shits for convention or authority (for his part, Hamish was somewhat cowed by authority). Gumede lived entirely by his own moral compass. He manned up to his indiscretions and accepted that if he chose to rock the boat, he would have to accept the waves.

One day, late in their Form IV year, the six boys of Miss Mkhize's Zulu class had been waiting for their teacher after break and had gathered in the sun next to a window that opened onto the gardens of the McCarthy Quadrangle. As three Sixth Form girls had walked over the lawn on their way to the Science laboratories, Gumede had wolf-whistled.

'Hello, sweet babes. Come over here and observe this fine piece of black magnificence!' He'd raised his arms to show his large, finely chiselled biceps.

Hitherto hidden by an exuberant green bush, Mr McAdams had exploded across the quad as fast as his ageing legs would carry him, appearing suddenly in front of the windows. The girls had made to move off.

'Please remain where you are, laaydees. This sort of unchivalrous behaviour will not be tolerated at Trinity College.' He'd glared through the window, his beaky nose, white hair and pale skin resembling a snowy crow. 'Which one of you reprobates whistled at those laaydees?'

For some reason he stared at Hamish, who had blanched.

Gumede stepped forward. 'It was me, sir.'

'Goomeedee! I might have known it was you. You are a constant disappointment.' The headmaster shook his head sadly – he'd rather hoped it was someone he liked less. 'Who do you think you are, whistling at those laaydees? Hey? They are human beings – not pieces of meat at a butcher's shop! This College prides itself on producing gentlemen who protect women – not scoundrels who leave here ready to defile anything that catches their lascivious eyes!'

It must be understood that Robert Gumede had stood in front of angry teachers all his school career – but the headmaster's passion made him back off from the open window.

274

'I can't even speak to such a despicable creature right now. You will come and see me in my office after school!' Mr McAdams stalked off to where the girls were standing. 'I'm so sorry for this shocking act of ungentlemanly behaviour – you can rest assured that I will deal with it swiftly and that Trinity College is a place where laaydees can feel protected and cared for.'

Sometime during the altercation, Miss Mkhize had arrived.

'Sit down,' she said sternly from the door.

As the class did so, Miss Mkhize walked round to the front of her desk, leant back on it and folded her arms. She looked at her pupils silently for some time, anger bubbling.

'Let me tell all of you *boys* something. Because that is what you are – *boys*.' She stood up and tapped her sternum. 'I don't *need* any man to protect me or make a safe space for me – I am not vulnerable, nor do I need or want any "gentleman" to look after me!'

Hamish realised with growing incredulity that this rant was directed at her boss – whose speech on chivalry he'd thought thoroughly rousing – and not at Robert Gumede.

'Do you all understand me?' She looked from one boy to the other.

Hamish nodded, despite his confusion.

'Yoh!' Gumede said from the desk closest to her. He raised his eyebrows. 'Ma'am don't like no old white McAdams!'

Miss Mkhize's right arm shot out like striking mamba, her open palm collecting Gumede over his left ear. The class gasped at the meaty thwack. Gumede sat stunned for a few moments and then coughed once, not daring to move. Miss Mkhize turned to the board and picked up a piece of chalk.

'We are doing palatalisation today – make some notes.'

Every time Hamish had spent time at hard labour for various minor infractions of the school code, Robert Gumede had been there. Together, they had sanded desks, cleaned bilges and dug trenches. They had chatted about rugby, school, music and women. The black boy had shared bits of his life growing up in a relatively salubrious neighbourhood of

Soweto. His father's name was often in the news – a senior negotiator in the talks that would eventually result in the South African constitution. Gumede had also shared his views on South Africa, authority, Trinity and social conventions. In many ways his attitudes resembled those of David Swart, although they were far less tempered.

So when Hamish Fraser, a senior (if somewhat unremarkable) Trinity pupil heard the story of Angelica Constable and Robert Gumede as told by Andrew Marsdorf, he felt a hot anger.

'Why is Angelica a slut?' His voice cut through the group and they swung round to look at him.

'What?' the great raconteur looked at Hamish and then shot a glance at Neil Long.

'What makes Angelica Constable a slut?' Hamish's mouth was turned down at the corners, quivering slightly.

'Well, she was …' Long tailed off.

'She was *what*?' Hamish was beginning to shake.

'She was sitting on Goomeedee, and he had his hand in her shirt,' snapped Marsdorf, irritated that his great revelation should be thus sullied.

'You've both done that. Is your girlfriend a slut?' Hamish glared at Long, whose girlfriend was Marsdorf's cousin.'

'That's not what I meant!' Long snapped.

'Well, what the fuck did you mean?' exploded Hamish.

'Goomeedee is black!' hissed Long.

Silence. Some of the boys nodded and others looked at their shoes. Some walked quietly away.

'That's what I thought you meant, you prick.'

'Don't talk to us like that – everyone knows you're a kaffir-boetie.' Marsdorf loomed over Hamish, and shoved the smaller boy in the chest.

Hamish, incensed, took a swing – a right cross aimed at Marsdorf's nose. It takes experience to land an effective punch to the nose of a much larger foe. Hamish Fraser was not experienced – in fact, this was the first punch he'd ever thrown – and it didn't come close.

Marsdorf swayed slightly as the small fist harmlessly passed his right cheek. He jabbed up into Hamish's exposed right ribs. The smaller boy collapsed to the black slate, an unspeakable pain rendering him breathless. Neil Long leant over him.

'Fuck you, Fraser – why you such a weirdo? Just because you do Zulu you think the zots won't stab you just as quickly as they'll stab anyone else? Don't fucken kid yourself.'

Marsdorf and Long disappeared as the bell began to peal in the tower above.

Hamish hauled himself onto the bench and allowed the pain to recede.

Later that day, Hamish saw Gumede in Zulu class and said nothing to him, but noticed an absence of the bigger boy's normal ebullience. Hamish longed to tell his only black teacher about the morning's incident and the circumstances leading to it, but felt the situation wasn't his to share.

The story of Marsdorf's discovery spread around the school with predictable speed and proportionate inaccuracy. By the end of the day, Robert Gumede and Angelica Constable had been caught having wild sex, and there was more than one boy who went home convinced that Marsdorf had saved the innocent and beautiful Constable girl from the lustful intentions of the Zulu. A whisper of rape drifted through the cloistered quadrangles.

Hamish arrived home that evening sporting a liver-coloured bruise over the bottom-right of his ribcage. He was angry and sad as he sat to do his homework – an English essay. After an hour he'd written two nonsensical paragraphs.

Stuart arrived in his room just after six, dressed in a pair of shorts and a T-shirt, expecting to catch the usual barrage of rugby balls.

'Hello, Dad,' said Hamish.

The fact that his son hadn't come to fetch him for passing practice indicated to Stuart a serious problem. Hamish said nothing for a while, and then stood and winced.

'Don't think I can play rugby today, Dad.'

'Oh dear,' sighed his father. 'What did you do to get thumped today? Come and tell me about it.'

The two walked out to the porch outside the front door and sat on the steps overlooking the rose garden. Caroline was picking late-summer blooms while Julia fed the budgies and murderous lovebirds in the aviary as Hamish began his account.

'... then, while I was lying on the floor, he said, "... you think the zots won't stab you just as quickly as they'll stab anyone else",' concluded Hamish.

'Phew,' whistled Stuart.

They said nothing for a few minutes, listening to the clicking of the sprinkler and the snipping of the secateurs. The budgies squawked as the lovebirds chased them off their food.

'And you're worried they're right – that you are nor perceived any differently from the other white guys,' Stuart assessed.

'I guess so,' replied Hamish. 'It's funny, it felt good to be called a kaffir-boetie in some ways – like some sort of honour badge.' Hamish touched his bruise. 'As I lay there on that cold black stone, I remembered visiting Rosie's place all those years ago and felt a sort of ... um ... pride, I guess.' He paused, looking at the sun disappearing behind a stately oak. 'But then also shame ... you know, I've hardly spoken to Ayanda since then and I've never been back to their beautiful home.' He touched his bruised ribcage and flinched. 'Anyway, anything those guys say is meaningless – they're just oxygen thieves and I don't give a damn what they think. I guess I'd just be honoured to be called a kaffir-boetie by the guys in my Zulu class.'

'You've never really given a toss what people think of you.'

Hamish took this as a compliment but knew it to be only partly true – he cared a lot about what some people thought about him.

'I'm a South African, Dad,' said Hamish. 'I want to be seen like that by other South Africans – I'd hate to be seen as just another racist white person.'

'Well, for what it's wurth, I don't think that's how you're seen at all, boy.'

'Ja, but … maybe those arseholes are right. At lunch, I sit with my Zulu classmates and sometimes they say a few things to me, but normally I just try and join in with whatever conversation they're having. I'm not sure why Robert should have much interest in my life, but it would be nice to think of him as my friend.'

'Have you ever invited him over here?' asked Stuart.

Hamish shook his head and shrugged. 'No – but that hardly puts him in a minority, does it?'

'I guess not.'

'I keep imagining him asking me to go to his place in Soweto. You know the kind of credibility that would give me? But then, I don't really have much desire to actually go to Soweto …'

'Did you say anything to him about the incident? Offer him your support?' asked Stuart.

Hamish shook his head and sighed. 'No. Maybe I should have – I just didn't know how.'

'Maybe you should tomorrow – he might really appreciate it.'

Presently Caroline arrived from the garden and sat down on the steps. Hamish gave her a brief rundown of the conversation, leaving out the bit about being punched.

'But, Hamish, you're a liberal. You're not a racist!' she said when he was finished, typically lenient of her son's myriad faults.

'I don't think I'm a racist,' Hamish replied, 'but I'm not a Zulu either.'

'You are a snob though,' said Stuart matter-of-factly.

'Stuart!' exclaimed Caroline.

'He is, and, my dear, in case it's escaped your notice, so are you!'

They sat quietly until Julia had finished with the birds. She picked up the well-loved rugby ball, scuffed by countless meetings with the rose bushes, and tossed a perfect torpedo pass at her brother. Hamish caught the ball and spun it back to her.

He smiled. 'At least someone's benefited from my obsession with this game.'

The next morning before roll-call, Hamish found Robert Gumede sitting on the lip of the Memorial Pond cramming for a *Macbeth* test.

'Sawubona, Robert,' said Hamish.

Gumede looked up, expressionless. 'Hello, Fraser,' he sighed. 'What's up?'

There was an awkward pause.

'I, eh, well … I'm not sure … I guess I just want you to know that I think it sucks what okes are saying about you.'

Gumede sniffed. 'You know I don't give a fuck what anyone in this shithole thinks about me.'

Hamish knew that he was included in the statement. It wasn't malicious, but it was emphatic.

'Ja, I know,' said Hamish, looking at the ground. 'Anyway, just thought I'd say it.' He turned to leave.

'But thanks, Fraser,' said Gumede.

The opening night of *Iolanthe* two weeks later was a triumph in some ways and not in others. It was certainly more amusing than anyone had intended it to be. Hamish Fraser was widely praised for his performance of Strephon. His depiction of the half-man, half-fairy was convincing and hilarious – he'd developed a technique for making his legs and torso look like they were moving in opposite directions. The final love duet with Natalie Smith was a beautiful combination of her rich soprano and his incongruously large bass. Hamish and Natalie played on their size difference subtly – they'd developed a mutual appreciation that bordered on friendship. Hamish's body language was confident in all interactions on the stage but for when Natalie was present – then he hunched his shoulders slightly and avoided eye contact. She played to this and became overly assertive when acting with Hamish, and more demure with all the other actors.

The chorus was less impressive. Neil Long, in a misguided attempt to impress Elizabeth Tresling, had suggested the men's chorus remove their pants beneath their long cloaks and blacken a few teeth. To the audience they resembled a gang of urchins bent on robbery rather than peers of the realm. Their nether regions, clad only in underpants, would have remained invisible under their cloaks but for Andrew Marsdorf's tumble. Too slovenly to tie his laces, he tripped making a turn at the front of the stage and his cloak flew open to reveal pale thighs and a pair of holey red briefs. He then stood on his cloak, spun and fell into the percussion section of the orchestra pit. There was a clanging of cymbals and rending of timpani skins. The hall fell briefly silent before erupting into hysterical laughter as the injured boy was removed via a subterranean trapdoor – his first and last stage performance complete. Backstage, Mr McAdams had delivered a tongue-lashing and eons of hard labour before any of the peers had returned to the stage (fully clad and toothed). Marsdorf was banned from the wrap party on the final night.

But it is was Robert Gumede who delivered the show-stopping per-formance. The Lord Chancellor's insomnia song was performed with astounding brilliance for an untrained voice. Gumede's haughty man-nerisms imitated a Johannesburg northern-suburbs snob rather than an English one and the audience was in such fits of laughter that he had to pause the song three times to allow the noise to die down.

For Hamish, the best part was Reggie's attendance.

Since their reacquaintance a year previously, Reggie had phoned the Fraser household almost every week – whenever she felt the need for a chat. Sometimes she would talk to Caroline only and then ring off, but the two teenagers would talk if Hamish answered and Reggie often asked to speak to him anyway. She especially loved the weekly updates in the lead-up to the play.

The weekend after the first rehearsal, she'd phoned while Hamish was lying on a sofa in the study, supposedly analysing Beethoven's Fifth for Music homework. He was just dropping off during the second movement when the phone rang.

'How's the Batbitch?' he asked after they'd said hello. 'Off murdering gentiles?'

Reggie giggled. 'Next door sharpening her broom before heading out, I think,' she whispered. 'How's school?' His tales of woe always cheered her up.

'Ag, it's okay,' he answered. 'I'm in a play but I think it'll be a disaster. We're doing it with Brighton College.'

'Why's it going to be a disaster?' She knew the answer would make her laugh.

'A few reasons. First, the men's chorus is so horny they can't figure out what to sing or when to come on stage. They just sort of ooze around staring at the girls.'

'*You* don't, of course,' she teased.

'Of course not! I am a professional thespian! I am above the, eh, frivo-lous extra-thespionic activities to which the randy peons I must act with succumb.'

'What else?' She was laughing.

'Well, then there's the girl I'm supposed to pretend to be in love with.' He paused. 'She is massive, like-a-bus massive. She's taller and much stauncher than me, and I'm frightened when she looks at me. I'm not sure if she's got a crush or if she's just hungry.'

'A crush?' Reggie giggled. 'Should I be jealous?'

He momentarily forgot how to breathe. 'Would you be jealous?' he rasped.

She fobbed him off. 'I'm just teasing, Hamish. Well, I'm coming to watch, so best it be good.'

Reggie attended the show with a friend's parents – telling her grand-mother she was going to watch a production of *Macbeth* at the Market Theatre. She'd pre-arranged to meet Stuart and Caroline and sat with them a few rows from the front. She laughed at Robert Gumede with the rest of the audience, but it was Hamish's comic and supremely confident performance that made her giggle the most, and she was disappointed each time he left the stage.

She had to leave before Hamish had emerged from having his make-up removed, but phoned the next evening.

'Fuck, you were funny last night,' she said before she'd even said hello.

He flushed – she could not have paid him a greater compliment.

'And that Robert dude was also hilarious.' She laughed. 'I see what you mean about the girl you were acting with – not a small unit. But, jislaaik, she can sing.'

'Are you jealous of her?' asked Hamish.

'Yes, of course – I *wish* I could sing like that!'

Silence. Hamish didn't know how to say that was not what he'd meant. She knew that, of course.

'You going to the Jersey Park show on Sunday?' asked Hamish, desperate for her not to ring off.

'Yes – are you?' She sounded excited, but Hamish couldn't tell if it was just because of the show jumping.

'Yebo,' he replied, happy at the thought of a full Sunday around her.

24

While the G and S musical was a huge part of Trinity's extra-curricular timetable during the first two terms, sport continued to play a huge role in school life. The first sporting event of the school year was the interhouse swimming gala.

Hamish's ability to propel himself through the water had not improved much. That said, he was still a better swimmer than Roger. For as long as anyone could remember, the last event at the gala was the Reserves Relay. Unofficially and inappropriately, it was known as the 'spastics' race' – a relay with two boys from each year group who were not allowed to have competed in any other race. The prize was a comically small and ancient brass cup.

Hamish Fraser was chosen to anchor the Iverson House spastics team. The other Iverson Matric was Robert Gumede, who detested being in the water because he hated the cold – he was never seen without a jersey.

The night of the gala was a warm summer's evening in late February. The atmosphere was festive – families came to watch with picnics, and countless trysts with other boys' sisters took place in the winding gardens and terraced rockeries surrounding the pool. The Ladies' Entertainment Committee filled the air with the smell of coal fires and cooking boerewors.

Hamish arrived late for the start after a riding lesson, but his race was not until the very end. He wandered through the cloistered corridors in the twilight, dressed in his school Speedo and tracksuit. While he considered the old adage 'school days are the happiest days of our lives' to be the work of a madman with no imagination, he felt a fondness for the college. As a Matric, he had a certain amount of freedom and, because he didn't have a reputation for deviance, he was left to do as he liked.

That evening, the old school was quiet but for the distant chanting of the boys supporting the swimmers. As he walked under the boughs of the trees in the Memorial Quadrangle, roosting pigeons cooed from the eves two storeys up. A few brave stars twinkled through the leaves. If there was a human sound, it was the almost imperceptible murmur of ghosts – footsteps and conversations of countless teenage boys over the last century.

At the end of the quad, Hamish passed under an archway and turned right down some stone steps and onto a landing. From there he could see the lights from the homes to the north, and the dying embers of the day glowing to the west. He paused briefly and chuckled.

In his Form I year, one of the Matrics, had gathered together the Iverson House juniors at the gala.

'Can you smell that?' he'd asked in hushed tones. 'That sweet cooking smell?'

The smaller boys had begun sniffing the air.

'It's Friday tonight – you know what they do at Wits Hospital on Friday nights?'

The small boys shook their heads, moving closer together as the darkness closed.

'Friday night is when they burn the bodies and amputated limbs at the hospital – always smells like cooking here on Friday nights.'

'Really?' Neil Long had asked, appalled.

'Really.' The Matric had nodded without the hint of a smile.

'I can smell it!' Angus Campion had agreed as the others concurred.

Hamish smiled at the memory. Down the next flight of stone steps, he walked through a raised garden fringed with purple agapanthus. He paused to listen to the crickets, extending the moment before he'd have to join the mass of cheering boys at the pool.

Finally, the spastics' race was called and Iverson House's hotchpotch team assembled. The two Form I boys looked like they hadn't eaten for weeks. One of the Form IIIs resembled a corpulent rain frog – his limbs seemingly meant for a much smaller human. Angelo Gramaticus, Form IV, was about six foot two, but if he turned sideways he was almost invisible such was the lack of muscle on his physique. Robert Gumede was dressed in his tracksuit, a scarf and a woolly hat (it was twenty-four degrees Celsius). He'd decided this would be a good race to win – he loved the underdog, and this was the underdog's race of races.

'Come, madoda,' he called. 'Gather round.' He put his right arm around Hamish's shoulders and his left around one of the Form Is as the team huddled. 'Now listen here, boys. This is my first and last swimming race at this school, and I don't expect to lose. You have one length to do as fast as you can – don't mind that this is the spastics' race. We're going to be the best damn spastics this school has ever seen. Understand?'

'Yes, Gumede,' the boys chimed.

Gumede's hazel eyes blazed.

The group split, half going to the shallow end, Hamish and the rest to the deep.

The race was an eight-length relay in age order. The gun went and the first Form Is leapt into the water. Every boy sitting on the stands went wild screaming for their houses. Iverson's Gerry van der Veen headed down lane four resembling a piece of bamboo with a fast-moving but misaligned propeller. He made contact with the lane markers four times before reaching the end of his length. Mercifully the standard of Iverson House swimming was by no means the worst: the East House competitor had to be retrieved from lane one after he slipped on the starting block and collected the concrete edge of the pool with his left knee.

Hamish detected a hesitance in Michael Gimble – the other Iverson House Form I, who seemed overawed by the screaming crowd. As Gerry van der Veen touched the deep end, Hamish shoved Gimble into the water. He belly-flopped, floated to the surface and began to flail in the vague direction of the shallow end.

By the end of the sixth length, Iverson House was lying fifth of five (East having been disqualified for two emergency rescues). The stringy Form IV, who Hamish dubbed Flat Stanley, made up three places. His counterpart maintained this position at the deep end and then it was the turn of Robert Gumede – who removed his woolly hat only as he dived into the water, his powerful thighs throwing him an astonishing distance into lane four. He passed the remaining houses such that Hamish would have a head start of two metres.

As Gumede motored towards him like a hypothermic torpedo, Hamish looked towards his competition for the final length: Andrew Marsdorf of Yates House.

Iverson House roared as Gumede slid through the water. He touched the edge and Hamish Fraser let out a mighty yell as he dived. He was still bellowing when he surfaced a second later and began swimming for all he was worth. The only way he could gauge his progress was from the screams of his house, which became louder and louder until with each breath he took he could hear, 'Fra-ser, Fra-ser, Fra-ser.'

And then he touched the end and looked left. Iverson House was going ballistic. To the right, Marsdorf climbed sullenly out of the water – he had closed the gap to a few centimetres, but those were Hamish's centimetres. Marsdorf walked past where Hamish was standing in the shallow end.

'Well done,' he said sardonically. 'You the fastest spaz in the school.'

The rest of the Iverson House team came around to the shallow end and Gumede pulled Hamish out of the water.

'Fraser the fish!' He slapped Hamish on the back.

Fraser the fish, thought Hamish ruefully. The fastest spastic at Trinity College. Thus ended Hamish's swimming career – and he wasn't sorry.

Hamish did have one sporting goal. He was desperate to play just one rugby match for the first XV. He lay in bed at night dreaming of donning the special navy jersey, the College's lion rampant embroidered on the left breast and a golden number on the back. He wouldn't even mind if it didn't have the number nine on it – he'd have happily worn a reserve jersey. He constructed a hundred scenarios in which he either created or scored the final try that gave Trinity victory over King James for the first time in living memory.

The universe had given Hamish countless unsubtle messages that he was not destined to achieve in the great game of rugby union. He was built like a waxbill, prone to concussion and not naturally skilled with a ball. The universe tried valiantly to push him in other directions – giving him wonderful musical talents, some skills on horseback and a love of performing. All of these messages Hamish studiously ignored.

At the end of his Form IV year, there'd been a special rugby training camp at Trinity. Invitations were extended to those considered possibles for the 1994 first and second XVs. Seeing the notice for the camp, Hamish had been surprised not to see his name and at break time he'd gone straight to Mr van Zyl's classroom.

The teacher was on his way to tea in the staffroom.

'Morning, sir,' said Hamish.

'Morning.' The master didn't look at the boy and made to leave.

'Sir, may I come to the rugby camp please,' Hamish blurted.

Mr van Zyl stared down at the tiny fellow, who he only dimly remembered. 'What's your name again?'

'Fraser, sir.'

'Why do you want to come, Fraser? Do you want to be a coach?'

'No, sir, I want to play for the firsts and seconds.'

Mr van Zyl just managed to stop himself scoffing. 'Well, I don't reckon there's any harm. You can come, Fraser.'

The course covered rugby training – there was no actual playing required. Hamish took fastidious notes and asked clever questions, which brought some respectability to the smallest attendee. It was clear to Mr van Zyl that Hamish Fraser had a deep interest in the game, even if that hadn't translated into on-field performance.

Hamish took those lessons very seriously. During the summer holidays and into the Easter term of his Matric year, he trained as much as his body and timetable allowed. He spent a few hours a week in the school gym trying to build the tiny muscles on his fifty-eight kilogram frame. Every afternoon that he wasn't riding, he ran down to the Inanda Club and sprinted up and down the polo field, kicking and chasing his rugby ball until the light was too poor to see. At school, if he found himself with any spare time, he'd head onto the main rugby field and pass at the posts. Again and again he would fling the ball at the metal poles.

His efforts were noticed – not by Mr van Zyl, but by Mr Smythe, Science teacher and the old under-13D coach. He confronted Mr van Zyl a few days before the first and second XV trials towards the end of March. The rugby master had just attached the list of trial invitees to the rugby noticeboard. It was a list of mostly Form Vs, but a few large and talented Form IVs were included.

'I say, Mister van Zyl,' began the Irishman. 'Dat young Fraser boy on your list der?'

The head of rugby wheeled around to the bristling lamb chops of the man two decades his senior. 'Roger Fraser? Almost put him on for flank but he needs another year.'

'No, his older brodder – Hamish. Little fella, passes de ball like a rocket.'

'No, he's not.'

'Ah, dat's a shame – he's put in a lot of effort. Why not give him a go, yeah?' Mr Smythe took a step forward. He knew how to use his six feet and six inches to good effect.

'I guess it can't do any harm.' Mr van Zyl grudgingly turned to the board and added the name of Hamish Fraser to the end of the list.

'Good man – little fella deserves a go!' He clapped Mr van Zyl rather too hard on the back and departed.

The next day, Hamish chivvied his brother, sister and father into the car with completely uncharacteristic urgency.

'Why the hell are you in such a rush?' asked Stuart as he buttered his second piece of toast.

'The trial invites are up today!' Hamish exclaimed, as though there wasn't a person in the world who didn't know this.

'What does that mean?' asked Julia, but Hamish was already out of the kitchen and packing his tog bag.

'It means the guys who'll be invited to the trials for the firsts and seconds go up today,' explained Roger.

Stuart sighed and set down his butter knife. 'I fear a large disappointment coming the way of your brother.'

'Is Hamish going to play for the firsts?' asked Julia, who, by no design of her own, was the most rugby-knowledgeable junior-school pupil at Brighton College.

When Hamish Fraser saw his name at the bottom of the list, albeit in a manner that suggested an afterthought, he was beside himself. Roger was standing with the who's who of the Form IV class, four of whom were also on the list.

'Rog! Rog!' Hamish blurted, looking up at his brother. 'I made it! I'm on the list!'

'Well done, Hamish!' Roger smiled as a few giggles went around the group.

'Trials are next week Wednesday!' Hamish turned and made to jog away, but tripped on a book bag and sprawled at the feet of some Form IIIs.

'Enjoy your trip, Fraser,' someone laughed.

For the rest of the week, Hamish was unable to concentrate on anything other than the rugby trials. His training increased in intensity – he destroyed four rose bushes and broke a window practising his box kicks in the garden.

At break on Wednesday morning, Hamish made his way down to

the field alone. He walked out into the centre and looked up at the College's magnificent façade. A few months previously, a motivational speaker had come to talk to the Matric body on 'Your Goals through Visualisation'. Mr Ron Dervish had been dressed in a perfectly tailored but slightly shiny blue suit, with not a hair out of place.

'You have to see your goals in your mind's eye,' he'd crooned. 'You've got an eye in the middle of your forehead – the all-seeing eye.' Ron Dervish looked wistfully to the back of the auditorium. 'You wanna win? You gotta *see* yourself win. You wanna be a success? You gotta *see* your success.' He'd tapped his all-seeing eye.

Hamish Fraser had been seeing himself in the blue first XV jersey for as long as he knew it existed. As far as visualisation went, he was willing to bet that he'd visualised himself in that jersey more often and in more scenarios than any other soul before or after. If Ron Dervish was correct, Hamish would not just be playing one game for the first XV, he'd be captaining the side from scrum half.

He sat cross-legged in the centre of the field, took a deep breath, closed his eyes and engaged his all-seeing eye.

Hamish is standing at the base of a scrum, a golden number nine on his back. The ball dribbles to the feet of the number eight. Hamish whips it off the ground and it rifles straight and true into the arms of Johnny Goodenough, standing at fly half.

Hamish is making a try-saving tackle on the King James wing as the College roars with admiration.

Hamish is breaking around the blind-side of a scrum. He evades the loose forwards, chips over the defending wing, collects his own kick and runs around to score under the poles.

At lunch, Hamish forced himself to eat a bit of rice and drink some sweet coffee for energy. He sat, as always, with his Zulu classmates, three of whom had also been invited to the trials. Robert Gumede had declined his invitation on account of an intense dislike for Mr van Zyl and very little affection for the game of rugby. Andile Ntunjwa would almost certainly make the hooker berth his own, and John Radatso was blisteringly fast on the wing.

Down on the field at two-thirty, it was a hot afternoon. Mr van Zyl and Mr McLintock surveyed the boys as they ran two warm-up laps. Some were horsing about, others lost in contemplation over how best to impress the coaches or outplay a rival for the coveted blue kit. Hamish ran at the back of the group, heart racing. His boots were perfectly polished, shorts clean, socks tied neatly in place and maroon practice jersey tucked in.

The first two teams of the trials were called out. These were the boys on the fringes of selection, and Hamish was assigned the scrum-half berth in one of the teams.

Gone were the days of leather balls. A synthetic white pill was drop-kicked and collected by one of the locks, who charged forward to take contact. Hamish arrived at the ensuing ruck to clear the ball to his fly half. Mr van Zyl was a fan of the dive pass and so a dive pass Hamish gave him: the ball plopped out of the ruck, Hamish put his hands on it, glanced towards his fly half and dived. At that moment, Neil Long, in an attempt to free himself from the pile of bodies on the floor, lifted his heavy left leg. As Hamish let go of the ball – body flying horizontally – his forehead collected Neil Long's left knee. The ball rocketed into the arms of the fly half and play continued – for twenty-nine of the thirty players.

When Hamish woke up, his vision was blurred and there were three medics peering over him, one calling loudly for a stretcher.

He closed his eyes.

Not for the first time in his life, Hamish spent the afternoon alternating between bouts of vomiting and lying in the foetal position. It took three days for him to recover from the concussion. The family doctor, who expressed surprise that an individual so constructed should be playing rugby at all, booked him off sport for a month, which meant Hamish played no further part in any trials – not for those of the thirds and fourths, or for those of the fifths and sixths.

In May 1994, Hamish returned to the rugby field for the first time since his second major concussion. For the first match of the winter term, he was placed in the sixth XV, the lowest open age-group side. It was a bitter pill to swallow – yet there he was at eight o'clock in the morning, in the bitter cold under a scudding grey sky, about to take the field for the sixths against St Steven's. They didn't even have a full team – on the wings were two co-opted hockey players who'd fancied a bit of a run before their match.

Perhaps the worst part of that Saturday was that Roger, a year younger and nowhere near as interested in rugby, was playing for the fourth XV. By the end of the day, Roger would be reserve flank for the thirds.

Hamish's match indicated at least one thing – he had no business operating behind the sixth XV scrum. The fly half for the day caught three passes that came his way; the rest just smacked into his chest and left him winded. He stood further and further from Hamish as the game progressed, terrified by the speed with which the ball shot at him from Hamish's diving form.

At half-time there was something of a conflagration in the Trinity huddle.

'Fraser, man, pass the ball softer!' said the extremely bright but less than sporty member of the Matric class, who was playing fly half merely out of a sense of duty.

'This is how I pass,' snapped Hamish. 'That's the pass a real fly half wants!'

'Fraser, this is the sixths, not the fucking All Blacks,' said a lanky and disinterested lock. 'Stop being such a doos. We're all doing our best.'

'No, you aren't,' Hamish whined. 'You okes just don't care!'

The scrum half's less-than-inspirational attempt to chivvy his side into some sort of enthusiasm did a lot to account for the twenty-point deficit the sixths ended with that cold May morning.

The next week, Hamish was promoted to the fifths – there was no sixth-team game and the incumbent fifth XV scrum half had asked to be excused. During the week, Stuart had called his eldest into the study for a serious word.

'Hamish,' began the father, 'wurd has reached me via Roger, who was approached by a few boys in the fifths and sixths, that there is general unhappiness with your attitude.'

'*My* attitude?' said Hamish, gobsmacked. 'I try harder than everyone else in the squad!'

'Someone described you, and I quote here, as "an arrogant little prick who thinks he's too good for the rest of us".'

Silence hung for a while.

'You need to understand that those boys don't live for rugby like you do. The best thing you can do to impress the coaches is put your head down and play as hard as you can.'

'But, Dad, I've tried so hard for this and now I'm in the sixths! The rest of the team is making me look like a fool! Roger doesn't even care about rugby and there he is playing for the fourths – and the thirds!'

'Hamish!' snapped Stuart. 'You're behaving like an ass! No one can make you look like a fool except you, and you are doing a great job of it!'

The sound of Tina placing dinner on the hot tray filtered through.

'You think it really matters in the greater scheme of things which team you play for? You've lost perspective completely. Rugby is for fun, camaraderie and fitness – nothing else. The wurld is filled with tragedy, death and sickness, and here you are worried about how hard your teammates play a meaningless rugby match. Think how many people died in Natal in the run-up to the elections! Get a grip on yourself!' Now Stuart was shouting. 'Get out! Go and think about your attitude and what's actually important.'

Hamish stalked past Tina as she loaded the bowl of peas onto the hot tray.

'Dinner's ready, Hamish,' she said. 'Please go and tell Mummy.'

Hamish sighed. 'Ag, ja, okay,' he snapped. Then the penny dropped, and a horrible feeling of self-loathing washed over him. 'Sorry, Gogo – yes, I'll tell everyone. Thank you for supper.'

But it was too late and Tina left without a word.

That Saturday, Hamish acquitted himself well – he kept his temper and passed well. There was an injury in the fourths and so the week after that he found himself playing in the fourth XV – with Roger.

Roger was playing number eight, so when the side lined up to take the field, the Frasers were standing next to each other. As they waited, he looked to the side to see his father sitting on the terraces, smiling. He raised a fist at his eldest son. Hamish waved, tears welling in his eyes – he felt a tremendous sense of pride and joy to be taking the field with Roger. His brother, now approaching six feet, turned and looked down at his older sibling.

'You alright, Hamish? What's wrong?'

'Nothing, Rog. Good luck!'

With that, the whistle blew and the team ran on.

Hamish played well by the lowly standards of the fourths. He passed accurately, kicked a conversion and scored a try off a penalty when he caught the St David's forwards napping. The highlight came when he broke to the blind side of a ruck. His peripheral vision caught Roger's unique, hunch-backed running style way out on the wing. The bigger Fraser yelled for the ball. It was not a pass many fourth team members could have achieved, but Roger, who'd suffered under Hamish's merciless practice regime, knew that if there was one person in the team capable of flinging the pill that far, it was Hamish. The white ball rifled twenty metres over the heads of the opposition and his own team, and into his brother's arms. Roger rounded a defender and scored in the corner.

After the game, Hamish played the move over and over in his mind's eye, feeling a deep sense of satisfaction. Curiously, he didn't mention it afterwards. He just patted Roger on the back and told him well done, perhaps realising that trying to relive the moment through its telling may, in some way, taint the perfect memory of it.

As Hamish's final season of school rugby progressed, he cemented his position in the fourths and played once for the thirds when Spencer Trotter had diarrhoea. He also slowly began to accept that he'd never don the beloved all-blue kit of the first XV and, while it was a bitter disappointment, he attempted – sometimes successfully – to put the failure in perspective.

The last match of the season was against King James – Goliath versus David all over again, except in this case David normally had his backside handed to him by Goliath. There was talk that the 1994 Trinity firsts might actually have a chance.

Catastrophe struck in the week preceding the match. An influenza epidemic ravaged Trinity, cutting a swathe through the rugby and hockey ranks such that the total number of available players nearly made Mr McAdams cancel the Saturday fixture. In the end, Trinity was only able to field three rugby and two hockey sides – and Hamish found himself in the third XV. The Thursday before the match, he was called by Mr van Zyl to attend the last part of the firsts and seconds practice – Hamish would have to be the reserve second XV scrum half.

The firsts and seconds were running their moves against each other. Hamish took the ball and prepared to feed it into a seconds' scrum. Bradford York, into his second year as the first XV scrum half, sized Hamish up and saw that he was shaking with nerves.

'Fraser, just pass the ball like you always do and you'll be fine – it's all the same.'

Hamish was not used to such kind words, and he smiled. 'Thanks, Brad.'

From behind the first XV scrum came a familiar voice: 'Fraser the fish.' The flu had placed Robert Gumede where he always should have been– anchoring the scrum for the best team in the school. While he'd always been stocky, Gumede was now also a touch over six feet. The recalcitrant Zulu had refused all offers and threats to join higher teams, and no one was surprised that, up to the last match, the thirds remained undefeated that year. Gumede had enjoyed playing in the thirds, but for his final match he would don the blue.

'Fraser,' yelled Mr van Zyl, 'put the ball in! This is not the fourths any more!'

Hamish turned, fed the ball under his hooker's feet, ran around to the back of the scrum and delivered a perfect pass to Philip Cobbler, the fly half.

Fifteen minutes later, the practice ended. It wasn't expected that Hamish would actually have to play for the seconds – his attendance was simply a precaution.

Saturday dawned crisp and bright. Unusually, Hamish didn't have to be at school in time to break the frost on the field because the thirds would play at ten o'clock (technically still the first game of the day because there were no lower teams).

The King James thirds were merciless and well drilled. They hammered their private-school counterparts. Hamish played well when Trinity had the ball, passing accurately and fast, and clearing for touch a few times. His concussions, however, had made him reticent to put his head in the way of too many flying King James knees, so his contribution to the defensive effort was below par.

The seconds fared marginally better than the thirds. Halfway through the second half, an up-and-coming Form IV and incumbent second XV scrum half was carried off with a broken tibia – the bone snapped clean through, so that it looked like he had two ankles. One of the medics passed out on seeing it, and the game was delayed by the search for a second stretcher.

Hamish was ecstatic to play the last fifteen minutes of the second XV game – by far the loftiest rugby position he'd ever held on a rugby field. He played well, breaking once to the blind side and then sending a perfectly weighted chip over the head of the defending wing for his fullback to collect and then dot down for one of his team's two tries.

So it was that, due to disease and injury, Hamish Fraser found himself facing Mr van Zyl at the end of the seconds' game. The coach took

Hamish aside and, with a look of pain in his eyes, told Hamish that he, as the second of only two remaining open age-group scrum halves in the entire school, would have to sit on the bench for the first XV.

'Fraser – this is a fu … *very* important game, see. We have a chance today. You just need to sit on the bench.' The rugby master paled visibly at the thought. 'Let's hope you aren't needed.' Then he handed Hamish a folded navy jersey, some navy shorts and a pair of navy socks.

The boy's face lit up, his braces gleaming in the sunlight as he unfolded the all-blue kit.

'Hey!' yelled Mr van Zyl, grabbing the jersey away. 'You don't just put that thing on! You're only allowed to wear the blue if you go onto the field. Understand?'

'Yes, sir.'

'Put the shorts and socks on – the blue is for those who play.'

The first XV match was an absolute cracker. While the flu had decimated most of the school, many of the regular Trinity firsts had escaped and there were a few key King James stalwarts either sick or injured. In the last game of rugby he would ever play, Robert Gumede decided to make an effort, delivering a performance of controlled aggression, strength and courage such that by halftime he was the de facto captain of the side. The spectating boys of the College roared his name as he made tackle after tackle, thwarting the efforts of the skilled King James backs.

At half-time, the scores were level at twelve all. Trinity had scored no tries but the unerring accuracy of Johnny Goodenough's boot kept his team level. Hope began to ripple through the Trinity boys and watching parents. Mr McAdams, sitting with the King James headmaster, was silent – he'd sat through countless matches like this, graciously acknowledging defeat. Now, perhaps for the first time in his twelfth and final year as Trinity headmaster, he would leave victorious. He began to imagine the post-match tea *not*, as was normally the case, hearing how Trinity had tried hard but they really weren't a rugby school. He dared to dream of egg sandwiches and Earl Grey accompanied by a stream of congratulations from the assembled staff and parents.

The second half exploded into life with the King James team determined not to fall like Goliath. They tore into the Trinity boys with renewed gusto, but Paul Simpson's half-time talk and Robert Gumede's tireless mangling of every attack inspired the team to new heights.

Hamish watched all of this from his position on the bench, not once letting go of the precious blue jersey in his hands. The other four reserves were wearing theirs – they'd all been capped for the firsts at one time or another. Only Hamish sat in his maroon match jersey – the same one he'd owned since Form I (at least it fit him now). While the rest leapt up and down with the ebb and flow of the match, Hamish watched Bradford York for any signs of injury or distress.

And there weren't any.

Fifteen minutes into the second half the deadlock was broken. King James was on the attack in the Trinity twenty-two metre area. Wave after red wave assailed the blue defensive line, but the screaming boys in the stand, the College's towering stone façade and the chance of a historic victory had driven the Trinity team into a bloody-minded frenzy.

It was possibly this frenzy that allowed the King James fly half to slip unnoticed into a deep pocket behind a ruck in front of the poles. When the ball rifled into his hands, instead of launching another attack, he dropped it onto the ground and kicked it through the uprights.

The score was now 15–12.

With just five minutes left, Robert Gumede broke from the back of a scrum on the King James ten-metre line. He charged at the fly half, but instead of flattening him, popped the ball inside to Bradford York. The Trinity scrum half ran a few metres and as the cover defence caught up with him, he passed back to the rampaging number eight. Gumede handed off his opposite number and broke into the clear with nothing but the superb King James fullback between him and the try line. All expected Gumede to mow over the top of the last line of defence, but just before he made contact, he dropped the ball deftly onto his right foot, stepped around the turning fullback, allowed his kick to bounce once, collected it with one arm and then dived under the posts to score.

Pandemonium exploded through the ranks of the Trinity spectators as Johnny Goodenough slotted the conversion, taking Trinity four points up with two minutes to play. As the euphoria of the try dissipated, the medics ran onto the field: a Trinity boy was sitting on the King James twenty-two metre line clutching his arm and moaning. It was Bradford York.

'Fraser, get off your arse – you have to go on!'

Hamish stopped breathing.

'Now, boy!' Mr van Zyl boomed.

Hamish stood up and ran onto the field.

'Fraser!' The coach was near apoplectic. 'Your blue, for godsakes!'

Hamish ran back, tugging off his maroon jersey. The atmosphere and the surging adrenaline left holes in his memory – he barely remembered pulling on the blue he'd so often dreamt of. He noticed the number twenty-one on it – in gold – but he couldn't recall any other noise from that moment until the end of the match.

'Now go and join the team,' said Mr van Zyl. 'All we have to do is collect the kick-off and put the ball out – tell them I said that. Then we win, Fraser, then we win!'

Hamish jogged out onto the field. He tucked in the reams of extra material that hung below his shorts and rolled up the sleeves as he took his place behind the forwards. Trinity would receive the kick.

Robert Gumede smiled broadly at him. 'Fraser the fish.'

'Welcome to the first XV, Fraser,' said Paul Simpson.

Hamish nodded.

A few seconds later, the King James fly half kicked off. Simpson plucked it out of the air and charged forward to set up the ruck. The forwards piled in after him and the ball plopped to the back. Hamish heard the voice of Johnny Goodenough: 'Right here, Hamish Fraser, straight behind you.'

Hamish extended his spindly left leg towards the fly half, put his hands on the ball and dived. The white bladder fizzed towards its target.

Johnny Goodenough, who'd never received a pass from Hamish before, was somewhat surprised by its velocity, and the ball went through his fingers and hit his chest. The brilliant fly half quickly regathered and aimed a kick at the touchline. That fraction of a second, however, was enough to shake him, and his normally raking torpedo kick sliced off the side of his boot and straight down the throat of the King James fullback.

With no one behind him in support, the fullback opted to go the aerial route. He dropped the ball onto his educated left boot and sent it rocketing up towards the Trinity posts. No one expected him to even receive the ball, let alone launch a counterattack, so the Trinity fullback was out of position. Hamish reacted before anyone else, and charged back to cover the up and under.

The ball hung in the air for an age.

'Watch the ball,' he said to himself. 'Just watch the ball.'

Up in the stands, Stuart mouthed exactly the same words, his heart in his mouth. Caroline covered her face in her hands and Julia's eyes widened as she saw the fate of the match falling, quite literally, into the arms of her brother. In the Trinity stands, Roger looked on, slack-jawed.

Eventually the ball began to fall – swirling winter gusts making it difficult to judge the trajectory. Hamish, moving backwards, kept having to look away from the plummeting pill to check that he wasn't about to run into the uprights. The reserve scrum half set himself in front and then behind the cross bar as the wobbling ball fell towards him. The King James fullback bellowed in frustration and, for a nanosecond, Hamish looked down as he realised that the charging fullback had overcooked the kick – the ball would reach his arms before the number fifteen would.

He shouldn't have looked down.

It's the golden rule: never, ever, take your eyes off the ball.

Hamish returned his attention to the ball just in time to see it smack into his forehead and bounce up in horrific slow motion. Before he could react, the King James fullback jumped up at full speed. His knees drove into Hamish's chest as he plucked the ball out of the air, fell to the ground and dotted down.

The King James stand went ballistic.

The Trinity stand was morgue-silent.

Mr McAdams's visage resembled that of a startled snowman.

Mr van Zyl vomited where he stood.

The game was over and Hamish, too winded to breathe, lay on his back, realising what he'd done.

The uprights creaked in the breeze above.

Hamish felt numb; some vague notion that if he lay where he was, everyone would disappear and he'd be able to leave unnoticed.

The first voice he could discern from the white noise was that of Andrew Marsdorf: 'Fuck you, Fraser. What a fucking loser you are.'

Hamish's eyes fixed on the sky and the careless clouds floating over-head. He vaguely heard his name whispered among his teammates as they gathered behind the poles for the conversion kick.

'No way that guy should ever have worn the blue.' Wayne Johnson.

'He was always a fucking gayboy co-ord.' Basil Anderson, lock.

The ball flew over the posts for the final time.

'Come, boys.' Paul Simpson. 'Let's go shake hands.'

The team departed, but for one young man. Robert Gumede flopped down next to Hamish.

'Fraser the fish,' he said. Then he began to laugh, a loud belly laugh that convulsed his body. After a minute or two, he calmed himself. 'Fraser, you should have seen your face as that oke climbed you like a jungle gym – geez, it was funny.' The laughing began again – genuine, unconcerned mirth.

After another minute, Hamish noticed that he too was smiling.

As Gumede folded once more into hysterics, Hamish too began to chuckle at the image his teammate had conjured. The two of them lay there for fifteen minutes as the field and the stands emptied.

Eventually the number eight sat up and tapped Hamish twice on the shoulder. 'Cheers, Fraser the fish. I'll see you on Monday.'

There was silence in the car on the way home, the whole family on eggshells – no one wanted to prick the balloon of Hamish's evil temper.

The humiliated boy just looked out of the window. A perfect flying pattern of sacred ibises on their way to Zoo Lake glided parallel with the car.

Back at home, Hamish went to his room, showered in silence and then sat for an hour playing his guitar – nothing in particular, just gentle strumming as the light faded outside.

On Monday morning, as Hamish was about to climb out of the car and walk under the College arch, Stuart turned to his son.

'I'm really proud of you, boy.' Tears welled in the father's eyes. 'You've handled Saturday's result with great philosophy. Don't you worry one jot what anyone says to you today.'

The Fraser brothers seldom walked into school together, the younger normally lingering with a friend or two. That morning, however, Roger walked to the right and one step behind his brother – past the statue of David, which Hamish scoffed at once again, under the bell tower and past the entrance to the chapel, where they met Mr van Zyl coming the other way. The teacher glanced towards the Frasers and pretended they were invisible.

'I fear I may have ruined your chances of playing for the first side,' said Hamish.

'He can get stuffed,' said Roger.

In the Memorial Quadrangle groups of boys littered the slate chatting, laughing, sharing last-minute homework. Many heads turned to watch Hamish Fraser walk towards Iverson House; whispers and pointing fingers followed the Fraser boys.

Hamish bit his lip and began to walk faster, his eyes dropping to his shoes, where they remained until his Science lesson halfway through the day.

The class was gathered in the laboratory, Mr Smythe standing at the front bench consulting his notes, when Hamish slouched in, a few minutes late. The master looked up.

'Fraser,' he shouted, 'a word wid ya in my office quick.'

'Oooooh,' quipped Dylan Crane. 'Fraser's in trouble.'

'Shut up, Crane, ya useless ingrate!'

Hamish followed the teacher out of his lab and into the tiny office next door. The desk was littered with books, papers and an array of organic-molecule models.

'Fraser,' Mr Smythe barked, sitting on the front of his desk.

'Yes, sir?' said Hamish, his shoulders hunched.

'Stand up straight, Fraser!'

Hamish stiffened to attention.

'Now look here, Fraser, I don't want to see ya slouchin' about de place after Saturday. Ya hear me?'

'Yes, sir.'

'Dat game was a fek up – scuse me language – no doubt about it. But what happened to ya could've happened to anyone. Ders one important ting to take from it. Ya listenin' to me, boy?'

'Yes, sir.'

'It's just a schoolboy rugby match. I'm sure it was surprising to ya, but as ya saw, de sun came up on Sunday morning, yeah?'

'Yes, sir.'

'It's not like anyone died, is it?'

Hamish thought about this for a second. 'No, sir. No one died.'

'Good. Ya did ya best and ya played for de firsts. No one can ever take dat from ya!'

'No, sir. No one can take that from me, sir.' Hamish sniffed.

'Ya know if ya grandfader fought in de war?'

'Yes, sir, he did. He died at Normandy on D-Day, we think.'

'Well, my dad died in France too – bit earlier in de war but dat's not de point. De point is dat whenever I'm feeling irritated or miserable, I tink of me dad and his comrades being shot at in France and I realise

I ain't got no problem. Yeah?'

'I see what you mean, sir.'

'Good man. Now let's go back to class and learn some chemistry!'

25

On the first weekend of the Michaelmas term, Trinity hosted the annual Matric dance. Hamish had known since the day he'd reconnected with Reggie that it was she who would accompany him to the dance. A month before the event, he had yet to ask her.

The first weekend of the August holidays, Caroline enquired when he was going organise a date.

'Soon, Mum – lots of time,' he answered, a quaver in his voice.

'Who are you going to take?' she asked.

Hamish pretended to arrange the stationery in his drawer. 'Um, well, I, eh, I'm going to take Reggie – well, I hope I'm going to take Reggie.'

'Ah,' Caroline nodded.

'You knew that already,' he guessed.

'Why do you want to take her?' Caroline sat on his bed and Hamish flushed.

'Because I, eh, I know her better than any other girl and she would like to go.' He lifted a pencil and sharpened it.

'So you want to take her as a friend?'

'Ja, I guess.' Hamish shrugged at his pathetic lie. In keeping with the advice to visualise his success, Hamish had frequently seen himself kissing Reggie for the first time on the dance floor. She was always wearing a navy dress, diamonds in her ears, hair tied up with one or two curls falling down her neck. They were dancing to 'Return to Innocence' by

Enigma, which built to a tremendous crescendo when their lips met. His mind's eye saw the scene from above, like in a movie, the rest of the dancers in the shadows, he and Reggie softly lit by the mirror ball and a golden spotlight.

'Hamish,' said his mother, 'you need to be sensitive to Reggie – she's a complicated person and, while I love her dearly, there are many things she needs to work out about herself.' Caroline had spent increasing time on the phone with the girl – helping her deal with the trials of being a teenager in a loveless home. She knew Hamish wasn't yet mature enough for Reggie. 'It's also going to be difficult to get her there without her grandmother's knowledge.'

'Mum,' sighed the boy, 'come on. She's the only girl I *can* ask. I can see you think I'm going to get hurt, but she's my friend – so I'm going to ask her.'

'Okay. But you must ask her soon, see? If you don't, she'll be busy and you'll be left with no one. Next time she phones, make sure you ask.'

Hamish didn't have long to wait because Reggie phoned that evening – ostensibly to shoot the breeze after the term and talk about the August holidays. Hamish answered the phone.

'Hello, Hamish Charles Sutherland Fraser,' said Reggie.

'Good evening, Regina Rebecca Fine,' replied Hamish in his most poncey accent.

She giggled. That was a good start.

'Watcha doin' in the holidays?' she asked using an American drawl she'd been perfecting of late.

'Going to the mountains again for a week,' he replied 'but then I guess I must do some studying for finals. My guitar, mainly – the prac exam is almost soon as I get back. You?'

'Oh, riding mostly, I guess – the Batbitch insists I'm in the A grades by the end of the year. She says to me the other day, "Rebecca, if you are not winning in the A grades by November, your grandfather and I will consider the money we've spent on your riding career a waste!"'

'You make her sound like a fairy-tale crone with a long, wart-infested

307

nose and no front teeth. And what of Grandpapa?'

'I think Grandpapa is losing it – he couldn't give a flying shit if me or my horse disappeared off the face of the earth. Years of being harassed by the Batbitch have cooked his brain.'

There was a pause.

'Reg,' he began.

'Ham,' she teased.

'Reg, I need to ask you a favour.' He swallowed.

'A favour – you actually sound serious. Of course I'll do you a favour, my oldest pal in the universe – anything. What is this favour?'

Hamish said nothing.

'It can't be that bad – come on, tell me.' The frivolity in her voice was replaced with concern.

Hamish sighed heavily. 'Will you come to my Matric dance with me?'

There was a brief pause and then she laughed.

'A favour? That's not a favour, Hamish – of course I'll go to your Matric dance with you. That's an honour, not a favour!'

A whoosh of air escaped Hamish's lungs. More giggles.

'You were really nervous to ask me, Hamish Charles Sutherland Fraser!'

'No, I wasn't!' Another lie, ruined by a ball-drag and the certainty that he could not fool her.

'Why would you be nervous to ask me?' she asked unkindly, knowing full well why he sounded like he was about to face a dragon in single combat. What's more, he knew that she knew. But she needed the affirmation and the attention – it was in such short supply at home.

Hamish changed the subject to discuss how to engineer her attendance without alerting her vicious grandmother. In the end, the plan was simple. On the day of the dance there was a show that they were both riding in – the Spring Festival. She'd ask permission to stay the night with a friend from the stables – which she often did – and then surreptitiously go home with the Frasers. She'd sleep in Inanda and then Stuart would drop her off at the gate of her home early the next morning.

'This is a risky business,' said Caroline to Hamish. They were on their way to the Oriental Plaza a few weeks later to buy Hamish a dinner jacket. Hamish was driving – he was nearly eighteen and preparing for his driver's test.

'Oh, come on, Mother, I'm not that bad.'

'You just react so late to things – PLEASE TRY AND BRAKE EARLIER!' she screeched, driving her feet into some imaginary brake pedals while adopting the brace position.

Hamish narrowly avoided rear-ending a minibus taxi that had slammed to a halt to disgorge its terrified passengers.

'Anyway, I'm not talking about your complete lack of driving skills.'

'Because that foul old bat could put a spanner in the works for my dance?'

'Hamish! PLEASE keep your eyes on the road!' The boy had the disturbing habit of looking at the passenger when talking and was drifting into the oncoming traffic, oblivious of the hooting, flashing remonstrations from oncoming motorists. 'For godsakes, just shut up and drive. I'll talk to you when we get to the plaza.'

They drove the rest of the way through the Indian suburb of Fordsburg with Hamish in sulky silence. He failed to understand why everyone who drove with him felt like death was both imminent and inevitable.

As they walked towards Pillay & Sons Luxury Suit Emporium, Caroline continued, 'I meant this whole dance plan of yours is risky business.'

'Don't worry about it, Mum.' Hamish eyed a shiny ice-blue faux-satin suit.

'Mrs Fine is unpredictable and volatile. She could change her mind at a moment's notice.' The mother stopped and regarded her son. 'That suit is disgusting, Hamish – you're going to a respectable school dance, not a costume party.' She took a deep breath. 'Darling, you've taken a real gamble, and if it doesn't come off, you're in for an awkward night.'

He grinned at her from under his unruly mop of hair, the neon light of the plaza reflecting off his mouth full of steel, a suppurating zit about to burst on the end of his nose. At least the top teeth would soon be free of steel, Caroline thought.

'She could easily decide that Reggie hasn't ridden well enough to warrant a night out, or that her academics aren't up to scratch ... anything like that.'

'Good morning, madam.' A man, presumably Mr Pillay or one of his sons, looked first at Caroline, and then at Hamish. 'And to you, young gentleman – it seems to me that you have come to be fitted for a suit, sir!' His thin moustache quivered beneath a perfect haircut.

'Well, sir, I'm not here for a haircut,' replied Hamish, smiling.

Mr Pillay roared with laughter. 'For a gentleman with a sense of humour, I've got a great deal on this black tuxedo.'

Caroline and Hamish departed half an hour later with a respectable-looking black dinner jacket. The label claimed the suit to have been woven from at least ten per cent natural fibres. The dress-shirt was possibly cotton. Hamish had spurned the clip-on bow tie, demanding the genuine article. He'd also insisted on a white scarf, an accessory made of a substance closer to fibreglass than silk, but which was so inexpensive that Mr Pillay threw it in for free. The shoes would be his school brogues, which he'd have to polish with Tina's help.

The day of the dance arrived – a glorious highveld spring day. Hamish woke feeling very excited about the next twenty-four hours. The first thing he did was run his tongue over his top teeth. For the first time in more than two years, they were free of metal. He then tried the same with the bottom ones and immediately yelped and withdrew his bloodied tongue – the bottom row still had a few more weeks of orthodontics. Before he could think about donning his ever-so-slightly shiny suit, which was hanging neatly pressed behind his bedroom door, he had to ride in a show and somehow extricate his partner from the event without her grandmother's knowledge.

Two hours later, Reggie rode past where Caroline and Hamish were sitting in the shade of a syringa heavy with blossoms, and Hamish's heart stopped briefly. She was wearing white jodhpurs, and as she came past, the flap of her navy jacket lifted to reveal her narrow waist and firm hips. Hamish, despite the distraction, rode well in the first class, but Sports Vision knocked a pole in jump-off and they finished unplaced.

As the A-grade class began, Hamish leant against the syringa and alternated between picking at its bark and trying to flatten a piece of hair that was rising from the back of his head like a curious cobra. A bacon-and-egg roll lay uneaten on his chair.

'Hamish,' said his mother, 'sit down and eat something, and please don't drink any more of that Coke – all that sugar and caffeine will give you a heart attack.'

He saw her coming from a long way off, stopping every so often to greet people she knew. Reggie's hair was tied into a thick plait that hung over her left shoulder. Hamish felt a stab of jealousy as she threw back her head and laughed at a quip from George Philips, a leading A grader. The greasy fellow touched her arm as she turned away.

A few steps later her smile vanished, and Hamish saw her sigh heavily. She flicked the plait onto her back, her eyes on the ground as she approached.

About twenty metres from where Hamish stood watching her, she looked up. For the briefest moment, he looked deep into her navy eyes. She smiled wordlessly and he did the same. The spell was broken by Caroline.

'Reggie!' She stood up. 'You rode so well!'

The two women embraced warmly and then Reggie turned to Hamish, who folded his top lip under itself and grinned stupidly. She laughed and shook her head.

'Hello, Hamish, you clown – what pretty incisors you have.' She hugged him and he returned the embrace, closing his eyes and inhaling the floral scent of her hair as it mingled with that of the syringa.

He'd happily have ended his existence on Planet Earth right then.

'Alright then, you can let me go now,' she giggled.

He released her immediately, blushing. 'I'm sorry,' he muttered.

'That's alright, old boy.'

Hamish was desperate to ask if she had her dress with her, if there were any potential hiccups. Had she fixed things with the friend? Was there any chance of her grandmother finding out? What would the Batbitch do if she realised she'd been hoodwinked?

His mother, as per usual, came to the rescue.

'All set for tonight?' asked Caroline, as Hamish pretended to peruse the programme.

Reggie shook her head and looked at Hamish. He went cold.

Then she laughed. 'Yes, it's all fine – you look like you need to sit down, Hamish.'

'That's not funny,' he said plonking onto his seat in relief. His mouth was dry so he grabbed the half-drunk Coke and then realised he'd taken the only other chair and stood up again. 'Sorry, Reg, you sit down.'

'I'll sit here,' she replied, sitting in the grass among the fallen blossoms, her back against the trunk. 'But I will have a sip of that Coke.'

Hamish handed her the can, his fingers feeling like they'd been inserted into a three-phase power supply when they brushed hers.

'According to the Batbitch, I'm going home with Jenna Murphy. Fear not, Fraser – you won't attend the illustrious Trinity Matric dance alone.'

'Thanks be to God and his angels,' said Hamish dryly.

Inspired by this confirmation, Hamish and Sports Vision won the next B-grade class comfortably and, with that, his ascension to the A grades.

Later that afternoon, the Fraser family and Reggie were drinking tea on the Inanda verandah among the myriad fragrances of Caroline's spring garden. Hamish watched his dance partner tease Roger about his new girlfriend (Roger was onto his umpteenth).

'But, Rog, really, Frances Merkel?'

'What's wrong with Frances?' He smiled, teeth full of chocolate cake.

'Well, she's pretty enough.' The bridge of Reggie's freckled nose crinkled up. 'But those feet, Rog ... I mean, have you seen them?'

'Her feet? What's wrong with her feet?'

'Well, they're not so much feet as they are skis.' Reggie winked at Julia, who giggled.

'I haven't noticed,' said Roger.

'You will when she starts borrowing your size elevens,' said Reggie.

Stuart looked at his watch. 'We need to leave in about forty-five minutes if you two want to be on time.'

'I'd better go get ready then,' said Reggie. 'We don't want Hamish arriving at the dance with a girl who smells like a horse.'

Forty minutes later, Hamish emerged from his room in high distress. He was garbed in his new suit pants and shirt, with a bowtie that looked as if he had attempted suicide by strangulation. His tardiness had been caused by the inordinate amount of time he'd taken trying to fix his hair and face. The stress of the event had created an infestation of acne, which Hamish had done his best to hide with some over-the-counter masking agent, the application of which made him look like he'd received a fistful of clay to the head. (He had washed it off, surmising correctly that the red pimples were better than the clay.)

He charged through the kitchen to the laundry, where his unpolished shoes were waiting. His socks failed to find purchase on the kitchen floor and he slammed into the closed stable door with a loud grunt: 'Ow, fuck!'

This brought Tina from the peace and quiet of her room.

'My shoes, I forgot my shoes!' he wailed, wrenching open the door and descending the stairs to the laundry holding his injured midriff.

Tina remained the only person in the world capable of calming Hamish when he was this agitated. 'Hamish,' she said firmly, 'look me.'

He came to a red-faced halt. A thrush called from a flowerbed overflowing with sweet peas.

'Where are your shoes?'

'In the laundry. I must polish them – I forgot – and now I'm late!' Hamish leapt into the laundry.

Tina wrested the polish box from the panicked teenager. 'Go ask Daddy to fix your tie – you can't polish in your shirt. I will do the shoes.'

'Thanks, Gogo.'

Hamish raced back up the stairs, skidded around the kitchen table and shot down the passage, where he tripped over the piano stool and sprawled onto the carpet leading into the hall.

He looked up to see the side of a black stiletto, above which stretched a smooth, stockinged and shapely calf.

A burst of laughter filled the space. 'Hamish Charles Sutherland Fraser, is that any way to receive your partner?'

Hamish stood up, dumbstruck.

There she was, embraced by the last shafts of afternoon sun coming through the front door. She lifted a teardrop diamond earring from the antique rosewood table and reached to place it in her ear, inclining her head towards to Hamish. He marvelled at her lips, the way the top one looked slightly too large for the bottom. Her navy eyes were darkly outlined and her raven hair was loosely tied, leaving a few ill-behaved strands to frame her high cheeks.

The dress was port-red velvet with a plunging neckline; it partially covered her finely crafted shoulders. The garment hugged her figure – over her breasts, into her narrow waist and around her hips. She was floating on impossibly narrow heels.

Reggie finished with the earring and ran her hands over some imaginary creases on the dress. She looked up into Hamish's eyes.

'Well, come on, Hamish – this is the part where you tell me how nice I look.'

He remained silent for a few seconds.

'You don't look real.' He spoke quietly, not wanting to disturb the delicate atmosphere.

'What does that mean?' she whispered.

'It means I don't have the words, Reg.'

There was another silence as she smiled.

'Is that a good thing?'

'It's perfect … just perfect.' He took a step towards her.

The moment was shattered by Julia's entrance from the garden.

'Wow, Reggie!' she gasped. 'You look so pretty!'

Caroline followed: 'Oh, Reggie, what a stunning dress.' Then she saw her son. 'Hamish, what on earth have you done to your tie? Quickly go and get your father to fix it.'

Half an hour later, the two of them stepped arm in arm through the Trinity College archway.

'I'm sorry I wore these heels,' she said as they walked under a thousand fairy lights. 'I didn't mean to be taller than you.'

'Don't be ridiculous,' he replied. 'The deficiencies of my physique are hardly your fault. You look perfect, as I said.'

The theme of the dance was *A Midsummer Night's Dream*, and so the floor leading to the hall was strewn with leaves (which resulted in more than one grazed knee for inexperienced wearers of high heels). The stone cloisters of the College were strung with twinkling lights and ivy from which peered effigies of the Bard's beloved characters.

The boys of the Matric Dance Committee (more accurately, their mothers) had created a mystical wonderland in the dining marquee and the hall where the dancing would take place. Most of the Matric boys brought girls from their small social circles, many of whom knew each other. None of them had met Reggie, and when she wafted down the slate steps into the marquee, she turned more than one head – largely because she was an objectively stunning creature, but also because she was on the arm of Hamish Fraser, hitherto known to have never had a girlfriend and suspected by many to be gay.

Their table was to be shared with another couple who would turn even more heads. Robert Gumede and Angelica Constable – the first mixed-race couple ever to attend a Trinity Matric dance – exuded a style that screamed 'we don't give a shit what any of you think'. He was dressed in an ivory dinner jacket, perfectly cut to his stocky physique. She wore a short, shimmering green dress and a pair of crimson six-inch stilettos.

After the starter, the first dance – traditionally a waltz – was announced. Hamish had made Stuart teach him the steps and had practised with his sister until she'd begged him to revert to throwing rugby balls at her. As the music began – Tchaikovsky's waltz from *Swan Lake* – Hamish turned to his partner.

'Would you like to dance, madam?'

'Why, sir, this is a waltz. Do you think you can manage?'

'Madam, I wager I'll do better than manage,' he replied, proffering his hand.

She kicked off her heels, stood and placed her fingers on his with a flourish. As on the stage, confidence surged as Hamish strode to the middle of the parquet floor, spun Reggie gently round and deftly placed his right hand on her waist, noting the firmness of the flesh beneath the velvet. As their left hands touched, Hamish moved with a natural sense for the music. Reggie's grandmother lived somewhere at the turn of the nineteenth century and had she succeeded in imposing her will completely, Reggie would have found herself at a Swiss finishing school. The upshot was that she'd been ballroom dancing for years, and she followed perfectly.

'Why, sir, you are a superb dancer!'

'And you, madam, move with the lightness of a sprite.'

Hamish felt twice his height as they sailed with Tchaikovsky, leaning into each other as the music ebbed and flowed. Reggie's thick hair came free of its moorings and flared out as Hamish spun her round. The leafy walls and low-hanging hessian roof strung with mirror balls and thousands of fairy lights cast the scene in an otherworldly lustre.

Hamish and Reggie's eyes were locked, and while their bodies had begun a respectable six inches from each other, as the music built to its

final conclusion, the gap had closed completely. The dance had the tim-
ing of a waltz and all the charge of a tango. As the deafening final chord
sounded, Hamish spun Reggie round, caught her, and dipped her back
over his arm. She swung up until her lips were millimetres from his.
Then, as rapturous applause broke out, she moved her head to the side
and nestled briefly in the crook of his neck.

'Thank you, Hamish Fraser.'

For the second time that day, he was ready for the end of the world.
Hamish led her out of the hall.

'Pff,' scoffed Dylan Crane quietly to Andrew Marsdorf, 'only gays
can dance like that.'

Back at their table in the marquee, Robert Gumede was laughing.
'That's Fraser the fish,' he said. 'Loves a big entrance. Nicely danced,
guys – that was very cool.'

He raised his glass to them. Hamish didn't have a drink, so Gumede
emptied half of his into Hamish's glass.

'Thanks, Robert.' Hamish took a large swig. Fire exploded all the
way down his oesophagus and into his belly. He was speechless briefly
and then began to cough.

'Easy, boy,' said Robert. 'You'll be under the table before dessert if you
drink that fast.'

Reggie reached for the glass and took a sip. 'Vodka, Robert?'

'Vodka.'

She pushed her glass towards him and smiled.

The meal progressed with pleasant banter. Robert Gumede, happy
and slightly drunk, played the role of host, teasing and cajoling his
tablemates in equal measure and filling their drinks from a seemingly
bottomless source of vodka-laced cola. Hamish drank the stuff sparingly
– he'd begun to feel woozy soon after the first gulp. Reggie, however,
drank as much as Gumede, but on a frame almost half the mass.

Hamish began to feel uneasy. As the pudding plates were cleared,
Reggie pushed her glass across to the host again.

'Reg, why don't you just have some Coke now – then let's go dance,'

Hamish suggested, hoping the activity would clear her system.

She turned to him, naked fury clouding her narrowed eyes. It took him back to the chestnut tree on the night she told him of her mother's illness.

Robert Gumede felt the atmosphere change. 'Let's all go dance – see if we can best Fraser the fish and his lady!'

The rest of the table stood to leave. Reggie's eyes blazed.

'Don't, Hamish – don't ever fucking tell me what to do,' she hissed.

He was stunned.

Reggie stood and tottered into the hall to join the throng of dancing teenagers. Hamish had very little experience of drunkenness or women, and none of that combination. He sat, unmoving, for the duration of Depeche Mode's 'I Just Can't Get Enough'. When no one came out of the hall at the end of the song, he stood and moved into the pulsing lights. Depeche Mode was replaced with a thumping remix of Madonna's 'Vogue'.

He felt discombobulated as he walked through the hall, now half the size he'd felt during the waltz. The pounding beat, flashing lights, heaving crowd and vodka had made him giddy. As he searched for his group, he felt like a wandering pinball in a nightmare – invisible Hamish Fraser again, losing his bearings and bumping into people who hardly noticed. How the hell had the night turned bad so fast? He crashed into Wayne Johnson – six foot four and weighing in excess of a hundred kilograms – and skidded across the polished floor into the tree-covered wall panelling.

There, he sat down heavily on a bench. Madonna ceased her wailing to be replaced by Midnight Oil with 'Beds Are Burning'. Hamish rubbed his eyes and looked up.

He saw her in the flash of a strobe light.

Heat surged up the back of his neck.

Waves of nausea caught in his constricting throat.

She wasn't dancing alone. She wasn't dancing at all.

Her perfect, sensuous top lip, the one Hamish had imagined kissing more times than he could count, was attached to Andrew Marsdorf's gaping mouth.

The earth turned beneath Hamish and he grabbed the bench to avoid toppling over. He couldn't take his eyes off the horrific scene playing out in front of him. It looked like Marsdorf was trying to eat the girl he loved, enveloping her like an ogre, one hand kneading her rump and the other behind her head. One of her hands hung limply to the side, the other cupped the back of his neck. As the horns played the final three chords, Reggie disentangled herself and staggered towards the door. Marsdorf followed.

The driving guitars of The Cult playing 'She Sells Sanctuary' galvanised Hamish Fraser. He ground his teeth, stood and marched after his ex-partner and the detested Marsdorf. He quickly spotted Reggie slumped alone at their table, another glass next to her. It took him another second to find Marsdorf talking to Dylan Crane and Neil Long – the latter two laughing and covering their mouths in disbelief. Long saw Hamish coming and flicked his head to warn Marsdorf, who turned in time for his nose to meet Hamish's flying right fist. This time the diminutive appendage found home. Marsdorf's head snapped back – more from surprise than the force of the blow.

This was a fellow who had played two years as a first XV lock – he'd taken countless knees and fists to the face. Marsdorf reached up slowly to his split top lip and then looked at the smudge of blood on his finger.

'Fraser, you fucken loser.'

As Hamish opened his mouth to respond, Marsdorf's left fist, backed by ninety kilograms of lean muscle, slammed into his nose. The smaller boy saw stars and fell onto his backside. A small crowd quickly formed.

'Stay down, loser – or I'll fucking kill you!'

Hamish shook his head and staggered to his feet, blood streaming from his ruined nose. Genuine surprise registered on the faces of the onlookers as Hamish, crimson dripping onto his new shirt, lunged again at Marsdorf. Before he could make contact, Paul Simpson – in one of his final acts as head boy, grabbed Hamish in a bear hug and pulled him away.

'No, Fraser – calm down, man. Just calm down.'

'Let that fucken loser at me,' said Marsdorf quietly.

Hamish pretended to relax but, as Simpson released him, he flew at his tormentor. Two other boys grabbed his arms but Hamish ripped out of their grip. The effect was to catapult him forward so that the crown of his head slammed into Marsdorf's snarling mouth. The larger boy's bottom lip split, his top teeth gashing Hamish's forehead. Once again powerful arms grabbed Hamish, wrenching him back.

'Let that little shithead at me,' Marsdorf roared. 'I'll show him how I fucken operate.' He charged forward but Simpson stopped him with an open hand to the chest that quickly became a pointed finger.

'You shut the fuck up, Marsdorf. What you've done tonight is incredibly shit – Fraser's never done anything to you. You're a bully and the only fucking loser standing here.'

Publicly rebuked by his hero, Marsdorf was humiliated.

'What is going on here?!' raged Mr McAdams as he arrived with a swathe of masters.

'Nothing, sir,' said Paul Simpson. 'All fixed now.'

Trusting the head boy to sort out the problem, the old master nodded and left.

Hamish walked away into the cloisters, onto the terrace that led to the chapel. He didn't know where he was going – it just had to be away from the hall, his peers, Reggie and his humiliation. Down the steps, past the crypt chapel and into the little garden of remembrance, where he sat on a weathered bench overlooking the spring gardens, the aloe-strewn rockeries and the main rugby field. The scene was lit dimly by a three-quarter waning moon in the eastern sky and the orange glow of the city. A cricket bowed gently next to him. Hamish shook his head, longing for an emotional explosion to take away the nausea and humiliation, but none came – no tears, no rage, just the constricted throat every time he pictured them kissing.

After twenty minutes he realised he would have to go and sort out the evening. It was impossible for him to attend the after-party – he couldn't face being with Reggie or anyone else, and he knew she was in no state to be going anywhere. Hamish toyed with the idea of leaving her at the dance to fend for herself, but knew this was simply vengeful. His only option was to call his father and to be fetched.

He stood, retched into the flowerbed next to him, wiped his mouth and walked back up the stairs to the tuck shop, where there was a payphone.

'Dad?'

'Hello, boy.' It was nine-thirty and Stuart and Caroline were watching a video. To say Stuart was surprised to hear from his son wouldn't be entirely accurate: the potential for disaster was never far from Hamish, and the two parents always found themselves slightly on edge when their eldest was out of the house. 'What's wrong? What's happened?'

Hamish was calm. 'I'll tell you later. I need you to come and fetch us now, please – as fast as you can.'

'Okay, no problem – I'll be there in ten to fifteen minutes. Is there a medical problem?'

'No. Just come – it'll be fine.' Hamish rang off.

He undid his bowtie, folded it into his pocket and walked back to the hall with dread. He found Reggie slumped in the same place at their table. Next to her sat Samantha Thatcher, partner and long-time girlfriend of Paul Simpson. The head boy appeared next to Hamish.

'You have to get her out of here, Fraser,' he said. There was sympathy in his voice and Hamish appreciated it.

Reggie's head lolled forward as Samantha tried to coax her into drinking some water.

Hamish looked at his partner. 'There's a car coming. Will you help me get her out?'

'Ja, of course.' Simpson patted him between the shoulders.

They supported the swaying, helpless young woman between them and walked her out through the Prep school, thus avoiding the staff table. Other than two unidentified smokers who scuttled into the shadows like nocturnal lizards, and Dylan Crane, who was in the process of being devoured by Elizabeth Tresling in the hydrangeas, they saw no one.

Stuart was waiting at the College archway. He opened the rear door of the Mercedes and the two young men laid Reggie on the back seat. She passed out immediately.

'I'm sorry, Fraser. This is really kak,' Simpson said with feeling.

'Thanks, Paul.' Hamish climbed into the passenger side.

'Sorry about this, sir,' the head boy said to Stuart.

'I doubt she or he were your doing,' he replied, looking at the girl in the back seat and then at his son's bloodied face.

Five minutes along the familiar road home, Stuart spoke for the first time through clenched teeth. 'I don't suppose you'd like to tell me what happened tonight?'

'Ag, a few guys had some booze – no one else is drunk, Dad. She just drank way more.'

'That doesn't explain your boxer's nose, cut forehead or the blood on your shirt.'

Hamish looked out of the window, eyes welling. 'Some real arsehole said some mean stuff to Reggie, so I hit him and he hit me back – that's all.'

His father decided to ignore the obvious lie, accepting that the evening had been sufficiently traumatic.

Back in the Inanda driveway, Reggie was conscious, but well beyond walking.

'You're going to have to carry her, boy,' Stuart said to his skinny son – knowing that if he didn't drop her on the bricks, he would at least take some heart from the feat.

They both pulled her from the car and then Hamish lifted her into his arms. The semi-conscious girl nestled against his shoulder. He didn't know whether to feel happy at her closeness or disgusted by the vodka fumes.

Hamish staggered into the house, where Caroline met them at the front door in a state of high agitation. When she beheld the comatose girl and her son's mangled face, she nearly passed out.

'Oh, Hamish!' she wailed.

'Mother, not now,' he snapped, walking past her, down the passage and into the spare room, where he laid Reggie down on the bed.

She seemed utterly helpless in the soft lamplight, her dark eye make-up smudged where she'd rubbed away the tears and her beautiful dress creased, the hem covered in dirt. His heart melted – he was simply unable to maintain a sense of anger.

His mother came to the door. 'I'll look after her now.'

Hamish nodded and went through to where his father was waiting in the sitting room.

'Looks like you could do with a drink,' Stuart said to his son for the first time ever. He went across to the cabinet, uncorked a bottle of Talisker, poured himself a generous measure and a smaller one for Hamish. He handed the cut glass to his son.

'Come, let's sit outside,' he said. 'You dinna have to tell me about it now.'

Hamish didn't sleep that night – or for many nights after. He lay awake as his mind played over the evening again and again.

The sense of wholeness and joy in the hallway before they left.

The intense connection during the waltz.

The shattering explosion of a pain and emasculation on seeing Reggie kissing one of the people he hated most. Hamish was beginning to see that his struggle to make friends was not entirely because the rest of humanity was in some way deficient – he'd began to appreciate that some of his own behaviours needed modification. Andrew Marsdorf, however, was beneath his contempt – a wilfully ignorant, arrogant, unprincipled, racist oaf.

That Sunday morning, while most of his classmates (and his partner)

323

were nursing their hangovers, Hamish rose early – the affection he'd felt for Reggie in her drunken slumber replaced with the same numb sickness he'd felt in the garden of remembrance. He forced himself out of bed, put on his riding kit, and told his parents not to expect him home until after lunch.

'What about Reggie?' asked his mother, who was making coffee in the kitchen.

'I really can't face seeing her.'

Caroline nodded and turned to her son. 'You know, while what happened last night is horrible for you, I'd like you to try and find it in your heart to forgive her – she's had a very, very hard time at home. She's obviously not lacked anything material, but she's grown up without love – with no mother, no one to talk to. But you know that as well as anyone.' She took two rusks out of a tin and placed them on a plate. 'Everyone deals with these things differently.'

The silence hung for a while and Hamish watched the steam from the cups catch the morning light.

'I know, Mum,' he replied sadly. 'I just can't see her right now.'

With that, he departed for the stables and the comfort of his cantankerous horse, Colin, the syringas and the oak.

26

The rest of the term progressed without further incident. As he approached his eighteenth birthday, Hamish, much subdued, enjoyed the spring. The smell of star jasmine as he bicycled to and from the stables reminded him that summer and the end of the year were coming.

In his spare time, Hamish did his best to study for the final Matric exams. During the week-long study break, he spent at least nine hours a day sitting at his desk, though the amount of time he actually occupied with absorbing information and not staring out of the window or listening to music made the activity largely wasteful.

He passed into legal adulthood with almost no fanfare – he didn't want a party – but much familial kindness. His grandmother grudgingly bestowed a watch on her least favourite grandchild. Despite the fact that her fortunes could have extended to a Rolex, the item was purchased from the local chemist.

'Thanks, Gran,' Hamish said as he unwrapped it.

'That's fine, but I tell you those Israelites who own the pharmacy charged an appalling price for it,' the old woman scoffed.

'Mum, please!' pleaded Caroline.

Hamish's most treasured eighteenth-birthday gift came from Tina, who had knitted him a cardigan of bottle-green wool. He wondered if he would ever actually grow to fill it. (He didn't.)

Three weeks after his birthday, he would attend his final Trinity carol service. The Matric boys in the choir were excused in order to study, but Hamish would not have missed his favourite concert of the year for love or money. All the Matric choir boys felt the same – this was, after all, their last hurrah. Before that, however, Hamish would ride in his first and only show as Junior A grade. Stuart had made it clear that if Hamish wished to carry on riding after school, it would be for his own account.

Sports Vision, all fifteen hands of him, was now twenty years old, and his life before arriving at the Inanda Club had been a difficult one. No one had expected Hamish to ride him for more than a year or two before upgrading to a larger and younger animal, but the Frasers' financial fortunes had not continued on the expected trajectory and a new horse for Hamish had never been a priority. It had taken almost four years for them to ride through the grades, and Sports Vision, depending on his mood, was not above refusing to jump halfway through a round. He was increasingly stiff, and Hamish wasn't able to practise his jumping as often as he needed to.

'In reality, this will probably be his and your last show – I think we have to try,' said Annabelle when Hamish asked if she thought the little chestnut was up for the A grades.

This was the argument Hamish had used to convince his parents that although he still had six exams to write after the show, he deserved this one last day to ride.

The Saturday of the show, Hamish slept in – as an A grade, he and Sports Vision only had to arrive by mid-morning.

The whole family turned out to watch that day. Roger was thoroughly sick of horses and the time they had sucked from the family over the years, but he was equally bored of studying. Julia loved the shows and horses. Stuart went along happy in the knowledge that he'd never have to sit through another one, although he acknowledged a slight sadness at the lack of Saturday-morning bacon-and-egg rolls. To Hamish's amazement, even Elizabeth insisted on coming.

'Finally, that strange child is going to achieve something worthwhile,' she'd said to Caroline on the phone the night before. 'I may as well be there to see it – I am not long for this world.'

The family found a plane tree to sit under on the northern side of the arena where the B-grade class was underway. Roger made a beeline for the canteen and an armload of bacon-and-egg rolls. Elizabeth had arrived with her own picnic of minute cucumber sandwiches, chipolatas and cheese puffs. These she intended to wash down with a bottle of unwooded chardonnay nestled in a cooler box of ice she'd insisted on bringing.

'What the hell is in here?' asked Stuart as he'd wrestled her hamper from the car. 'The eighth army could have dined on this!'

'Do you expect me to drink water or cola?' she'd remonstrated.

'Oh God, no. Please let it never be said that pure H_2O ever passed your lips.'

'You know I hate it when you mutter so,' the old woman snapped, tottering in her half-heels towards her chair.

Hamish went in search of a programme, twinged slightly with the fear that he'd have to face Reggie, but comforted in the knowledge that the chance of her grandmother allowing her to ride in the middle of her Matric exams was negligible to zero. At the judges' box, he paid ten rand and leafed through the printed pages as he made his way back to the family – his mind working through the amount of time he'd need to warm up. As Sports Vision stiffened with age, it was taking increasing periods to loosen him up – almost double what it had four years previously.

Halfway back, Hamish froze in his tracks.

There was her name – number eleven in the A-grade class, Rebecca Fine and My Fair Lady. The comforting smell of the breakfast kiosk suddenly made him bilious.

Reggie had tried to speak to him on the phone every Sunday for a month after the dance. Each time, he'd refused to take the call – not knowing what on earth he'd say to her. She had then written a letter.

My dear Hamish,

I wanted to say this to you in person, but your Mum says you don't want to talk to me on the phone. That makes me so sad. So, I'm just going to say what I wanted to in this letter. I hope you will write back to me, but I understand if you don't want to.

I am so sorry about what happened at the dance. What I did to you that night was so cruel and it makes me sadder than you can imagine. You and your family have been so kind to me and you didn't deserve to have a partner like me at your dance. I'm so sorry I got drunk. I'm so sorry I kissed that guy – I don't even know his name and I wouldn't even recognise him. That's so gross, but I don't want you to think I'm having something with one of your classmates.

I need you to know something about how I feel about you and your family. You are my oldest friends in the world and you, your home and your family remind me of a time when I was happy. I love spending time around all of you. It makes me so sad that we can't do it more because of the shitty Batbitch. Those times sitting with you at shows and even talking on the phone have been like precious holidays for me. With you, I can just be myself without all the pressure of being the most righteous, academically brilliant, superbly athletic and religiously observant Jewess in the world. I don't have to pretend to be happy like I must at school. I am so exhausted all the time.

You also need to understand how much of a help your mother has been to me. She has given me comfort and advice that I guess most young women would get from their mothers, but I get nothing but a list of goals to achieve from the Batbitch. Without your mother, I am not sure I could have got through the last few years.

I think I understand you enough to know that you have read this thinking 'Yes, but what about me?'

I am going to be very honest with you now, so I beg you to read this with an open mind and heart.

I think you are a very special person, Hamish Fraser. I love your quirky attitudes and your sarcastic sense of humour. I love the hundreds of stupid facial expressions you pull. I love that you haven't compromised on being you (although some changes perhaps wouldn't be so bad). I love how hard you try against the odds – the story of your debut for the rugby firsts is hilarious, tragic and a tribute to you. It sums up so nicely the things I love about you.

Despite the limited time we've spent with each other, I know you understand me – you get me. I know that because you know what I'm going to say it before I open my mouth. If we spent more time together, we wouldn't even need to speak – we'd just know. You get what I'm saying?

Here's the difficult bit.

I can see from the way you look at me and hug me that friendship is not what you want from me. Well, it wasn't what you wanted from me until the dance. Now you might want nothing at all to do with me but I'm going to pretend that isn't the case. I have never discussed this with your mother, just in case you are worried.

So I guess you might want to know how I feel. The truth is that I don't know. There is something that stops me giving in to some sort of romance between us – impossible as it might be. Maybe we've known each other too long, maybe I don't want to ruin what we have. Sometimes when I lie in bed at night, I think about what it would be like to have you next to me, to hold me and it makes me smile. Other times I think it would be the worst idea in the world. I have hurt many people in my life and I couldn't bear to do that to you and now look what I've done!

Anyway, I'm not going to phone any more unless you write to

me and ask me to.
  I'm so sorry.
  All my love,
  Reggie

A week and several thousand readings of the letter later, Hamish finally replied in his illegible scrawl.

Dear Reggie,

Thank you for your honest letter, which I appreciate.
  I too am going to be as honest as I can and I think some of this will be hard for you to read so I'm sorry in advance.
  This has been a really hard thing to write because I feel so conflicted. I want to be angry with you, but I can't for some reason. I want to write you off as a human being, but as I was told after the debacle of my rugby debut, 'No one died.' And no one did die that foul, shitty night. I thought a piece of me had died for a while, but it didn't. I think I just grew up a little more, became a little less nayeev (I know that's not how you spell it but I really can never remember how).
  Anyway, you hurt me horribly, Reggie, but I accept your apology. I know that you've had a very difficult life and that I really haven't – even if I feel sorry for myself a lot of the time.
  I always think I'm being so subtle when I have a crush on a girl, but it seems that my emotions are painted across my forehead. I am not going to lie – ever since I saw you at that show two years ago, I've been smitten (that's a good word, isn't it?). The breath catches in my throat and I actually ache sometimes when I think about you. I too have lain in bed at night wondering what it would be like to have you there with me – I have never felt anything other than wonderful under the illusion. When I saw you standing in the hallway in your dress, I wanted to freeze time

*forever. During the waltz you made me feel like I was a man –
the only man in the whole world. Afterwards, it was more worm.*

*I'm really sad that you don't feel the same way but to be hon-
est, why would you? I'm sure there are older boys courting you
– probably men, actually. Anyway, it doesn't matter.*

*Thanks for your letter. I don't know what happens now. I'm
still not sure I can talk to you but I want to find out what you are
going to do next year. And wish you a happy birthday.*

*Whatever happens, I hope that you will be happy when you can
finally leave your grandparents.*

Love,

Hamish

There was another paragraph that he had inserted and then removed
because he hated the self-pity in these words, though it was true.

*After much thought, I know that the thing that I feel the most
right now is shame. I am ashamed to face the guys in my class –
everyone in the school knows what happened. Everyone knows
that Hamish Fraser's partner was taken from him just after pudding. As the boys in my class have grown up, so their jibes about
the choir and my riding have almost disappeared to the extent that
I have a few friends now and have even been invited to a few parties. But this thing has eroded my confidence and takes me right
back to being little Hamish Fraser, the co-ord who is probably
gay.*

The last thing he wanted was for her to feel sorry for him.

'Hello, Hamish.' Her voice was softer than the breeze – so much so that
he thought, hoped even, that he'd imagined it. 'Hamish?'

He looked up, and there she was in her white jodhpurs and a

331

pale-blue shirt, her face expressionless. And there he stood, completely in her power.

She knew everything now – not that she hadn't before, but before the letters they could at least both pretend.

'Hi, Reg.' He managed a wan smile and was suddenly overcome with the desire to hug her. He took a step forward, felt ashamed and stopped. 'How are you?'

'I'm okay.' She shrugged. 'You?'

'Yeah, I'm alright.'

They were standing alone behind the grandstand. Hamish looked west over the rolling hills of smallholdings. The silence wasn't awkward; they'd known each other for too long. Their energies balanced in the quiet.

'How are you allowed to ride in the middle of exams?' he asked eventually.

'The Batbitch expects me to win – in all things. She doesn't see this as a pleasure – winning here is almost as important to her as my achieving straight As. It was pretty easy to con her.'

'Con her?'

'I guessed this was going to be your last show. I don't know if I'll ever see you again.'

He was surprised.

'So here I am.' She smiled.

'I'm riding first,' he said eventually. 'I'd better go and warm up.'

'I'll see you afterwards.'

Then they were holding each other beneath the highveld summer sky dotted with puffy cumulus, a flock of queleas whirring in the long grass next to them. Five minutes later they wordlessly let go, both wiping their eyes.

As the first to ride, Hamish had to salute the judges on behalf of the other riders. Sports Vision, comfortably the smallest and oldest horse in the competition, seemed to realise the significance of the occasion. Instead of doing his best to bite the marshal as they waited at the gate, or lunge for the thick Kikuyu fringing the arena, he stood to attention.

Hamish was lost in thought, nervous about the huge fences. More than that, he was thinking of the end of an era: the last show on this old horse, the final Trinity carol service that night.

An uncertain, if exciting, future.

The gate opened and the marshal shouted the order: 'Sports Vision and Hamish Fraser, in you go.'

As they walked in, Sports Vision began to canter on the spot, his muscles bunched under him. Colin's grooming and Hamish's disciplined schooling had turned the horse into a sublimely statuesque, if small, picture of equine magnificence. The rider sat deep into the saddle and thrust out his chest as a fanfare greeted their arrival.

'Into the arena for the A-grade welcome stakes is Sports Vision and Hamish Fraser to take the salute,' the announcer called.

Eager spectators whispered their appreciation for the chestnut horse cantering sideways along the eastern side of the arena. The animal snorted with each stride. His neck arched, the sun glistening off his powerful, compact physique. Hamish felt as if he too was blessed with a compact (true) and muscled (false) physique. He was, however, the perfect size for his horse, and the two of them cut a dashing sight.

As the pair approached the judges' box, the judge rose from her seat to receive the salute. Hamish, Sports Vision cantering on the spot, took the reins in his left hand and with his right removed his hat and bowed his head to the judge, who acknowledged him with a subtle bow. The formalities thus complete, Hamish could concentrate on his round. But an idea struck him – it was a beautiful day, his horse and he had never looked better, and who knew when or if there would ever be another opportunity.

Hamish replaced his hat and, instead of making his way to the start poles, turned the prancing horse towards the main grandstand. He cantered sideways along its length until he reached the middle. Sitting in the front row was Reggie, her grandmother and various others from her stable yard. He brought Sports Vision to a halt in front of the girl he loved. As her grandmother looked on, wide-eyed recognition register-ing, Reggie stood, her eyes welling. For a second time, Hamish removed his hat in salute.

The bell rang for his round and the old horse, so used to the sound, began to prance again. Hamish replaced his helmet and cantered through the start poles to commence his first A-grade round. The fences were bigger than he or Sports Vision had yet seen, but despite the doubts of his mother (who watched him with her hands over her eyes), the pair rode a beautiful clear round. Polite applause accompanied them as they cantered through the finish poles.

There was one loud cheer as they cleared the final fence. 'Yaaaah!' Colin yelled at his charges.

Hamish returned to the family feeling a subdued sense of pleasure at his achievement.

Annabelle smiled. 'You know I wasn't sure that horse would manage that,' she said.

His mother was crying, but no one was surprised at her tears.

'Well done, Hamish!' said Roger and Julia.

Stuart patted his son on the shoulders and handed him a Coke. 'Good lad,' he said.

'It's not like he's actually won anything yet,' muttered Elizabeth, sip-ping her Chardonnay.

The other competitors rode with varying degrees of success. Hamish watched Reggie with his heart in his mouth – unsure as to why he was so nervous for her. She went clear.

The next time Hamish's heart rose towards his throat was as his name was called for the jump-off. There were twelve clear rounds and the winner would be decided over six fences against the clock.

Hamish and Sports Vision walked into the arena, the rider going over the round in his mind. There was one tight corner that he knew Sports Vision could make because he was small – but it was risky. His route planned, he waited as the course-builder raised the last of the fences. To the south, the beginnings of what would become a late-afternoon thunderstorm billowed into the sky. North, the endless blue vault of Africa. Hamish smiled in appreciation at the culmination of his riding career. He patted Sports Vision lightly on the shoulder.

'Thanks, old boy,' he said quietly as the bell rang.

Hamish gathered the reins and Sports Vision collected underneath him. They cantered one small circle and then Hamish turned to the first fence and urged his horse forward. The chestnut's hindquarters exploded three strides to the first upright. The risky turn was on the approach to the final obstacle.

As they landed after the fifth fence, Hamish sat down hard into the saddle and hauled on the left rein. Sports Vision – four years of disciplined training under his belt – responded beautifully. He came around the corner on a daring line. As the horse straightened, Hamish saw that the three strides he'd allowed were going to be long – perhaps too long.

'Come on, boy!' he encouraged.

Sports Vision's back right hoof seemed to slip as his hindquarters pushed towards the jump. Maybe it was a piece of uneven ground. Perhaps Hamish was overambitious. It is possible the horse had simply had enough of show jumping. Whatever the case, the huge blue-and-white oxer was a fence too far.

Sports Vision took three fast strides and then dug his front hooves into the ground, swinging sideways to avoid colliding with the poles, panels, bales and uprights that made up the oxer.

Hamish, blinded by adrenaline, fully expected his horse to take off and was thus completely unprepared for the abrupt cessation of forward momentum. As Sports Vision swerved viciously, Hamish flew out of the saddle and clattered into the timber, straw and steel. He reflexively turned his body mid-flight to protect his head, with the result that his left shoulder took the first impact on the top pole while ribs and back accounted for the planking panels below. As the front section of the jump took the impact of Hamish's sixty-three kilograms propelled at high velocity, the whole edifice collapsed. Four heavy steel uprights fell inward, one of them landing on Hamish's lower right leg. The back pole came down next and collected the left side of the rider's face, splitting his bottom lip and bruising his eye socket.

Hamish was pinned beneath the debris.

For a second or two he lay there, his breath the only sensation he could perceive. Then he heard voices.

'Fuck, he can't have survived that,' said the course-builder, running to his ruined construction.

'Oh, Christ.' An unknown female.

'Catch the horse, Phineas,' ordered another woman (unnecessarily, as Sports Vision was calmly helping himself to a hay bale that had once been part of the jump).

An eye-watering pain exploded in Hamish's right ankle – the joint was pinned by a winged steel upright. He gasped and was further racked by a stabbing sensation in his ribs and the taste of blood. Slowly the myriad pieces of apparatus were removed from above him and the sky appeared. Then his father's voice, struggling for calm.

'Are you alright, boy?'

'Don't move, I'll need to assess you – let's bring the ambulance,' said the medic, ever ready to drive someone to hospital at high speed with the sirens wailing.

Hamish ran his tongue over his split lip and winced.

'I'm okay, Dad. Please help me up.'

'Don't move!' yelled the medic.

Hamish ignored this and began to sit.

Stuart helped his son sit up. 'Are you alright, boy?' he asked again.

'I've been better,' Hamish wheezed.

Annabelle, seeing that her pupil was alive and as yet unparalysed, took control. 'Come on, Hamish, you've got fifteen seconds to get back on or you'll be eliminated,' she urged. 'Don't let it end like this.'

Truth focused the boy.

'Take my arms,' he said.

Stuart and Annabelle pulled him to his feet. Pain shot through his ankle as he tried to put his weight on it. He winced and then hopped twice to where his horse was standing. Annabelle shoved him into the saddle just in time.

'He's not going to jump again?' asked the course-builder.

'Oh yes, he bloody is,' said Annabelle.

While the fence was reconstructed, Hamish gathered the reins and put his feet back into his stirrups. There was no way his right foot could bear any weight, so he wrenched the stirrup off the saddle and tossed it over to Annabelle. He put his hand to his swollen lip and wiped away the drying blood. Reaching to his left eye socket, he felt the graze the pole had left.

The course-builder finished and gave a signal to the judges' box. The bell rang indicating Hamish could finish the round – or retire.

'One more jump, boy. We ain't finishing like this,' he said to the little chestnut.

They cantered a circle, Hamish's ribs and shoulder on fire, his right leg hanging loose. He turned Sports Vision to the fence and saw a perfect five strides. 'Come on, boy!' he said, resisting the urge to hold too tightly to the reins.

The horse responded to his voice, lifted his head, tucked his hocks underneath him and surged forward.

'One, two, three, hup ...' Hamish urged.

Sports Vision took off with a grunt and Hamish sat awkwardly without his right stirrup. Then they were coming down, without any accompanying sound of falling timber. As the horse landed, Hamish knew there was something horribly wrong. Sports Vision pulled up immediately and took two painful steps forward, unable to put any weight on his back right hoof.

The rider instinctively swung his uninjured leg over the saddle and dropped to the floor.

'Ow, fuck!' he hissed under his breath as the injured ankle touched the ground.

The horse was breathing in ragged snorts, his hoof hanging off the ground. Hamish turned to the bridle and undid the noseband. Then he looked up. They were standing in front of the main grandstand.

'Come on, boy,' Hamish said, tears filling his eyes. He took the reins in one hand, patted the gasping horse on the neck and whispered into his ear. 'We have to walk out of here, see.' He turned, gritted his teeth and took a tentative step. Nausea flooded his body as fresh waves of pain exploded from his ankle.

He limped forward once and Sports Vision did the same. Then they took another step and another. The spectators began to stand silently as the horse and his rider hobbled past the grandstand.

On the northern side of the arena, Julia, Caroline, Stuart, Roger and Annabelle began to clap. Even Elizabeth managed some perfunctory applause. Soon everyone around the arena was clapping. Hamish looked to his right and saw Reggie, tears streaming down her beautiful face, hands clapping together.

Then he felt a presence next to him. Wordlessly, Colin pulled Hamish's arm around his shoulders, taking the weight off the now-swelling ankle – an ankle from which the riding boot would have to be cut.

It was clear to all that this would be Sports Vision's last outing as a show jumper. If the injured fetlock could be repaired, he could look forward to retirement or an easy life as a school horse. If recovery wasn't possible, then it would be the dog-food cannery. Hamish knew this as he fought the tears during the painful walk out of the arena.

These thoughts were playing on his mind later that day as he added his voice to the basses in the second verse of 'Once in Royal David's City'. He leant heavily on a crutch, the ankle strapped and twice its normal size. From the bottom of the bandage stuck his bruised bare foot. The left side of his face was a kaleidoscope of yellows, purples and reds, the tumid eye almost closed, the lip swollen but recovering.

After a visit to the emergency room had revealed a grade-two tear in his ankle ligaments and a cracked rib, his parents had tried to convince him to take the night off. But Hamish was determined to sing in his final carol service. He loved the quiet atmosphere, the anticipation of Christmas, the incense mixed with the fragrance of star jasmine floating into the chapel on the summer-evening breeze. Mostly he loved the music. The meditation of 'In the Deep Midwinter', the souring descant in 'Hark the Herald Angels', the infectious joy of 'I Saw Three Ships'. Trinity always ended with 'Oh Come All Ye Faithful', and even the most hard-hearted boys sang their lungs out in competition with the mighty organ. It always left Hamish feeling inspired.

When Stuart had suggested that he sit on the sofa and watch a movie instead of singing, Hamish had looked at him as though he'd just cursed the family.

'No, Dad, I'm going to sing tonight. I'd have to have broken both legs and have a rib lodged in my lung not to go,' he replied. 'Besides, Roger has to go anyway.'

They'd arrived just in time for the service. Hamish was the last of the choir boys to shuffle into the gallery. Mr Danhauser was normally incensed by tardiness, but when he beheld the fact that Hamish was stuck together with bandages, he relented. The hobbling invalid made his way to the rear where the basses were seated.

During the service, Hamish noticed the choirmaster casting anxious glances at the door from time to time but thought nothing of it – so enraptured was he by the music and the healing effect of the atmosphere. It cleansed the sadness of the day.

Three quarters of the way through the service, Hamish was examining the blue tinge his toes were assuming when he felt Andrew Wilkinson, one of the basses, tap him on his shoulder.

'Sir wants you,' Wilkinson said, indicating the choirmaster at the front of the gallery.

Mr Danhauser was beckoning frantically. Hamish stood slowly and, as quietly as was possible with his crutch, made his way to the front of the gallery while Mr Huddle was reading the lesson about the wise men travelling from the east.

'Sir?'

'Jared hasn't arrived!' the choirmaster said.

The choir stood to sing their next carol – 'The Three Kings'.

'Oh,' said Hamish. Then realisation dawned. 'What, you want me to sing it?'

'You know it, don't you?' Mr Danhauser whispered, wide-eyed, as the congregation began looking up to the gallery in expectation.

'The Three Kings' by Peter Cornelius was written for baritone solo and choir. The ethereal piece of music had been Hamish's favourite since he'd first sung it as a treble, when the sublime purity of Simphiwe Buthelezi's tenor had threatened to lift the roof off the chapel. Hamish had known the solo, note for note, from the very next year, hoping that one day he might be invited to sing it. Such notions had been put from his mind with the arrival of Jared Bennington – a boy with a voice that could one day make him a very good living.

This had not stopped Hamish from imagining performing it.

Hamish took visualising his goals very seriously. Countless were the hours he had dreamt of kissing Reggie. In his mind's eye, he'd scored more tries for the first XV than he'd had hot breakfasts. His careful planning for glory in the riding arena had cost innumerable hours while sitting at his desk 'studying' Afrikaans. When the fragrant warmth of spring arrived each September, Hamish's thoughts had always turned to singing in the carol service. He'd imagined stepping onto the soloist's platform – checking the wood's integrity first – and then belting out 'The Three Kings'. And until this very moment, Hamish could safely say that nothing he had visualised had ever come to pass.

'Hamish!' hissed the choirmaster. 'Can you sing it?'

The young man looked down into the congregation, remembering the last time he'd been on the platform. People were staring up at his battered face.

'Yes, sir.' Hamish leant his crutch against the railing over which he'd fallen five years previously. 'I can sing it.' He straightened his blazer and drew himself to his full height.

The organist played a D.

Mr Danhauser lifted his hands and the choir, as one, fixed their eyes on him. He gave two beats and Hamish opened his mouth.

Three kings from Persian lands afar, he sang.

Mr Danhauser smiled and the choir came in on cue. Hamish continued,

To Jordan follow the pointing star ...

As he sang, childhood memories flittered unbidden through his consciousness. Reggie, the walnut tree and the horse at Jumping Jacks.

And this the quest of the travellers three ...

The blissful joy of driving to Kenton for the Christmas holidays.

Where the newborn King of the Jews may be.

The day his little sister had arrived home to the sound of the pipes.

Full royal gifts they bear for the King ...

Precious afternoons listening to Colin under the oak tree.

Gold, incense, myrrh are their offering.

Nicholas Cullinan's constant bullying and ultimate humiliation on the bus.

During the pause between the first and second verses, Mr Danhauser winked at Hamish and gave him a smiling thumbs-up. The soloist glanced down into the congregation to see his mother and father looking up at him. Stuart's cheeks were wet. Hamish looked back up to the rood screen.

The star shines out with a steadfast ray ...

Throwing endless passes at his dad in his mum's peaceful, gorgeous garden.

The Kings to Bethlehem make their way ...

The night at the Ntunjwa's beautiful homestead.

And there in worship they bend the knee ...

Roger's silent but consistent loyalty.

As Mary's child in her lap they see ...

The birth of the baby in the car park at the stables.

The royal gifts they show to the King ...

The green cardigan Tina had knitted for him.

Gold, incense, myrrh are their offering.

The volume of the music increased and Hamish looked to Mr Danhauser, who seemed to be in a rapture. It was one of those rare moments when the unfocused energy of myriad persuasions, creeds and opinions coalesced into a sacred harmony – the silence of the candle-lit void beneath the gallery, the ethereal music, the incense and summer jasmine.

Mostly, it was the emotion of the battered soloist singing his heart out.

Thou child of man, lo, to Bethlehem...

Single-handedly losing the first XV match against King James.

The Kings are travelling, travel with them!

The horrific sight and the humiliation of Reggie kissing Andrew Marsdorf.

Hamish reached up and loosened his tie as the tempo increased.

The star of mercy, the star of grace ...

At the thought of his brave, cantankerous little horse, tears began to flow.

Shall lead thy heart to its resting place.

Winter mornings, eating porridge with Tina in her room.

Gold, incense, myrrh thou canst not bring ...

The feeling of Reggie in his arms.

Offer thy heart to the infant King.

Soaring over Hamish came the trebles, the congregation hardly daring to breathe in an unconscious effort not to break the spell.

Offer thy heart.

It wasn't the most musically brilliant solo ever performed in the old chapel. Hamish's voice, not yet settled, didn't have quite the range for the top notes and they sounded more Springsteen than Kings College, but the carol was delivered with a sincerity and passion that no one sitting in the congregation or the choir that evening would easily forget.

The last note faded quietly into the roof and a pigeon fluttered off the rood screen and out of the window into the night. There was silence in the chapel as the power of the moment slowly ebbed. Then, from the front, a voice cut through the candlelight.

'Yoh! That's old Fraser the fish,' laughed Robert Gumede

Acknowledgements

For someone of my writing skill and ability to focus, a little yarn like this doesn't come about without a substantial effort from many people.

To Andrea Nattrass, Terry Morris and the team at Pan Macmillan for placing their faith in my writing again. Without this, the words above (unrefined) would have remained in my long-suffering parents' inboxes.

To Craig Mackenzie, Jane Bowman and Nicola Rijsdijk for their superb editing skills.

To Laura Goldsworthy for her invaluable and wise advice on early versions of the manuscript.

To my brother and sister whose various character traits appear in these pages without their permission. Eish, but sorry.

To South Africans of all persuasions who have coloured the characters and stories in these pages. You are the most infuriating, amusing, inspiring, frustrating, conflicted, tear-jerking and fascinating people on Planet Earth. This might be a gentle yarn about a privileged little white fellow, but it is also his way of trying to make sense of himself and the country he loves.

To my special Mum and Dad, who have soldiered through most of my writing efforts from the very first shocking efforts at wildlife description. Much of this book was read to them in the Kenton kitchen over Scotch, wine and the smells of their superb culinary skills.

CPSIA information can be obtained
at www.ICGtesting.com
Printed in the USA
LVHW090740110220
646323LV00014B/35

9 781770 106420